Language Arts

BOOKS BY
STEPHANIE KALLOS

Broken for You

Sing Them Home

Language Arts

Language Arts

Stephanie Kallos

Houghton Mifflin Harcourt
Boston   New York   2015

For information about permission to reproduce
selections from this book, write to Permissions,
Houghton Mifflin Harcourt Publishing Company,
215 Park Avenue South, New York, New York 10003.

www.hmhco.com

Library of Congress Cataloging-in-Publication Data
Kallos, Stephanie.
Language arts / Stephanie Kallos.
pages; cm
ISBN 978-0-547-93974-2 (hardcover)
1. Divorced fathers — Fiction. 2. Life change events — Fiction.
3. Domestic fiction. I. Title.
PS3611.A444L36 2015
813'.6 — dc23   2014034439

Book design by Greta D. Sibley

Printed in the United States of America
DOC 10 9 8 7 6 5 4 3 2 1

Excerpts from *Caps for Sale* by Esphyr Slobodkina,
copyright © 1940 and 1947, © renewed 1968, by Esphyr Slobodkina,
are reprinted with the permission of HarperCollins.

Lines from "Handwriting Analysis" are from *The Alphabet Not Unlike
the World* by Katrina Vandenberg (Minneapolis: Milkweed Editions,
2012). Copyright © 2012 by Katrina Vandenberg. Reprinted with
permission from Milkweed Editions. www.milkweed.org.

The lyrics from "White Christmas" by Irving Berlin,
copyright © 1940, 1942 by Irving Berlin, are reprinted with
the permission of the Irving Berlin Music Company.

Lyrics from "The Bigger the Figure," words and music by
Marshall Barer and Alec Wilder, copyright © 1952 (renewed)
by Hampshire House Publishing Corp. & Ludlow Music, Inc.,
New York, New York, are reprinted with permission of
Hampshire House Publishing Corp. & Ludlow Music, Inc..

Per il mio dolce Bill . . .
dalla tua baffuta, con amore

Truth has nothing to do with words. Truth can be likened to the bright moon in the sky. Words, in this case, can be likened to a finger. The finger can point to the moon's location. However, the finger is not the moon. To see the moon, it is necessary to gaze beyond the finger, right?

— Zen master Hui-Neng

You may in fact be wondering what I even mean when I use the word "prayer" . . . Let's say it is communication from one's heart to God. Or if that is too triggering or ludicrous a concept for you, to the Good, the force that is beyond our comprehension but that in our pain or supplication or relief we don't need to define or have proof of or any established contact with . . . Nothing could matter less than what we call this force . . . I called God Phil for a long time . . . Phil is a great name for God.

— Anne Lamott

Love, and be silent . . . I am sure my love's more richer than my tongue.

— William Shakespeare, *King Lear*

Pointing at the Moon

When my brother Cody was about two years old (and for reasons our baffled parents were never able to fathom), the word *God* entered his vocabulary.

Where could he have heard it? Certainly not at home.

Early one weekend morning, my mother and father were awakened by the surprising sound of Cody's clear, piping voice repeatedly proclaiming *Hello, God!* from behind his closed bedroom door.

Hello God hello God hello God hello God hello God HELLO!

Coming into Cody's room, my parents found him standing in an erect, commanding attitude — his hands positioned a couple of feet apart, grasping the crib rail, his stance wide, his face rascally — addressing a spot on the wall above his window. The overall effect was of a pintsize politician delivering an especially entertaining whistle-stop speech while being buffeted by a bracing wind.

Hello Mama hello Daddy hello God HELLO! Cody proclaimed with great largess, as if to a crowd of cheering constituents whose votes had already been won.

For the next few weeks, this set of behaviors became a morning ritual. Cody's consistently presidential manner of greeting the day inspired my parents to start calling him Mr. POTUS. This in turn provided my brother with a game that very young children love: the opportunity to catch adults in a mistake.

Good morning, Mr. POTUS!

Poh-Tuhs, no! Cody would assert with offended pride. *COH-Dee! COH-Dee!*

Who? Who *did you say you are?*

COH-Deeee!

When it came to improvisations like this, my mother was game enough, but reserved; extemporized hilarity has never been her strong suit.

My father, however, thanks to the advent of parenthood, had discovered a previously unexpressed thespian alter ego —

Oh! Of course! *COH-Deee!*

— a kind of nineteenth-century burlesque funnyman that he trotted out at every opportunity for my brother's entertainment and delight.

COH-Dee! COH-Dee! my father would emote, mock horrified, feigning news of some biblical-size calamity, smiting his forehead and falling to his knees. *How could I have forgotten? Can you ever forgive me?*

Daddy! So-kay! No sad! So-kay, Daddy!

Likewise, at bedtime, whenever my father read that lengthy, comforting litany of farewells from one of our favorite childhood books, *Goodnight Moon,* Cody chimed in:

"Goodnight cow jumping over the moon . . ."

— *Goodnight God, Goodnight God* —

"Goodnight light and the red balloon . . ."
— Goodnight God, Goodnight God —

Sometimes, long after my parents assumed Cody had fallen asleep, they would hear his small voice wishing God a good night.

What do you make of it? my mother asked.

It's probably what we deserve, my father joked.

We? my mother countered, archly. You're *the atheist. I'm still on the fence.*

Ha! my father replied. *Point taken.*

A few months later, the symptoms of Cody's illness began to emerge; among the most obvious of those symptoms was regressed speech.

Language left him gradually, a bit at a time. One would expect words to depart predictably, in reverse order — the way a row of knitting disappears, stitch by stitch, when the strand of working yarn is tugged off the needle — but that was not the case.

Cody's earliest and most used words — *mama, daddy* — were the first to go, while more recent acquisitions lingered.

Eventually, though, all of his words abandoned him.

God was the last holdout; at least, that was the word my parents assumed Cody was trying to say when he'd let loose with a long, agonized *Gaaaaah!* at the usual times: first thing in the morning and again at day's end.

He began applying that amorphous sound to everyone and everything: rice cakes, peas, string cheese, sippy cups; shoes and hats and coats and mittens; Thomas the Tank Engine; Babar the King; his pull-toy pony and plush orca whale; his library of board books; wooden puzzles; foam blocks; eyes, ears, nose, mouth . . .

It was *Gaaaah!* as well — not *sister* or *Emmy* (two words my brother never acquired) — that was his name for me.

PART ONE

Absent Child

Grief fills the room up of my absent child,
Lies in his bed, walks up and down with me,
Puts on his pretty looks, repeats his words,
Remembers me of all his gracious parts,
Stuffs out his vacant garments with his form.

— William Shakespeare, *The Life and Death of King John*

Cloud City

It was such a small news item — a few hundred words in the Around the Northwest section — that even a scrupulous reader like Charles might have missed it altogether if the headline hadn't included the name of the school he'd attended from kindergarten through fourth grade, a name so charmingly archaic that it could easily figure into a work of nineteenth-century literature:

FORMER NELLIE GOODHUE SCHOOL SLATED FOR DEMOLITION AND SALE BY SCHOOL DISTRICT

Up to the moment he noticed the headline, Charles had been happily settled at his favorite café table, wedged into a windowless corner beside a big-leafed philodendron that was in such dire need of transplantation that its roots, black and thick as cables, had begun to extrude from the potting soil; nevertheless, the plant seemed to be thriving. Situated thus, he enjoyed a camouflaged obscurity, a public solitude.

Cloud City Café was a bustling establishment within walking distance of Charles's house. It was where he spent every Monday through Friday morning (except holidays) from six o'clock until seven fifteen — even when school wasn't in session, as was the case on this day, a Wednesday in mid-July.

As it happened, it was also his daughter Emmy's birthday.

He had just finished his regular breakfast — black coffee, a pair of poached eggs (one whole, one white), unsweetened oatmeal — and gotten his cup refilled. He'd been making his way through the *Seattle Times* at perhaps a slightly more leisurely pace than usual.

Seattle Public Schools will sell the former Nellie Goodhue School, a 3.2-acre property in North Seattle that real estate advisers estimate could fetch at least $2.75 million.

During the summer months, Charles adhered to his workday routines as much as possible, refusing to drift into the never-never land of exotic locales and amorphous time as did many of his teaching colleagues: sleeping in, socializing on weeknights at trendy downtown bistros, taking spontaneous trips to the beach or the mountains, attending midday street fairs and festivals, going to movie matinees; in short, letting themselves *go* completely, making it that much harder for them to get back into the swing of things come September. Charles pitied them, really. How could they reliably forget on an annual basis that the disciplines of day-to-day living, so hard won, are so easily unraveled?

Nellie Goodhue is the sixth and last of the school district's major surplus properties to be sold.

It startled him, seeing the name of his alma mater in print after all these years — up for sale and slated for demolition?

Charles checked his watch. He imagined that, back home, Emmy would be awake by now and getting ready to go to one of her jobs: she had a part-time internship at the Gates Foundation; twenty-five hours a week, she managed the neighborhood video store where she and Charles had been renting movies since she was two; and she was a frequent volunteer at Children's Hospital, giving swim lessons and leading games in the hospital's therapy pool. Not surprisingly, her social life was limited (her best friend was her brother), and at her request, the birthday celebration was to be low-key, family only.

After laying the newspaper aside, Charles refolded his napkin and began consolidating the tabletop clutter — actions he habitually undertook after he'd finished reading the paper and was about to walk out the door but that today for some reason he felt impelled to expedite.

The Nellie Goodhue School was featured in a 1963 story in the Seattle Times, "Fourth-Graders Predict the Future." In conjunction with the recent World's Fair, the students of Eloise Braxton's Language Arts class were asked to reflect on what they thought life would be like in the 21st century.

Perhaps if Charles had returned for fifth grade, there would have been an entire unit centered around Miss Goodhue, an innovative syllabus in which reading, writing, and social studies (and maybe even math, science, and art!) were all linked to a single remarkable historical figure, a course of study that included screenings of old newsreels, fascinating classroom visits from living descendants, and multiple field trips to the Museum of History and Industry, where an extensive, interactive exhibition about Nellie Goodhue's impact on the Pacific Northwest would be on permanent display. Even typically dreary tasks like memorizing vocabulary lists and writing reports would be enlivened by the subject at their center: the indomitable, brave, visionary, self-sacrificing, and beautiful Nellie Goodhue.

The Nellie Goodhue property, which was converted to a warehouse space in the late 1970s, is now known as the North Annex.

But Charles hadn't returned. Abruptly, a few weeks after the end of the 1962–63 school year, he and his parents moved out of their Haller Lake rambler to a house where the neighborhood school was Greenwood Elementary and where he navigated fifth grade at an under-the-radar altitude, achieving neither academic success nor social distinction — which, after his experiences at Nellie Goodhue, was exactly what he wanted.

The district tried to sell the North Annex two years ago, but the soil was contaminated from heating oil leaked from underground storage tanks.

Charles's mother told him at some point that even if they hadn't moved, he would have been enrolled in a different school. *After what happened on that playground,* she declared, *there was absolutely no question of you going back. Your father and I were in complete agreement about that . . .* Charles could never tell whether these statements were offered as reassurance or blame; his mother could be hard to read that way.

When he dreamed of her, she was rarely in view but standing within the presumed enclosure formed by hundreds of bulging cardboard boxes, stacked too high, mildewed, dangerously unsteady. Charles knew she was in there, somewhere, unspeaking, inscrutable, her presence revealed by the occasional sound of agitated ice cubes and the intermittent appearance of cigarette smoke signals telegraphing mild to moderate distress.

Charles took a sip of coffee. His stomach suddenly felt raw, abraded, ulcerous, as if it were empty, as if there were nothing down there to absorb the acidity.

As soon as the district completes its plans to tear down the former school, the property will be ready to put on the market.

He'd read the article several times, not because he couldn't retain its contents — in fact, by the sixth reading, they were practically memorized — but because an enchantment had befallen him: whenever he tried to move on to a different story, the words were incomprehensible; he might as well have been reading Urdu or Arabic.

Could he be having a stroke? He looked up and across the room and was relieved to discover that he could still decode the title of a framed poster near the café entrance: 100 WAYS TO BUILD COMMUNITY. He leaned forward in his chair and squinted, seeing whether or not he could make out anything else. Eventually he noticed two women sitting beneath the poster were staring at him in a way that suggested they were thinking of alerting the manager.

Charles ducked behind the philodendron. A blade of sunlight sliced across the café; the temperature of the room shot up and his face began to sweat. He reached for his water glass, but even though he felt parched, he was mouth-breathing so deeply and erratically that the thought of forc-ing himself to take a drink made him even more anxious.

The women were no longer staring; they'd resumed their conversation. Their torsos tilted toward each other, inti-mately, foreheads almost touching, so that they formed the A-frame shape of a pup tent. Every now and then, one of them sat back and made a broad, sweeping surveillance of the room that always included Charles's corner, no longer camouflaged, no longer safe.

Feeling a panic of indecision — His routine had been so thoroughly disrupted, but how? Why? What had gone wrong? — Charles stood up, intending to bus his table. His water glass was still full; so was his coffee cup. How would he manage everything in one trip?

He dumped the contents of the glass into the philoden-dron pot; instantly, water began pouring out of the bottom, forming an expanding puddle beneath his feet and draw-ing the stares of several other café customers, who prob-ably thought he was incontinent or — worse still — one of those unhinged, misanthropic types who urinate in public as a demonstration of defiance and rage. The police could be on their way at any moment.

Charles downed the rest of his coffee, shouldered his school satchel, and arranged the dishes — plate, then bowl, then cup, then glass, then cutlery — in a precarious but man-ageable stack. *Like the Cat in the Hat!* he thought, feebly try-ing to jolly himself by imagining how Emmy might describe his predicament.

He made it to the BUS YOUR DISHES HERE cart without incident but, experiencing another attack of empty-headed-ness, found he couldn't manage the complicated task of separating the items into their appropriate receptacles, so he dumped everything into the cutlery tub; the noise was astonishing, a cymbalist's egregious error amplified by microphones and broadcast over the civil air defense system. By now, the entire population of Cloud City had fallen silent and was staring at him.

When he started to walk, he discovered that his knees had locked, as if immobilized by orthopedic steel braces, so that he was forced to execute a series of mini–goose steps across the room and out the front door, no doubt looking *exactly* like a man who'd peed his pants.

Had he even paid the bill?

Halfway home, still breathless and hot (although having thankfully regained the full use of his legs), Charles realized with a sinking heart that he'd forgotten the newspaper. The most cherished part of his morning ritual was making a start on the daily crossword puzzle and then bringing it home to Emmy.

Today he'd grappled unsuccessfully with a four-part quote by Albert Einstein, getting only as far as

ACROSS
1 _ _ I N _ I D E _ C _
57 _ _ G O _ S _ A Y _ F
DOWN
5 R _ _ _ I _ _ _ G
38 _ _ O _ Y _ _ U S

But even the most obvious answers eluded him — *retire* for "quit the rat race," *avenge* for "retaliate," *hedges* for "suburban barricades" — so he was never able to finish without her help.

Signare

How many times over the course of a life do you think a person writes his or her name?

It's probably an unanswerable question — unless we're considering someone like Cody; during the brief period my brother was capable of making those four letters, I'm guessing he managed it fewer than a dozen times.

My father, Charles, however: fifty-nine years old, reared at a time when cursive was a required element of an elementary-school curriculum, someone who, as a child (for reasons of his own), took great pains to develop that expression of identity known as the signature — from the Latin *signare*, "to sign, to seal" — and for whom writing by hand is still a common practice, as he insists on conducting his personal correspondence via pen and ink (he's been writing to me since I was a baby), paying by check for groceries and dry cleaning, and eschewing the convenience of online banking . . . surely he has penned his name thousands, if not tens of thousands, of times.

Consider now the fact that every time my father writes his signature, he is reminded of a distant era that he wishes he could forget — all because his surname happens to end with a *w*.

To explain: the Palmer Method of handwriting, in which my father was rigorously schooled, requires that the letters *t*, *w*, and *g* be written differently when they occur in a terminal position.

Charles Marlow

For years, he considered making a small alteration by adding a final, silent *e*. Such things are done. He did some investigating and was surprised to discover that the process of legally changing one's name is fairly simple; it takes only a few weeks.

But in the end he realized that, in this situation, a silent *e* would be anything but silent.

Besides, it would make his name look like a placard of pretension or irony: Harbour View Pointe. Sweet Thyme Tea Shoppe. Ye Olde Charles Marlowe.

One cannot crowd out pain with pomposity. One can't obliterate memory with artifice.

The first time he wrote the word *father* in a fresh context — on a hospital release form, on an occasion of great joy — he was, of course, legally required to write his signature as well.

father

In that moment, he realized that even in the light of a new, much-yearned-for identity —

— he was still obliged to authenticate himself with that old sign. It wasn't fair.

On that occasion, my father tried to alter his signature — just a little — by changing the way he inscribed that terminally positioned *w:*

Charles Marlow

Three years later, when hospital protocol again mandated that he write the word *father* — under very different circumstances, on an occasion of great sorrow

father

— he realized that escape was impossible. He might be able to change his signature, but he would never be able to alter the invisible seal of a condemned life.

Natal Charts

Dear Emmy,

It's a relief to know that you've safely arrived at JFK and are on your way into the city. I've been thinking and <u>worrying</u> about you (I know, I know, but it's a father's prerogative) ever since I put you on the redeye.

When I got home, the house was already too silent. Not in an overtly discernible way obviously — although there's surely an instrument sensitive enough to register the reduction in decibel level resulting from one fewer set of inhales and exhales. You've always been a quiet dreamer, never a snorer or a chatterer, although you sometimes laugh in your sleep, have done since you were a baby, and I have to say that's a trait that speaks volumes about you.

I stretched out on the living-room sofa and tried to fall asleep, but every time I closed my eyes, I pictured you winging your way across the country buckled into an aged Boeing 747 that, somewhere over Kansas, was beset by unexpected turbulence. This created a "thunderous silence" — a phrase I use in my ninth-grade Language Arts class as an example of oxymoron, along with Shakespeare's "ravenous lamb" and "beautiful tyrant" — as well as a palpable heaviness in the region of my solar plexus. I felt like one of Salem's accused, being bullied into self-incrimination by the laying on of stones.

I confess: there was a moment when I thought I was experiencing cardiac arrest.

Instead of dialing 911, I called your mother, who in her wisdom advised me that I was probably having a panic attack and should take a few deep breaths and ingest two of those nonaddicting homeopathic sleep-aid tablets she buys for me, allowing them to dissolve, slowly, under my tongue.

"You can't chew them, Charles," she reminded me. "They're not Tums. They won't be completely effective unless they mix with the enzymes in your saliva and are ingested sublingually." I heard her stifle a yawn; ever polite, your mother, even when roused from a sound sleep in the wee small hours by her hypochondriac ex-husband. "Just think of them as under-the-tongue Communion wafers, okay?" Between you and me, I've not had the heart to tell her that although the tablets do indeed induce sleep, they often incite very disturbing dreams. I'll choose insomnia over nightmares any time.

I breathed deeply. I brewed some chamomile tea — another one of your mother's suggestions — and am drinking it now as I write this, sitting outside on the front steps. It's a beautiful night, really, unusually clear; even against the bleached background of an artificially lit city sky, the constellations are asserting themselves in a rare, vivid way.

I'm reminded of a girlfriend I had in college (the only other serious girlfriend I had besides your mom) who was a great devotee of astrology. Her name, appropriately, was Ursula, from the Latin ursus, meaning "bear," the name given to the greater and smaller star formations also known as the Big and Little Dippers.

While the rest of our crowd worked part-time jobs flipping burgers at Dick's, parking cars at Canlis, or shelving books at Suzzallo, Ursula earned an impressive under-the-table, tax-free income from the comfort of her dorm room by reading fellow students' natal charts.

Her clientele — a fifty-fifty coed mix — came to her with questions like, Which fraternity should I pledge? Should I change my major from premed to business? Is this a good time to lose my virginity? Is it pointless to try and make my 7:00 a.m. class when Mercury goes retrograde?

While Ursula and I were dating, she tried to convince me that human lives are profoundly influenced by planetary and lunar movements, that it is the stars that are responsible for those periods when one is unaccountably bombarded with riches or woes, joys or disasters, or those times when every attempt at forward motion is thwarted, or when one has stopped evolving and is stuck, indecisive, in stasis. She used to caution me that moving through life without this celestial awareness was like driving cross-country at night on an unfinished interstate highway, one lacking lane lines, reflectors, and signage. True, one could navigate such a road, but at great peril.

I have to say, I found it all fairly ludicrous, and — with a combination of condescension and cynicism (apparently byproducts of the Virgo-rising element in my natal chart) — I eventually shut down her sweet, earnest attempts to convert me. It's no wonder she broke up with me.

I thought about trying to find her after you were born, to ask if she'd do your chart; Cody's too. Your mother would have had a fit, but I did find myself curious. I suppose I could try again. It's easier to locate the long-lost than it used to be.

Dear Emmy, Emerson Faith Marlow.

I want to say to you: Please try not to worry. This separation will be difficult, for all of us. I know you're scared about being away from home for the first time. And you'll be missed, of <u>course</u> you will. But I wouldn't have nudged you out of the nest if I didn't think you were ready. It's time for you to start living your own stories, guided by whatever navigational instruments you choose.

Charles's writing hand stalled. He stared at it, dramatically backlit by the front-porch light, a close-up in some atmospheric art-house film.

A marvel of evolution, really, the human hand in deft possession of a writing implement, in this case a rare edition Montegrappa Italia produced in the 1970s and now valued, Charles guessed, at several thousand dollars. The pen had been given to Charles by his ex-wife on an occasion of no little significance: the very night they met. It would be given to Emmy in four years' time, upon her college graduation. Cody had no need for pens.

Glancing once more at the sky — lightening now, its stars losing their gloss and reconfigured — Charles drank the last sips of cooled tea and headed inside.

What to do? Four thirty Seattle time; seven thirty in Manhattan. Charles felt vaguely dismayed to realize that he'd be thinking in two time zones until Emmy came home for Thanksgiving.

The sensible choice would be to try to get some sleep, so he rinsed out his mug, turned off the kitchen light, headed to bed, and waited for the soporific effects of Celestial Seasonings to kick in. He even took the homeopathics, five of them, for good measure.

He continued to imagine Emmy, settling into her dorm room, meeting her roommate, resident adviser, and fellow freshmen. He hoped she wasn't feeling overwhelmed or out of place. He hoped she'd heed his advice: *Find one person, just one to begin with, someone on the fringes, someone who's hanging back, a fellow introvert, or maybe another girl who's far from home. Introduce yourself. Ask her name. Find out where she's from. That's it, honey. That's all you have to do.*

As he closed his eyes and began to drift off, he tried to locate a feeling of deliciousness from having nowhere to go and nothing to do on this Labor Day weekend, the official end of summer. But in truth, the novelty of summer vacation had long since worn thin, and now Charles found himself looking forward more than ever to the start of the school year, the ringing of the alarm clock, paperwork, accountability, regularly scheduled human contact, welcoming into the fold a new group of goofy, amorphous sixth-graders, sending forth another twelfth-grade class of self-assured young adults . . .

Mrs. Braxton stood in front of the blackboard, wearing a nun's wimple. Her arms were draped with long white strips of fabric (could they be bandages?) and she was teaching a lesson about some aspect of Palmer penmanship, but the sound was on mute. There was a mummy propped up in the corner, completely encased, slumbering, larvalike. Mrs. Braxton called Charles to the front of the room. His assignment was to unwrap the mummy; this action was in some way pertinent to the lesson topic. Charles approached the mummy; it was his height, freestanding, unsupported by a coffin. How was it able to remain upright? Charles tried to find a place to begin, a cut edge he could pry up, but the material enclosing the mummy was solid, like a cast. There were words written on it, clues to a puzzle he needed to solve, but he couldn't make them out. Mrs. Braxton sighed with exasperation; couldn't Charles see what he needed to do? Someone had bound her arms to a pair of yardsticks; she flew across the room and began whacking and sawing at the mummy, and then, in a weak, plaintive voice, whatever was inside began calling Charles's name: "Char-Lee! Char-Lee Mar-Low!"

He awoke — his heart skittering, his breath a series of convulsive gasps — to the sound of a garage door lumbering open. A radio station was blasting Journey's "Don't Stop Believin'," a song Charles could expect to hear several times before the day was out and to which he knew all the lyrics; he attempted to slow his breath by singing along: *It goes on and on and on and on . . .* It was almost entirely thanks to his next-door neighbors' listening habits that Charles was familiar with the greatest hits from the '60s, '70s, and '80s and thus able to fake a cultural connection with his peer group.

Eight thirty? How could he have slept so late? He needed to get up, head downstairs, start his day.

As he waited for the coffee to brew, Charles gazed out the kitchen window, a view dominated by the neighbors' garage and driveway. Gil Bjornson, a retired career Marine, and his thirty-five-year-old computer-game-designer son, Erik, spent most weekends together; this morning they were already at work on their latest acquisition: a 1959 baby-blue Austin-Healey bug-eyed Sprite suffering from metastatic rust and leather rot and looking hopelessly ruined to Charles, but then he was neither skilled nor passionate when it came to automotive restoration.

It was nice, though, watching the two of them. Charles noted the intuitive interplay of their movements, the way they found words when words were needed but fell into a purposeful easy silence when conversation was superfluous.

Drinking the last of the orange juice, barely more than a splash, he became aware again of the peculiar energetic *absence* in the house, the cessation of that gentle, ruffling molecular motion that always trailed in Emmy's wake. Not only would nights be quieter, he realized, but he wouldn't be hearing her come and go throughout the day, experiencing the awareness one has when there's another resident in a house, whether one actually *sees* that resident or not.

Oh, he should have known this was coming, this tidal wave of longing and loss. Alison would have had this day planned months in advance, a universally momentous one for parents, the day after a youngest child heads off to college. She'd be having lunch with one of her friends or going on a day trip with that fellow she was dating, Mark or Doug or Dave (Charles could never remember his name, but he had a PhD in psychology, taught aikido, and made a living doing something that involved power tools).

Yes, that definitely sounded in character for Ali, distracting herself with scenery.

Not that Charles's ex-wife was a cold person. He didn't doubt for a moment that she was every bit as aggrieved by Emmy's exodus as he was. However, Alison was also intensely pragmatic and would consider this kind of solitary emotional indulgence a waste of time and energy.

If you're going to feel sad, Charles could imagine her saying, *you might as well feel sad while you're driving to the Lavender Festival in Sequim, or even just grocery shopping.* Do *something, Charles, some one little thing that will get you out of the house and give you the chance to belong to something besides the noise in your head. Don't hibernate. When you hibernate, you* wallow.

It was then that Charles noted the capacious wine rack, each diamond-shaped cubby occupied by a dust-covered bottle, the wine rack and its contents being one of many shared possessions Ali left behind when she'd moved out more than ten years ago, a relic from a distant era in their married lives.

It suddenly occurred to him: he no longer entertained. He didn't concoct wine-based marinades. How the hell was he supposed to get rid of this stuff unless he started drinking it himself?

He reached into the wine rack at random and ended up with a 1992 Lacryma Christi del Vesuvio, surely expensive; something someone must have brought to a party, years ago, before the divorce anyway, and never opened. Charles uncorked the bottle, filled his juice glass — the wine was a deep garnet red — and took a sip.

It was surprisingly soothing: mild, luxuriant, plush. He finished the first glass and poured another.

This was unorthodox behavior, to be sure — even a bit dodgy. Nevertheless, Charles felt justified; after all, it wasn't every day one became a dues-paying member of the Empty Nester Club, and under such special, heart-sore circumstances, he figured he was entitled to a bit of conduct unbecoming.

Besides — Alison's advice to *do something* notwithstanding — it wasn't as if he had anywhere to go. It was Saturday. No need to operate any machinery heavier than a Mr. Coffee. With the exception of orange juice, the larder was stocked. His clothes were back from the dry cleaner's. The DVD player was still loaded with the digitally remastered copy of *The Best Years of Our Lives* that he and Emmy had watched the other night as part of their recent Teresa Wright film festival and that he wouldn't mind seeing again.

Charles finished his second glass of wine, poured a third, and checked on Gil and Erik; they were standing side by side, holding coffee mugs and staring meditatively into the depths of the Austin-Healey's corroded innards, a father and son at ease in companionable silence. To imagine himself and Cody sharing such a moment was to imagine nothing less than a miracle.

Why not? Charles thought suddenly. Why not amp up this indulgent *wallowing,* this willful *hibernation* by visiting the old father-daughter clubhouse, the multipurpose site of countless tea parties, story times, and beauty-parlor makeovers (at least until Emmy was too old for such things); the game-and-puzzle room; the meeting place of the After-School Homework Society.

During the many years when Charles was banished from the optimistically christened *playroom* upstairs — where Alison and a revolving cadre of specialists never played but rather worked with Cody on various strategies, therapies, evaluations, modalities, et cetera — he and Emmy appropriated another room in the house as theirs, the one farthest away from these sad, officious doings: the crawlspace.

Charles grabbed the wine bottle and made his way (somewhat unsteadily) to the laundry room, where a door not much taller or wider than a kitchen cupboard had been artfully cut into one wallpapered wall; a casual observer wouldn't even notice it was there.

Feeling giddy from the wine and the out-of-character recklessness of it all (what would Emmy think of her stodgy father, thoroughly squiffed on a Saturday morning and headed all by himself to their secret hideaway?), Charles got down on his hands and knees, yanked the door open by its cunningly camouflaged knob, and (how else?) crawled inside.

❖

"*Aspergillus, Cladosporium, Penicillium, Stachybotrys,* or — possibly — *Chaetomium strumarium.*"

"Excuse me?" Charles said. He glanced at Alison, hunched over in the chair next to him.

Her bearing — which until very recently had been as reliably erect as a dancer's — now suggested a case study in severe osteoporosis, her spine the rigid shape of a shepherd's crook, a recalcitrant question mark. She scrawled on a legal pad that was balanced on her knees; the pad was on top of a rapidly thickening file folder labeled CODY MEDICAL.

It was 1994. Cody was twenty-seven months old and something was wrong with him. Dr. Indu Gayathri — an MD/ND specializing in the treatment of persons afflicted with fungal-borne neurotoxicity — was the latest in a long line of experts Charles and Alison had consulted in the hope of learning what, exactly, was wrong with him and what, as parents, they could do.

Surely there was something they could do.

Something *new,* that is; their faithful compliance with the behavioral, environmental, pharmaceutical, dietary, chiropractic, craniosacral, homeopathic, Ayurvedic, and acupunctural recommendations put forth by Dr. Gayathri's predecessors had had no effect on Cody whatsoever.

If anything, he was getting worse, vacillating between a globally expressed rage and a private, mute dwindling; an inward collapse into capitulation and despair. Charles and Alison looked on, useless, as the affectionate, puckish, inquisitive little person they had been coming to know and cherish began powering down, shutting off, shrinking into the farthest corner of some doorless, windowless inner sanctum to which they could find no access, his small hands clinging to a penlight with a failing battery. All this occurring at the same time that around him, his body (cruelly) continued to be under construction, ever expanding, structurally sound.

At least he's not medically fragile, one of the specialists had chirped.

"I'm so sorry," Alison said, shaking her head as if rousing herself from a deep sleep. "That last one. *Chaetomium* . . . ?"

". . . *strumarium.*"

"Yes. Could you please spell that?"

"Certainly. *C-h-a* . . ."

Charles studied his wife as she transcribed.

Ali's postural decline was yet more evidence of trauma, a physical byproduct of what they'd been through over the past months, what they continued to go through, with no foreseeable end. Cody wasn't the only one who was shrinking.

Dr. Gayathri finished spelling and then continued. "Please know that *Chaetomium* would represent a worst-case scenario." She fixed her eyes on Charles and abruptly flung up her hand: a crossing guard halting the oncoming traffic of an exceptionally negative aura. "Hopefully we're just dealing with standard, run-of-the-mill black mold. In which case, the protocols are clear and have proven to be very effective."

Charles reached over and gently pressed his hand against the flat winged bone of Ali's sacrum. She continued to scribble with ferocity but registered his touch with a soft intake of breath and by unfurling into an upright posture: a fiddlehead fern in a fast-motion film.

"I'm going to step out for a moment," Dr. Gayathri continued, "and assemble some literature for you to look at. In the meantime" — she swiveled around in her desk chair, stood, and opened a pair of doors on the large credenza behind her desk to reveal a television and video player — "I'd like you to watch a short film on neurotoxicology, sick building syndrome, and mold infiltration."

Charles opened his mouth to ask if they couldn't please just talk about Cody specifically (something they had yet to do), but once again Dr. Gayathri's hand flew up.

"I know, I know . . ." She made a halfhearted expulsive sound that Charles assumed was her version of a laugh, although he couldn't imagine what the joke could be. He glanced over at Alison; she was still focused on note taking, but her expression was now softened by a slight smile. What was it about women and their sense of humor? They could be so enigmatic.

Dr. Gayathri went on. "Please disregard the fact that this video is a promotional tool for a mold-detection-and-mitigation company. I offer this particular program as a patient resource only because I have found it to provide a clear and compelling explanation of what exactly we are facing here. May I bring you some herbal tea?"

"Do you have coffee?" Charles asked.

"I'm afraid not."

"Water would be nice."

"Yes, water," Alison murmured. She had finally stopped writing and was staring down at the legal pad as if it were the entrance to a condemned mineshaft.

"Very good. I'll be right back." The doctor loaded the video, pushed the play button, turned off the overhead lights, and left the room.

Golly, Charles thought, *it's just like health class on sex-ed day.*

Before he could share this insight with Alison (who probably wouldn't find it funny anyway) a new-agey musical score began playing: marimbas, drums, Peruvian flute.

Seconds later, brightly lit images of various molds began to float into view; these pictures alternated with a black screen on which the molds were identified and described.

Chaetomium strumarium turned out to be an especially entrancing-looking organism; columnar in structure, it was composed of stacks of fluffy-looking orbs, cotton-ball kebabs that spun and tilted languidly in a pastel pink-and-blue environment.

Isn't that one of the oddest things about dangerous organisms seen in this way, Charles thought, *microscopically enlarged and illuminated. Their alien beauty belies their devastation.*

A choir joined the musical score; they sang in a language Charles couldn't identify, perhaps even an invented language. He had to admit, the musicians were talented; the production values were very good. Perhaps the composition would be credited at the end: *Chaetomium Symphonium no. 1 in C Minor. Cladosporium Chorale. Ode to Mold.*

Alison was watching the television screen, slouching again, mesmerized.

Charles began to question the wisdom of the producers behind this benign, color-saturated, musically lush presentation. The overall tone of the program didn't exactly inspire dread or prompt one to action; it was a little like watching an episode of *Teletubbies.*

Eventually, however, the hypnotic parade of floating fungi, mold, and spores gave way to identifiable and disturbing images alternating with text: a close-up of a severely deformed toenail — it looked more like a talon — and the surrounding blistered skin (*intractable nail fungus*); a crying toddler (*severe asthma . . . debilitating respiratory ailments . . . fatal idiopathic pulmonary hemorrhaging*); a pained-looking grandmotherly type (*hypersensitivity pneumonitis . . . memory loss*); a computer-generated image of the human brain (*a high incidence of fatal brain abscesses among long-term intravenous drug users*).

"*That's* certainly germane," Charles said.

The video continued like this, a succession of pictures

along with a litany of life-threatening ailments attributed to mycotoxins, and then, finally, a list of prescriptive actions the afflicted homeowner should take, beginning with HIRE A MOLD-DETECTION-AND-MITIGATION SPECIALIST.

"This all makes so much sense," Alison said, her voice flat, her eyes fixed on the screen. "Something invisible. Something in the walls. In the Sheetrock. Or underneath. It can only be this. I can't believe we didn't think of this before."

Charles stared at her. He wasn't entirely sure she remembered that he was in the room.

Dr. Gayathri returned. The overhead halogens oozed back to life.

"Informative, yes?" she said, reaching between them to set two glasses of water and a collection of pamphlets on the desk. She resumed her place behind the desk, deftly pushing the pause button just as the company name appeared: *Emerald City Mycotoxin Assessment and Remediation: Seattle's #1 Mold Busters!*

"This all makes so much sense!" Alison repeated, her voice now animated, her spine erect. "We'll get started on the house right away." She leaned toward the television screen and started writing down the 800 number. "It's the crawlspace. It has to be. We're probably all sick — or sickening — and don't even know it, right?"

"That's quite possible," Dr. Gayathri replied, nodding, her delivery so deadpan and earnest that it bordered on caricature.

Charles shifted in his chair; he felt a growing suspicion that he and Alison were being played, a pair of marks in a health-care-industry shell game. Maybe Seattle's #1 Mold Busters rewarded referring medical professionals with a commission. Maybe the CEO was Dr. Gayathri's cousin.

"It wouldn't be a bad idea for the two of you to go over

the symptoms checklist with your own health in mind," the doctor continued, "as well as your son's. But, naturally, a child's immune system —"

"— is so much more vulnerable!" Ali chimed in.

"Precisely. Therefore, any toxic effects — physiologic, behavioral, et cetera — will be both amplified and intensified."

"Of course!" Alison nodded with enthusiasm. Charles realized that up until today, they'd been in sync at these confabs, spring-loaded bobble-head twins, their reactions *amplified and intensified* by stupid hope and blind desperation.

"And at the same time, because of your son's age —"

"Cody," Charles interrupted. "His name is Cody."

The doctor smiled. "He's between two and three, yes?"

"Twenty-seven months," Alison answered. "His birthday's in May."

"So, he's experiencing as well all the *normal* limitations of this developmental stage; restricted language, for example —"

"Cody knows a lot of words," Charles said. "He can write his name."

The doctor smiled again but sped on. "A keen frustration when encountering impediments to his growing sense of independence; an erratic control of physical abilities and functions . . . Is he toilet-trained?"

"He was," Alison answered, "but he's been a little . . . inconsistent lately." She'd begun to dwindle again.

"That's not unusual," the doctor replied, but she frowned and made a note. "Is he tantrumming more than usual?"

"Yes, you could say that," Alison replied, smaller still.

When did tantrum *become a verb?* Charles wondered.

"With increased vehemence?" the doctor prompted.

"Yes . . ."

It seemed to Charles that Alison was being pummeled by

the sledgehammer of Dr. Gayathri's relentless queries; she'd shrunk by half and was practically inaudible.

"We've been reading to Cody since he was born," he said. "Until a few months ago, he could repeat whole stories by heart. He could say the alphabet."

"I understand, Mr. Marlow." Dr. Gayathri's smile had acquired a petrified quality that Charles found perversely satisfying. "Believe me, I'm not trying in any way to suggest that your child isn't a marvelous and extremely intelligent little boy."

"We're not here for your corroboration," Charles countered. "Nobody — certainly not a stranger who's never even met him and can't be bothered to remember his name — needs to tell us how *marvelous* and *intelligent* Cody is. We're his parents. We know him better than anyone. We're here to get some *help*, for Christ's sake."

Alison shifted in her chair and cleared her throat. "I think what Dr. Gayathri is trying to say" — she spoke softly, her head bowed and tilted submissively, her gaze focused in the vicinity of Charles's feet — "is that Cody can't express himself about something this complex, about feeling *sick*, if what's happening to him isn't the usual way he understands what being sick means, like having a tummy ache or feeling feverish, right?"

"Exactly so," the doctor replied, her expression steely. "And finally, there's the heredity factor . . ." She began babbling on about the effects of mycotoxicity, how whatever genes Cody had inherited from the two of them would determine the nature and severity of his reactions. He might experience some of the same symptoms they were experiencing, or he might manifest the presence of mold in a completely different way.

All in all, her monologue served to do what all such

monologues did: indict and baffle. It was their fault, always. That was what it all came down to. They'd doomed Cody from the beginning by dealing him a bad genetic deck, they'd wrought further damage by not recognizing and protecting him from hazards, and they'd compounded everything by not noticing sooner that something was amiss, not taking immediate action. (As if they didn't spend every waking moment with Cody *noticing* and *doing,* or at least *trying.* They loved him. They didn't leave him in a locked car on a ninety-five-degree day while they roamed the aisles of Walmart or smoked crack. And yet, for all the implied condemnation laid upon them at meetings like this, they might as well have.)

But they had a chance now to make things right, because here was yet another new prescriptive action to take, one that — like all the previous failed prescriptive actions — would not be covered by insurance.

The doctor paused. She looked down and shuffled some papers around — exactly, Charles thought, like a television news anchor filling that awkward interval before the camera cuts away to the commercial break.

When she finally spoke, Charles realized that she'd spent the entire office visit delaying the moment in which she'd have to ask one final question:

"Has anyone suggested that Cody might be . . . on the spectrum?"

"Excuse me?" Charles said.

"The *autism* spectrum."

Charles heard Alison inhale sharply. Her writing hand opened, slack, as if it had gone numb; her pencil dropped to the floor.

"No," Charles said.

Dr. Gayathri seemed, for once, to be bankrupt of speech.

"No," Charles repeated. "No one has mentioned autism."

"Well," Dr. Gayathri said, "there is a great deal of evidence that mycotoxicity can be a significant triggering factor in the disease . . ."

Autism, Charles was thinking, and it was as if he'd spoken the word into an electronic device that caused it to reverberate — not receding, like an echo, but exactly the opposite, gaining in volume and intensity, like the ringing of an unheeded alarum: *autism, Autism, AUTISM, AUTISM!* He was vaguely aware of Alison reaching down to retrieve her fallen pencil.

"This company . . . ," Ali began, her voice barely audible over the crescendo of the repeating word in Charles's head. "Emerald City." Nodding toward the video screen, she wet her lips and swallowed with effort. "They could refer us to a house excavation contractor, couldn't they?"

Auto-, from the Greek autos, *"self,"* Charles thought. *How does that fit with* -ism?

"Yes, absolutely!" the doctor answered. "There's a full list of resources related to mold mitigation right there in the informational materials I've provided."

Alison snatched up the pamphlets and began studying them.

Dr. Gayathri went on. "I would like to schedule another appointment very soon. It's extremely important that we start finding ways to support and strengthen your child's immune system during this transition; that is, while you decide what to do about the environmental issue. Supplements, dietary changes . . . these can all have a very positive effect in the interim."

"Oh God!" Alison cried out. "Is Cody safe, do you think? Do we need to move him somewhere else until the problem is fixed? Maybe we should send him to my parents . . ."

"Alison," Charles said, but she didn't seem to hear him.

"I don't think that will be necessary if we take immediate precautions and implement a dietary program right away. But it would be appropriate for the two of you to have a discussion as soon as possible about how you'd like to proceed in terms of your house. In this case, I do believe we're dealing with SBS as caused by biological contaminants."

Alison began to cry.

"SBS?" Charles asked.

"Sick building syndrome."

"What are you suggesting?"

"I don't think we can move," Alison managed to say. "It's the only home Cody has ever known; he loves the house, the garden . . . We live on a corner lot, you know, and there's this big stand of old trees. Cody calls it his forest . . ." She took off her eyeglasses, swiped at her nose, her eyes, her forehead. "And his room, he just loves it, all his things, the colors . . . We've tried so hard to make it . . . *his*." She gripped her hands together in front of her face, a gesture of entreaty. "I think uprooting him would do more damage than good."

"That is of course your decision," the doctor said, and — to her credit — she looked at both of them.

Alison nodded sharply and put her glasses back on. "We'll need to replace the windows right away," she said, "all of them, probably, but certainly those 1950s aluminum ones in the kitchen and bathroom. They're always sweating, I'm sure they're a factor in the mold . . ." She turned over a fresh page on her legal pad and resumed writing; it was a to-do list, Charles noted, beginning with ASK DAD ABOUT CONTRACTOR RECOMMENDATIONS and GET CASH OUT OF 401(K). Her eyes were too big, too bright, her pupils too dilated, her breathing too rapid: a wild creature in flight mode.

"Alison," Charles began again, reaching for her hand, but she gestured him away.

"We'll make this work," she muttered, pressing down hard with her pencil, adding item after item to her list, all emphatically capitalized in block print. "We'll do whatever it takes. I know what you're thinking, Charles, I *know,* but we can't be proud about asking for help, not anymore. It's all for Cody. From now on. It all has to be for him."

Ephemera

Charles pulled the crawlspace door closed behind him, turned on the overhead fluorescents, and surveyed the room. It looked far less like the father-daughter playhouse he'd remembered with such fondness and more like a hopelessly jumbled catchall: a scattering of tools, paint cans, odd bits of leftover construction supplies, Alison's abandoned sports equipment, and dozens of unlabeled cardboard boxes.

How could he have let this happen?

Charles despaired. Organizing clutter was not his strong suit.

If he and Alison were still married, she could have directed him instantly to the boxes he'd come down here to find. There were three.

One contained the earliest evidence of Emmy's existence, its inventory inscribed in painstaking detail in the ledger of his memory: an ultrasound photograph with the technician's crude drawing of a word bubble coming out of

Emmy's already-formed mouth (*Hi, Daddy!*); a Post-it note
the same technician handed him on the sly with the words
It's a girl! (Charles had been eager to know the gender of their
second child, but Alison preferred to be surprised); congratulatory cards scrawled with exuberant addenda: *We couldn't
be happier for you! Wishing you and your little one every blessing! We can't wait to meet your perfect new baby!* (it was clear in
retrospect that all the exclamatory excess was in direct proportion to Alison and Charles's fears — although they were
in perfect, complicit, and unspoken denial about that at the
time); a scrapbook of photos from the baby shower.

Another box contained Emmy's baby things: the layette
(gender-neutral, in yellow, green, and white); the silver rattle;
an assortment of soft cuddly things, wild creatures tamed
by their plush exteriors and beribboned necks; the wind-
up crib mobile playing "Somewhere Over the Rainbow" and
setting a small flock of bluebirds in slow circular motion; the
set of Beatrix Potter books, sized for a child's hands . . .

And there was at least one more treasure chest of sentimental savings down here as well, boxed relics documenting
Emmy's journey from toddlerhood through high school: the
handmade birthday/Valentine's Day/Father's Day/get-well
cards; the letters from camp; the school projects . . . (Had
Cody provided him with these kinds of treasures while he
was growing up, Charles would have felt just as sentimental
about them and saved every scrap.)

Where to begin? How would he be able to find Emmy's
boxes in this mess?

Intending to pour a refill, Charles reached for the wine
but discovered he'd left his juice glass upstairs. He considered
drinking directly from the bottle, but that was just *too* scan-
dalous, *too* dipsomaniacal. Besides, with the low ceiling, he
wouldn't be able to tip up the bottle without risking spillage.

The problem solved itself as soon as he spotted Emmy's miniature china tea set — he'd forgotten about that! — stored in its original packaging, sitting in plain sight on top of a larger cardboard box in the farthest darkened corner, opposite where he was crouched. Charles crawled toward it, sliding the bottle along the floor with him, shoving aside the boxes in his way, creating a narrow but traversable path.

The tea set was packaged with a clear lid, so its components — teapot, creamer, sugar, saucers, and teacups — were in full view, nestled into molded plastic niches. *Who gave this to us?* Charles wondered. It was real china, from what he could tell, hand-painted with orange and yellow flowers, in pristine condition. He could picture Emmy sitting down here playing hostess to him and her favorite stuffed animals, serving up imaginary refreshments in the style of a Jane Austen heroine.

Would you care for a cucumber sandwich, Mr. Charles?

Yes, indeed, Miss Emerson. Thank you ever so much.

With care, Charles extracted one of the cups, filled it with wine — a little more than a thimbleful — and drank it down.

He might as well commence his archaeological dig here, by exploring the contents of the box nearest the one upon which Emmy's tea set was resting. The moment he began easing open the flaps, he knew exactly what he'd found.

There is no smell in the world like old magazines.

On the very top was the August 10, 1962, issue of *Life* magazine: a jaunty Janet Leigh on the cover, proudly buxom in a lemon-yellow sleeveless dress and wearing on her head a towering stack of red fezzes, eleven of them, their tassels swinging wildly, impossibly, illogically, so that one had to conclude that they were being animated not by the pedestrian mechanism of an out-of-frame wind machine but by Ms. Leigh's breezy insouciance. Next to Janet, a headline read THE FULL STORY OF THE DRUG THALIDOMIDE: THE 5,000 DEFORMED BABIES, THE MORAL QUESTIONS OF ABORTION . . .

The box contained several other issues as well, their covers featuring photos of John Wayne, Marilyn Monroe, JFK, John Glenn . . .

This smell, old Life, Charles thought. *How does one describe it?*

This was exactly the kind of exercise he gave his creative-writing students, so it was only fair that he attempt it himself.

He refilled the teacup, closed his eyes, inhaled deeply, and spoke: "A dense, gluey, chemical musk that comes on strong but soon dissipates, growing elusive, trailing in its wake the faint aroma of a de-ivoried piano key in a Sunday-school classroom."

That was terrible. Heavy-handed. Verbose. Self-consciously clever. Resoundingly average. He'd give himself a solid C.

Was *de-ivoried* even a word? And yet, how else would one describe it — *bald, scalped, denuded*? None of those quite got it somehow . . .

Charles lifted the magazine out of the box and set it on the floor. *Too late to stop now,* he thought, so he began to inventory the rest:

Fourth-grade report cards
A framed certificate of merit for Palmer penmanship
    bearing his name
Cursive-writing workbooks, most filled to capacity
Yellowed copies of a *Seattle Times* article from 1963 enti-
    tled "Fourth-Graders Predict the Future"

A stack of red-and-blue-lined newsprint, hole-punched and held together, just barely, by three still shiny butterfly brass brads. The front cover was a sheet of faded, dog-eared, orange construction paper bearing the block printing of his much younger self:

FLIPPER BOY by Charles Marlow
Room 104
Mrs. Braxton

Also in the box were several remaindered copies of this opus printed in grape-pop purple on slick white paper and emitting another distinctive smell, that high-inducing chemical blend known as mimeograph ink, the clearest evidence of a far-distant, toxic childhood. Astonishing. Someone had taken the time and trouble not only to transcribe Charles's words into typewritten form but to make mimeographed copies.

Who? The Nellie Goodhue secretary? Mrs. Braxton?

Why on earth had his mother saved this stuff? Did she think Charles would want it? To him, it was criminal evidence.

Fourth grade was a landmark year, the one in which Charles experienced his proverbial fifteen minutes of fame as well as the fall that inevitably follows such a sudden, unearned ascent.

It was the year he'd started wearing a crucifix, mastered the Palmer Method of penmanship, and become obsessed with doomsday scenarios — especially those resulting from pharmaceutical disasters.

It was the year he became a fan of sci-fi/horror movies and began collecting the names of film stars with the same fervency that his better-adjusted contemporaries collected baseball cards and merit badges.

It was the year his best friend moved to Minnesota. The year his parents' marriage went to hell.

Mainly, though, it was the year he met Dana McGucken.

Charles picked up the magazine and began thumbing through it.

The coffee table in his childhood house was two-tiered, glass on top with a lower shelf shaped like a shallow tray. Each week, when a new issue of *Life* arrived, his mother relegated the old *Life* to the tray below. She spritzed the glass top with Windex, wiped it until it was free of fingerprints and the circles left by coffee cups and martini glasses, and then, with precision, placed the new *Life* in its designated position: intriguingly off-kilter, so that its edges did not align with those of the table.

For a while, the cast-off issues of *Life* remained on display in the tray below. They were stacked neatly, in three side-by-side piles, their covers continuing to change, and then at some point they went into the garbage can.

By contrast, *Playboy* magazines were harder to access; they were secreted in the garage in a footlocker that bore Charles's father's initials (GDM) and on occasion was left unlocked. *Playboy*s were interesting in a puzzling way — although the photos of women's breasts were a revelation, making Charles understand why his mother always spoke in such self-derogatory tones about being *flat as a pancake*. The centerfold feature was intriguing from an engineering standpoint, but Charles's curiosity was piqued mainly by a man named Hugh Hefner (in his mind, the first name was pronounced "hug"); he was always wearing a bathrobe and seemed to be married to a lot of women dressed as rabbits. Charles was puzzled as to why *Playboy* warranted such out-of-the-way, secretive placement. The cartoons weren't even *funny*. Nonetheless, *Playboy* exerted enough of an influence on his imagination to inform certain sections of "Flipper Boy" — although not to nearly the same extent as *Life*.

Janet Leigh's oddly contrived chapeau — its whimsy clearly intended to provoke delight — had filled Charles with a terrible trepidation for the state of her immortal soul. He interpreted the image as a grave insult; more than that, as a *sin* — for surely that tower of hats was meant to mimic, or perhaps even *mock*, the papal headdress.

Whoever she was, Janet Leigh looked like a nice enough lady. Maybe she didn't know she was being used as Satan's pinup girl.

Now, seeing the photo anew, and at a slightly narcotized remove, thanks to the wine, Charles was able to rouse himself from these morbid reminiscences just a little, enough to recognize that Janet Leigh and the eleven red fezzes resonated differently, reminding him of one of his children's favorite stories: *Caps for Sale*. It must be boxed up somewhere down here as well, along with Cody's and Emmy's other books.

Caps for Sale was the tale of a solitary peddler who wore his merchandise — an assortment of red, blue, gray, and black caps — balanced in a tall stack atop his head.

Caps! he proclaimed as he wandered the empty countryside calling out to an unseen clientele. *Caps for sale! Fifty cents a cap!*

Hours passed. The peddler found no takers for his wares and, growing weary, decided to lie down under a large tree and have a nap. When he awoke, he discovered that his caps had been filched by a band of mischievous monkeys who taunted him from the lofty sanctuary of the tallest branches.

You monkeys, you! the peddler cried. *Give me back my caps!*

And they did, eventually, once he learned how to trick them.

Cody loved that story. Charles used to read it to him over

and over in a variety of ham-handed accents — Russian, German, Scots, Yiddish — and it always made him laugh.

Charles reached for the wine, but the Tears of Christ were all gone. Just as well.

Deciding to take a cue from the country peddler, he lay down on the floor and closed his eyes. The crawlspace was very quiet.

Caps for sale! an old voice echoed from a great distance.

It was Charles's voice, he realized, the voice of himself as a young father, lulling himself to sleep as if he were his own child.

Fifty cents a cap . . .

Enigmatology

The facility known as Madonna's Home is located in North Seattle and situated on a deep, narrow lot. There are many places like it, with more and more of them springing up every day, for the need is great. Some of these facilities have large, noticeable signage that clearly identifies their function; this one does not. Most first-time visitors get lost on the way; even people who have visited on numerous occasions find it difficult to locate.

Its overall appearance is indeterminate. It seems somehow adrift, transient. Whereas navigating to most destinations is a mindless process (one need only announce SCHOOL or HOME or DRY CLEANER'S or GROCERY STORE to the brain, and the autopilot function is engaged), getting to Madonna's Home requires a sustained exertion of consciousness and will. It is never quite where one remembers.

Consisting of two colorless, architecturally bland structures — one street-side, shadowed by an aged Douglas fir

and a weeping birch, the other shoved to the back of the lot
at a distance of about a hundred feet — the site offers few
overt clues as to its purpose.

In the middle of the grassy expanse separating the buildings is a courtyard with a concrete patio. Rain mixed with
city grime pools in the recesses of plastic chairs and um-
brella-topped tables; wooden picnic tables are covered with
amorphous patches of bilious-green moss.

There is no apparent interest in projecting what real
estate agents refer to as *street appeal.* The prospect of hospitality within is called into doubt by two kinds of fences:
protecting the front of the property is a battalion of black,
wrought-iron bars with spiked finials; on the other three
sides, wide cedar planks form a ten-foot-tall privacy screen.

Globular silver doorknobs extrude from the front gate
entrance at a peculiar height, and a complicated system of
chains, steel rings, lockboxes, keypads, and bolts gives rise to
several questions, all worrisome:

*Is this place a frequent target of thieves? The urban compound
of a religious cult? The domicile of a conspiracy theorist?*

Abutting single-family residences (small, mostly shabby-
looking prefabricated post-WWII houses) on the north and
commercially zoned apartment complexes and businesses
on the south, Madonna's Home perfectly exemplifies the
ideal marriage of form and function: a temporary, aggressively secured storage facility for people who are neither
here nor there.

Only when standing on the sidewalk outside the iron
fence is one able to read a small metal placard affixed to the
gate: *CAUTION! VISITORS PLEASE TAKE NOTE: THIS IS
A RESIDENCE FOR PEOPLE WITH DEMENTIA AND THERE-
FORE THE GATE MUST BE LOCKED AT ALL TIMES.*

Inside the facility is ample evidence of *elder-proofing* (the bookend to childproofing), various kinds of safeguards with specific names that are relatively new arrivals in the lexicon of dementia care: *kill switches* on the stoves to prevent residents from starting fires; *traveler's locks* on windows, doors, cabinets, and closets, intended to keep patients from venturing into unsafe areas like stairwells or simply to direct them to where they are expected to go. Outlets are fitted with *tamper-resistant electrical receptacles.* Walls are decorated with *faux windows,* posters that simulate real views into worlds to which residents no longer have access.

Nonetheless, there remain doors that cannot be secured, forms of travel that cannot be restricted, conduits that are yet unhindered. There is still some recourse for these souls, trapped as they are in what Shakespeare called "second childishness and mere oblivion."

For within the mind, of course, travelers are free — movement continues, unencumbered; views remain panoramic; all destinations are possible. We can tell ourselves whatever stories we choose.

In the back seat of a van that has just pulled up to the curb is one such teller of tales, Sister Giorgia Maria Fiducia D'Amati. The van driver and the front-seat passenger, unaccustomed to city driving and befuddled by the absence of signage, consult a Seattle street map to make sure that this is indeed where their appointment is to take place.

Which story will Giorgia tell today? Will it be a variation on one of the old ones? "A Love Like Salt"? "The Sunflower Bride"? "Life Among the Changelings"? Or will it be — at long last! — a *new* story, one of reunion, with her family, her students, her son?

She does not yet know. She can only wait in silence and

stillness until the details become clearer and the characters begin to appear.

◆

Gaaaaah, Cody says to whatever might be listening, his voice little more than a whisper. *Gaaaaaah . . .*

On the other side of his eyelids, light.

On the other side of his closed bedroom door, sounds:

The soft, measured shufflings of slippered not-Cody feet; the muffled suction-y sound of the refrigerator door as it opens and then the pillowy thump when it shuts; quiet low-pitched not-Cody voices; the first gurglings of the machine that makes the hot black drink, the thick rich smell getting stronger until the machine sputters to a stop.

There are things that happen here the same way every day, so he knows —

Soon, someone will come.

He stays very still, like a small creature in the under-brush: a rabbit.

But not Foolish Rabbit, the one in *Animal Tales from Around the World,* Foolish Rabbit who cries out *Eagle! Eagle! I am so afraid of you! Do not eat me!* so loudly that he gives his hiding place away and Eagle comes at once and eats him.

No; Cody is Wise Rabbit, who stays still and silent and hides until it is safe to come out, and who never gets eaten.

He squints his eyelids apart, slowly, as if they are unoiled doors that might squeak if opened too abruptly or carelessly.

Likewise, he has a trick of keeping his eyes unfocused at first, so that everything is indistinct, shapeless, colors with-out definition.

He needs to make sure that everything is as it should be, that his room is exactly the way it was before he went to sleep. He looks around and sees:

First, the blurred colors of his bedspread — blue, yellow, brown, red, white.

Next, on the table by his bed — the hazy shape of his cowboy lamp, still turned on; his picture book, closed.

Then, curtains — blue.

Finally, walls — mostly white, but with a fuzzy patch of color across from him, and now he slowly brings his vision into focus to look at the picture of wild ponies. The ponies are purple. Behind them are orange and gold and lavender mountains and a sky full of stars and a big round moon like the *o* in his name.

No people. Just ponies.

Like the real ponies he visits some days.

Is today one of those days?

There are footsteps approaching his door. Not the footsteps of his mother (who is often the first person to say *Good morning, Cody*) or his father (who is never the first person to say *Good morning, Cody*); they are the footsteps of one of the others.

Cody closes his eyes again, tight, as he hears his door being opened.

Good morning, Cody!

He knows this voice, this person: Esther.

No playing possum now, mister. I know you're awake in there!

Once again, he opens his eyes the tiniest bit, ever so slowly allowing the outside world in, the not-Cody world.

His door is wide open. Esther stands there, a dark shape against the brightness of the big room beyond.

Well, hello there, big brown eyes. How we doin' so far?

Her shape changes as she turns and tapes a sheet of paper to his door —

Oh boy, a new day, a new chance for Cody to earn lots of stickers . . .

— and then she comes into his room and starts moving around, opening the curtains and letting in more light, patting the covers over his feet — just once — as she passes the bed, turning off his lamp, going to his closet.

Cody, unmoving, continues to stare at the ponies.

Come on now, Cody, time to get up. Here's your bathrobe and your slippers. Sit up. Sit up, Cody. I just know you wanna get your first sticker today, so let's get your bathrobe and slippers on and go to the bathroom and see how you did last night . . .

Cody sits up.

All right, good job . . .

Cody slides his feet into his slippers. Esther helps him stand up and get into his bathrobe. He is allowed to wear his bathrobe and pajamas while he is eating breakfast, but then he has to put on his day clothes and wear those until after dinner. Even if he has a big accident, he has to put day clothes back on.

Sometimes if he is having a *bad* time he is allowed to put his bathrobe on over his day clothes but he's never allowed to be in his pajamas during the day unless he is sick, and then he has to stay in his room with the door open.

If he has been *good* he is allowed to wear his pajamas and bathrobe while he watches TV and has a snack before *Good night, Cody.*

Cody does not like changing clothes. But if he doesn't take off his pajamas and his bathrobe he won't get his changing-into-day-clothes sticker.

Let's go to the bathroom and see how you did. I sure do hope you get a sticker!

Esther takes him by his arm and leads him out of his room and down the hall, and now he is aware of the others in the house making sounds and moving around: Raisa, Big Mal, and Robbie-Myles-Felix-Angie-Melody.

In the bathroom, Esther changes his old diaper — *Darn, you've got a wet one so no sticker, but at least there's no number two* — and puts on a new one.

Okay, Cody . . . let's go back to your room to get your picture book . . .

Cody avoids looking at the others. Taking Esther's hand, he closes his eyes and makes a big, loud, long yawn all the way down the hall until they are back in his room.

Open your eyes now. Come on, Cody. Now get your book; go on, go get it.

Cody takes his picture book from its place on the table next to his bed.

They go to the kitchen. On one wall, there is a big white-board, the calendar, where they look every morning to find out what is happening today.

Esther says the names slowly as she points: *There's Robbie, Myles, Felix, Angie, Melody, and . . .*

Cody lost most of his letters around the same time he lost his words, but he still remembers the way his father helped him identify the letters that make up his name. He was sitting in his high chair, eating a face snack; his father wrote on the kitchen chalkboard and drew pictures to go with the letters.

Here's Cody's name, his father said, drawing.

Here's Cody's name, Esther says, pointing.

C

(horseshoe)

O

(moon)

D

(Santa's fat belly)

Y

(martini glass)

Esther goes on.

Today is . . .

She points at some other letters, lost ones.

S . . . u . . . n . . . d, a, y, and . . . look! There's something here. Something is happening for Cody today.

Cody gets out his book. He flips to a picture.

No. Not ponies. You don't go see the ponies today.

Cody flips to another picture.

No, you don't go to church for art lessons.

Cody closes his book and sits on the floor.

Cody. Get up. Get up! *You're not gonna get any stickers if you keep acting like that.*

Cody lies down.

Okay. Fine. Hey, everybody! No stickers for Cody today! And then, to the cook, *No breakfast either, I guess, Raisa, since boys who lie on the floor don't get breakfast.*

Is somebody having a bad day already? Raisa says. *Too bad, because for good children I make bacon and eggs and potatoes, children who sit up and act proper and come to the table.*

Cody, Esther says, *don't start with me like this. Look . . .*

She tries to take his book from him. Cody grunts and holds it tight.

Okay, that's it. I'm done. I guess you don't want to know who's coming to visit today.

Cody sits up. He flips to a photograph in his book.

Yes, Mom, but who else?

Cody flips to another photograph.

Esther sighs. *No. Not Emmy. Can I show you?*

Cody hands over his book. Esther finds a picture and shows it to him.

Who's this? Who's this, Cody?

Cody signs: a *D* to his forehead.

Dad! Yes, your dad is coming today. Won't that be nice?

Cody scowls and begins shaking his head with such adamant force that his entire torso swivels in protest. Then he flips to another picture and again thrusts his finger at it with blunt insistence.

No, Cody. No! *I already said no to the damn ponies.* No. Po-nies. Today. *Okay? Now come on, get up, it's time for breakfast . . . Lord, give me strength. Raisa, is that coffee ready yet?*

The Boy in the White Suit

When the end-of-recess bell rang on the first day of school
in the fall of 1962, the twenty-seven fourth-graders who had
been assigned to Mrs. Eloise Braxton (a group that included
Marlow, Charles Simon) dragged into room 104 with a sense
of dread.

Charles was especially glum that morning, not only because he'd been condemned to spend the year with the
teacher famously known as Brax the Ax, but because his best
friend, Donnie Bothwell, had moved to Minnesota over the
summer — suddenly, unexpectedly — when Mr. Bothwell got
a better job working for Hamm's.

An inescapable reminder of this sad truth came in the
form of a frequently aired television commercial. It began
with a black-and-white film of a full moon shining on a dark,
gently lapping lake; an announcer intoned, "This . . . is the
Land of Sky-Blue Waters. This . . . is the Land of Enchantment"; then came the sound of Indian tom-toms accom-

panying a velvet-voiced choir singing, "From the Land of Sky-Blue Waters . . ." Finally, the camera view widened to include a man and woman seated at a lakeside table raising their glasses in a toast while looking longingly into each other's eyes. Charles thought that Minnesota must be a wonderful place.

Then, as now, he did not make friends easily, so on that first day he was doubly worried about the things all nine-year-old boys worry about: Who would eat lunch with him? Who'd sit next to him on the bus during field trips? Who would offer the sanctuary of tribe during the wilderness of recess?

As the children filed in, they discovered a new kid; he was sitting at a front-row desk, smiling with unstinting benevolence, diffusing the laser beam of malice emanating from Mrs. Braxton, who commanded each child to state his or her full name and then — ominously, silently, not unlike the Ghost of Christmas Yet to Come — slowly lifted her arm and pointed to the child's assigned seat.

The fact that this new student was in the front row didn't elicit any special note on Charles's part; in his elementary-school career to date, he hadn't given much thought to the significance of seating charts, although he would soon enough.

No, what was odd was the fact that this boy was already *there*, as if conjured by magic. No one had seen him on the playground that morning. No one had ever seen him *anywhere*.

On the way to his desk, Charles heard the new boy mutter something in a strange, hollow voice that he took to be a greeting.

"Hi," he replied. "I'm Charlie."

"Dana McGucken!" Mrs. Braxton yapped. The force of her

voice set her famously bulldoggish face jiggling. "No talk-ing!" She rethrust her finger at Charles's fourth-row aisle seat and he moved on.

Dana burped. A couple of children laughed out loud; the rest snickered.

"Silence!" Mrs. Braxton marched to Dana's desk, leaned close, and hissed something. He bowed his head. His body curled in on itself, like a traumatized potato bug. At first, Charles worried that he might be crying, but once Mrs. Brax-ton's back was turned Dana looked over his shoulder, graced the class with a diffusely aimed smile, and stuck a pencil up his nose.

As the second bell sounded and Mrs. Braxton began roll call, Charles became aware of the three other children who had been assigned front-row placement: two thuggish types who looked like Boys Town rejects (because of their hard-ened appearance, he suspected they might be fourth-grade repeaters), and Astrida Pukis, who was brilliant but myopic and always sat in the front row. (They'd been in the same class since kindergarten.) But he barely noticed them.

Dana was the one; he had all Charles's attention.

He was small for a fourth-grader, elfin. His upper back was bent, and his head and neck retracted into his shoul-ders, giving him the appearance of someone who'd spent his formative years stuffed inside a tree. It made him seem ancient, wizened. He had chalky white skin and a weasel-shaped face. His teeth were impossibly crooked: a handful of Chiclets in a crazy-angled row.

There was a pale, cyanotic blush on the very tips of his ears and fingers, as if he were in the early stages of being cryogenically preserved. His hands were elegantly shaped, portrait-worthy, like those of some eighteenth-century aris-tocrat, poet, or pianist; his fingernails were long, oval, opalescent — weirdly feminine — but rimmed and clouded with grit.

He was dressed entirely in white: a rumpled, oversize three-piece linen suit (vest, jacket, cuffed and pleated trousers) and buttoned-up shirt. No tie. This getup, in combination with his cringing physical attributes, suggested the character of a slightly crazed, furtive foreign spy who'd been stationed for too many years in a politically unstable tropical country, one of those Peter Lorre types who keep laughing and grinning even as they're being slowly driven insane by the demands of the espionage business.

"Attention, children!" Mrs. Braxton began moving through the room depositing single half sheets of lined paper on the desks. "I'd like you to print your full name — first, middle, and last — in your very best writing."

Astrida's hand went up.

"Yes?"

"Where would you like us to print our names, Mrs. Braxton? On the top line?"

"That would be fine, Astrida. Thank you for your attention to detail."

Astrida swiveled in her chair, enough to make sure everyone could see her satisfied smirk.

"However," Mrs. Braxton continued, "let me repeat: what is most important is that you use your *very best penmanship*. If you make a mistake and wish to start over, raise your hand and I will give you a fresh piece of paper. *No erasing!* You may begin."

The children ducked their heads and set to work — everyone except Dana, who began to exhibit the first of several behaviors they would all come to know well over the course of the school year: he started swaying, back and forth, side to side. Not in a frantic way, but dreamily, serenely, at a

tempo that would align nicely with a group of tipsy, frater-
nal, schmaltz-affected partygoers singing "Auld Lang Syne"
with their arms slung round one another after the clock
strikes midnight and the new year begins.

Charles was fascinated.

He was also horrified, because in that moment he understood the reason for Dana McGucken's front-row placement
and, more crucial, the enormous social gaffe he'd made in
speaking to him as if he were a normal kid.

How could he not have known?

Dana McGucken was *a ree-tard.*

In 1962, the word *retarded* was the best, kindest, and
frankly most accurate description there was, a linguistic
catchall that has since been divided and subdivided into
dozens, perhaps hundreds, of categories.

Who knows what Dana's real story was?

He might have had attention deficit disorder, attention
deficit hyperactivity disorder, Asperger's syndrome, obses-
sive-compulsive disorder, phenylketonuria, fetal alcohol
syndrome, Pitt-Hopkins syndrome, or some combination of
the above.

Or maybe he was put on the planet as a miracle-in-
reverse, a punch line for a joke that nobody gets but God, a
test for the rest of us, something to interpret, translate, decode. A mystery of faith — *Can you accept never knowing? Can
you love without condition?* — made manifest.

"I'm going to put these away until June," Mrs. Braxton announced as she collected the work, "at which time we will
compare them with your end-of-the-year signatures, which
will be in *cursive.*"

She moved on to other subjects. There were the usual
assessments in reading and arithmetic; as these proceeded,
Dana showed off more behaviors in his repertoire: staring

at the ceiling or out the window, rocking, picking his nose, sticking pencils in his ears, kicking his feet.

Near the end of that first day, Mrs. Braxton delivered a lengthy sermon, its subject the value of good penmanship in general and the virtues of the Palmer Method in particular. In little time, there wasn't a child in room 104 who wasn't cross-eyed — even Astrida had the look of a hypoglycemic on quaaludes.

At the conclusion of her lecture, Mrs. Braxton once again handed out sheets of paper. "Now, class, to see how well you've been listening, I'm going to ask some questions. Please write your first and last names on the top upper left line, and below that, the numbers one through four."

Dana was demonstrating a new behavior: he'd started moving his arms in a grand, angular fashion, at the same time emitting rhythmic, grunting noises. Perhaps he was semaphoring an inspirational coded message — NEVER NEVER NEVER GIVE UP! — or telling a morale-boosting joke.

"Again," Mrs. Braxton said, striding through the ranks, stopping briefly at Dana's desk to take hold of his arms and firmly resettle them on his desk, "please demonstrate your very best penmanship. For today, and today *only*, do not worry about spelling."

Stationing herself at the blackboard, Mrs. Braxton took up a piece of chalk and began writing her questions in cursive as she simultaneously spoke them aloud.

Brax the Ax was a squat, heavy woman, broad of beam, who wore high-heeled pumps that were obviously too small. Seen from behind, her silhouette suggested Humpty Dumpty balanced precariously on a pair of golf tees.

But there was no denying that to watch Mrs. Braxton write in cursive was to witness a transformation: she became a figure of impressive grace and strength. Her technique was so smooth and effortless that she might have been writing with a fountain pen; the chalk made almost no sound on the blackboard. And she wrote quickly too.

"Number one. The first objects to be written upon were tablets made of . . ."

Charles knew that one: *Clay.*

"Number two. The name of the person who invented the penmanship style we will be learning in fourth grade is . . ."

Unsure, he guessed: *Mister Arnld Pahmer.*

"Number three. The proper angle for writing cursive is . . ."

The only child to dive for her pencil in response to that question was Astrida.

"And, finally, complete this quote: 'To know how to *write* well is to know how to *blank* well.'"

Dana filled in the blank with an impressively thunderous fart.

The room erupted in laughter.

"Silence!" Mrs. Braxton shouted.

Dana turned around and beamed. His pale complexion acquired the satiny sheen of a newly harvested pearl. His white suit seemed to emit a dazzling glow.

"Silence!" Mrs. Braxton repeated, taking up a ruler and rapping it on her desk. Eventually, the children of room 104 regained their composure.

By the time the final bell rang on that first day, Charles Simon Marlow's attitude toward the boy in the white suit had undergone another change.

Whether Dana McGucken's courage was born of genetically programmed stupidity or genuine spirit was impossible to know, but the truth was, from the very beginning, Charles admired him.

Password Strength: Weak

Charles's academic year — his twenty-second teaching at the sixth- through twelfth-grade private school known as City Prana (CONFIDENT INDEPENDENT THOUGHTFUL YOUTH PROMOTING RESPONSIBILITY, the ARTS, and NOBLE ASPIRATIONS) — was off to a dreary start. Not because anything had *changed;* on the contrary, everything was exactly, reassuringly, as it always was. It was quite puzzling.

Charles always looked forward to the first day of school, the way the students' arrival transformed the main building from a mausoleum to a ballroom. A perplexing stylistic mashup of French Moroccan and English Tudor, the structure had been the original carriage house/servants' quarters adjacent to a nineteenth-century mansion that had been demolished decades ago; the forlorn and lesser surviving twin of an architectural duo that now, standing on its own, no longer made any sense.

He was grateful too for the way that the strictures and demands of his profession provided him with a vessel, one that contained the intrinsic messiness that is human interaction.

Above all, he relished the clean-slate, newly-emerged-from-the-confessional feeling: *Today, we begin. Today, and today only, there is achievement amnesty; anything is possible and everyone is excellent until proven average.*

But as Charles trudged upstairs to his second-floor classroom, he couldn't summon anything but a weary, resolute calm, oddly impermeable to the effervescent energies of students and staff. It was as if he'd been encased in the emotional equivalent of a hazmat suit.

He was tired, that was all; exhausted, really, since he was still having trouble sleeping. He'd even found himself drifting off during the required faculty meetings that had filled the two days before the students' arrival. One of his colleagues, art teacher Pam Hamilton, actually had to nudge him out of a sound sleep during the requisite yearly seminar on Diversity Awareness.

Was there such a thing as late-onset narcolepsy?

At least today's schedule was a reduced one: after checking in with their homeroom teachers, all students went to a fifty-minute welcome-back assembly in the gym, which was housed in one of the new buildings next door.

Charles decided that, having sat through two decades' worth of these first-day revels, he could skip today's and get a head start on reading the paperwork that had already amassed in his mail cubby — a daunting stack that included the latest edition of *The City Prana Senior-Project Guide for Teachers.*

The sounds of footsteps, laughter, and spoken words faded. Charles could almost hear the old building sigh with disappointment: *What? Gone again? They're leaving already?*

Taking a seat at his desk, he began to read.

Because senior project was the cornerstone and culmination of senior year, every homeroom teacher was expected to spend an inordinate amount of time going over *The Senior-Project Preparatory Handbook Packet*. After this, students were required to fill out the paperwork contained within *The Senior-Project Workbook* and produce rough drafts of their project ideas; finally, each of them turned in a contract confirming every detail and requiring only slightly fewer initials and signatures than a home mortgage.

Charles found this growing trend toward excessive accountability in education worrisome, one of the things that often made him feel less like the shepherd of young minds and more like a bank officer at a savings and loan — the beleaguered George Bailey from *It's a Wonderful Life*.

As he continued making his way through the pile (wasn't the whole point of e-mail to avoid paper waste?), he was surprised to discover that the bulk of this mass consisted of the rough drafts of several senior-project proposals.

This was unprecedented. Charles couldn't remember ever receiving proposals on the first day. Was this year's senior class exceptionally motivated?

Naomi Barstow planned to volunteer with vets suffering from PTSD at the VA hospital; Carlos Fontana wanted to study community-sponsored agriculture and produce a local Farm Aid concert; Kaisha Woodward intended to explore a potential future career by shadowing women firefighters and interviewing them about their experiences in a male-dominated field; Ethan Chichester was composing a klezmer/jazz oratorio for an intergenerational orchestra and choir on Mercer Island to be performed as part of a community center dedication. Clearly they'd all assimilated the *noble aspirations* element of the school acronym.

Emmy would have been a model student at City Prana, but because their home environment was so tightly controlled, it was decided that a less rarefied atmosphere would be better for her — one in which she'd have to assert herself to achieve notice and wouldn't face the stigma of being a teacher's kid. It had been a wrenching decision, but a good one: their bashful, humble homebody of a daughter (with her off-the-charts IQ) had graduated summa cum laude from Roosevelt High School at the age of sixteen.

The fifth proposal came from Romy Bertleson, one of Pam Hamilton's art-student standouts:

"A Picture's Worth": Photography and Text
(Combined Focus in Studio Art and Creative Writing)

PROJECT GOAL: *to produce a series of photographic portraits and short texts for an art exhibit sponsored by Art Without Boundaries, an organization that provides arts-enrichment programs for persons marginalized by socio-economic, mental-health, and intellectual challenges.*

When Charles saw her sitting in the back row of his homeroom this morning, he'd barely recognized her.

My current interests are studio photography and science. At this point I hope to have a career in medicine, possibly in the field of neuroscience research. These interests dovetail in this project proposal . . .

Gone were the defiantly geeky horn-rimmed prescription glasses, the oil-spotted mechanic's overall, machine-embroidered with the name *Alonzo D.* and overlayered with thrift-store articles: Catholic school plaid skirts, crinoline tutus, men's boxer shorts. Today she wore a pair of jeans and a mannish-looking shirt over a plain T. Period.

Art Without Boundaries offers classes for people with conditions such as Alzheimer's, dementia, and developmental disabilities. I have been given permission to attend classes and take photographs.

The one fashion item that had withstood every costume change through the years was Romy's camera, worn on an embroidered strap and slung diagonally across her body, an accessory that — depending on the accompanying fashion context — had suggested everything from Miss America's silk moiré ribbon to Rambo's bandolier.

The culmination of the project will be the inclusion of my work as part of an exhibit that showcases the art and writing of professional artists and program participants and raises money for the organization.

What eventually confirmed her as *Bertleson, Romy Andrea*, was her voice — still a husky, high-pitched chirp — and that pleasant citrus odor that Charles had noticed for the first time a few years ago while Christmas shopping at the mall.

What's that smell? he'd wondered, retracing his steps until he stood in the entrance of The Body Shop, and Emmy replied, *Satsuma Body Butter,* and Charles asked, *Do you think your mother would like some?* and Emmy considered, doing that funny thing with her mouth where she yanked it sideways, her default expression whenever she was contemplating something with gravity, and then she shook her head and said, *Some women are florals, some women are fruits, and some women are herbals; Mom is* definitely *a floral.* Charles asked, *How about* you? And she answered with tolerant exasperation, *Daaad, I'm twelve. It's too soon to tell. Ask me again when I'm sixteen.*

Charles lifted Romy's proposal off his desk, laid it against his face, and inhaled deeply. Yes, even the pages were infused with the fragrance of oranges.

"Good morning."

Charles's feet jolted off the floor, as if some unseen, punitive researcher had flipped a switch, causing the test subject to experience a low-voltage electrocution.

It was Pam Hamilton, leaning against the doorjamb, stock-still and smiling in a fond, amused way that Charles found unsettling. Even immobile, she gave off a hovering, silent, intensely vibratory energy, like a hummingbird. Charles wondered how long she'd been watching him.

"You playing hooky too?" she asked. Her hands were wrapped around one of those pathetic, lumpy paperweights-passing-for-coffee-mugs that her beginning pottery students were always making.

Charles tapped the edges of Romy Bertleson's proposal into alignment and turned it face-down on his desk. "I think it's safe to say we've both assimilated the content of the 'Welcome to City Prana' assembly."

Pam gave a subdued, single-syllable chuckle and sauntered into the room.

This habit she had, of strolling in without being formally asked, had been annoying Charles for at least a decade, but what ultimately made her intrusions bearable was the manner of their execution: Pam moved lightly, almost noiselessly, and in an indirect path, not looking at him but surveying various aspects of the room — ceiling, floor, walls, windows — as if she were here in the capacity of a building inspector, and Charles's presence was purely coincidental.

"I've been trying for half an hour to change my damn password," she said, staring with apparent fascination at the electrical outlet next to Charles's desk. Her focus was so steadfast that Charles found himself following her gaze, noticing for the first time that stacked grounded outlets looked a little like smiley faces — vertical slashes for eyes, arch-shaped holes for mouths — except they weren't smiling; they appeared to be chorusing the word *Oh!*, as if witnessing a spectacularly horrific social blunder.

Pam moved farther into the room and shifted her eyes toward the ceiling; she began studying the smoke detector, which was, thankfully, featureless. "You got that e-mail, didn't you, about how some kid has already hacked into the system?"

"Yes. It's inconvenient."

"At the risk of validating a passel of stereotypes, I have to say that I *hate* all this tech stuff." She immediately slapped a hand over her mouth and emitted a muffled *Oops*. "Sorry, not the way we teach the kids to talk is it? *Despise? Disdain?*" She started roaming the room again. "Personally, I find embracing technology to be a challenge. Why can't we go back to the good old days: attendance books you actually *write* in, with actual writing *implements?* Report cards?" She squatted beneath one of the windows, showing an acute fascination with the shoe molding. "You're old enough to remember report cards, aren't you?"

"I am."

Nimble knees, Charles thought, admiring Pam's flexibility. She had to be in her early sixties. His own joints suddenly felt sticky and unyielding, as if they'd been lubricated with tar. He wanted to get up and stretch. He wanted his solitude back. He liked Pam Hamilton but was always slightly discomfited in her presence; there was something too well-adjusted about her, too bright, too incisive, even when she wasn't looking directly into his face. *But then,* he thought, *that's a set of artist's eyes for you.*

"Thank God," she said. "Ever since becoming a card-carrying member of the AARP, people's ages are impossible to figure out."

Charles inhaled sharply enough for her to shoot him a worried look. Although he'd trained himself out of the (according to Alison) extremely disagreeable habit of verbally correcting grammar infractions, he still experienced an intense reflexive repugnance for dangling participles.

He grinned in Pam's general direction and then took up his pen and a notepad and wrote, *I cannot determine people's ages.*

Pam stood and ambled through the circle of desks to the far end of the classroom, where a trio of folding screens formed three walls of a smaller room within a room: a student lounge that Charles painstakingly furnished and arranged over the years with a rotating assortment of beanbag chairs, sofas, footstools, oversize floor pillows. There were thick-pile rugs on the floor, and a pair of HappyLight floor lamps allowed students to study beneath illumination gentler than that supplied by the twitchy fluorescent tubes overhead and helped combat seasonal affective disorder.

The intense, demanding work of a Language Arts class — reading, reflection, discourse, writing — put students in the path of risks and hazards that were (in Charles's opinion) every bit as dangerous as those encountered in chemistry, metallurgy, or glass blowing. It was his job to make sure that the young people in his care felt sufficiently protected to take those risks. Two decades of teaching experience had taught him that teenagers feel safest when they're allowed to slouch.

"A person could live in this room, practically," Pam observed. This was exactly how Charles felt, but this concurring remark from his colleague was disturbing, especially since there were in fact many times when he'd opted to spend the night here. What if Pam Hamilton got it into her head to do the same? They all had master keys.

"Do you mind if I sit for a minute?" Pam went on. "There's something I wanted to talk to you about."

She eased down onto the sofa so that they were facing each other across the room's expanse and took a sip of whatever was in that atrocious mug.

"Have you seen Romy Bertleson today?" she asked.

"Yes, she's one of my homeroom kids."

Pam had an understated, unfussy elegance: no makeup; a nimbus of curly, blond, flyaway hair generously scribbled with silver and battened down on either side of Pam's face (just barely) by a pair of tortoise-shell combs; wire-rimmed glasses; boyish figure; khakis and a cardigan and slip-on Merrells. "She's changed, hasn't she?" Pam said.

"God, yes."

Pam had been at City Prana as long as anyone; she and a group of young parents/educators had started the school back in the 1970s. All three of Pam's children had gone here. Now she was a grandmother.

"Don't you love it? When kids transform like that?"

Not really, Charles wanted to say.

Pam absent-mindedly fingered her multistranded, multicolored necklace — beads and carved stone, animal fetishes (Alaskan, was Charles's guess; he remembered that one of her daughters lived up that way) — there was something rosary-like about it. Charles wondered from time to time if Pam was another lapsed — or even practicing — Catholic. Not that they discussed personal matters.

"Have you had a chance to speak with her about her project idea?" Pam asked.

"Not yet, but she turned in a rough draft proposal."

"Have you read it?"

"Not all of it."

Staring at the contents of her mug, Pam raised and lowered her tea bag a few times. "I don't want to steal her thunder. She'll tell you about it."

Charles glanced at the clock. "Well . . . ," he said, hoping the up-inflected word would have the effect of lifting Pam off the sofa.

"I just wanted to make sure it's okay with you."

"Sorry; whether what's okay?"

Pam looked up. "Romy's proposal? Art Without Boundaries? Her taking photographs? That's not an issue for you?"

"Why would it be an issue?"

"Well . . . Cody participates in that program, doesn't he?"

Charles was surprised that Pam knew this, but then he remembered that she and Alison had stayed in touch after the divorce. Ali had probably mentioned it.

"Yes. He goes to classes twice a week."

Clearly, Pam was waiting for him to elaborate, but what else was there to say? He certainly wasn't going to object to Romy's proposal because it would put her in contact with his son. Was that what Pam was worried about?

"How is Cody doing?"

"Fine."

Charles avoided her eyes; he became entranced by the way she continued to raise and lower the tea bag, rhythmically, precisely; it was like watching a miniature offshore oil-rig operation.

"Okay, then," she said finally. "One more thing . . ." She withdrew the tea bag, tossed it into a nearby receptacle, and settled back into the sofa cushions with the demeanor of someone intending a long visit. "Because Romy's including both art and creative-writing elements, I think she's going to ask us to be co-advisers."

"What? Why? I mean, it's not something I've been asked to do before."

"I have, by other kids with dual-focus projects. There are advantages. We can share the load."

"True," Charles said, although he had no idea how that would work.

"Do you have her proposal? She's got something in there about people without language." Pam looked at him expectantly.

Charles turned over the proposal and began leafing through it. "'Who tells the stories of people who have limited or no language? Is there a way to help empower such people to tell their own stories?'"

"Good stuff, don't you think?"

Charles grunted in the affirmative but he was mostly thinking about how much he hated (*despised, disdained*) the word *empower.*

"She's got this kind of Diane-Arbus-meets-Dorothea-Lange-meets-Allen-Ginsberg homage going on, unconsciously, I think, and obviously derivative, but you know what they say: Imitation is the sincerest form of flattery."

A child who cannot imitate cannot learn.

The response was so ingrained and automatic that Charles thought it was subtextual, but when there was a silence, he looked up to find Pam staring at him again, and he realized he'd spoken aloud.

"Right," she said flatly, and stood. Her thin figure seemed older now, stiff; her movements contained a quality of angularity, like a card table being set up, or an ironing board. "Well, let me know how it goes with Romy and what you decide about the co-adviser thing. Have a good one."

After she was gone, Charles left his desk and began moving through the room, feeling compelled to touch the desks, tidy the books, re-angle the folding screens, refluff the sofa cushions — in reassurance, perhaps, or to reinforce his proprietary relationship to this sanctuary.

The upholstery was lightly scented with whatever Pam had been drinking, something herbal and spicy. The smell reminded Charles of the ginger-molasses cookies that were a daily staple of the Cloud City pastry case — and Emmy's favorite.

He must remember to buy some and send a care package soon.

❖

By twelve forty-five, Charles's exchange with Pam Hamilton had been excised from his awareness. He'd closed the door to his classroom, had eaten some soup, and was hunkered down in one of the beanbag chairs reading Ted Kooser's *100 Postcards to Jim Harrison* when someone knocked.

He jerked the door open to find Romy Bertleson. Wide-eyed, she took a half step back. He'd frightened her.

"Hi, Mr. Marlow," she said in her high-pitched, scratchy voice: Tweety Bird with seasonal allergies. "Sorry to interrupt. I was wondering if you had time to talk . . ."

Although his hospitality was a lie — he was still struggling with an overwhelming feeling of just not being *ready* for all this — he said yes, of course, invited her to come in, left the door open as protocol mandated, and assumed a seat behind his desk.

"Did you get a chance to look at my proposal?" Romy asked.

There was that smell again: citrusy, lush, confectionary, complex.

"I did, yes, but . . ." Charles hastily retrieved Romy's paperwork. He remembered now that she'd asked him at the end of homeroom if she could stop by during lunch; he should have been prepared. "Why don't you tell me more about what you have in mind?"

And so she began, a scatter shot of words, enthused, heedless, optimistic, in that wonderfully unguarded way that belongs to the impassioned young, telling him that the only thing she'd settled on for sure was the idea of creating photographic portraits paired with some kind of text, maybe poetry. She mentioned the unit Charles taught in tenth grade, Allen Ginsberg's American Sentences: seventeen syllables, haikus unspooled.

"I'm not a poet, not like . . ." And she named a few classmates, young people Charles knew to be connected with Seattle's poetry-slam scene and who — Charles could only guess, for he'd never actually *been* to a poetry slam — likely shouted amplified obscenities with a rapturous sense of discovery, ownership, and invention, as if Lenny Bruce had never existed. But that too Charles found charming and worthy of commendation; at some point, he imagined, the trend would swing in the opposite direction, and notions of what was radical would involve unplugging and reciting hymnic poems, as if Emily Dickinson had never existed.

"But American Sentences," she continued, "I like those, and having the creative-writing component would be a way of stepping outside my comfort zone, like we're supposed to. That's why I was hoping you'd be a co-adviser with Ms. Hamilton."

She fell silent and blinked several times, re-agitating the air and sending a satsuma-scented squall in Charles's direction. She'd been talking for so long and with such run-on patterned inflections that it took him a few moments to realize that some sort of query had been posed and she was awaiting a response.

"You've obviously given this a lot of thought," he said, buying time by stating the obvious.

What had she asked? He looked down — Had her eyes always been this huge and luminous? Had she always looked so much like Emmy? — and shuffled through her proposal. "You said something about having a personal connection to your project . . ."

"Yes." She swallowed hard and readjusted her position, sitting back, crossing an ankle over her thigh, a habitual posture that didn't carry its former cockiness since she held her hands in a demure, meditative fashion: two small nested bowls, precisely placed in the center of her lap. "My grandma had Alzheimer's. We used to be really close until she got sick. She died over the summer. Toward the end, she didn't know any of us, not even my mom, and . . . well, I'm just sorry that I didn't find out more about her, and about the disease, before it, well, took her away from us."

Here then, Charles understood, was the deeper circumstance beneath Romy Bertleson's transformation. *Sometimes,* he thought, *they really do flower right before your eyes.* "I'm sorry," he said, recalling that blooms do not always emerge in sunlight but can be *forced* by prolonged darkness and isolation, by sorrow.

Charles paused, waiting to see if Romy had more to divulge. Or ask.

She didn't, and — recognizing a fellow tortoise when he saw one — Charles made no further attempt to invite her confidence. In his opinion (one in opposition to the current trend), teenagers had just as much right to hide within a carapace of privacy as adults.

"I'd be happy to be your adviser," he said, "along with Ms. Hamilton."

Romy's eyes widened briefly — a toddler on the playground swing getting pushed just a little too high — but then she frowned and stared down into her upturned palms with such intensity that Charles wondered for a moment if she'd been conducting the interview with the aid of crib notes.

"Just get on the paperwork," Charles continued, rising from his desk and ushering her toward the door. "I know it's a pain, but it's the way we do things."

"Thanks, Mr. Marlow."

Suddenly shedding her diffidence, she stood up straight and readjusted her camera in a resolute manner that made Charles afraid she was about to shoot his picture at point-blank range.

But she merely added "See you tomorrow!" and then clumped away on those heavy clog-like shoes with the urgency of Dorothea Lange on a deadline. Teenagers could be such chameleons.

Charles checked the clock: seven minutes until the bell.

After closing the door, he crossed the room and sank back into his beanbag chair, intending to resume reading. But he found that he was too distracted by shafts of light and shadow bending and crisscrossing as they fell between the satsuma trees.

Homo Scriptor, Homo Factum

Once in a while you might notice an elderly person — or even someone of my father's generation — doodling a long series of loops like this:

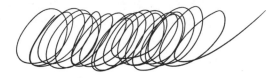

Try it. It's harder than it looks.

I said *doodling,* but it's the wrong word, implying as it does a kind of mindlessness, an absence of awareness and intent, a physical correlate, perhaps, to *daydreaming.* A more accurate verb would be *producing.*

This will serve as your introduction to the handwriting system known as the Palmer Method. We'll begin with basic loop practice.

What you're aiming for is threefold: a perfectly smooth line, uniformity of loop size, and evenness of pen pressure. (A superior writing implement — my father's Montegrappa Italia, for example — is a great assist in this regard, by the way.)

All of this requires maintaining a balance between control and relaxation — a challenge in *any* endeavor — and to this end, finding the right speed is both a vital part of the process and a highly personalized one, since most human beings move through life in a predetermined metronomic comfort zone. Going too fast will lend a frantic quality to the experience; going too slow will make one feel clunky, impatient, stalled, uncalibrated — a cog out of whack, a set of misaligned zipper teeth. One person's largo is another person's allegro, so when it comes to tempo, do not expect to succeed by emulating someone else, not your penmanship teacher, not a fellow student, not even that amazingly proficient little woman sitting in the Madonna's Home waiting room. Success in the execution of Palmer loops demands that you locate the beat of your inner drummer.

Try again. Don't lose heart.

When executed correctly — to the exacting standards imposed by the Palmer Method of business writing — the loops start to take on a three-dimensional look.

No worries. You'll get it.

Trust me: practicing Palmer loops with dedication and sincerity is a worthy pursuit. Potentially beneficial side effects extend well beyond improved penmanship and include the following:

1. Loop practice lights up little-used or even failing connections within the brain.
2. It offers a low-cost, minimal-effort option for stress reduction, engendering the same kind of meditative tranquility that some people find from other kinds of repetitive physical actions: swimming laps, shooting hoops, kneading bread, knitting. No need for special equipment, fancy footwear, innate agility, or a gym membership; one need summon only enough energy to pick up a pen.
3. In rare cases, among the ascended masters, Palmer loops can open up traversable wormholes, portals through which the space-time traveler may access the distant past.

❖

Sister Giorgia Maria Fiducia D'Amati finds herself sitting alone at a wooden table in a large room with big windows. These surroundings — they are familiar, *aren't they?*

She must be in one of the church-school classrooms.

Yes, that's it.

Two of her sisters are over there, across the room, talking to a third person — perhaps the mother of a new student, for she is dressed in a modest and attractive manner, as mothers often are: skirt, cardigan, blouse. Or maybe she is a newly arrived novitiate. God knows they could use some new blood.

She's a bit old to be entering the convent, but then, one answers when one is called.

Their voices are quiet, indistinct; occasionally, they all turn to look at her.

There is no sign of the students, which is puzzling. Maybe they are still sleeping, or at recess, or at Mass.

To pass the time and to prepare for their arrival, Giorgia begins doing some loop practice. Her hands are all but useless now for anything but this:

Up, down, around . . . Up, down, around . . .

She feels the eyes of her sisters and the other woman upon her.

It might be best if you say goodbye now, the unknown woman says, *before we take her to her room. It usually makes the transition easier.* Giorgia's sisters nod. Sister Martha brings a handkerchief to her face and dabs at her eyes, her cheeks. *Please don't worry,* the woman adds. *We'll get her settled after you leave . . .*

Their conversation continues. Giorgia has no idea who they are talking about or why this woman, this stranger, is speaking with such authority — and such composure! Why are they not, *all* of them, *worried,* as she is, about the whereabouts of the students?

Maybe the classroom location has been changed and Father forgot to tell her. (That would make sense. She has never been one of his favorites.)

Construction, renovation, fortification: could it be under way at last? Giorgia squints at the ceiling. The parish school roof has been in need of repair for so long. A disgrace, really. They've been teaching among buckets, paint cans, soup pots, and frying pans for months, maybe years, their voices all but drowned out by the incessant, tinny *plinkaplinkaplink* of falling water so that sometimes there's nothing to do but abandon whatever lesson was planned, declare recess, hand out the Noah's Ark bath toys, and read from Genesis (*and the waters prevailed upon the earth one hundred and fifty days*), hoping by such actions to reassure their God that they *understand* and *preserve in their hearts* the lesson of this *weather:* they are to pray *as the rain falls, without surcease.* The occasional sun break, dear Lord, would not cause them to forget.

It is holy water falling on the heads of God's unanointed children! some of her sisters joke when the roof leaks, but to Giorgia it is no laughing matter. An unbaptized child deserves all their prayers, and she makes of her sisters' levity a weighty plea:

Lo, how He directs even the rain to bless them!

Giorgia slides off the chair seat and kneels.

O Lord, grant these unfortunates entry into Thy eternal kingdom, these, the mute, the broken, discarded as chaff upon the earth. And yet does not the chaff provide nourishment for the birds of winter — the quail, the cardinal, the sparrow? Surely, dear Father, Thou has prepared a kinder place for them in the life to come, and for these special ones it shall not *be in heaven as it is on earth — where they are labeled imbecilic, defective, idiotic, retarded.*

Where *are* they?

Maybe she is to teach outside today, in the meadow or on the beach. The students enjoy being outside when it is fine.

Giorgia looks out the picture window, the one facing the courtyard. The light is pale, the day is gray as usual, but the rain has stopped, at least for the moment, so perhaps . . .

Of course, even the picnic tables are soggy, but she could bring the parachutes.

No, wait. Not parachutes. Something else. Large and billowing, just the thing that is called for at a picnic . . .

Then it occurs to her — *Oh no, please, no!* — that perhaps Father has ordered that the students be reassigned, to Sister Frieda or (God forbid) Sister Elspeth. Maybe Giorgia has been deemed unfit and relieved of her responsibilities.

But to what place has she been sent and for what reason? What sin did she commit to be separated from her pupils in this manner?

Ah! There is one other explanation, the most likely yet.

She is being tested.

This would not be unprecedented; her life since girlhood has been replete with tests, trials, and sufferings, and God knows, she has passed them all. She has kept her faith. She has never doubted or relented, not once.

Getting up off her knees and resuming her place at the table, she begins again.

Up, down, around . . . Up, down, around . . .

She looks up. Her sisters stand before her, their expressions strangely pitying; the woman stands behind them, and now, a few feet behind her, another stranger has appeared: a man, huge, dressed in white, his expression austere. One of God's fallen? All that's missing are his wings.

Sister Martha gathers Giorgia into a lengthy, firm embrace; she is crying, that's obvious now, but why?

Sister Frances hugs her as well. Her mustache and chin whiskers need tending. She too — *is it possible?* — has tears in her eyes.

Goodbye, Sister, they are saying. *Goodbye, God bless, we will see you again soon.*

Giorgia is irritated. Of *course* they'll see one another again soon — at supper, at evening prayer, at vespers. How can they leave when there is still no sign of the children? Why do they not answer her questions?

Giorgia waves them off brusquely, adding, *"Bene! Fuori,"* causing Sister Martha to produce a new storm system of tears. *"Risolvo il problema da sola! Dio mi aiuterà!"*

Her sisters depart, arm in arm, their heads bent. Giorgia is still angry with them, although she cannot help but feel a twinge of sadness and regret as well. Her temper has always been a problem; temper, pride, recklessness, foolhardiness. It's been thus since she was a girl.

But now, she has work to do, and she strides off in search of her pupils.

The woman intercepts her, blocking her path. The tall man takes her by the arm, his grip firm. Giorgia struggles, but she cannot get away. Even Giorgia's strength — and she is strong, *forte,* like a man — is no match for a fallen angel. Is he taking her away? *No. No!*

"Devo rimanere qui e aspettare per gli studenti!"

They wrestle her down the hall, past other rooms with open doors —

Who are those blank-eyed people? Giorgia wonders, growing more and more fearful. *All old, all alone. Is this hell? Where are the children?*

— and into an unfamiliar, smaller room with a bed, a table, a bureau, a chair, and a window; the view is of a sunflower field.

The fallen angel releases his grip. The woman speaks in a calm voice. *This is your new room, Giorgia. See? All your things are here.*

At least there is a desk, small but serviceable. She sits at once and begins to comfort herself in the best way she knows, shaping her hand around what only she can see, beginning again: practice and prayer, prayer and practice. God knows. God sees. God understands. It is but another way of saying the rosary.

If only the students would come. Even one would be enough. Just one . . .

O Raphael, Angel of Happy Meetings, lead us toward those we are waiting for, those who wait for us, those dear ones we seek!

Until then, she waits. She works. She holds fast to her faith and remains diligent in her industry.

Up, down, around . . .

God or His angels will send someone. Sooner or later. Here or elsewhere.

Till then, she goes on.

◆

They are watching a Thomas the Tank Engine video in the big room after lunch — all except Big Mal, who always goes outside after they eat to smoke a cigarette and talk on the phone — when there's the sound of the front door opening.

I bet I know who that is, Cody, Esther says from her chair. *I bet that's your dad.*

It is. It is Dad. He is carrying a grocery bag.

Hello, Cody. How are you, son? I brought you something . . .

Dad reaches into the bag: *Here you go, buddy. Have fun.*

He pulls out two large blocks of packaged ramen noodles, sets them on the floor, and then steps back several feet.

Cody rushes across the room and snatches up the blocks. Securing them against the side of his torso, he gallops to the counter that separates the kitchen from the living room: this is where he is allowed to do this work, here and nowhere else.

Dad follows, coming around to the kitchen side of the counter. Raisa is leaning against the sink, looking at a magazine.

How you doin' today, Mr. Marlow? Esther asks from her chair.

I'm okay, Esther, how about you?

Fine. Just fine, thank you.

Dad sets a small white plastic tub on the counter directly in front of Cody. This is a tool Cody needs. Soon the work will begin.

How about you, Raisa? Dad says.

Not bad.

Do you mind if I make a fresh pot of coffee?

Not a bit.

And could I trouble you for some aspirin?

You bet.

Raisa's hands unlock and open one of the drawers and give Dad a bottle — *Here you go* — Dad pours three pills into his hand, the bottle goes away, Raisa locks the drawer, all this while Cody stands and watches and waits. He needs to get to work.

Cody starts tapping his hand on a block of noodles so that it makes a noise. Raisa reads; she doesn't look up. Dad pours a glass of water, puts the pills in his mouth, takes a drink, swallows.

Cody grabs Raisa's magazine.

Hey! Raisa says.

Cody! Dad says. *Give that back to Raisa. Right now!*

Cody holds out the magazine, Raisa takes it and moves out of reach.

Cody grabs both blocks of noodles and starts banging them together.

Okay, Cody, I get it. Dad rubs his head. *Just give me a minute . . .*

He brings out the other needed tools: Cody's mortar-and-pestle collection. Cody is not permitted to keep these in his bedroom.

Dad places the mortar-and-pestle sets on the kitchen

counter: marble, wood, clay, stone, granite; little, medium, big, bigger, biggest.

There you go. Everything okay now?

Cody smiles; he enjoys seeing all his tools — but he does *not* enjoy Dad leaning on the counter and looking at him, too close, even though he is on the other side. Cody reaches across the counter and pushes Dad's face away.

Cody! Raisa says. *Too rough! You hurt your father? After he bring those noodles for you?*

Cody looks down and crosses his arms, wedging his fists into his armpits.

It's okay, Raisa, Dad says, backing away. *My fault.*

I'm sorry, Mr. Marlow. You have your coffee.

Raisa puts the other tools away.

Cody waits.

I set timer now. Raisa's voice is quiet but mad. She points a finger. *Ten minutes. No more.*

That's right, Esther says from her chair. *You want a sticker, you have to put those noodles away the second that timer goes off. No fussing.*

Finally, he begins. This is how the work is done:

First, he rips the wrapping off one of the big blocks and tosses it into the plastic tub.

How has he been today? Dad asks Raisa.

Inside are twelve smaller packages.

Rough at start, but things better since after lunch . . .

He stacks these smaller packages in four piles of three.

Look at him go! Esther says. *He sure does love playing with those noodles . . .*

He takes a package from one of the stacks, tears away the wrapping, and locates the small silver square package inside; this too goes into the bin.

Hey, Mr. Marlow. Big Mal comes back inside, smelling of

smoke. Cody hunches over; his head is so low that his nose almost touches the mortar's rim.

Hi, Mal, Dad says.

After Cody places the block of noodles in the mortar, he takes up the pestle and begins, setting up a rhythm:

Down-up, down-up, down-up, down-up . . .

He smashes for a while, and then he changes to grinding:

Twist-twist-twist-turn, twist-twist-twist-turn . . .

It can take a long time to grind the noodles until they are just right: small and fine, like sand. The timer almost always goes off before then, and sometimes he can't help making a fuss. On those days, no sticker.

But if he finishes, he is able to run his hands through the noodles in their new form and feel what he has accomplished: the blocks of noodles started out one way — wrapped and separate — but now they are all one. All the same. He can do that.

And now Dad is going. He walks around the counter but stops far away. He doesn't make that mistake of coming too close again.

Goodbye, Cody. Goodbye, son. See you soon.

Cody doesn't look up. *Twist-twist-turn, twist-twist-turn . . .*

The timer is still ticking.

A Good Hand

Charles's mother, Rita Marlow, was a master when it came to preparing what is now a category of haute cuisine known variously as *small plates, mezes,* or *tapas* — although her culinary artistry was a byproduct of maternal obligation and went by the term *after-school snack.*

When Charles came through the front door after that first day of fourth grade —

Mom! I'm home!

— he realized that the house was empty.

Mom?

The kitchen table was set with two napkins, two glasses of milk, and two plates, each of which contained a mandala-like display: peanut-butter-and-jelly-sandwich triangles alternating in a complex pattern with circular slices of Little Debbie Ho Hos, cut crosswise to reveal their spiraling jellyroll centers. All of this framed a perfectly centered Red

Delicious apple filleted to look like a flower in bloom. A scattering of carrot curls added color and unified the overall design.

In the center of the table was a note:

Hello, Charles. I had to run an errand. You and Donnie may watch cartoons in the TV room after you have your snack if you wish. Please clear your dishes. Your father won't be home for dinner. I'll be back soon. Mom.

Charles and Donnie had been walking home from school together since kindergarten. Their kinship began when, after being toppled by a stampede of heedless upperclassmen charging onto the playground for morning recess, they ended up occupying side-by-side cots in the Quiet Room adjacent to the nurse's office.

While recuperating, they learned that being human bowling pins wasn't the only thing they had in common: they both went to a Catholic church; they both were only children; they both had a tendency to magnetize playground mishaps. For these reasons, they ended up meeting many more times over Mercurochrome, gauze, and the apple juice and Vanilla Wafers that the Nellie Goodhue nurse dispensed to every patient, a comforting reminder of the Blessed Sacrament.

It was in the Quiet Room that they invented their own version of a blood-brother ritual by swapping Band-Aids that had been applied to their ravaged knees. Their allegiance endured through third grade even as they noticed other clubs acquiring larger memberships, strong identities, cachet.

They enjoyed christening these evolving social circles. Charles started bringing a small flip-top spiral notebook to school, tucked into his shirt pocket, and — just like a TV police detective — he recorded findings and observations, taking down the names given to the groups as well as their membership rosters:

The Bullies, the Pretties, the Fatties, the Lonelies, the Good-at-Sports, the Jokers, the Smarties, the Cheaters, the Chatty Cathys . . .

What did they call themselves? What was the name of their club?

They didn't have one. They didn't need one. They were just Donnie and Charlie, best friends.

And now Donnie had moved away.

Charles crumpled his mother's note into a tight ball. How could she not have remembered?

After finishing his snack and his absent friend's glass of milk, he dumped the remaining food in the garbage and put the dishes in the dishwasher.

Where *was* she?

He walked into the living room and looked out the window. The garage door was open; both cars were gone. He recalled a recent conversation between his parents in which his mother reiterated her ongoing difficulty in raising and lowering the garage door: it was heavy, she was ruining her manicures. Garrett Marlow said, *Well, maybe if you're a good girl this year, you'll get a surprise from Santa,* to which Rita Marlow replied, *If I'm going to ask for something from Santa, it's sure as hell not going to be a garage-door opener.*

Charles was restless. Now that Donnie wasn't around to trade comics with, his own collection had quickly grown stale and boring. He was about to go to the TV room and watch cartoons when he noticed the display of *Life* magazines on the coffee table.

So as not to disturb his mother's careful tabletop presentation of the most recent *Life,* he sat down on the sofa and decided to look at the older magazines on the lower shelf.

That was when he discovered Janet Leigh.

Opening the magazine in search of information about those mysterious red fezzes, he found stories with titles like:

THE MASTER OF AGENT 007

WHICH PHONE NUMBER DOES SHE DIAL TO STOP A MURDER?

BOYS AND GIRLS TOO OLD TOO SOON

Eventually, he located more photos of Ms. Leigh, part of an article on page 39 called JANET, THE BELLE OF THE BRAWL. The pictures showed her wearing a scanty, circus-performer-type getup and being passed around by a roomful of men who'd apparently stolen her fezzes. These images only increased his concerns on Ms. Leigh's behalf.

But none of the photos were as gripping as those that accompanied the story called THE DRUG THAT LEFT A TRAIL OF HEARTBREAK: pictures of deformed, dwarflike creatures, real-life monsters that were easily as grotesque and fascinating as those in any *Amazing Adventures* comics or *Creature Feature* movies.

Except they weren't monsters. They were children.

Charles had no idea that *Life* contained such wonders.

He was still lost in thought when he heard his mother's voice from the kitchen.

"Hello? Helloooooo! Anybody home?"

"I'm here," he replied, before realizing that his mother might not approve of his sudden interest in adult periodicals. He was about to replace the magazine and assume an innocent expression when she strolled into the living room. Immediately, she froze and gave a sharp gasp, followed by a humorless but relieved chuckle.

"Well, look at you," she said. Her expression was odd, as if *she* were the one who'd been engaged in covert activity. "So grown-up, sitting there on the sofa, reading a magazine. For a minute I thought you were your father."

She sat down beside him.

"What have you been up to since you got home?"

She smelled of hairspray and cigarettes. Wherever she'd been and whatever she'd been doing had made her happy.

"Nothing much."

"Did you find your snack?"

"Yes. Thank you."

"How's Donnie?"

"Fine. I guess."

There was a pause. Charles pretended to study an ad for men's slacks.

"I'm sorry I'm so late."

"It's okay."

"Did your father call?"

"No."

"Were you worried?"

"No."

"Are you angry?"

"No."

She lit a cigarette. Charles felt her staring at him, thinking. As an acute observer of adult behavior, he'd recently realized that, in cases such as this, whatever his mother said next would *not* be the thing she'd been thinking about.

"How was your first day of school?"

"Fine."

"Do you like your new teacher?"

"She's okay."

"What's her name?"

"Mrs. Braxton."

"Is she pretty?"

Charles shrugged.

"Well, I suppose I'll be meeting her soon enough . . ."

She got up and went into the kitchen. Next to the sofa, she'd left deep tamped-down toe/heel imprints in the shag carpet, as if she were a heavy piece of furniture that had been in the same place for a very long time.

Charles heard her cracking an ice cube tray and filling a glass as she spoke, her voice sometimes loud, sometimes soft: "Your father won't be home, he has a Jaycees meeting, or maybe Shriners or Sultans or Elks or moose or caribou who the hell knows, one of those anyway, so it will be just you and me and a couple of TV dinners. Aren't we *lucky* to live in The Age of Convenience? Isn't *all this* just a dream come true? Lucky, lucky, lucky . . ."

After gathering up several more issues from the lower coffee-table shelf, Charles tiptoed down the hall.

"We've got Salisbury steak, Mexican, fried chicken . . ."

He stashed the magazines in his bookshelf, out of sight, behind his comic books.

If his father could keep a hidden stash of *Playboy*s and his mother could be gone when he got home from his first day of fourth grade and forget all about Donnie Bothwell and not say where she'd been, then he was entitled to his own secrets.

He wouldn't even tell her about Dana McGucken.

❖

Mr. Austin Norman Palmer invented his famous method of business writing in response to the needs of a rapidly changing planet — one in which science and technology were advancing at a rate that left many people wondering where the telegraph left off and God began.

It was also a brawling, bold world, epitomized by America's president at the time, Theodore Roosevelt.

To get a sense of why Mr. Palmer might have felt it necessary to offer a pared-down version of cursive writing, consider the lettering style used by the Coca-Cola company. That's Spencerian script, the preferred penmanship of the late nineteenth century. It was high-minded and heavily embellished; built for beauty, not speed.

My father has many ideas involving handwriting — its significance, its evolution, its relationship to history. He believes that the metaphoric big stick of President Roosevelt's diplomatic policy found a correlate in Mr. Palmer's revolutionary approach to the pencil.

Here's why:

The Palmer Method requires tremendous physical strength, confidence, and tenacity. Early on, Mrs. Braxton informed my father's fourth-grade class that for these reasons, it was also referred to as Muscular Movement Writing.

With that in mind, we're going to revisit those basic loops you tried a while ago. You'll need to clear your desk and roll up your sleeves.

Now, instead of punishing your pencil with white-knuckle force and controlling its movement in a stingy, restricted way by using the small muscles of your wrist and fingers, you're going to move from your shoulder joint.

This means:

1. Your forearm and wrist form a long, unbroken line.
2. The muscles of your fingers are almost completely passive, engaged only to an extent that allows your pencil to ride in the seat formed where the bases of the thumb and index finger meet.

3. Your hand slides along on the fleshy cushion of its
    pinkie-side edge, losing its connection to the table
    only when you pick it up to begin a new line of
    writing.

Go ahead. Give those loops another try.

Remember, you're still seeking the holy grail of speed
combined with size-and-pressure consistency, but you're
using your arm as one large unit.

When it comes to teaching this element of the Palmer
Method, Mrs. Braxton's method — which you're about to observe in action — might strike you as extreme; however, it
certainly drove home the point that the Palmer Method required real chops.

Many people insist that this forearm-and-passive-hand
approach to writing — using the grosser muscles of the arm
to propel something as lightweight as a pencil in service of
something as delicate as thought (although one could argue,
and many have, that *thought* is one thing the Palmer system
didn't require) — represents the *real* challenge of mastering
Palmer penmanship. A roomful of people practicing loops,
ovals, and push-pulls look less like they're learning cursive
and more like they're taking PE. It's rigorous. It's calisthenic.
It's exhausting.

As a schoolboy, Theodore Roosevelt wouldn't have
learned Muscular Movement Writing, but it's fun to imagine him in a Palmer penmanship class. He would have been
a natural.

❖

By late September, Charles had achieved a more complete understanding of the significance of Mrs. Braxton's seating chart.

The smart kids — aside from Astrida — occupied the classroom hinterlands. Apparently Mrs. Braxton trusted them to remain intellectually engaged and behaviorally appropriate, although in Charles's experience Smarties were just as disruptive and mean-spirited as anybody else, forever correcting, ridiculing, and shushing, even if all you did was drop a pencil or start coughing when you inhaled a mushroom cloud of eraser dust.

It likewise became clear that he'd been assigned to a seat in the center of the classroom because, in four years of public-school education, he'd firmly established himself as a boy who was neither bright nor riotous but merely obedient, occasionally distracted. Teachers had already come to expect a middling and nondisruptive effort from him (his report cards routinely featured words like *adequate, sufficient,* and *satisfactory*); therefore, he sat in the middle.

"All right, class. In preparation for today's penmanship lesson, I will require three helpers."

Instantly, the hands of three Smarties shot up: Astrida and two back-row girls.

"Thank you. Will you please go to the supply closet, locate the rulers, and pass out one ruler to each student?"

While the class helpers executed their orders, Mrs. Braxton went to the blackboard, erased the morning's social studies lesson (Theodore Roosevelt and the Rough Riders), and began transcribing the quote of the day:

Corresponding on paper lets you elevate a simple pleasure into an art form. — Margaret Shepherd, calligrapher

"What should we do now, Mrs. Braxton?" Astrida asked.

"Please come back to the front of the classroom."

After retrieving a cardboard box from beneath her desk, Mrs. Braxton began moving through the room, reaching into the box, pulling out long strips of plain white fabric, and depositing them on her students' desks, three per customer.

"Leave these items alone for the time being," Mrs. Braxton instructed, needlessly, as she continued her rounds. Everyone knew better than to touch anything without further commands — everyone but Dana, of course, who immediately tied the fabric strips to his ruler and then began waving it around, a battle-shredded miniature Fourth of July flag.

"Dana McGucken!" Mrs. Braxton said, passing him on her way back to the front of the classroom. "Leave it!"

Dana lowered his banner but not before making his opinion known with a crisply executed toot: a single musket shot aimed at the battlement of Mrs. Braxton's backside.

No one laughed. They were too anxious about Mrs. Braxton's plans for those fabric strips. Maybe this was the day she'd start expecting the class to execute perfect push-pulls while blindfolded. It didn't seem out of the realm of possibility.

"Today we are going to focus on a very crucial aspect of Palmer penmanship, that of learning to use the forearm, wrist, and hand as one solid unit. In order to do this," she continued, "we are going to bind our arms to our rulers."

The collective unspoken subtext in response to this proclamation couldn't have been clearer: *We're going to* what?

"Astrida," Mrs. Braxton said, wielding one of the rulers and a clutch of fabric strips, "may I demonstrate using you as our model?"

Astrida froze, wide-eyed and mouth-breathing, and said, faintly, "May I please be excused to the girls' room?"

"Yes, but hurry back."

Astrida scuttled away. Mrs. Braxton surveyed the room in search of another assistant.

It was at that moment that the weather system of eraser dust — a massive bank of thunderheads that had been drifting in a slow but steady southwesterly direction — arrived at Charles's desk, and he began to cough uncontrollably.

"Charles," Mrs. Braxton said. "You may go to the sink and get a drink of water. Then join us for the demonstration."

The course of personal destiny is determined by such small moments.

"All right, children," Mrs. Braxton continued. "You may stand at your desks so that you can better see the presentation. You will work in pairs with the people sitting closest to you. I will assist as needed. Now, pay attention . . . Charles?"

Mrs. Braxton instructed Charles to sit at Astrida's desk, roll up his sleeve, and extend his arm, palm up — a position suggesting an imminent vaccination. She held the ruler so that it bridged from just below the bend of his elbow to his hand.

"The cloths are to be wrapped and then tied in three locations . . ."

Throughout this demonstration, Dana yawned, swayed, and gazed contentedly at the ceiling. Although he occasionally expressed a quality of engagement during math and science, penmanship was a subject for which he had neither interest nor innate ability.

". . . first, around the palm of the hand like this, between the thumb and forefinger, so that there is no impediment to the correct pencil grasp . . ."

It's possible that Dana didn't even know how to *say* his ABCs much less *write* them in any recognizable form.

". . . then, at the wrist, to prevent bending at that joint . . ."

So, during the extensive periods Mrs. Braxton set aside each day for penmanship practice — what she called *writing a good hand* — Dana was usually allowed to freely indulge in any of his habitual nondisruptive behaviors, including napping.

". . . and finally, at the forearm just below the elbow . . ."

However, for some incomprehensible reason, it was *this* lesson among all others that Mrs. Braxton chose as the one in which Dana's participation was mandatory.

"Questions? All right, then, you may begin. Please keep talking to a minimum."

What could she have been thinking?

Astrida returned and, seeing that her desk was occupied, glared with indignation. Mrs. Braxton — who had gone to work binding Dana's forearm to his ruler — gestured brusquely toward Charles's vacated fourth-row desk, indicating that Astrida should take a seat there. Incredulous, her face bloomed beet red; her eyes filled with the tears of one wrongly accused.

With Mrs. Braxton occupied with Dana, and Bradley and Mitchell paired off, Charles was the odd man out, with nothing to do but look on.

Dana was clearly puzzled, but passive. At least Mrs. Braxton hadn't required him to remove his suit coat. She worked efficiently and quickly; Brax the Ax would have made an excellent triage nurse. Once Dana's arm was firmly secured to his ruler, she leaned close, spoke a few quiet words into his ear, and then began moving through the room helping other children.

Immediately, Dana started experimenting with his splinted arm, making sweeping arcs in all directions, tapping it against his desk.

All was well until Mrs. Braxton resumed her place at the front of the room.

"All right, children. Please sit up straight, position yourselves properly, take up your pencils, and begin your two-minute timed loop practice . . . *now.*"

Mrs. Braxton swooped behind Dana with surprising speed and agility and wrapped her arms around him; the impression was of a huge, powerful bird descending from on high and capturing its prey within a pair of massive wings. After pinning Dana's left arm to his desk, she forced a pencil into his right hand, laid the length of her right forearm atop his, and began trying to guide his first loop-practice efforts.

Dana let go of the pencil immediately. It rolled to the floor. He began grunting and shaking his head, then bucking in his desk chair, then screeching as if in pain.

"Dana," Mrs. Braxton said, undeterred, her voice steady. "You can do this. Come on now . . ." She produced another pencil, placed it in his hand, and clasped her own hand over it.

Dana's panic exploded into rage, and he began to thrash against Mrs. Braxton's substantial bulwark of a body so forcefully that she almost toppled. Unbelievably, she persisted throughout the eternity of those two minutes, keeping one eye on the clock even as she tried to wrestle Dana into submission.

". . . five, four, three, two, *one!*"

By now, Dana was screaming. The rest of the class sat, stunned into silence by the force of his resistance and Mrs. Braxton's inability to contain him.

"Dana!" she kept shouting. "Dana McGucken! That's enough! Calm down!"

Take it off, Charles thought as Dana continued to flail and cry, his primal fear endangering both student and teacher. *Take it* off *him.*

Mrs. Braxton struggled with Dana well beyond that two-minute mark. Finally, she stopped trying to combat or control Dana's thrashing and began moving in sync with him, so that eventually the two of them were rocking, side to side, at

Dana's usual tempo. His screams diminished to wails, then whimpers, and finally to a kind of subdued keening.

"I'm sorry, Dana," Mrs. Braxton said gently, breathlessly, as she began removing the strips. "I'm very sorry. It's all right. You won't have to do that again."

When she turned around, her expression was frankly startled, as if she'd forgotten that there were other children in the room. A few of them gasped when they saw her face.

"Mrs. Braxton," Charles said quietly. "Your nose is bleeding."

She darted her eyes at him, then nodded. A series of self-composing gestures followed: she pressed her handkerchief to her face, replaced Dana's fabric strips in the box, slid his ruler into a desk drawer, smoothed her hair, and looked up at the clock.

"Let us continue," she said nasally, still occluding one side of her nose with her hankie. "Please begin your two-minute timed bedspring-oval practice . . . *now.*"

Dana remained mute and downcast, and on that day he exhibited a new behavior: using the thumb of his right hand, he aggressively massaged the triangular web of skin and muscle between the thumb and forefinger of his left hand. He looked down and watched himself do this with a bleak desperation, as if administering a last-resort drug that might not take effect in time to save the patient's life. (Years later, in the process of researching Cody's condition, Charles learned from a medical dictionary that this area of the hand is known as *the anatomical snuffbox,* and that Dana's massaging habit is often seen in people with fragile X syndrome.)

Mrs. Braxton's last instruction to the class as they left that day was to return the rulers to the supply closet and the fabric strips to the box on her desk. Charles was almost out the door when she spoke to him.

"Charles. You did exceptionally well today during penmanship practice. You seemed to have no trouble with the immobilizing technique."

"It's like wearing a cast," he said.

"Excuse me?"

"I broke my arm when I was seven and had to wear a cast. Being tied to the ruler today, it . . . Well, it felt like that."

Mrs. Braxton nodded. "That is an excellent insight, Charles. Would you be willing to share that with the class on Monday?"

"Sure. I guess."

Charles should have been cheered and flattered by this exchange, but it only served to remind him of his missing friend — the games of tic-tac-toe they'd played on his cast, the cartoons they'd drawn.

He wondered if, way up there in the Land of Sky-Blue Waters, Donnie Bothwell was also learning the Palmer Method and, if so, whether his experiences were proving to be as dramatic.

Art Without Boundaries

Rain or shine, Tuesdays and Thursdays at precisely 9:15 a.m., a few select residents of Madonna's Home are led outside; some walk unassisted, others use canes or aluminum walkers or wheelchairs. All are closely supervised. It is a slow procession.

They are guided into a small bus, helped to their places, secured with safety belts.

The caregivers take their seats.

The journey begins.

The bus driver, like most of us, maintains run-of-the-mill notions involving time and space. He takes his work seriously. A heavy rainstorm has started moving through the city, and he's worried about getting his passengers to their appointment on time.

A complex series of maneuverings over surface streets and freeways will eventually bring them to a Catholic church on Capitol Hill. The bus driver checks his watch. So far,

they're making good time. They usually do, going this direction on weekdays, midmorning. It's the trip back, after
lunch, that's the wildcard. It could be a breeze; it could take
an hour.

The Madonna's Home residents pay no attention to traffic conditions. They are free of travel-related anxieties. They
don't consult clocks. They abide by internalized and highly
individuated global positioning systems. Each one tells a different story as to what is happening; each one has his or her
own ideas about the destination.

Giorgia D'Amati — a newcomer among these pilgrims;
she has made this trip only two other times — sits immediately behind the bus driver.

She perches on the edge of her seat, bright-eyed, smiling.
Occasionally she pats her hair, tugs at the hem of her dress,
and mimes the actions of applying lipstick, her small, olive-
skinned hands fleet as swallow's wings.

Only she knows the truth.

They are going to Italy.

❦

It is 1943, a midday in spring, and Giorgia is in a chapel in
the Tuscan countryside having her photograph taken.

She is in the company of three soldiers. *"Come sono dis-
tinti!"* she says. *"Come sono belli!"*

Giorgia stands on the steps leading to the dais, her back
to the altar. Next to her is a tall, gangly boy wearing a U.S.
Army uniform: wool, filbert brown.

Standing at the base of the steps is the best man; next to
him is the other groomsman, the one who is taking the picture.

She sees herself from the photographer's point of view:
dowdy and plain-featured, the opposite of voluptuous — Giorgia D'Amati is built like a deck of playing cards.

But today, the silhouette of her body is indented slightly at the presumed location of her waist; skipping breakfast made it possible for her to cinch the thin belt of her home-made dress one notch beyond comfort.

Giorgia is an excellent seamstress, but fancy styles and colorful fabrics are forbidden, even on such an occasion as this.

From where the photographer stands, at a distance of several feet, the yard goods used for Giorgia's short-sleeved shirtwaist appear to be a mottled black and gray, the result perhaps of a laundry accident. But a closer look reveals a faint, all-over pattern of dainty flowers bound together by swirling ribbons: clouds of blurry-edged bouquets floating in a night sky lit by a weary moon and overlaid with mist, everything in gradated shades of gray.

Giorgia has taken special care with her hair; her head is covered with marcel finger curls that she learned to make from an American magazine. According to the magazine, a homely face and an unremarkable figure can always be off-set with attention to hygiene and style. Only in America do women think like this.

Now her viewpoint shifts and she is standing in her own skin, looking down at her bare, thick-calved legs (at least she remembered to borrow Father's razor and shave) and her newly polished but ugly shoes (no remedy for this).

The photographer — pudgy and freckle-faced — calls out, *Say cheese, Giorgia!* And she replies, *Romano, formaggio, Asiago, Parmesan!* It is a standing joke among them and they all laugh.

The camera clicks.

Once. Twice. Thrice.

She would have liked one more photo of her wedding day: she and her bridegroom kissing, or walking down the aisle, or at the rectory table, signing the banns — and she would have had one too, except at that moment, the chapel door bursts open, blasting them with a gust of cold, wet air (*when did it start to rain?*) and revealing a silhouetted figure backlit at the sanctuary entrance.

An unexpected guest, a presence so startling and compelling that Giorgia loses all awareness of her bridegroom, the best man, and the photographer. *Girl or boy?* Giorgia wonders. *Bridesmaid or ring bearer?*

Indeterminable at the moment, but apparently and in either case born in a barn and not dressed at all as one should be to enter the house of God: an odd style of dungarees, threadbare in places and yet unpatched; a man's shirt, unpressed and too large, with tails untucked and sleeves rolled up; and heavy Dutch-boy-like shoes that — *who would have believed it possible?* — are even uglier than Giorgia's.

The gender question is resolved soon after, for not even an excess of rumpled fabric can obscure the undignified jiggling of two ungirdled breasts.

No bridesmaid then, and definitely not one of Giorgia's sisters; none of them would dress for church in such a manner — dungarees, a man's shirt, and no brassiere!

Worst of all, the girl's head is uncovered.

But then — slowly slipping back into an awareness of her own physical body — Giorgia realizes with shame that she is bareheaded as well. Her vanity over the marcel curls made her forget!

Giorgia locates the picnic basket she stashed beneath the altar (they packed a lunch to have after the ceremony), hurriedly plucks up a large cloth napkin, and flings it atop her head. It lands askew and off center, forming a floppy awning that substantially narrows Giorgia's peripheral vision. As she whirls about to face the Intruder — attempting to project a theatrical combination of distinction and haughty disdain — the napkin slips farther, so that one corner droops over Giorgia's left eye. She immediately feels a fool, deservedly ridiculous for attempting such pretensions. Hardly the desired impression. And yet, at least she has made an *effort.*

As the woman continues to walk down the aisle (*she does not even take the time to genuflect!*), the soldiers begin to back away, receding into the storm, for the rain is now torrential.

Giorgia calls out to them — *"Tornate qui!"* — and then she notices something, a puzzling alteration to this story, "The Sunflower Bride," a story she has enacted in one form or another many times and that has always been under her control:

The Intruder is now wearing the camera.

Did the groomsman give it to her? Why would he do such a thing?

Looking beyond her, Giorgia sees that the soldiers have gone, without a word of goodbye. The chapel door is closed. She is alone and face to face with this person, this *trespasser,* who has ruined everything — not a woman, after all, but a young girl, maybe sixteen or seventeen, around the same age as Giorgia herself.

The girl's absurd masculine attire (*she even wears that stolen camera on a strap across her chest like a man!*) cannot obscure a delicacy, a feminine essence that Giorgia lacks and, furthermore, could never attain were she to swath herself in miles of ribbons and flounces.

Giorgia begins to pace. She mutters, *"Io sono la sposina."* Then she turns to the Intruder and makes a shooing motion. *"Non dovreste essere qui. Voi andate, io resto!"*

The girl asks a question, using words that Giorgia does not recognize. Not that it matters; Giorgia has no intention of interacting with her in *any* language.

Giorgia draws the napkin lower so that it covers her face. She carefully realigns its position so that one corner falls over the exact center of her sternum and then pins it there with her right extended index finger; it presses firmly through her flesh to her breastbone and is angled precisely toward her heart.

Steal my picture now *if you want,* Giorgia thinks. *Crook, heathen, killjoy.*

And the girl does; Giorgia hears a faint click.

Giorgia remains like this, a statue, no longer caring how foolish she appears, ignoring the girl, who has started to murmur in that incomprehensible language. Her voice, not unpleasant, is still an irritant — such presumptuousness.

Eventually, the murmuring ceases, the girl stops taking pictures, and there is the decrescendo of slow-moving footsteps in retreat.

Giorgia peeks out from under her napkin/veil. The Intruder has departed.

At last! She is alone again in the sanctuary. Hungry, too, and tired from so much standing. Her feet feel bloated, sweaty, too ample, as if they are balls of dough that have risen inside her shoes.

After sitting down on the altar steps and freeing her feet — *what a relief it is!* — Giorgia wiggles her warm, yeasty toes. How good it is now to feel the cool, rain-washed air against the skin of her soles.

She pulls another napkin from the picnic basket and smoothes it across her lap. She extracts a panettone from the picnic basket, remembers to loosen her cinched-in belt before she eats.

My bridal feast, she thinks, happily.

She is just about to take a bite when another person barges into the chapel: that woman, the one Giorgia foolishly believed to be a mother or a new novitiate. She too is bare-headed. What is the world coming to?

Come along now, Giorgia. You know you can't be in here by yourself. Come back and join the others. It's lunchtime.

"Naturalmente, è ora di pranzo! Che male c'è a starsene un po' da soli? Lasciatemi in pace! Questa è la casa di Dio!"

Giorgia folds her arms across her chest, ducks her head, and applies the force of her will toward making her body as heavy as possible.

Oh, Giorgia. I wish you didn't make me do this . . .

The woman calls out to someone beyond Giorgia's field of view, and he appears; Giorgia might be inclined to like him, his fallen state notwithstanding, were it not for his loyalty to that witch of a jailer.

She steels herself for a battle. Just let them try to banish her from God's house. She is no match for a fallen angel; she knows she will lose. But she can still put up a fight like a man.

❖

A sudden commotion in the church basement makes Cody look up: one of the people in the not-Cody group is being carried through the room where they are eating lunch; a big man — as big as Big Mal — holds her as if she were a baby. She isn't a baby, but she's very small. She is struggling and shrieking in a language Cody hasn't heard before.

He watches for a while. Then he looks away, stuffs a handful of rice crackers into his mouth, and starts chewing. The sound is loud enough to block out the sound of that tiny woman's screams until she is gone.

Storybook Cottage

Charles was in his office, grading. An assignment that he gave to all of his students near the start of the year — Seven Postcards — had come due. He'd been at it for hours, ever since he got home from school, stopping just long enough to make a sandwich. It was getting late.

Feeling restless, he pushed himself away from the desk, rubbed his eyes, twisted from side to side in his desk chair, and pondered the options:

He could put off finishing until the weekend.

He could brew another pot of coffee and soldier on.

Or, he could take a break and resume his archaeological efforts in the crawlspace.

Part of the problem: he was distracted. His eyes kept straying to the answering machine, where a pinprick of red blinked at him, incessantly, accusingly. There were two messages. Both required a response.

Message one:

Hello, my name is Mike Bernauer, I'm a reporter with the Seattle Times, *doing a follow-up article about a piece that appeared back in 1963. I'm calling to find out if you're the Charles Marlow who attended the Nellie Goodhue School that year and...*

Message two:

Charles. Stop avoiding me. Call me back. Tonight. I'll be up.

Charles thought of himself as being *in* his office, even though there was, in fact, no door. It wasn't even a room, really, but an efficient at-home workspace wedged into a triangle-shaped niche next to the stairs. It had been created in the first couple of years following Cody's diagnosis, after Alison felt it necessary to repurpose the upstairs bedroom that used to serve as Charles's office.

She'd found the design in an issue of that magazine Martha Stewart published — Charles could never remember the name but thought of it as *Martha!* — and then, voilà: she'd unveiled this marvel of organization.

It was touching, really, her heroic effort to solve a wrenching domestic problem, a deprivation counterbalanced by a gift. That was Ali all over.

The earliest structural alterations to the house — Charles's under-the-stairs office and the mold-mitigation remodel — were necessary at the time, and both turned out well. However, there was an unintended result: the bifurcation of their family — Ali and Cody retreated upstairs to the playroom, Charles and Emmy to the crawlspace, and from that point on, the divide between them continued to grow.

Charles pitied the poor house sometimes. Built in the 1930s, exemplary of an architectural style known as *storybook*, it retained its charming, eccentric exterior: exaggerated peaked roofline, intentionally off-kilter brickwork, small in scale but expansive in whimsy. True, Charles had let the yard go a little, the herb and vegetable garden completely, but overall it looked pretty much the same as it had when they'd moved in as newlyweds, the large down payment a wedding present from his in-laws.

It was the house's interior that told the real story, whimsy's opposite, a former war zone showing evidence of battles, vandalism, lootings: scarred parquet floors, pockmarked walls, chipped archways, boarded-up fireplace, architectural details — wall sconces, ceramic tiles, and plastered porticoes — severely damaged or excised altogether, changes wrought either directly by Cody or in the interest of keeping him safe.

Alison was always asking Charles how he could bear to keep living there, why he didn't sell. She wouldn't mind. He could get a nice two-bedroom condo like hers; there were so many new ones on the market right now, LEED-certified, and several were even within a few blocks, so he could stay connected to the neighborhood, the café, the video store, all of his routines, if that was the issue.

It wasn't.

She didn't understand.

For Charles, the house was perfect.

❖

"He's different when he's with us, you know," Alison's mother was saying. "I've never seen him have one of those meltdowns you and Alison talk about."

"That's good," Charles said. "I'm glad." He found it hard to imagine his genteel, diminutive mother-in-law in Cody's presence when he was shrieking like a cornered possum or smearing feces on every available surface.

"Fussy, yes. The occasional tantrum. But a meltdown? No. Never."

It was a Sunday evening in August, still light outside, about a week after their consultation with Dr. Gayathri.

Alison's parents, Victor and Eulalie Forché, were being given a pre-dinner tour of the house exterior. A light wind was moving in from the southwest.

Victor and Alison led the way; Charles and Eulalie sauntered along a few paces behind. Some unspoken protocol mandated this arrangement, that a precise distance be maintained between them.

Energetically, they were already miles apart, Victor and Alison exuding edginess and exigency, a pair of generals about to lead a battalion to the front lines. Eulalie, in stark contrast, was relaxed and gracious, as if *she* were the one hosting this gathering and they were strolling through the formal grounds of the Forché estate in the Highlands.

Cody was in one of his clingy moods, demanding that his mother carry him, so Alison was having a hard time keeping up with her father's brisk pace; Victor, in turn, seemed either oblivious of or indifferent to her difficulties. He squinted at the house as if perusing a legal brief naming him as chief defendant.

"It might be because of the space, you know?" Eulalie wafted one of her manicured hands in a series of vague, looping gestures. "The size of the rooms, the ceiling height . . ." The vestiges of Kentucky roots were still evident in her languid delivery; a person could practically recline on those airy, musical vowels and feathery consonants. "This is a dear, sweet little house, don't get me wrong, and it's been perfectly adequate for the two of you, but now that you've finally started a family, it is awfully confining. And this teeny yard . . . Where do you run him?"

"At the park."

"Not too far, is it?"

"No, just a few blocks."

"That's good, because little boys, you know, they need a

lot of room." Eulalie gazed up at the house and sighed. "Are you sure you want to stay? You wouldn't rather look for a new place?"

"Alison thinks it would be too upsetting for Cody if we moved."

"Ah, well, we know all about Alison's determination, don't we?" Eulalie took Charles's arm, gave it a gentle squeeze, and leaned into him in a playful, teasing way.

Charles had learned in the years since he and Alison had wed — suddenly, unceremoniously, and with only the most perfunctory introductions to the Forché dynasty — that when it came to Eulalie, it was best not to ponder any possible subtext; to do so meant risking intense feelings of inadequacy, if not outright paranoia. Eulalie did seem genuinely fond of him, so he chose to believe that her remarks weren't meant to underline the differences between them or the fact that — using the expression of a former century, one from which Eulalie often seemed to have been lifted — Alison had married *beneath her station.*

Eulalie took a sip of the cocktail Charles had prepared to her specifications — a dirty martini made with pickle brine and garnished with skewered grape tomatoes and caper berries. "I love my daughter to bits," she continued, "she is a lioness in every sense of the word, but those qualities . . . Well, they cut in both directions."

The rules of engagement with Alison's father were more difficult to ascertain. Victor was pleasant enough in a hale and hearty way, but Charles had seen him be just as congenial to strangers and underlings: the waitstaff at Canlis, the salesclerks at the Bon Marché. Charles suspected that Victor's expansiveness was in direct proportion to his distrust. Eulalie may have had issues with Alison's choice in a husband, but she didn't appear to hold Charles at fault; with

Victor, however, Charles often felt less like a son-in-law and more like a parolee.

Eulalie inhaled deeply and looked upward. The wind was drawing a series of connected clouds across the sky: shape-shifting pull toys. "I believe that we are in for some rain tonight. It's starting to feel like autumn already." Charles helped her resecure her linen stole around her shoulders. "Where has the summer gone?"

Up ahead, Victor and Alison had come to a stop. Alison was gesturing toward the house with a manic intensity, jabbing, pointing, slicing. Her stance was wide and lock-kneed; her spine rigid. It struck Charles that her body language was in exact opposition to Cody's diffuse restlessness.

"Tell me more about what this Indian doctor said," Eulalie prompted, gazing into the contents of her martini glass as she swirled it rhythmically in a small circle.

Before the evening began, Charles had been thoroughly coached by Alison as to their respective roles: she would handle her father, appealing to his practical side by laying out the contractor recommendations and stressing the fact that the proposed alterations to the house would increase its resale value; Charles would emphasize their concerns over Cody's health with Eulalie — although Ali was emphatic that the word *autism* not be uttered.

"Do you and Alison trust her opinion?" Eulalie asked.

"Oh, yes. Absolutely."

Victor and Alison started walking again. Eulalie and Charles followed.

As Charles began to recap the major points supporting a link between mycotoxicity and Cody's mild developmental delays, he overheard fragments of Alison's monologue: ". . . the floor will have to be entirely concreted . . . below forty percent humidity . . . Visqueen and additional venting

. . . fogging versus pump spraying . . ." She was trying hard, Charles could tell, to sound knowledgeable and confident, but these efforts were being undermined — not only because she was carrying an unwieldy twenty-six-pound child, but because she was extremely nervous.

"So the primary concern is mold and moisture," Eulalie said, "is that right? And it's mainly located in the crawl-space?"

"Yes, but we've found problems in other parts of the house as well."

Eulalie clucked her tongue. "Victor is going to pitch a fit with the inspection company he hired before he offered on the house. He certainly won't be doing business with them again. He'll probably have a few choice words for the friends who recommended the company as well — *good* friends too . . ."

Cody was growing more agitated — he'd started grunting, fidgeting, burrowing his head into Alison's hair, forming a tangled nest; she was trying to restrain him against her hip with one arm while gesturing toward the house with the other.

Charles wished he could help, but Cody had begun to express a fierce preference for his mother. Attempting to relieve Alison could result in one of the very meltdowns Eulalie had been spared. This was not the occasion to risk that.

"This is an *excellent* martini, Charles. I might have to have one more before we open the wine. We brought red and white, by the way. I wasn't sure of the menu . . ."

Alison had made it a point of pride her entire adult life not to dip into the deep well of her parents' wealth. *My older brothers drank the Kool-Aid years ago,* she wrote in a letter to Charles early in their courtship. *Kendall and Grant graduated and went right into Dad's law firm, they didn't even try to get away, and poor Aidan — Dad's just waiting for him to fail as a musician so he can say "I told you so." We're all expected to fail if we don't do what my father thinks is best, which is basically to marry money in all its forms.*

I understand now why you're attracted to me, Charles joked in reply.

It's weakened all of them, she wrote back. *I will not let it weaken me. Once you give in, once you let wealth define who you are, you can't go back.*

Eulalie was old money, Victor was new money. Charles was not privy to the details of their net worth — nor did he care to know — but his general assumption was that between them, they could subsidize a small country.

"When does she plan on making the Big Ask?" Eulalie remarked. "After dessert?"

"Excuse me?"

"Oh, come on now, Charles. Don't play innocent with me. I'll be surprised if she hasn't catered the entire meal and hired a master of ceremonies."

Eulalie was shrewd, that was certain; no emcee, but the feast awaiting them in the dining room — laid out on good china next to a lavish floral display — had indeed been prepared by a caterer recently featured in the *New York Times* as a Northwest regional best.

"I wish someone would tell her that she doesn't have to treat us like potential corporate sponsors," Eulalie continued. "Lord knows we get enough of that from total strangers . . ."

The five of them were curving around to the east side of the house. Alison was pointing out the aluminum windows, the place where a proposed drainage system would siphon water away from the house.

"All this fuss, this strategizing . . . she really needn't make it so complicated." Eulalie downed the rest of her drink. "But that's my daughter, always choosing the path of most resistance . . ."

Up ahead, Alison shifted Cody to her left hip. She must have been getting tired.

Immediately, Cody began to thrash against her in protestation, moaning and keening, shaking his head. His long hair — which Alison had gone to great pains to detangle and neaten into a ponytail before Victor and Eulalie arrived — came undone and fell around his face like a thatched roof, making him look even more feral.

Victor reached for him, Cody's screams intensified, and the three of them turned the corner and disappeared from sight — at which point, Eulalie gripped Charles's arm with sudden firmness and came to a stop.

"I have a confession to make," she began. "I haven't been entirely truthful. It is a fact that I've never witnessed one of Cody's full-blown fits, but I've . . . *sensed* something, nothing I could put a finger on, just a feeling that things weren't quite right . . ."

Charles felt a sudden rigidity seize his chest; he was taken back to the day when he too began to *sense* something, a Saturday when Cody was about a year old.

Alison was working that weekend, and the two of them were on their own. Charles had put Cody in his high chair for his morning snack. He had made the wonderful discovery that children would eat anything that was arranged to look like a face, and he'd improvised an especially inspired and colorful meal: a rice cake with spaghetti-squash hair, a necklace of peas and blueberries, apple-slice lips, elbow-macaroni earrings, cucumber-and-black-olive eyes, yam cheeks, and string-cheese eyebrows.

He offered it up to Cody with a flourish.

Here you go, buddy. Eat up!

Cody stared at it, expressionless.

Charles pointed. *What's this, Cody? Cody? What do we call this?*

Cody continued to stare; slowly, he opened and closed his mouth. He did this a few times, inhaling and exhaling with increasing panic: a beached guppy gasping for air.

It's okay, sweetheart, Charles said, stroking his head. *These are eyes, right? Can you say* eyes? *And this is . . . This is the* hair. *See? Hair? And these are . . . ?*

Ears, *Cody,* Charles thought. *Those are* ears.

His own breath had begun to quicken; it was as if Cody had never seen a face before. Yesterday he could say *ears, eyes, mouth* — all the parts of a face. He could say a lot of words, but that morning, he couldn't find a single one of them.

Cody started to weep, not cry, but weep, as if for all the world's tragedies, all of life's great irredeemable losses.

What is it, Cody? Charles said, picking him up, but he thrashed against him and moaned, inconsolable. *What's wrong, little man?*

That was really when it started, the long, slow decline.

Eulalie went on. "I didn't feel that I could say anything, not with Alison being the way she is." Eulalie grimaced; it was an unguarded, inelegant expression, the likes of which Charles had never seen on her. "That sounded unkind," she added, "but you know what I mean."

Charles nodded, staring ahead into the darkening area between their house and the stand of trees that separated them from their neighbors to the east: Cody's forest.

Out of sight, presumably in the front yard, Cody was still wailing, but he sounded less distraught — almost certainly because Alison had relented and resituated him on the right side of her body. Their son's desperate insistence that he be held on the *right,* never the left, was just one of many accumulating enigmas.

"I've raised three boys," Eulalie continued. "I'm a grandmother seven times over. I may not be good for much, and I'm no medical expert, but I've always been a keen observer — as, I believe, are you. Did you try to get Alison to see it?"

"Eulalie . . ."

"I love my daughter dearly," Eulalie repeated, "but she has a tendency to let hope outlast the truth. I believe that in modern-day psychological terms, this would be known as *denial.*"

Charles felt an urge to sprint away, to catch up to Alison and Cody, but Eulalie held him fast; her body seemed suddenly intractable, geologic in weight and density. He'd need a backhoe to move her off this spot and into the house.

"You *did* say something, didn't you? How long ago? How long have you known?" Eulalie's voice had lost all its softness. "Never mind, you don't have to answer that. I'm not asking you to indict yourself . . ." Her grip loosened. Charles felt her body drain of energy so quickly that he feared she might collapse.

"What do you think is wrong with him, Eulalie?" he asked. "What's happening?"

Before she could answer, Cody exploded into view, rounding the corner of the house, completely transformed from the child they'd seen only moments before: joyful, laughing, anointed with garden soil and jam as all young children should be, bounding toward his grandmother looking like any other toddler who hates getting a haircut.

There he is, Charles thought. *There's Cody.*

But on the heels of his relief and joy came another thought, because now there was this *word*, this ugly word, and Charles found himself suddenly seeing his son differently, judgmentally. There was, *wasn't there*, something disorganized about his movements as he ran, something *not quite right*, and from there he thought, *Yes, of course, I see it clearly now, Cody runs like that because he has autism* instead of *Cody runs that way because that's the way Cody runs.*

"There he is!" Eulalie cried. "There's my snuggle bunny!" She handed off her martini glass to Charles and sank into an open-armed crouch, instantly muddying the hem of her designer dress. "Hello, sweetheart! Hello, darling!" she cooed, just barely maintaining her balance as Cody collided with her. She hugged him fiercely and then set him at arm's distance and regarded him with solemnity.

"Eskimo kiss." They touched noses.

"Horse kiss." They pressed their foreheads together.

"Butterfly kiss." They blinked against each other's cheeks.

Eulalie wrapped her arms around him and, with a strength that belied her small size, stood up and settled him in his preferred position. Gently, Cody freed a few strands of hair from her chignon and began brushing them against his face.

She started toting him back into the house. Stopping partway, she looked over her shoulder and added, "My opinion doesn't matter, Charles. Not in the long run. It's what you and Alison believe that's important."

Charles remembered a remark Alison had made near the end of their first session with Dr. Gayathri; it had surprised him.

I know what you're thinking, Charles, I know, but we can't be proud about asking for help, not anymore . . .

The funny thing was, he hadn't been thinking anything of the sort. Knowing how Alison felt about her parents' wealth, he would never in a million years have suggested that they solicit their financial support in this way. This evening, the whole plan, every part of it: it was entirely Alison's idea.

❖

Charles got up, stretched, and started another pot of coffee. While waiting, he decided to take a break from Seven Postcards and scan through the eighty-seven e-mails that had accumulated in his inbox over the past few days.

He noticed a new message from Romy Bertleson (bertle theturtle@gmail.com), CC'd to Pam Hamilton and with the subject heading first photos!

Hello Mr. M and Ms. H, i thought you'd like seeing some pictures from my first day at art without boundaries. thanks and see you soon, romy

There were three attached JPEGs; Charles wondered if one of them would contain a picture of his son.

But all the photos were of the same elderly woman. She was standing next to a tall young man (uniformed, likely a caregiver) on what looked like a church dais. The setting was puzzling until Charles remembered that Art Without Boundaries conducted classes at a Catholic church on Capitol Hill. The pictures had obviously been taken in quick succession; they formed a triptych, a pictorial narrative of some sort.

It was odd, Charles thought, how sometimes you could see in the faces of old people an underlayer, something not entirely obscured, the kind of thing he imagined an art-restoration specialist might discover, a painting beneath a painting. *Pentimento;* that was the word for it. Beneath this woman's face was strength, humor, intelligence, Charles could tell. But even on the surface, she did not look like a woman who was losing her mind (he assumed the subject must be suffering from some form of dementia); quite the contrary, in fact — in the worn parlance of pop psychology, she looked like a woman who'd *found* herself.

The phone rang. Charles let the machine pick up.

"Charles. I *know* you're there, it's a school night. Pick up. *Pick. Up!*"

He picked up.

"We need to talk about Cody."

Immediately, even after all this time, that six-word sentence incited a physiologic, primal fear, a fast-moving flood of adrenaline, the fight-or-flight response.

"Charles," Alison said, her voice sharp and reprimanding, as if they'd been engaged in crucial face-to-face negotiations for several minutes but his eyes had glazed over. "Are you there?

"We *need.*

"To *talk.*

"About *Cody.*"

Charles felt his heart rate double and his breath grow shallow. He was enveloped by a hot, prickly sensation, a dangerous electrical storm of unknown origin, his own personal St. Elmo's fire.

"Charles! Did you hear me?"

"Yes," he managed, finally. "I'm here."

"The clock is ticking," Alison went on. "He'll be twenty-one in May. That's less than eight months from now."

"I realize that, Alison," Charles replied, not able to keep the faux-offended snippiness out of his voice, because, of course, he *hadn't* realized that, or was engaged in avoidance or denial or whatever; it basically amounted to the same

thing, with the bottom line being that *there was no excuse.*
Having an autistic son who was about to become a legal
adult and age out of state-supported care should have been
at the forefront of Charles's awareness, so on this occasion,
as on so many others, he felt ashamed of his paternal failings. The fact that Cody had no more awareness of Charles's
failings than he did of Alison's Herculean efforts on his behalf was moot.

"So when do you want to meet?" Alison went on. "We
need to talk in person." Charles could hear the sound of
pages being turned: Alison in consultation with her day
planner.

"Right."

"I've got aikido tomorrow, synagogue Friday night and
Saturday morning . . ."

"What?"

"Synagogue? Shabbat? Torah studies? Charles. Really?"

"Oh," Charles said. "Right."

Why did she always act so annoyed when he forgot about
the conversion business? She'd announced it, completely
out of the blue, a few months ago —

*This is important to me, Charles. I've gotten to a point in my
life when I need . . . Well, I'm not asking you to understand, but
please. You have to promise you won't . . .*

Won't what?

You know . . . scoff.

What are you talking about? Why would I scoff?

*Because it's a loaded issue and you have very firm ideas on the
subject, and when I get serious about something you tend to, well,
get silly, make jokes, try to lighten me up.*

*No. Really? Did you get a PhD in psychology when I wasn't
looking?*

I get it, Charles, why you do it. I've always gotten it, and there have been many times when I've loved you for it. But about this — please. I don't want to debate; I don't want to win you over; I just need you to understand that I'm doing this for myself, for reasons that have nothing to do with you. So: promise me that you won't make fun.

All right. I promise. I solemnly swear not to mock, jeer, ridicule, or scoff.

— but it wasn't as if she'd chosen to share anything further on the subject. In fact, it had been so long since she'd mentioned anything, he'd been hoping she'd given up on the idea. He should have known better.

"The rest of the weekend's no good either . . . ," Alison went on.

He could ask her about it, he supposed. What version of Judaism was she converting to, exactly? Christmas was out, obviously, but would she have to wear a wig?

"How about this: We've got our monthly meeting next Wednesday at six — you have that on your calendar, right?"

"Yes."

"Why don't we go for drinks afterward and talk then? Someplace close to the hospital, maybe U Village? I know you don't like to be out on school nights, but —"

"It's fine."

"I've done some research, so all I'm asking you to do is help narrow the choices and then spend a Sunday visiting these places with me . . ." Then she launched into a briskly paced monologue that Charles found himself only minimally able to follow — although he did pick up his pen and attempt to take notes.

There were so many abbreviations and acronyms involved whenever Cody was the subject of discussion; Charles was able to readily interpret some of them — DSHS, UWAC, SIB — but due to some shortfall in his own brain wiring, he found calling up the meaning of many of these linguistic expediencies a terrible struggle. It was as if the acronyms constituted toeholds on some gigantic climbing rock and Charles was unable to continue his ascent until he'd laboriously translated each one.

Alison, by contrast, was a fantastically agile and practiced climber, completely fluent in this bureaucratic cipher, so that by the time Charles finally anchored his foot in the recollection that ICF/MR stood for intermediate-care facility for the mentally retarded, she'd scaled all the way up to the rock's pinnacle.

Trying to remember what ARCHWAY stood for brought Charles's listening efforts to a full stop.

Alison, a perceptive listener, soon recognized this.

"Charles, are you with me?" was what she said. What he heard was *Charles, why can't you keep* up?

"Yes, yes, I'm listening. Go on."

Charles never ceased to marvel at the irony that their son, someone who hadn't spoken an intelligible word in seventeen years, continued to stimulate so much heated discussion, intellectual debate, soul-searching, *cris de coeur* — so much *language* — all of it ultimately useless, because none of it brought any of them closer to understanding anything about the inner workings of Cody's unique mind.

Charles followed the conversational thread (or, more aptly, the climbing rope) all the way through Alison's comically huge understatement "At least we have some financial resources," but he soon fell hopelessly behind once again.

He looked down at his notes; they included a list of abbreviations transcribed in the order they were uttered:

CRM
RCSD
HCBBS
FEATWA
LIHTC
CDBG
HCV

Charles was fascinated by the way these randomly spoken acronyms formed a graceful, organized shape: when viewed vertically, a subtle convex curve to the right; when viewed horizontally, a gently swelling hillock. And they were perfectly, symmetrically ordered in terms of number of letters: 3-4-5-6-5-4-3.

"You've stopped listening again," Alison said.

"Sorry, I —"

"Never mind. I'll see you next Wednesday at PLAY then?"

Charles knew this one: Parents Loving Autistic Youth. "Yes."

"Six o'clock?"

"I'll be there."

"Drinks and discussion after."

"Sounds good."

Charles became aware that they were now speaking in another kind of verbal shorthand: nothing extraneous, nothing revelatory, as if they were criminal suspects under surveillance. Or the opposite — complete strangers whose conversation might be monitored for quality-control or teaching purposes. It was sad that to someone reading a transcript of this exchange, either scenario would be plausible.

"Have you seen him?" Alison asked.

"Tomorrow."

Charles visited their son twice a week.

"He's been very calm lately," Alison continued. "We're finding a good balance in terms of his meds."

Ali visited every day. She had a high tolerance for pain in all its forms.

She went on to apprise Charles of Cody's latest regimen of pharmaceuticals and supplements; she also gave an enthusiastic testimonial for a new treatment she was eager to procure, an oxytocin nasal spray. "It's still in trials," she said, "but the military is spending millions developing something similar for returning soldiers, an antisuicide nasal spray, so clearly they're really onto something. It's very exciting."

No giver-upper, my ex, Charles thought. *She is fierce. She is undaunted.*

Of course, that had been one of many things that had attracted him to her in the first place.

After saying goodbye, Charles noticed that his right hand was in spasm; he released his hold on his pen and began shaking it out.

He looked down at the legal pad on which he'd been taking notes; it was covered with a series of scribbled loops. They traversed the entire page, line after line, row after row, smooth, controlled, uniform in size at the start but eventually becoming wildly erratic, so heavily executed that the paper was shredded in places. The acronyms and abbreviations were now obscured, as if standing behind the densely curled razor wire of a prison-yard enclosure.

Charles had no memory of making these marks — the transcriptions, obviously, of a madman.

He tore off the page and folded it into halves, quarters, eighths, and sixteenths before dropping it into the wastebasket.

He took up his pen again and began to write:

Dear Emmy,

Do you remember the Seven Postcards exercise? I bring out the boxes containing my collection, give the kids an entire class period to browse and choose a week's worth of favorites each, and then — with the caveat that "having a great time wish you were here" is not an option and that the per-postcard word count (excluding the address) must exceed twenty — tell them to compose one postcard a day to a thoughtfully chosen friend or relative, someone they miss sorely and aren't likely to see any time soon.

Over the years I've found this exercise to be a low-pressure way to reintroduce students to the act of putting pen or pencil to paper in the service of their imaginations, especially since it's likely that the only writing many of them did over vacation was accomplished with the assist of a keyboard too small to be operated by anything other than thumbs.

I find myself increasingly obsessed with the sorry state of penmanship. I'm starting to wonder if I should go back to college; perhaps I could better serve today's youth with a degree in corrective graphology. Or maybe it's called something else: handwriting therapy? That has a less punitive ring to it . . .

I'm joking.

But not entirely.

Here's my point: no one expects anyone to have decent handwriting anymore.

It's no wonder, when not only business but social interactions are conducted via the striking of keys, the thumbing of buttons.

As an example, almost half the consolatory messages I received after my mother's death were in the form of e-mails. Given that sad state of affairs, it seems likely that "sorry 4 ur loss" isn't far down the road.

This begs the question: At what point will elegant linguistic languor be permanently usurped by text-speak expediency?

When will we humans abandon the ability to generate long, complex, lusciously worded emotional expressions — like Elizabethan sonnets! — in favor of:

Pls b my wif xo

Left u 4 him ☹

My . a wk L8 ☺

2 sad 2 have 2 kdz

Whenever my students are called upon to produce something without the aid of computers or cell phones, their script is usually in the form of block printing that has a rushed, out-of-control, slightly panicked look, as if they're all suffering from visual or neurological impairments.

But of course, I'm as much of an offender as anyone else. How far I've fallen from my Palmer penmanship certificate-of-merit days. Writing letters to you by hand is one of the few ways I'm able to keep up my handwriting chops.

So Seven Postcards remains an important curriculum element, intended to be both a creative assignment and athletic training, the Language Arts equivalent of a football scrimmage.

Up next is a stack of postcards from Abe Kaparsky, one of my new crop of sixth-graders. From what I can tell so far, he has chosen to write to a long-deceased hamster named Houdini.

I mean, really: Who wouldn't love getting mail like this?

The phone rang. Charles let the machine pick up.

Hello, Mr. Marlow, sorry to trouble you so late, but this is Mike Bernauer from the Seattle Times, *calling again to see if you got my earlier messages . . .*

Charles muted the sound, turned off his office light, and headed to bed.

Alluring Objects

My father has always been deeply comforted by the sensory delights of office supplies — the smells of different kinds of paper; the feel of pens in hand, their varying weights, textures, mechanisms; the degree to which writing implements embrace or resist contact with the page. He's savored the dense resinous scent of wooden pencils, enjoying an across-time kinship with Henry David Thoreau for his entrepreneurial efforts on behalf of that homely instrument. He's relished the look of corrugated, flat-roofed tunnels formed by lengths of conjoined staples, the smooth, streamlined elegance of paper clips.

His well-stocked home-office cupboard provided my brother with some of his favorite playthings when he was small; one of Cody's early pastimes was building whimsical, rainbow-colored structures out of cellophaned stacks of Post-its mortared together with double-sided tape. He also

loved arranging and rearranging unsharpened Ticonderoga
no. 2s in intricate patterns on the floor.

Around the time of my birth, my brother (who had not
yet lost his fine-motor skills) had begun to design and manu-
facture an impressive line of paper-clip jewelry.

On our last day at the hospital, before I was released into
my parents' custody —

Charles Marlow — father

— Cody solemnly presented our father with a special gift.
That was the moment he permanently retired his crucifix
and began wearing an intricately assembled, beaded paper-
clip necklace next to his heart. He never takes it off.

Should anyone ask, he'd testify to feeling far more solaced and protected by the powers of his Cody original than
he ever felt by that fuddy-duddy symbol of Christ's suffering.

❖

It would be logical to trace a straight line from Charles's affection for office supplies to his life as a teacher. He often
wished he could say that he'd felt called to his profession,
that the idea of nurturing young minds came to him early
and unbidden, but in truth it was a simple question from Alison on the night they met — followed by a conversation with
a friend — that nudged him in that direction. Not toward becoming a Language Arts teacher specifically, but toward the
radical notion that another version of himself — updated,
improved, rebooted — might yet be possible, that his life
story wasn't over yet.

He was thirty-five years old and happily living the unexamined life of a country-club bartender, work for which he'd always felt temperamentally well suited and to which he was still occasionally tempted to return.

But it wasn't just temperament that predisposed Charles to success as a mixologist; it was his early apprenticeship to Mrs. Eloise Braxton, Palmer penmanship zealot. By the time he was ten, Charles was able to execute a series of repetitive movements consistently, efficiently, and in a relaxed manner over long periods, often while experiencing substantial anxiety. Eight years later, casting about for a job that could keep him well stocked with weed while his parents funded four years of college and living expenses, he'd discovered that mixing one cocktail after another for the clientele of a happy-hour rush wasn't all that different from producing a long succession of lowercase *m*'s in the presence of the formidable Mrs. B. It certainly wasn't as stress-inducing.

So after graduating with a major in philosophy and a minor in linguistics, Charles decided that mixology was an excellent career match for both his academic interests and his recreational needs.

Early on the evening of Friday, April 1, 1988, he was sacked out on the sofa, looking forward to spending the weekend reading, watching movies, and smoking dope (his chief downtime occupations for the previous two decades), when the phone rang.

It was Zach Dennehy, the country club's head bartender, asking if there was any way Charles could fill in for him the next two days.

"I hate to ask, Charlie," he said, "especially on such short notice, but I'm kind of in a bind." He sounded terrible.

"Absolutely. No problem." Zach never missed a shift, never called in sick. "What's up?"

"Oh, it's stupid, really. I'm in the hospital."

"What happened? Are you okay?"

"Yeah, it's just that I finally went to see the doctor about this damn cough. They took a couple of x-rays and guess what — I've got pneumonia."

"Holy shit." Charles's heart gave an arrhythmic jump, and he experienced an odd, ill-defined panic that did not have the familiar feel of pot-induced paranoia.

In spite of the seven-year age difference (Zach was in his early forties), Charles considered Zach his best friend. They had a fair amount in common, neither of them aspirants to anything beyond earning a generous salary plus tips. As bartenders, they conversed with interesting, successful, and, for the most part, pleasant people, including attractive single women who were occasionally interested in commitment-free sex. Their camaraderie was founded on shared identities as affable, intelligent, middle-class slackers who'd successfully infiltrated Seattle's social stratosphere but had no ambition to rise through its ranks, much less attain full membership.

"Listen," Charles said, detaching himself from the couch and shrugging into his jacket. "Why don't I come over?" Zach's gestalt was of the Clint Eastwood variety, lean, laconic, attractively rough-around-the-edges, and, above all, *invincible;* Charles's mental picture of him — alone and bedridden in a hospital room on a Friday night — violated world order in a deeply disturbing way. "Where are you? I'll get some takeout. I could even bring the VCR and we could watch a video."

"Nah, thanks, I'm okay, really, but thanks. I'm kind of worn-out. I'm just gonna get some rest, take advantage of the weekend off." He coughed hoarsely. "You should rest up too. You'll need it."

Zach went on to remind Charles about the Stanford/Bettencourt wedding reception, a supersize fête scheduled the next day from four until midnight in the Broadmoor's largest party room. It would be a huge amount of work, pouring and mixing drinks, supervising two rookie bartenders, and overseeing a cadre of over-hire waitstaff who'd be roaming the room serving pre-dinner hors d'oeuvres.

"I can't believe Meghan Stanford is getting married," Zach said. "I was working poolside the summer she had her first swimming lesson; she must have been two, three. She was a funny little kid, comical, I mean, her daddy's girl from the very beginning." Zach adopted a mock grandfatherly tone, something he did whenever he started sounding like a senior citizen. "Of course, my son, that was *way* before your time."

"Right," Charles said, trying to laugh, sinking back down on the sofa without taking off his coat. Suddenly, he felt exhausted. "Hey, are you sure this whole hospital story isn't an April Fools' joke?"

Zach emitted a single, hollow sound, more cough than chuckle. "Ah, bro. I wish. Good luck tomorrow. Let me know how it goes."

That was how, on the chilly first weekend of April 1988, Charles ended up managing the no-host bar for the Stanford/Bettencourt wedding reception. Among the three hundred and fifty guests was a twenty-five-year-old law student named Alison Forché.

❖

Around seven thirty, there was enough of a lull that Charles felt comfortable entrusting the bar to his less experienced colleagues, a pair of overcaffeinated, undernourished graduate students with the hollow-eyed seriousness Charles associated with overachievers (pity the poor kids): Pre-Law Patrick and Biochemistry Kate.

He left a message at the hospital for Zach letting him know that everything was going well (a nurse informed him with obvious irritation that the patient was already asleep), and then — because he considered it important to enforce a strict boundary between his dual identities (Charles the Pothead and Charles the Barkeep) — he removed his mono-grammed, country-club-issue jacket and took a brisk walk to the sixteenth green to smoke a joint.

By seven forty-five — as the toasts were wrapping up and the cake-cutting was about to begin — Charles had taken a piss, freshened his breath with mouthwash, renewed the whites of his eyes with Visine, and resumed his place behind the bar before any of the guests noticed he'd been gone. At least, that's what he thought.

After announcing his return to his battle-weary subordi-nates — neither of them had worked an event of this size be-fore, and both of them looked exhausted — Charles added, "Why don't you take a break for half an hour, get some din-ner. I can handle things."

"Are you sure?" Patrick asked.

"Tell you what," Charles went on. "Take forty-five min-utes. Just come back when you hear the band start up, okay?"

Kate began gathering up her things with such rapidity and desperation that Charles wondered if she intended to bolt. "Sure," she blurted. "You bet. Thanks. Bye."

Reaching for his jacket, Charles noticed what looked like a small handkerchief tucked into the chest pocket. "What's this?"

"One of the waiters left it." Patrick raised an arm and pointed. "That one. A guest asked him to deliver it to you. See you later."

It was a gold-lettered cocktail napkin — the first of its kind Charles had seen that day. Supple and soft, feeling more like cloth than paper, it was the same warm persimmon color as the bridesmaids' gowns and had probably cost almost as much:

Meghan & Kyle

Together from This Day Forward

"Love Life Us Up Where We Belong"

April 2, 1988

On the non-lettered side, in black ink, someone had written:

BARTENDING EXAM

1. Name the ingredients in a Moscow mule.

Charles was no graphologist, but given a reasonable-size writing sample, he did have the ability to make assumptions about a person's penmanship background and training. And in the same way that an elocution teacher can detect the slightest trace of a regional accent in even the most neutrally executed speech, Charles could locate vestigial influences in the script of anyone who had come into contact (however briefly) with the penmanship techniques of Austin Norman Palmer.

The woman who wrote this message — and Charles knew it was a woman, not because of the handwriting but because of the perfume — used a combination of print and cursive, a sure sign that she was younger than Charles, schooled at a time when learning cursive was no longer a priority. And yet somewhere along the way she'd been exposed to the Palmer Method; the words *bartending* and *Moscow* made use of Mr. Palmer's distinct, special variants for the letters *g* and *w* located in a terminal position.

Charles perched on a stool behind the bar, assumed the position, and began to write.

2 oz. vodka

It had been years since he'd written with a consciousness of technique —

juice of ½ lime

1 split ginger beer or ale

— and being so out of practice, he was nervous —

Combine and serve in beer mug with two cubes of ice.

— but at least he didn't have to improvise the content of his reply.

Drop in lime shell.

Charles examined his penmanship as if judging a blind submission to the national Palmer system handwriting competition. Muscle memory had served him well; it was an acceptable effort, so he flagged down the waiter Patrick had pointed out and asked him to deliver the napkin to its original sender. Charles tried to follow his figure through the crowd, but there were too many people and the postdinner drink orders were starting to come.

A few minutes later, another napkin arrived:

Correct.

2. What is the proper glass in which to serve a Bacardi buck?

Charles wrote his next response on a Broadmoor letter-head note card, tucked it into an envelope addressed "To Examiner," and posted it with the waiter/mail carrier.

Another question: *How do you make a blood 'n' sand cocktail?*

Then others: *How do you make an absinthe frappe? A Bobby Burns cocktail? A horse's neck? A maiden's prayer? A merry widow? A point of no return?*

Charles penned and posted his replies as quickly as he could.

The questions kept coming (none fired his anticipation more than *How do you make a between the sheets?*). And then — as the clock inched toward midnight and the band began its last set — the final question arrived:

How do you make sense of the fact that you're working as a bartender?

❖

Once the room started to clear, Charles scanned the remaining crowd and guessed that the person most likely to be his mysterious correspondent was the one sitting alone at a table on the far end of the reception hall.

Wearing horn-rimmed glasses and one of those simple, A-line dresses that look best on lean, long-boned women, she was watching the band and sipping on what looked like the remnants of a hot buttered rum. Mahogany-colored hair shorn into a boyishly messy ruffle; no makeup. She'd kicked off her shoes and stretched out her legs, using a small shipping box as an ottoman.

Great gams, Charles thought as he made his way across the room; *Big feet,* as he got closer.

"Designated driver?"

Startled, she looked up, quickly shifting her body as if she'd been caught in some trifling infraction, and then she readjusted her eyeglasses, leaving another set of smudges on their already murky surface. "No, actually," she said, "designated Sherpa."

She thrust out her hand; they shook like businessmen at a Rotary Club lunch.

"Alison Forché. Nice to meet you . . ." — she squinted at his chest — "Charles."

"With whom are you on expedition?"

She looked startled and (for some reason) amused. Twitching her head toward the reception-hall stage, she said, "My brother Aidan is the drummer — please, have a seat — and we made a deal: I promised to help him haul his gear around this weekend and he promised to help me haul my books across Manhattan next month."

"What happens next month?" Charles asked as he sat.

"I'm moving. And graduating."

"Ah," Charles said, immediately starting to strategize a polite exit. *Too young.*

"From Columbia Law School," she added, not with hauteur but with a wry emphasis that made it clear she'd read his subtext. "I'll be clerking with a firm that's paying enough so that I can finally have my own apartment."

So she wasn't twenty-two; she was still much younger than Charles. He'd concluded that this person couldn't possibly be the authoress of the cocktail-napkin epistles; she was too straightforward and deadpan, too *earnest.* She didn't exude even a trace of flirtatious intent.

"Are you a friend of the bride or the groom?" Charles asked.

"Groom."

Charles checked to make sure no one needed him at the bar (he'd dismissed the rookies at eleven o'clock) and then let his gaze wander.

The reception was in its death throes, the guests gathering their things, leaving the tables, and somberly drifting away in twos and threes. Occasionally there was a truncated blurt of laughter, but it sounded canned, like the soundtrack of an embarrassingly unfunny sitcom with irredeemably lousy ratings. At the coat check, people looked as if they were swimming in gloves, hats, jackets, and overcoats that, inexplicably, were now two sizes too large; they examined their claim tickets with disbelieving expressions: *Is this really mine? Why does it feel so* big?

It was always like this after a newly married couple departed the postwedding festivities: a steady leak of high spirits, a mysterious physical shriveling. Charles suddenly pictured the big inflatables at the Macy's Thanksgiving Day Parade, all those ten-story Snoopys and Bullwinkles and Hortons and Spider-Men. They had to surrender their buoyant contours sometime, somewhere, and as he watched the last deflated guests depart the Stanford/Bettencourt wedding reception, he felt as if he were witnessing the end of the line, looking on as Whoever's-Sorry-Job-It-Was pulled the plug, setting off that long tragic exhale of stale helium.

Jesus, what was *wrong* with him?

Charles concluded that his cocktail-napkin correspondent had to be long gone, having chosen to remain anonymous. He checked his watch. Twelve fifteen. Time to clean up and head home.

He turned to bid a polite farewell to the odd Mademoiselle Forché and found her staring at him. She looked different somehow.

"You didn't hear me, did you?" she said.

"Sorry?" She'd removed her eyeglasses; that was what had changed.

"I said, I didn't think you were going to find me."

"Find you?" The floor in their corner of the room began to upend like a huge curling linoleum tile; Charles could feel a dull, potent headache gathering force between his brows. *Stupid,* he thought, remembering that he hadn't eaten all day and wishing that he'd forgone his habitual end-of-shift Irish coffee. "I'm sorry, I'm not following."

Leaning forward slightly and looking into Charles's eyes with purposeful intensity, she said: "Have you thought about my question?"

"What?"

The muscles around her mouth quavered into a tilted, suppressed grin. She took a sip of her drink and re-angled her body to reveal a small spiral-bound book: Charles's dog-eared copy of the 1952 edition of *A Guide to Pink Elephants: 200 Most Requested Mixed Drinks on Alcohol Resistant Cards;* it usually lived in plain sight on a shelf behind the bar. She picked it up and handed it to him.

"Sorry about filching this and inundating you with those napkins," she continued, filling the conversational void while Charles grappled with vocal paralysis, a side effect of being gobsmacked. "The groom's mother put me in charge of getting rid of them, but they're so lovely, I couldn't bear to toss them."

"Hey!" a voice called from the stage. The musicians had started breaking down their equipment. "Alison! Need you!"

"Be right there!" She stared at Charles for another moment, then reached down and hoisted the box of napkins into her lap. "I should go," she said.

"Why were you supposed to get rid of them?" Charles asked. "The napkins."

"Because of the typo."

"The what?"

"Hey! Roadie!" A tall fellow — presumably Alison's brother, since he was thwacking a pair of drumsticks together — stepped to the front of the stage and bellowed, "Sis, time to schlep!"

"Be right there!" she hollered again. She reached into the box, plucked up one of the napkins by its corner, and smoothed it out: a miniature picnic blanket unfurled on the field of her upturned palm. "See?" she said, holding it toward Charles and pointing with her other hand: "'Love *Life* Us Up Where We Belong.' It's a mistake."

"Ah. Is that a quote from something?"

"Not a big fan of popular music, are you?"

"No, not really."

"Well." She replaced the napkin and hugged the box. "I should go help my brother. A promise is a promise."

Charles stood. She stood. He'd guessed that she was tall, but he hadn't expected them to be eye to eye. They looked at each other from either side of the boxed-up inventory Alison clasped to her chest: hundreds of costly, exquisitely soft, obsolete, and typographically flawed rejects, neatly packaged and facing an uncertain future.

"I'd like to see you again," Charles said.

"I'll say goodbye before I leave."

"No, I meant —"

"I know what you meant," she said. "I'm thinking about it."

As Charles finished washing glasses and wiping down the counters, she made several trips in and out of the reception hall, toting band equipment with impressive fortitude.

When fifteen minutes went by and she hadn't returned — by which point Charles was the only person left
in the reception hall — he figured that was the end of it, but
after he hung up his bartending jacket and started heading
to the kitchen to clock out, he heard the sound of hurrying
footsteps.

"It's a lot of work, being a roadie." Her voice was a little
breathless.

Reaching into her coat pocket and withdrawing a small
rectangle of paper, she walked toward the bar, parked herself with her back to him, and, bending close to the counter,
began writing something. "I'm flying back to New York tomorrow," she announced. "I prefer written correspondence
to telephone conversations."

When she finished, she turned around, stood up straight,
and held up her pen at the precise midline of her face, so
that it aligned perfectly with her nose. "You are under no
legal obligation to return this," she said. "However, you
should know that it's my favorite. So, please, either use it or
regift it, but don't throw it away."

She handed over the pen and the piece of paper: lightweight card stock. It was her claim check. When she didn't
immediately depart, Charles kissed her.

He could have stood there kissing her forever, but when
their breathing started to deepen and synchronize, she pulled
away.

"Goodbye, Charles," she said. Then she turned on her
sensible heels and walked away.

The pen she'd handed him was no ordinary Bic Roller
Ball (So Smooth It Almost Writes by Itself) or even a Sheaf-
fer Slim Targa (Revolutionary Inlaid Nib) but the brand
used by Ernest Hemingway and John Dos Passos during

their World War I ambulance–driving days: a Montegrappa Italia.

On the claim check, she'd written two addresses and a brief note:

> The first address is good through the end of May. After June 1st my law books and I will be living on West 10th. It was a pleasure meeting you, Charles. You're an excellent bartender; nevertheless — and no matter how things turn out — I do hope you'll give some thought to that question.
>
> Best wishes, Alison
>
> P.S. I'll want to have children right away.

❖

"Crazy, isn't it?" Charles took a long hit and leaned back into the reassuringly firm resistance of Zach's Italian leather sectional. They were sitting in the living room/kitchen of Zach's condo; with its ascetic design and expansive views of Elliott Bay, it looked like it had just been featured in an *Esquire* photo shoot. In contrast to Charles's cramped and squalid U District studio, Zach's place was clearly the abode of a grownup.

"And just think," Charles concluded, offering Zach the joint, which he declined, "it could have been *you* on the receiving end of that girl's weirdness."

It was Monday night. To celebrate Zach's release from the hospital, Charles had invited himself over, toting a bag of takeout from El Puerco Lloron, a couple of videos, and a six-pack of Corona. Charles had just finished a rambling

monologue in which he recounted the story of the Stanford/
Bettencourt reception and how he'd narrowly escaped falling into the clutches of a humorless nutcase.

"Of course, if *you'd* been the one working the gig," he
went on, "she probably would have missed her flight. Hell,
she'd probably be in this room right now."

Zach smiled. "I'm not so sure about that."

He started gathering dirty plates and glasses, clearing the
mess of bags, napkins, beer cans, and tinfoil scattered on
the coffee table. "Stay put," he said when Charles had trouble getting up. "I got this." Zach crossed to the kitchen and
began washing dishes.

Charles breathed in another long, sustained hit of weed
and worldview. *Lucky guy,* he thought. *So fucking lucky.*

What Zach had was what Charles aspired to: personal
freedom, elegant surroundings, the tidy, dignified sphere of
a man unfettered by connections to anything but his own
desires, untouched by the emotional and environmental
chaos that's an inevitable result of letting other people into
one's life.

Zach was saying something over the sound of running
water.

"What's that?"

"I said, do you like her?"

"Who? Loony tunes?" Charles shrugged. "Sure, I guess,
aside from the fact that she's obviously insane."

"You said you kissed her."

A small warning light went off in Charles's mind when
Zach brought up this minor detail.

"Yes, and . . . ?" Because Charles's version of the story was
carefully abbreviated, emphasizing Alison's eccentricity and
youth and his levelheaded maturity (and downplaying his

devolution into a man with a terrifying case of kiss-induced tachycardia), the extended version of their make-out scene ended up on the cutting-room floor. "So?"

"Come on, Charlie." Zach raised his voice just enough to be heard over the clink and clatter of glasses and plates being returned to the cupboards. If Charles hadn't been so stoned, he would have realized that there were complex maneuverings in play: tableware in the hands of a bartender as experienced as Zach did not clatter. "Just tell me," he prompted. "What was it like?"

Charles redirected his attention to the nachos and settled deeper into the sofa cushions. He was aware that he was acting like an adolescent but remained clueless as to what other behavioral choices were available.

"Okay," Zach said when Charles didn't respond. "Here's the thing: based on my experience and wisdom . . ." His old man voice sounded disturbingly authentic, and he abandoned the effort when he started to cough.

"Are you okay?"

"Yeah, I'm fine." Zach crossed the living room and stood at the picture window, looking out at the bay. It was getting dark. "I just wanna say: What the hell? What could it hurt to follow up?"

"What do you mean?"

Zach turned around and, with an uncharacteristic gravitas that Charles perceived even from the depths of his stoner haze, said, "Do it. Write her a letter. Even if she *is* crazy, she's three thousand miles away. It's not like you're gonna need a restraining order. Hell, if you're that worried, don't give her your phone number. Come on. What can you lose?"

Zach's counsel was sound, reasonable, brotherly. And there had been that kiss.

So Charles wrote to Alison in his best Palmer cursive,

making use of her pen. She wrote back, making use of the typographically flawed napkins.

He told her about his parents and their volatile marriage, the mixed blessings of being an only child, the small embattled country that was their three-person family, his love for books and movies, philosophy and language. Yes, for years he'd been aimless in his aspirations, superficial in his relationships. He blamed no one but himself.

He did not write of his landmark fourth-grade year or Dana McGucken, although — in a lighter vein — he did share reflections related to the Palmer Method and suggested that Alison might benefit from daily loop practice if her work at the law firm became too stressful; to that end, he sent a vintage Palmer Method handwriting workbook he found at an antiques mall.

She told him about her family, their legacy of wealth, privilege, and visibility within Seattle society, her conflicted feelings about a life for which she'd always been grateful but also felt guilty about, her desire to do something worthwhile, *earn* her way, and eventually practice the kind of law that would involve advocating for the powerless instead of protecting the privileged. She expressed theories about Charles's lack of direction and drive, his fears of intimacy; she elaborated on what she saw as his gifts: patience, kindness, an ability to listen and mentor. She reiterated her belief that he had more, so much more, to give to the world than a superlative martini, and didn't he owe that to himself as well? She had unbounded faith that anyone with self-awareness, discipline, courage, and intent could change for the better.

It was an epistolary courtship that lasted until the fall, when the effects of chemo and radiation made it impossible for Zach to continue hiding his cancer diagnosis.

"Marry me," Charles said, arriving on the doorstep of Alison's Morningside Heights apartment at six thirty one September morning after taking a Seattle-to-JFK redeye.

He kissed her for the first time since the Stanford/Bettencourt reception, *Love life us up where we belong,* rewinding time to that moment, confirming what he'd known since then but had been too frightened to acknowledge, because it was impossible for this to be happening to him; surely there had been some sort of mistake, a major gaffe at the highest managerial levels.

But no, apparently not, so *Thank God,* he thought — his first prayer since childhood — and he kept on kissing her; she did not pull away. They'd exchanged thousands of words over the past few months, *So now let words go,* he thought, feeling the emphatic *yes* of her body in reply and agreement.

"Marry me," he said again later. "Come back to Seattle and marry me."

"Today?"

"Today. Tomorrow. Soon."

"What's the rush?" she asked lightly, bemused — as if all of this were sweetly commonplace, nothing out of the ordinary, merely what was merited. It frightened him for a moment, for this was no small disparity: she was a person for whom happiness and good fortune was a given; he lived in constant expectance of sorrow. But maybe she could teach him; maybe he could learn.

"My best man is dying," he replied.

She kissed his eyelids, pulled him close, and said, "It won't take me long to pack. I travel light."

Where Are They Now?

"All right, then, Mike," Charles said, adding, "I look forward to meeting you," before hanging up. He immediately retracted his hand from the receiver, as if he'd grasped the handle of a cast-iron skillet he'd forgotten was blistering hot.

I look forward to meeting you?

A polite end to the conversation, but a blatant lie.

Charles stood next to his home-office desk, still wearing his coat and shouldering his satchel. After school, he'd rushed home to get ready for his date with Alison at Children's Hospital; when the phone rang, he thought it might be her calling with a change in plan, so he picked up.

"Mr. Marlow? Mike Bernauer here, from the *Seattle Times* . . ."

"Oh, hello," Charles said dully, fighting an impulse to disguise his voice, say, *Sorry, wrong number,* and hang up.

After Charles confirmed that yes, he was the Charles Marlow who'd attended Nellie Goodhue during the 1962–63 school year; yes, he was the Charles Marlow quoted in the 1963 *Seattle Times* article; and yes, he was the Charles Marlow who'd written "Flipper Boy," the reporter reprised the information he'd left on the answering machine: he was doing a follow-up piece about the fourth-graders who had been in Mrs. Braxton's Language Arts class, where were they now, what were they doing, had their predictions of twenty-first-century life come true, that sort of thing.

It sounded benign enough.

The reporter mentioned the names of several others who'd consented to the interview. Charles recognized but one: *Astrid Overmeyer.* The surname was different, the first name devoid of that final schwa, but it had to be her.

Probably he'd consented for no other reason than curiosity and to reconnect with one of the few other people who might be able to corroborate — or refute — his version of what had happened at the end of that school year.

With his Montegrappa Italia, Charles made an entry on his desk calendar for three days hence: *10:30 Mike Bernauer Seattle Times interview @ Center House next to Monorail.*

◈

It was Alison's idea that they keep going to these things. Charles suspected that she had a hidden agenda, that she worried about his lack of a social life and these monthly PLAY gatherings were her way of getting him out now and then.

Usually there were guest speakers — scientists addressing some aspect of the brain, therapists offering helpful tools in terms of communication, dietitians recommending some new nutritional theory, and so on — and Charles almost always took away something to contemplate.

"Good evening, everyone!" announced a voice over the microphone.

The PLAY director, Leslie Eisenberg-Zimet, an anesthesiologist and the mother of three autistic sons, began gesturing the crowd toward the front of the room, away from the potluck-dinner tables. "If you could, please start wrapping up your conversations, grab something to drink if you'd like, and take a seat. Tonight's presentation is about to begin."

Charles poured himself another cup of coffee while Alison finished chatting. She'd developed close relationships with many of the people in this room, often seeing them in social settings, but Charles preferred to enforce certain boundaries in his personal life — such as it was. He kept a polite distance, not considering the shared experience of having a child *on the spectrum* a good foundation on which to build potential friendships.

"Ready?" Alison said, taking his arm. "Let's get seats."

There was a larger-than-usual turnout, as many as fifty people, Charles estimated. It was the time of year, Charles was sure of it. There was no more anxiety-provoking month than October, our bodies remembering the ancient cave days, anxious to secure sources of light and warmth and companionship before the arrival of winter.

Once the room had quieted, Dr. Eisenberg-Zimet took up the microphone again and addressed the assembly.

"This month, in the interest of doing something a little different and giving us all more of a typical parents'-night-out experience . . ."

She paused for laughter, and it arrived, ranging from the timid-forced variety to the gregarious-forced variety.

". . . tonight's presentation will be — surprise! — a movie screening of an award-winning independent Australian film called *The Black Balloon.*" Referring to a small piece of paper, she continued, "This is from a synopsis I found on the Internet: 'When Thomas and his family move to a new home and he starts a new school, all he wants is to fit in. But that proves difficult with his autistic brother . . .'"

Oh boy, Charles thought. *Here we go.*

"'. . . who likes to wear a monkey suit, play computer games, and find every opportunity to escape.' It's supposed to be a great film, full of heart and humor. I'm just sorry that I didn't think to provide us with popcorn" — again, she paused for an anemic wave of laughter — "but nevertheless, I hope you'll enjoy it. Okay, let's hit the lights. The film isn't terribly long, so if you're able, please stay for a postscreening discussion."

❖

"Oh, come on, Charles," Alison said after the waiter deposited their drinks on the table: cabernet sauvignon for her, a nonalcoholic cocktail for Charles. They'd driven to a bar in University Village, not far from the hospital, and were sitting on a sofa in a large sunken area with a fire pit. "You had to at least have liked the *acting.* It was good, right?"

"Yes, very good."

"And the writing?"

"It was excellent, Alison. Really."

"Liar," she said playfully. "You hated it, I can tell." She hefted her briefcase into her lap and began looking for something. "The actress who played the mother, she looked familiar."

"Toni Collette."

"Have I seen her in anything else?"

"She was the mom in *Sixth Sense.*"

Alison looked up, frowned briefly. "Oh. Right." It was a performance that had infuriated her: *No mother of a special child would ever act like that,* she'd said.

"Okay . . ." She brought out two crisp sheets of white paper, placed one in front of each of them. "We should get started."

At the top of each page was a typed heading — POSSIBLE HOUSING CHOICES FOR CODY — followed by a long numbered list.

Charles took up his copy, settled into the sofa, sipped his mocktail, and for the next half hour or so nodded and made appropriate interjections as Alison enumerated the pros and cons of each facility. He knew that his opinion wasn't really required; she'd already made up her mind about which places they should visit.

"So we're in agreement about this? I do think these are our best bets for him," she concluded, referring to the check marks she'd made beside the three acceptable choices.

"Sounds good."

"Okay, I'll make the phone calls and arrange the visits as soon as possible."

Charles looked at his watch. Ten thirty. He still had papers to grade.

"There is one other thing I wanted to talk to you about," Alison added as she made notations in her day planner, "another possible option, just in case we're not happy with what we see at these facilities."

Her voice remained nonchalant; only because Charles knew her so well did he recognize that the content of this statement hinted at a deeper significance, a subtextual brewing of some radical idea.

"What do you mean?" he asked.

"Well, I've been talking with other families who are facing this same thing — you know, kids aging out — and a few
of us got to brainstorming . . ."

She went on to describe what was clearly much more
than *another possible option;* it was a fully fleshed-out plan —
although she would never allow herself to acknowledge that.
It had always been important to Alison to feel that she was
including Charles. Only once in the course of their conjoined lives had she made a major, irrevocable decision
without consulting him.

Occasionally Charles's vision blurred, a compensatory
reaction to his ex-wife's crisply enunciated, impassioned
voice, her laserlike focus. More than once, he found himself
drifting off, staring into the fire.

❖

"I have a surprise for the two of you," Eulalie announced.
She and Alison were in the living room; Charles was in the
kitchen, setting the kettle to boil and trying to figure out
what was on hand that he could use to improvise dinner.
In the pantry, rice, quinoa, potatoes; in the fridge, desic-
cated, whiskered carrots, boxed baby lettuce gone slimy, and
a few end-of-season beets and beans from the garden; in the
freezer, chicken thighs, ground turkey, a lactose-and-gluten-
free entrée. There'd been no time to get to the grocery store
this week.

It was a Friday afternoon in October of 1994; the remodel
was in full swing, the rains were upon them, the house was
a disaster, and Cody had regressed substantially. Not a day
went by that Charles didn't fear the whole enterprise was
going to ruin them.

Atypically, and to Alison's obvious displeasure, Eulalie had
dropped by without any forewarning or prearrangement.

"Your father and I are taking Cody for the next four days so the two of you can spend some time on your own."

"What? Mother," Alison protested, "no! We can't possibly leave with everything going on, the construction, Cody —"

"I've reserved three nights at a B and B in La Conner, and —"

"Three nights?"

"Yes, I checked the school calendar and saw that Charles has a long weekend. Isn't that right, Charles?" she called to him.

"Indeed," he called back.

"There's absolutely nothing to worry about. Go and pack. If you get on the road in the next ninety minutes or so you'll arrive in time for dinner; I made a reservation at a phenomenal restaurant that your father and I discovered over the summer."

"Mother, this is insane."

"What's insane about it? Wouldn't you like to get away? Where's Cody?"

"Upstairs, with the therapist. They just got started."

"Fine, I'll stay until his lesson is over; I can pack his things while I'm waiting. Your father and I have all sorts of fun activities planned. We'll have a lovely time."

"Mother, I just don't think you and Daddy understand how complicated our life is right now. I know you're trying to be helpful, but —"

"I understand perfectly, Alison." Eulalie's voice was stern. She exchanged a frustrated look with Charles as he came into the living room carrying a tray bearing a teapot, a French press, two cups, and a plate of Walkers shortbread, Eulalie's favorite. "And that is exactly why you and your husband need to get away. Thank you, Charles."

Charles sat on the arm of the sofa next to Alison; he tried

to pull her close, but her body was resistant, taut. He knew that her protestations weren't entirely related to Cody and the remodel; she was surely just as anxious as he was about the prospect of spending time alone together, attempting adult-to-adult conversation over a good meal and a bottle of wine, and, maybe, possibly, having undistracted, unrestricted sex.

"Eulalie," he said, "this is an amazing offer. Thank you. What do you think, Ali? It sounds like everything's worked out."

Alison sipped her tea, frowned.

"Come on," he said, keeping his voice dispassionate, as if he really didn't care one way or the other, when in fact he was so elated by the idea of having his wife to himself for a few days that it was all he could do to keep from pulling her into a Bogart-Bergman lip-lock. "Cody will be fine."

"Of course he will," Eulalie chimed in. "You mothers today: so protective. My Lord, your father and I went out at least twice a week when you children were little. It's so important for a marriage."

Eulalie and Victor Forché — like Rita and Garrett Marlow — came from a generation of couples who did not consider themselves subordinate to their children but rather stepped out, regularly and often, regardless of the state of their unions and for no other reason than to have *fun*, choosing to put their identities as husbands and wives in front of their identities as fathers and mothers. Alison, however, epitomized a more current trend: on the rare occasions she and Charles went out, their babysitters were vetted with a scrutiny typically reserved for Supreme Court nominees and paid three dollars in excess of the current minimum wage. Charles knew he needed to interrupt this line of persuasion as soon as possible.

"It would be great for Cody too, don't you think? Getting away from all this?"

Alison considered. "Okay," she said, getting up, her intonation conciliatory but skeptical. When Eulalie started to stand as well, Alison made a preemptive gesture. "You stay here, Mother. I'll get Cody's things together."

My wife, Charles thought fondly, *genius, legal advocate, fierce fighter, acting like a petulant tween who's been unjustly grounded instead of a thirty-one-year-old woman who's been gifted with a responsibility-free weekend.* But then, Ali remained a case study in regression whenever her parents were involved.

Forty-five minutes later, their bags were packed and they'd said a brief goodbye to Cody. (*Don't linger,* Eulalie advised, *don't make a big production out of it.*) Alison handed over a pamphlet of written instructions pertaining to Cody's care — which, Charles felt sure, Eulalie would mostly ignore — and they were off.

The trip did not begin well. On the way, they argued — as parents typically do when cut loose from the distracting and role-defining presence of their children. Weekend traffic slowed the journey to a crawl. When Alison fell silent, Charles sensed an impending, irreversible decline in her spirits; he feared the weekend was doomed.

"Do you remember the last vacation we had?" he asked. "Just the two of us?"

"We've never had a vacation."

"Yes, we have."

"What are you talking about?"

"I'm talking about our prenuptial honeymoon in New York. The day I proposed?"

"Oh," she said, her mouth softening. *"That."*

They'd lingered in Alison's Cathedral Row studio apartment for hours, but eventually, famished, they went out. They ended up going into a Morningside Heights deli and designing a deluxe gift basket. *It's for some friends who just got engaged,* Charles explained. *They're planning on having a big family.* The deli owner smiled broadly, tucked in a box of menorah candles (*Free with big spending!* he said in heavily accented English), and then proceeded to shrink-wrap and beribbon their purchase. On the way back, they sat in the garden of St. John the Divine, decimated most of the roast chicken, couscous salad, and bialys, and then made out madly until a pair of territorial peacocks chased them away.

"That was a good day," Alison said.

It was nearly nine by the time they left the restaurant in La Conner. The B&B was a few miles out of town, situated on a prairie next to a barley field, with a misty view of Mount Baker to the north and tidelands to the west.

Their room had a fireplace flanked by shelves holding the complete works of Shakespeare in small, exquisite, separately bound editions; volumes of poetry; a bouquet of flowers; a basket of fruit and chocolates; a bottle of wine.

They lit a fire.

They slipped into the skins of younger, softer selves.

They found each other again, in that room, in that house bordering a fruited prairie.

And that was how they got their daughter.

❖

Dear Emmy,

How are you, sweetheart? How are midterms going? It feels like a long time since I've written, probably because I've had an atypically full dance card this week.

In fact, this will be a short letter; I have an appointment at the Seattle Center later this morning and have to leave in a few minutes.

Your mom and I saw a film the other night — the first time I've been to a movie in a while. It was about a family dealing with autism, a good film, very heartfelt. Your mom loved it. So did everyone else, from what I could gather.

I hate to sound cynical, but good God — they shoved every possible cliché into the narrative. Which is not to say that it wasn't spot-on accurate, clichés being based in truth after all. But really, it got to be a bit much:

1. Scene of PWA escaping due to negligence, leading family members on a frantic chase culminating in near tragedy but ultimately comic — check.
2. Scene of PWA smearing feces everywhere — check.
3. Scene of PWA masturbating in public — check.
4. Scene of PWA freaking out in public as misunderstanding and/or insensitive onlookers are either appalled or interfering — check.
5. Scene of PWA and family coming to blows, hurtful words spoken, combatants injured, dishes broken, walls punched — check.
6. Scene of forgiveness — check.
7. Scene of triumph — check.
8. Scene of bittersweet acceptance — check.
   The End.
   Credits roll.

I couldn't help but wonder how a mainstream audience would respond to this film. They'd probably depart feeling good about the experience, the acquisition of insight and sympathy infused with laughter. Having purchased this bit of karmic goodwill—and with no need to revisit the subject until the statute of limitations on compassion expires—they could then feel free to spend their next moviegoing bucks on something like *Die Hard 6*.

◆

"Okay, I think I've got everything I need," Mike Bernauer said, collecting his notes. The six of them were gathered around a circular table in the Center House food court, which, at some point in the years since Charles was last here, had been rechristened the Armory and redecorated by someone whose aesthetic ran to sleek and sophisticated and who obviously disdained any color but an exceptionally morose gunmetal gray. "Thanks again for doing this."

Mike was a tall, friendly guy with a strong Chicago accent who was probably around Charles's age. One of the first things he'd asked after they'd settled in was what they did for a living. One was an investment banker, one worked for a computer software company, one was an Eastside art-gallery owner/mom heavily involved in philanthropy, and Astrid(a) — not surprisingly — had become a neurosurgeon. With the exception of Charles, they all seemed to have lived up to Mrs. Braxton's expectations: wealthy, high-achieving pillars of the community. Of course, Mike had located and/or chosen only the five of them; perhaps the other students in Mrs. Braxton's class were somewhere up in the Okanagan manufacturing meth, although, when Charles thought about it, that too required no small amount of mental acuity and ambition.

"One last thing: our photographer would like to get a few shots outside, and then we're done."

"When will the article be out?" the banker asked.

"Probably sometime early in the new year. It'll be in the *Pacific Magazine* section of the Sunday paper."

They headed out, the photographer snapped pictures of the group in front of a couple of iconic locations, and then they were free to go. It wasn't even noon.

"Whatever happened to Mrs. Braxton?" the computer fellow asked as they were about to part ways.

"She passed, back in ... let's see ..." Mike consulted his notes. "I did manage to get a phone interview with her daughter ..."

A *daughter?* Charles was thunderstruck. He'd never considered the possibility that Mrs. Braxton had a family.

"Yeah, here we go ... Patricia, only child, told me that her mother taught in the Seattle school system right up to retirement; she received a special award for her service a couple of years before she died, age eighty-five, in 1996."

Charles was only half listening. He was still thinking about Patricia. He wondered what *her* handwriting was like.

"Nice to see you all!" the banker said, handing out his business cards.

"Can't say that I remember any of you, but this sure was fun!" the computer guy shouted.

"I hope to see you all at the auction!" the Eastside mom/ art dealer added.

Astrid turned to Charles. "Which way are you headed?"

"I'm in the stadium lot."

"Me too. I'll walk with you. We didn't really get a chance to catch up."

They made their way past the former location of the Fun Forest, where city kids used to be able to get a taste of messy, gooey, thrilling, and, yes, slightly sordid carnival life.

The Fun Forest had recently been bulldozed into oblivion to make room for the Chihuly Garden and Glass Museum — a disheartening state of affairs, in Charles's opinion, exemplifying the current ethos that exposing young people to a fragile, pristine, humorless, and hands-off environment of *culture* was preferable to the gut-dropping rush of riding a roller coaster.

"I know you're an English teacher," Astrid said, "but that's about it. Where do you teach?"

"City Prana. Do you know it?"

"Capitol Hill?"

"Right."

She nodded. "We looked at that one for the kids but ended up at Lakeside. How long have you been there?"

"My whole teaching career, basically, so . . . since around 1990."

"That's a long time."

"How about you? Did you get your medical degree here?"

"No, I went away, to Johns Hopkins, and I really didn't want to end up back here, but . . . well . . . you know. The Northwest kind of *imprints* on you. Like on the salmon."

"I get it."

"So? What else? Family?"

"Divorced. Two kids."

She chuckled. "Sorry. It's just that, at our age, that's pretty much the way we summarize our lives. At least for a few more years, until we start listing our ailments. Amicable?"

"Now, yes. Not at first. You?"

"Divorced. Three kids."

Charles laughed, or tried to.

"You changed your name," he remarked.

"Hell yes. Wouldn't you? I sometimes think I married my husband as much for the chance to escape my maiden name as anything. How old are your kids?"

"Seventeen and almost twenty-one. Yours?"

"My oldest is thirty-five, a pediatrician, and about to make me a grandmother, *finally.* Young people today seem to take their time when it comes to procreation."

"Very true," Charles murmured.

They walked on in silence for a while.

Surely she was going to ask him. Surely that was the real reason she wanted to speak with him in private.

"Well, this is me," she said as they arrived at her Audi, spotlessly clean, liberally stickered: MY CHILD IS AN HONOR STUDENT AT LAKESIDE; PROUD STANFORD PARENT; CO-EXIST. "It was good to see you again, Charles. I wish you all the best."

"You too."

Was he relieved or troubled? Charles wondered as he walked to his car. Had Astrid forgotten the most significant experience they'd shared that school year? The cast of characters involved?

He supposed it was possible. Not everyone had the proclivity, as he did, to be imprinted by the desert of exile instead of the garden of home.

Teacher's Pet

By mid-October, Mrs. Braxton had granted favored status to a single student. No one was more surprised by her selection than the designee himself.

"Perfect, Charles."

The Ax was so enthralled by her protégé that she had even started to smile, which was unfortunate; when the nearly atrophied muscles responsible for smiling drew her lips apart, they revealed a set of preternaturally white, store-bought dentures that were as eerily eugenic as Dana's God-given teeth were flawed.

In all areas of study but one, Charles remained consistently undistinguished, nonexemplary, neither exceeding nor falling short of his average status. But ever since Mrs. Braxton had given a lecture on the unexpected benefits of becoming a Palmer penmanship gold medalist (handwriting could build *muscles?*), he'd been driving himself strenuously.

"All right, class. Present arms!" This was the cue for students to take up their writing implements with no less vigor and intensity of purpose than if they were hoisting broadswords.

Each day, when the time came for penmanship lessons, Mrs. Braxton asked her star pupil to vacate his desk, station himself at the chalkboard, and lead the class in what she called preparatory calisthenics.

"Notice the evenness with which Charles writes," she remarked, "the steady pressure he applies to the chalk."

Producing a row of perfectly uniform Palmer loops extending the length of the chalkboard was clearly number one of Mrs. Braxton's criteria for academic success. Her gusto for the study and practice of penmanship so far exceeded her enthusiasm for any other subject that Charles sometimes wondered if she had a personal relationship with Mr. Palmer. Maybe they were pen pals.

"Notice how he keeps his arms relaxed, his movements completely smooth . . ."

That particular day, while Mrs. Braxton droned on and made her rounds, Charles began replaying the events of the previous evening, when he'd discovered the benefits of Palmer practice at home.

He and his parents were in the TV room. The evening news was on, the martinis were poured, and his mother was recapping the events of the day, which included a bridge-club luncheon at one of her friends' houses.

I just don't understand why some people don't make an effort to speak correctly. It's not rocket science, it's not brain surgery, it's a simple matter of opening up a dictionary, but I guess some people can't be bothered — but I mean, really, how can anyone hope to rise above their situation if they still sound like they're from, well, you know what I mean; in this country we can be whoever we want; *we can* all *make something of ourselves, and speaking properly is one of the simplest ways to improve our social standing; it makes an impression, the way we talk; people are sadly misinformed if they think it doesn't; I mean, think about it, Garrett: you'd fire your secretary in a heartbeat if she sent out a business letter with misspelled words or improper grammar and yet people think nothing of saying* Warsh-*ington or* git *or* melk *or —*

Suddenly, Garrett Marlow threw his newspaper down in a mangled heap and yelled, *Jesus Christ, Rita, you can be a pretentious BITCH!*

He stormed out of the room. A minute later, he could be heard slamming the door to the garage, gunning the engine of his car, and speeding into the night.

"Notice the steady tempo," Mrs. Braxton continued now, "the balance between energy and relaxation . . ."

While Walter Cronkite had reported on Wally Schirra's space orbit, Charles withdrew a cursive practice table from his satchel and began trying to slow his heart rate by executing a series of up-downs. His mother finished off the pitcher of martinis.

You may eat in the TV room tonight if you want, Charles, she'd said after a while. Her voice sounded faint and quavering, as if she were speaking from inside the freezer. *I'll heat up a potpie — we've got a turkey; that's your favorite, isn't it? — and then I think I'll take a little nap.*

In the safety of his bedroom, Charles retrieved his pocket dictionary; *bitch* was easy to locate, but it took a long time to find *pretentious.*

"Look how consistent he is!" Mrs. Braxton marveled, her voice exuberant enough to penetrate Charles's reverie. "Really, that is quite *exceptional.* Textbook *perfect!*"

"*Egg-SHEP-shun-all,*" Bradley whispered, giving a sustained, reptilian emphasis to the *s*'s.

"*Puh*-fect." Mitch's aggressive, plosive articulation of the *c* and *t:* a linguistic shiv.

Charles felt the ping of spitballs hitting his shoulder blades.

"Bradley! Mitchell! Shall I send you to detention?"

There was a momentary silence, followed by an impressive cadenza of farts.

Mrs. Braxton shot Dana a poisonous look. His head was resting on his desk, cushioned by his forearms, and up to this point, everyone had thought he was asleep. But now he roused himself. His weasel's grin expanded into a full-fledged smile and he craned his head around, basking in the accolades of laughter.

An eggy fragrance was permeating the air; the Ax pursed her lips, strode to the other side of the room, and threw open a window. She sighed heavily, then spoke in an uncharacteristically small, defeated voice. "I had so hoped that we might move on to more complicated letter forms today, but clearly that is not to be the case."

She seemed unaware that Dana's contribution to the atmosphere had been dissipated by a sudden, bitterly cold wind blowing in through the open window and that the sky, the color of dull paper clips, was starting to spit snow — a meteorological event that, in Seattle, borders on the miraculous and fills students with the not-unreasonable hope that school will be canceled at any moment.

Whoa, students began to whisper. *Look outside, it's snowing.* Children telescoped their necks to get a better view. Some dared to detach their bottoms from their desk chairs; others poked the unaware and then, gluing their forearms to their chests, allowed single, cautious fingers to unfurl and point.

Snow snow snow snow snow snow snow . . .

The word gathered force with each repetition, the *s*'s and *o*'s filling the room, a two-letter alphabet soup spiraling around and around: a spell, a charm, an invocation.

When Brad hollered, *"Holy shit, it's snowing!"* Mrs. Braxton shook herself out of her melancholy, glared at him, and spoke a single word: "Go."

Brad rose and exited. The class was riveted by Mrs. Braxton's sudden recovery of her godlike powers. She turned to the window and pushed down on the casement with such force that the glass rattled and the snow stopped falling. (By the time recess arrived, it had vanished without a trace.)

"All right, class," she began. "Let us resume with a series of lowercase *a*'s. Charles will continue to lead. I will call out a rhythm. Present arms! And . . . up, down, up, down, up, down, up, down . . ."

She was near the back of the room when Dana spoke. His strange, denasal voice was not, for once, too loud; it was almost within the bounds of normalcy.

"You do good with that, Char-*Lee* Mar-*Low*," he said.

A hush fell over the room. Even Mrs. Braxton was temporarily stunned into silence. Charles turned around.

Dana wasn't looking at him — Dana never looked directly at anyone — but his head and gaze were spiraling around Charles's general direction. He looked like he was tracking the movements of an inebriated bumblebee whose flight path was roughly at the level of Charles's face. He was smiling too, in a genuine, easy way, revealing his train wreck of a mouth. "Char-Lee, Char-Lee Mar-Low," he repeated.

"Dana," Mrs. Braxton said, less sharply than she normally spoke to a disruptive student. "Quiet, please."

Dana bobbed his head, as if shrinking from a blow. He drew his hands toward his chest, squirrel-like, in a way that was usually the precursor to his hand-massaging habit. But then, very slowly, as if encountering terrific internal resistance, he separated them and inched his right hand to just above the level of his head. In this diffident and clearly difficult way, Dana McGucken was asking to be called on. Never had he employed this basic schoolroom protocol before.

"Yes, Dana." If Mrs. Braxton was as astonished as everyone else by Dana's unprecedented use of classroom etiquette, she gave no indication. "Do you have something to contribute? You may put your hand down if you wish."

Dana spoke at a normal volume, slowly, but with exceptional clarity:

"That boy . . . that Char-Lee Mar-Low . . . He do good work with . . . those . . . those . . . *Pah*-mer loose. He do real good work."

It was the most anyone in room 104 had ever heard him say.

PART TWO

The Palmer Method

On the first day of fourth grade, Mrs. Hunter
collected our penmanship samples to save
until June; by then, she said, we'd write
in the handwriting we would have all our lives.
. . .
We were writing ourselves into the future.

    — Katrina Vandenberg, "Handwriting Analysis"

I almost think we are all of us ghosts . . . It is not only
what we have inherited from our father and mother
that "walks" in us. It is all sorts of dead ideas, and life-
less old beliefs, and so forth. They have no vitality, but
they cling to us all the same, and we cannot shake
them off. Whenever I take up a newspaper, I seem to
see ghosts gliding between the lines.

    — Henrik Ibsen, *Ghosts*

Every childhood has a lexicon.

    — Priscilla Long, *The Writer's Portable Mentor*

Giorgia's Boys

The Intruder continues to disrupt the orderly workings of the many worlds Giorgia inhabits, an idle tourist with too much time on her hands. Maybe *she* has nothing to do but sightsee, chitchat, and take photographs, but Giorgia has obligations.

Most concerning of all, however, is the fact that the Intruder (whose name, Giorgia has learned, is Roma) has begun to evolve into something far more than a meddlesome, gossiping nuisance; she has become a *threat,* aggressively inserting herself into Giorgia's stories.

She has made herself a character in "A Love Like Salt" — a *sixth* sister in the *panificio,* when it is Giorgia who has always been the youngest! — parading around, showing off her strength and beauty, trying to supplant Giorgia as Papa's favorite.

She is the newest teacher at the school on "The Isle of

Rain," a novitiate seeking to endear herself to Giorgia's special students, some of whom are starting to prefer her when it comes time for handwriting lessons.

And she has also somehow gained access to Giorgia's convent cell, where Giorgia is the title character in "The Epistles of the Banished Princess." Earlier this morning, she became aware of the girl crouched beneath her writing table, spying, peering over the edge through that camera lens, trying to distract Giorgia from her responsibilities as a wartime pen pal.

As if anything could keep her from that story and that work, *l'opera di Dio!* How wrong it would be to abandon her correspondence, written in an unperturbed, flowing female hand with the greatest of care, telling of ordinary things, affirming the enduring existence of places exempt from horror. The war is escalating. The body count is rising. Not every boy is fortunate enough to have a sweetheart or wife assuring him that there is at least one person in the world advocating for him morning, noon, and night with God the Father and with the saints in His special employ, the patron saints of soldiers: Saint Ignatius, Saint Joan, Saint Martin, Saint Maurice, Saint Sebastian, and Saint George — Giorgia's namesake.

Ha! There is no Saint Roma! It is a satisfying thought. *I bet she's never written as much as a* postcard *to a boy in uniform!*

One thing is certain: this Roma had better not dare to step foot in the chapel again, or into any part of the story of "The Sunflower Bride."

It remains a puzzle. For so long, Giorgia has moved easily and alone between worlds on paths she believed that no one else could travel; how is it that the Intruder is able to follow?

It matters not. She has come up with a way to shield

herself. In one of the church classrooms, she found a large, lightweight white board with two folds, a standing screen that she can situate wherever it is most needed. It affords her privacy and separation. It allows her to concentrate. She can carry it with her wherever she goes, and she does, from world to world, country to country, across the seas and back again.

One world materializes as another recedes. It is difficult sometimes knowing where she is and who her allies are. But at least, always, she has this protective barrier that serves her many needs: portable confessional, *panificio* kitchen, convent cell, the walls of a classroom, the palace of her shame.

She has this wall, and her hands, and her ceaseless industry.

◈

Now she is in the story "Life Among the Changelings."

Giorgia's pupils at the island convent school are among God's most special children: eyes tending ever upward, roaming the skies; speaking (if they speak at all) in a private, individuated language; typically oblivious to ordinary earthly concerns; often outright resistant to traditional forms of human connection — touch, eye contact, conversation; attentive first and foremost to celestial voices only they can hear and decipher. In this sense, Giorgia considers her role to be less teacher and more code-breaker.

Yes, of course, her students can be difficult, even dangerous. Within their grown bodies (her students are all boys), they are still children. A stern hand, sometimes even physical restraint, is called for, but Giorgia can handle them. As Papa always said, *Sei forte, Giorgia, come un uomo, quasi.*

(He called her something else too, something besides

strong; what was it? A mandolin? A mango? A pair of hand-cuffs? A sleeve? Oh, well. It doesn't matter.)

The student she is working with now is an easy one. Tall, tame as a domesticated geriatric bear, he is one of the mutes — although he occasionally sings snatches of cheerful songs, some of which sound familiar: *The bigger the figure the better I like her the better I like her the better I feed her the better I feed her the bigger the figure the bigger the figure the more I can love* . . . Consistently attentive to personal hygiene (this cannot be said for all of Giorgia's boys), he presents a clean-shaven face, combed and Brylcreemed hair, and today wears neatly pressed trousers and a corduroy jacket over a plaid shirt. His expression is slack, his arm dead-weight heavy when Giorgia lifts it. She has to mold his fingers around the pencil and adjust his forearm so that it is angled appropri-ately in relation to the table. He watches these gentle ma-nipulations with baffled interest, as if they are happening to someone else.

They begin.

Up, down, around . . . *Up, down, around* . . .

This student is moderately advanced; very soon he'll be able to attempt his first letter, a lowercase *i*.

Giorgia is no fool; she doesn't expect her students to mas-ter cursive writing, but she believes it is important for them to *try* (how else but by attempting human gestures such as writing will they lay claim to the highest expressions of this earthly existence?) and just as important for their families to *watch* them try (how else but through observing these imperfect but brave efforts will their families begin to love them?).

Far more than demonstrations of social courtesy or proper hygiene — although these things are important as well — Giorgia has discovered that what makes her students' families most hopeful is watching their boys attempt to write. Why this is so, Giorgia is not sure, but clearly there is deep comfort and joy to be found in observing a son, grandson, nephew, uncle, or brother who has never spoken a word in his life try to write one.

The boys sense this happiness too, the fact that they have surprised other human beings in a positive way. It makes them more content to stay on earth, to keep trying.

Giorgia focuses on her students' divinity and mystery, not on obsessive repetitive gestures, nonresponsive expressions, or inappropriate outbursts. She knows they are capable of far more than competency and compliance. The key lies somewhere in penmanship practice.

After rewarding this student's effort with a brief, feather-light pat on the shoulder and a chocolate chip cookie, Giorgia stands and waves him on his way with a briskly executed series of bedspring ovals written in the air. She then reclaims her seat and waits for whoever is next.

❖

Giorgia hears the sounds of many footsteps approaching. She peers around her screen.

The rain has stopped! The sun has come out! The room is filled with the golden light of the countryside.

Home.

Toscana.

This must be a new scene from "The Sunflower Bride"; her wedding reception, perhaps? That's why all these people are here. The old ones have already taken their seats. Of course, that is as it should be, the elderly deserve preferential treatment, respect, and safekeeping; and now the young people are arriving, all the young people of Giorgia's village — her friends!

Giorgia looks for her sisters, her uncles, and Papa, who will surely soon be toasting her happiness from the head table.

Where is the head table?

And why are there not flowers? There should be flowers, *girasoli,* from the fields outside their village — hundreds of them, in milk bottles, on all the tables. Her sister Felice used to set them out like that, on the counter at the front of the *panificio,* a cheerful welcoming sight for their customers.

Where is Felice? Giorgia is growing anxious. As Giorgia's maid of honor and best friend, she should be at her side. And where is her groom? He will be in uniform, of course, as will the groomsmen.

Across the room, near the church basement entrance, Giorgia sees her, Roma, greeting each of the young guests, calling them by name. She guides them to their places around the room.

That is not her job! Giorgia is the bride! Only she knows the seating chart!

"Ma io *sono la sposa,"* Giorgia says, getting up and leaving the seclusion of her small screen. *"Non quella ragazza."*

Things have gone too far. This is more than inexcusable rudeness or even a threat — this is mutiny; this is a coup d'état.

Now the Intruder has begun to take pictures of the wedding guests.

But she is not the wedding photographer! It should be her bridegroom's friend, the pudgy redheaded boy.

There he is! And there is Giorgia's groom next to him, both in uniform, *si bello,* standing beside a table where one young villager, a gangly-bodied boy with dark hair and pale skin (*he needs to get out in the sun, that one*), sits alone.

"Hello, Mrs. D'Amati," the Intruder says when Giorgia draws near. "How are you today?"

How does she know my name? Giorgia wonders. *We've never met. It is time to make it clear. She is not and will never be a character in any of my stories.*

Giorgia reaches for the camera.

"Togliti di dosso quella telecamera," she says.

"I'm sorry, Mrs. D'Amati, what is it? Do you want me to take your picture?"

Giorgia shakes her head. *"Non sei stato invitato,"* she says, wrapping her hand around the camera strap and giving it a sharp tug.

"Mrs. D'Amati, I don't . . . can you just tell me what . . . please, let go . . ."

Giorgia yanks the strap so hard that the Intruder topples toward her. *"Fuori!"* Giorgia yells. *"Non puoi stare qui!"*

Suddenly Giorgia's bridegroom steps in and breaks her hold on the camera strap.

The Intruder moves behind him, cowering. She places her hand on his arm.

"Togli le mani di dosso a mio marito! Io sono la sposa!"

"Stop that, Giorgia." Her bridegroom's voice surprises her; it is hard and cold, like Papa's. "Leave Romy alone or I'll have to take you outside and put you in the bus."

Giorgia is incredulous; he is taking the Intruder's part! She has bewitched him! She has stolen him away!

"Io sono la sposa!" Giorgia shouts at her. *"Io sono la sposa! Lui è mio marito! Mi ama!"* And then she hurls the full force of her ninety-eight pounds against her bridegroom, bull-dozes him out of the way, and slaps the Intruder in the face.

Instantly, her bridegroom and his friend van-ish — *poof!* — and in their places the fallen angels appear, with their massive arms and thick necks.

Where are her allies? Why do none of her friends come to her rescue?

"Aiutami!" Giorgia cries out in desperation to whoever might hear and understand. *"Dio in cielo mandami un angelo custode!"*

◈

Cody is sitting and watching. It is the first time he has seen the tiny woman up close. He has studied her from across the room many times before. She too prefers to sit alone. She speaks a strange language. Sometimes she talks to other people, but mostly she talks to herself. She does things with her hands that interest him.

A small crowd has formed near Cody's table. At the center is the tiny woman, screaming — she is having a bad day — while Big Mal and the other man who is like Big Mal are trying to get hold of her. A few steps away is Romy, the girl who takes pictures and helps Cody and his group do art; she is talking to someone Cody doesn't know.

"It's all right," Romy is saying. Her face is red. "Really, I'm fine. You don't have to take her outside, I'll just . . ."

Cody stands up. No one notices; they are all too busy grappling with the little woman, who is strong, mad, and afraid. He walks around his table and comes closer.

"Cody," Big Mal says when he sees him. "Sit down and finish your lunch."

But Big Mal is too busy with the tiny woman to make Cody do anything, so he keeps on standing there. The tiny woman has started to cry.

Finally she notices him.

"Tu?" she says. She stops fighting the big men. Her eyes are large and brown and shiny. *"Sei tu? Sei venuto ad aiutarmi? Grazie. Grazie a Dio che ti ha mandato."* Everyone else has

stopped moving too. *"Vieni. Cerchiamo di dargli una lezione. È passato troppo tempo."*

She tries to take Cody's hand. He jerks it away and steps back. She nods — *"Bene, ho capito,* A-Okay" — and makes a gesture letting him know he should follow.

❖

Giorgia leads the student back to her place. She hasn't seen him for such a long time. Thanks be to God the Father for sending *him,* one of her favorites! She's forgotten his name — Dario? Dante? Delmo? — but it will come to her.

She sits. She pats the table surface next to her.

Roma has followed, but she isn't wearing that camera anymore, and she keeps a respectful distance, so Giorgia is no longer worried. She showed that girl what's what and then some.

Of course, Giorgia shouldn't have let her temper get the better of her. It was wrong to strike Roma, even if she is a flirt. Giorgia will need to say many prayers of contrition in her cell tonight. In the meantime, she looks Roma in the eye and says, *"Mi dispiace. Ti prego perdonami. Ho un cuore invidioso."*

The girl's face softens slightly, almost a smile, and she takes a few steps closer, so that she is next to the boy.

As soon as Giorgia sees them standing side by side, it all makes sense; the resemblance is so clear. Of course: they are brother and sister! Why did Giorgia not see it before?

This, at last, is a story she can live with, a way for the Intruder to have a place in Giorgia's world. Roma can be a character in "Life Among the Changelings":

It is visiting day. The three of them will eat lunch together — Giorgia, her student, and his sister from the mainland — and then, afterward, Roma will see the progress her brother has made.

Giorgia pats the table again, one hand on each side of her. They sit.

Giorgia touches the boy's hand.

He pulls away; he doesn't like to be touched, she'd forgotten.

The best thing is just to begin.

And so she does.

She starts with the basics. It is never a waste of time to go back to the beginning:

"Su, giù, intorno . . . Su, giù, intorno . . ."

Beyond the triptych of her screen, Giorgia is aware, others draw close, watch with respect, with reverence. Even the fallen angels and the prison warden!

That's fine! That's good! Let them all observe what it is to work with diligence and care in this small way.

God sees everything. It is not for the showy that He opens the gates of heaven, nor for the clamorous. It is for the small and resolute; the meek, the humble, the patient, the silent.

Let them all watch and learn.

The Art of Ukemi

It was Thanksgiving break, the day itself. Cloud City was closed, but Charles had risen at five thirty as usual and was already busy.

He had nothing but time over the long weekend and was determined to make some headway in the crawlspace. He really wanted to locate Emmy's childhood keepsakes — going through them together would be something fun to do — so in a way, he was grateful she'd decided to stay in New York and wait until Christmas to come home.

It's fine, sweetheart, he'd told her when she broke the news.

Are you sure, Dad?

Absolutely. Traveling over Thanksgiving break is a nightmare, especially cross-country. So much can go wrong.

Please tell me that you have plans. I don't want you to be alone.

I won't be.

Well, give Cody my love, okay? I miss him so much.

He misses you too, Emmy. Have fun, get some rest, and I'll see you next month. I will recognize you, won't I? I mean, you won't be coming home with a shaved head or a tattoo or a nose ring or anything, will you?

Very funny, Dad. Ha-ha. But just wait; one of these days I'll surprise you.

Charles had made coffee, eaten breakfast, chosen another dusty bottle off the rack and set it in the fridge to chill: French, white, a *piquepoul.* He learned from a quick Internet search that the literal translation was "lip stinger" but he'd decided to try it anyway. He liked the lettering on the label.

The day was all planned.

Later this morning he'd visit Cody at the group home, watch a few minutes of whatever college football game was on, and wish the caretakers a happy holiday. He wouldn't stay for the special lunch, most of which Cody probably wouldn't eat anyway.

Alison had made a point of inviting him this year; she'd be bringing Mike/Dick/Harry — *Don't you think it's time you met him, Charles?* — but Charles demurred; he was fairly sure that sitting down to cranberry sauce with his ex-wife's gentleman friend would not put him in a count-your-blessings mindset.

Then, back here by three o'clock Seattle time (six o'clock in New York, when Emmy would be sitting down to dinner in Brooklyn with her roommate's family), he'd open the wine, warm up a single-serving Traditional Thanksgiving Meal from Whole Foods, and settle in front of the television to watch his DVD of *The Accidental Tourist;* all in all, a perfectly acceptable way to spend the holiday.

But for the next few hours, his focus would be exclusively on the Box Project.

Charles donned his 3M 8293 respirator; he'd discovered a stash that Alison had purchased in quantity for Cody when they were mitigating mold. Although the crawlspace was now mycotoxin-free, the *dense, gluey, chemical musk* of old magazines lingered, and after developing a slight cough, Charles became worried about the potential side effects associated with long-term exposure to *Life*. Respirator secured, he headed purposefully down the stairs.

The agenda was simple and straightforward: move one box at a time upstairs, open it, assess its contents as quickly as possible, distribute those contents into one of three large plastic tubs labeled DISCARD, DONATE, SAVE, and repeat.

He would not allow himself to loiter. He needed to be efficient. He needed to focus. *No wallowing.* He would not spend time wondering which box to explore; he would simply lay hold of the first one that caught his eye (*That one, right there*) and get on with it.

It was small, not terribly heavy. Using the top of his head, Charles nudged it across the crawlspace floor as he made his way on hands and knees: a one-trick pony nosing a bale of hay across the least exciting ring of a three-ring circus.

Outside the crawlspace, non-equine, bipedal, he toted the box up the stairs and into the living room.

When he scissored it open, he discovered a haphazard jumble of newspaper clippings and magazine articles; mixed in with these were the persimmon-colored napkins that had served as Alison's notepaper during their epistolary courtship.

Charles reached into the box, gradually submerging his hand as if testing the temperature of a bath, feeling the clothlike suppleness of the napkins, the brittleness of the newsprint.

It saddened him to find these two types of archival material mixed together and in such disarray. But he had to admit, from a curatorial point of view, it made a certain sense: Alison's letters (chronicles of buoyancy and hope) mixed in with the articles (uniformly bleak stories related to persons with autism) — these relics bookended their life together.

What was odd was that Charles had never gone looking for these articles; they had found him: in the teachers' lounge, at the dentist's office, in the grocery store. Some were in the nature of profiles: informational calls to action, full of sobering statistics. Others were exposés: shocking, reform-inciting, the kind of major, serialized stories that are frequently collaborations between two or three investigative reporters whose efforts end up winning them a Pulitzer.

Charles wasn't cynical about such things; the commendations were well deserved, the work these journalists did was vitally important.

Whenever these stories appeared in his field of view, Charles felt he had no choice but to filch or purchase the publications in which they appeared, clip them out with his blunt-nosed scissors, and preserve them. He had cast aside his crucifix decades ago, but God wasn't about to let him forget that he was still under surveillance.

In a way, journalists were to be envied; objectivity gave them an ability Charles lacked. He was always trying to come up with ways of describing Cody.

He didn't think of his son as *backward* or *flawed* or *withdrawn* or *challenged* ... The word *pale* sometimes seemed right — before, Cody had been an oil painting, dense, textural, color-saturated, layered. He was still the same person, but his portrait had thinned and flattened, changing to a watercolor, one in which the *absence* of paint — the white space — was as defining as the colors.

Did Charles love him?

Yes.

Was it the love he'd imagined?

No, because there was always this overlay of bewilderment, disconnectedness.

A haze, an impediment, what was it?

Charles couldn't help himself, he couldn't stop trying to describe his love for Cody through language. Words were what he had, what he sought — what he'd reached for since childhood in times of fear, sorrow, confusion.

It was the Catholic in him, he supposed, the habit of prayer forever outliving the loss of faith.

He'd stopped collecting the articles after Alison moved out; with her departure, there was no one in the house who needed reminding that happy endings weren't always possible.

So why had he kept all this?

In a way, this material provided the ephemera that Cody could not; in lieu of school reports, report cards, certificates of merit, tournament trophies, and Father's Day cards, there were these articles.

DISCARD? DONATE? SAVE? Charles had no idea.

So once again, he found himself sitting on the floor, full stop, rubbing up against inky, tattered old newsprint, acquiring the smudgy fingertips of a disreputable archivist.

Ah, this one, he thought, lifting out one of the largest articles in his collection — and the only one that had found its way into his possession by way of Alison:

Three full pages from the *Seattle Times* dating back to 1998.

On their tenth anniversary that year, Alison presented Charles with a gift certificate for a ten-week Introduction to Aikido series.

"Ha!" he said. "Clever you. Very nice."

"I signed up for it too," she answered. "We can go together."

"Aikido," Charles mused. "That's a martial art, right?"

"Yes, but not like karate or tae kwon do or jujitsu."

"I see," Charles said, even though he didn't. Obviously and as always, Alison had done a good deal of research in advance of this conversation so that her knowledge already far outpaced his.

"It means 'the way of harmony,'" she continued. "It's essentially nonviolent, based on the idea that it's possible to practice self-defense in a way that doesn't inflict harm on the attacker."

Cody was only six, but he was tall for his age and getting stronger every day. What would happen once he reached adolescence, Charles wondered with apprehension, when that surging hormonal stew makes lunatics of us all? Words like *violence, self-defense,* and *attacker* had taken on a whole new meaning in their family. But Alison seemed to be using them in a completely guileless way.

She read Charles's silence as reluctance. "Of course," she joked, squinting through her spectacles in a familiar sendup of her lawyer persona, a character they referred to affectionately as the Honorable Judge Ball Buster, "if the plaintiff would rather have an anniversary gift that lines up with tradition, I could sentence you to a pair of tin cufflinks or a tenpiece set of anodized cookware . . ."

At the ten-year mark, it was presumed that a marriage had revealed itself as durable and flexible; the traditional tin or aluminum gift was supposed to remind the couple that a marriage can perhaps be bent, but never broken.

Charles laughed. "No, this sounds great."

He'd avoided tradition entirely that year, finding the metallurgical metaphor lovely in theory but completely uninspiring. Instead, he'd presented Alison with ten yellow long-stemmed roses, a gift certificate from her hair salon, and a current best-selling novel about a man trying to find his way back to his wife after the Civil War. It sounded good. Alison was hard to buy for.

"This will be fun," Ali said, reaching out and giving his upper arm a light squeeze. "Something for just the two of us. The sitter will be here at five thirty."

"What, wait, it starts tonight?"

"And she can stay until nine. That gives us time for dinner."

"Dinner. You mean, *out?*"

"We've got a seven-fifteen reservation at a little hole-in-the-wall sushi place across the street afterward. It's supposed to be excellent."

Viewed objectively, the gesture was sweet.

And yet, it was so obviously underpinned by Alison's preeminent love for Cody. Ten weeks of dates, yes, but these arrangements, they weren't for the two of them, not really; not dinner and a movie, not a hand-holding stroll on the beach, not sweaty sex at a nice hotel in Pike Place Market, but a martial-arts class.

It was for Cody, as always.

After being welcomed to the dojo — an open, airy place with picture windows looking out toward Lake City Way — they sat side by side on the white, expansive, canvas-covered mat as the instructor, Sensei Richard (a ginger-haired, bearded fellow with a scant ponytail and pale beefy feet), informed the class that there are two components of aikido, *nage* and *ukemi.*

"How many of you have done some form of martial-arts training before?" he asked genially.

A couple of hands went up.

"How many of you have an impression of martial arts based on what you've seen in the movies?"

More hands went up, including Charles's.

The instructor grinned and nodded. "Well, it's a common misconception that the person who throws is the one with all the power —"

Throws? Charles thought. *Throws what?*

"— when in fact it is the *uke,* the person being thrown, who is in control. That's why we'll start by learning *ukemi,* the art of falling."

"He's kidding, right?" Charles muttered to Alison.

The philosophy behind aikido, Charles soon learned, is a worthy one; unlike other martial-art forms, which *stop* the flow of energy, aikido is about redirection, about acknowledging that an aggressive force is in play but shifting that force slightly so that it is aimed elsewhere. Its movements are largely circular and flowing, as opposed to angular and sharp; the sounds of an aikido class are predominantly rustlings, swishings, like the gentle abrading of a broom being swept across a slightly roughened surface.

Alison took to it right away — to such an impassioned extent that any outward signs that she and Charles were there *together* soon disappeared. There was Charles, sitting back on his heels, wary but polite, and there was Alison, leaning forward as if tethered to the sensei by an invisible wire fastened firmly to a spot between her furrowed brows.

Ali's zealotry for aikido sparked with a suddenness that was startling but, in retrospect, hardly surprising. Not that she liked falling; she hated it. It was so antithetical to anything she had ever done before: giving in, giving over to another's manipulations, even if the fall itself — an orchestrated roll on a padded floor — was highly controlled and concluded by the *uke* with a firm thump against the floor, for it was the *uke* who in that way announced that the fight was over; one of many aspects of the philosophy behind aikido is that *uke* and *nage* are equal partners.

But the idea the instructor put forth time after time, that *falling does not equal failing*, was one that intrigued her even as she was frustrated by it. Learning to embrace the art of *ukemi* became the latest in a long line of battles she was determined to win.

She would fall, but she would not by God fail.

Charles quit after the first three sessions. He hated to fall too but, unlike Alison, had no desire to learn.

"Can't you *try*, Charles?" Alison said repeatedly, pursuing what had become their regular date-night conversational topic. At least they weren't talking about Cody; although, of course, they were. "I could help you, if you want," she offered. "We've got a perfect place to practice at home . . ."

By this time, the room that was formerly Charles's office had been re-appropriated; Ali had installed a thick, soft, wall-to-wall wrestling mat that allowed her and Cody to work comfortably on the floor. It also minimized injury.

"It's just not for me, sweetheart," Charles said. "But I'm glad you like it. Really. I hope you'll keep going after the series is over."

Each week, Charles accompanied Ali to the dojo. He remained in the waiting room, out of view of the class, perusing the dojo's lending library of books on Japanese culture, philosophy, language, history while Alison learned to fall.

It was there that he first came across the word *koan.*

A fundamental part of Buddhist lore, a koan is a story, dialogue, question, or statement, the meaning of which cannot be understood by rational thinking.

Everyone knows the famous ones — *What is the sound of one hand clapping?* and *If a tree falls in the forest and no one is around to hear it, does it make a sound?* — but these don't do justice to the tradition. A koan is not simply an unanswerable or even absurd question; it is a question that requires deep thought. It is only when the student has truly committed to the thought — detaching from any outcome, any desire to please the teacher or be correct, any *expectations* — that he or she solves the koan. The answers are often ridiculous-sounding, producing laughter in the teacher.

Charles and Alison continued to go out for dinner afterward, but to one of the fast-food places that dotted Lake City Way, not to the sushi restaurant. It had been a disappointment: too slow, and they had to be home no later than eight thirty, not so much for the sitter but for Cody, who had lately taken to lashing out at anyone who tried to get him to go to bed. This included Alison, but his attacks on her were less intense and didn't last as long.

Charles's *real* reason for quitting aikido was one he couldn't share: soon after their first session, he'd dreamed of Dana McGucken.

They were at the dojo. Dana was kneeling across the room from Charles wearing not a white *gi* and belt like the other students but his signature three-piece suit. When Mrs. Braxton ordered them to stand and choose a partner, Dana began running toward him, calling *Char-Lee! Char-Lee Mar-Low!*

In his wake, staining the expanse of the white dojo mat, was a wide swath of gleaming, viscous blood.

◆

Charles initiated the conversation. He had to; Ali would never do it.

"What is it going to take, Alison? A broken nose? Fractured eye socket? Knocked-out teeth?"

She was sitting on their bed, holding a bag of frozen peas to her cheekbone.

"I've got it under control."

"Are you listening to yourself? Have you looked in the mirror? When I come home, I don't know whether I'm going to find the police waving a domestic-abuse warrant with my name on it or you comatose on an ambulance gurney."

"Don't be ridiculous."

"You think that's ridiculous? What do you tell your friends, the people at work, about the bruises, the scratches, the bite marks, the bald spots? What are you telling your parents? Do you really think no one but me is paying attention?"

When she didn't respond, Charles sat down on the bed. "It just isn't working," he said. "You've done everything possible. No one could have done more. We have to start facing the fact that —"

"No," she said. "*No.* I will not accept that. I will not hand him off to strangers. Nothing bad is going to happen."

"And you know this how? Do you want him to *kill* you, Alison? Because something bad *is* going to happen, there is no other way this is going to play out, and if you can't see that, maybe you need proof. I have plenty . . ."

Charles crossed the room and yanked open the top drawer of his bureau; it fell on the floor, scattering several

years' worth of clippings. He grabbed a stack at random and
began reading: "'Ballard Resident Attacked by Disabled Son
Suffers Miscarriage, in Serious Condition.' 'Fierce Protec-
tion of Mentally Challenged Son Costs University Professor
Her Life.' 'Autistic Child Who Started Fire Survives; Mother,
Sibling Die'—"

"Stop it, Charles," Alison said. "Please. I understand that
you're worried about us, but I have to keep trying. I can't
give up."

"I'm not suggesting that you give up, Alison. I'm just suggesting that there might be another setting where he could
be better cared for, and our family could be safe."

"But he's our *son*, Charles," she appealed, "he *is* our family, and he's only six years old."

Not long after, Charles arrived home late from school and
found her in Cody's room, sitting on his bed, watching him
sleep.

It was the fact that one of her hands was resting lightly
on their son's head that made Charles know something was
seriously wrong; touching Cody, awake or asleep, was a calculated risk. Her other hand was clutching a section of newspaper.

"Alison," Charles whispered. When she turned around,
Charles saw that she'd been crying. "What's the matter?"

She got up, careful to shift her weight in a gradual manner. Her weeping continued, noiselessly, and she didn't
speak until they'd passed out of Cody's room, closed the
door, and made their way down the hall and to the first floor,
where they stood next to the efficient, under-the-stairs office
she had so meticulously crafted.

"We can't . . . ," she said, turning to face him and then
starting to cry again.

"Ali. Honey. What is it? What?"

"No matter what happens, we can't let something like this happen. We can't *ever* see his picture in an article like this."

Her body went limp and she leaned into him, dropping the newspaper to the floor at their feet.

❖

It occurred to Charles that he was sitting in almost exactly the same spot where he'd held Alison that night, where he'd seen this article for the first time.

LAWSUIT ALLEGES THREE DISABLED MEN WERE ABUSED; THEY WERE LEFT AT GROUP HOME AFTER STATE HAD BEEN WARNED.

The accompanying photograph — yellowed now, but still just as striking and memorable as it was the first time Charles saw it — was a close-up of the oldest victim. He looked much younger than he actually was.

The faces of some disabled adults can be like that, Charles thought. *Cody's is; smooth, ageless, unmarked, the sinless portrait of Dorian Gray.*

The man had pale skin, neatly trimmed light brown hair, luminous aquamarine eyes; *cherubic* would be an apt description. His hands cupped a small stuffed animal he held next to his cheek, as if protecting it: a beanbag puppy that had one black-spotted eye. He spoke infrequently, the article said, but when he did, it was through this small creature, whose name was Boo. He'd been repeatedly beaten and sexually abused by his caregivers. At forty-two, he had the mental capacity of a five-year-old.

Heartbroken parents left with few options . . .

The subjects of the article faced dismal futures. One would have to move back in with his sixty-eight-year-old father, who was suffering from mesothelioma; another would likely be institutionalized, since his retired parents had depleted all their funds; a third was being taken in as a charity case by an order of Catholic nuns who ran a small, underfunded experimental school for boys with autism on Shaw Island.

We spent everything we had, we thought it was safe, we love our son, we'd never knowingly put him in a situation like this, what parent would, we don't know what will happen, who will take care of him after we're gone?

Charles stood up. He still couldn't decide which bin was appropriate for this material, so he returned all of it to the box, leaving it where it lay.

Dad, I have a question. A big, important question. It was the voice of Emmy as a child. *How can you tell if a cardboard box is a girl or a boy?*

The question — unexpected and perfect in its koan-like absurdity — made him start laughing so convulsively that his knees gave way and he fell back to the floor in a quivering heap.

Given this giddy state of affairs — and the fact that his resolves toward efficiency and decisiveness had all but vanished — Charles figured that he might as well uncork that wine.

We Now Conclude Our Broadcast Day

The person who made Garrett and Rita Marlow's social life possible was Catherine Bernadette Ryan. In the lexicon of Charles's childhood, it was *Catherine* who defined the word *babysitter*.

The Ryans lived in a nondescript one-story brick rambler that was across the street and two doors down. It looked far too small to accommodate the two adults, nine children, and numerous pets that poured in and out each day, and for that reason it laid hold of Charles's imagination.

Maybe the Ryans had a hidden bunker — or (inspired thought!) a *bomb shelter.*

In the wake of the Cuban Missile Crisis, *bomb shelter* was one of several new terms that had begun infiltrating adult conversation. Charles had learned from a recent *Life* ad that an adequately stocked, standard-size bomb-shelter unit could provide a safe habitat for five people for a period of three months. *Hell, Garrett,* he'd heard their next-door neighbor Hank Helmsdorfer remark while flipping T-bones on the backyard grill, *think of the money we could save if we went in on one of those things together!*

Charles understood the reasoning: Mr. and Mrs. Helmsdorfer were childless, the Marlows were only three, so the standard five-person size would be perfect; however, even though he was as worried about nuclear annihilation as the next nine-year-old, he was even more worried about what it would be like spending ninety days cooped up with a group of adults that included his parents, whose escalating aggression toward each other would probably erupt in a mushroom cloud the minute they sealed the shelter hatch, so they'd all end up dead of radiation poisoning anyway.

If and when the air-raid siren went off, Charles planned to make a beeline to the Ryans'; they'd surely ordered the deluxe-model bomb shelter designed for Catholic families.

The Ryans were not part of the Marlows' social sphere; Charles suspected that their fecundity was an issue: they were *real* Catholics, they *procreated.*

They also worshipped. Every Sunday, the voices of the Ryan family could be heard raised in a choral free-for-all as they crammed into their wood-paneled station wagon and barreled across town for early Mass at the Cathedral of St. James. The Marlows slept in. They could leave as late as eleven forty-five and still arrive in time for noon Mass at the newer, more progressive congregation, St. Matthew's, a mere three miles away.

Catherine was fifteen — old enough to be responsible, too young to have a boyfriend (or so Rita Marlow believed); in birth order, she was somewhere in the middle, so she knew her way around children, and her proximity was another plus.

For all of these reasons, Catherine enjoyed regular gainful employment at least twice a week for periods far outlasting the length of a level-one aikido class followed by five minutes in the Burger King drive-through.

One of the many reasons Catherine had earned Charles's special affection was that she always let him stay up late — not because she was unreliable or disobedient, but because they had a long-standing secret pact upheld by the promise of mutual, illicit rewards: from ten o'clock until midnight, Charles ate popcorn and watched *Creature Feature* in the TV room while Catherine rendezvoused with her boyfriend out in the back alley, in his car.

One typical date-night afternoon, Charles was watching cartoons waiting for Catherine while his mother got ready. She often came in and out a few times, modeling possible wardrobe choices.

"Do you like this dress?" she asked without preamble. "It's brand-new. It came from Frederick and Nelson's." She pointed to an embroidered bouquet of large, colorful flowers and leaves winding up from the hem to the bodice. "See this? It was done entirely by hand. It's called *crewelwork.*" She regarded Charles and sipped on her martini, in which floated a translucent pearl onion; it looked like the shrunken orb of a blind midget. "Your father picked it out especially."

"When is Catherine coming?"

"Soon . . ." She lit up a cigarette and glanced out the window toward the Ryans' front yard. "God, just look at all those kids," she mused quietly. In an uprising three-note melody, she added, "Bing-bing-bing," a chipper vocal flourish that was at odds with her masklike face.

Is this the right moment to ask? Charles wondered. He decided to risk it.

"Why don't we have more kids?"

She turned from the window. "Phrase the question properly, Charles. What you *mean* to ask is, 'Why don't you and
Dad have more children?'"

"Well, why don't you?"

Rita Marlow patted her helmet of hair and took a long
drag on her cigarette. "Probably because God knew that I
could only be a good mother to one," she said, gazing again
at the Ryan youngsters through a cloud of smoke. "Like
Mary."

After popping the pearl onion in her mouth, she rolled it
around a few times before trapping it between her back mo-
lars and biting down on it, hard.

❖

"And the certificate of merit for Palmer penmanship goes
to . . ."

Mrs. Braxton paused for dramatic effect, as if there were
an official-looking sealed envelope stashed within the depths
of her Playtex Cross Your Heart, as if terrific suspense surrounded the identity of the honoree, and her teasing delay
would prolong the audience's tortured anticipation.

". . . Charles Simon Marlow!" Mrs. Braxton gestured her
meritorious pupil to the front of the room, presented him
with a framed certificate, and then stood aside, initiating a
round of applause that was taken up dutifully if weakly by
the rest of the class.

Only Dana showed exuberance, bowing his head so that
his gaze seemed directed at his sternum, ducking and bob-
bing his upper body in an odd manner, extending his fully
straightened arms, anchoring his triceps to his ears, and
clapping quickly and rhythmically, a kind of performing-
circus-seal effect.

"Yay! Yay! Char-Lee! Char-Lee Mar-Low!"

Was Charles proud for having risen above his usual me-
diocrity?

Yes.

Would he have preferred to hear Donnie Bothwell cheering his accomplishment? An ally who was neither a reviled
teacher nor a ree-tard but a fourth-grader from the ranks of
developmental normalcy?

Absolutely.

But in Donnie's absence, Charles gratefully received the
peculiar fanfare offered up by Dana McGucken, and it was
to him that he raised his eyes and muttered, *Thanks.*

The class's energy soon lagged, but Mrs. Braxton allowed
Dana to continue his huzzahs and applause a while longer.

"The ree-tard *loves* him," Mitchell mumbled.

"The ree-tard is his *girl*friend," Bradley added.

"Fruit."

"Faggot."

"Creep."

"Queer."

"Yay!"

"All right, Dana," Mrs. Braxton said, resuming her place
at center stage. "That's enough. I'm sure we're all very proud
of Charles."

Dana kept clapping and cheering as Charles headed back
to his desk.

"Yay, Char-Lee! Char-Lee Mar-Low!"

"Dana McGucken," Mrs. Braxton admonished, her voice
assuming its familiar edge. "Quiet down."

But Dana swiveled around in his desk, his extended
arms now suggesting a giant compass needle pointing to the
true north that was Charles's location, and began chanting:
"Char-*Lee* Mar-*Low!* Char-*Lee* Mar-*Low!*"

"Dana McGucken! Silence! Now!"

Startled, Dana's smile collapsed, his face blanched even paler, and he folded in on himself and began frantically massaging his hand.

◆

Charles looked forward to the Saturdays when his parents left shortly after breakfast and were gone until the wee hours; long days, to be sure, but Catherine kept them interesting and varied. They took walks to the drugstore or rode bikes if the weather was nice. If it was cold and rainy, they played gin rummy and Parcheesi, built with Legos, read books. Once, Catherine taught him the recipe for Charlie's Chicken of the Sea Surprise, a casserole that alternated layers of canned tuna, Campbell's Condensed Cream of Mushroom Soup, and potato chips. (Years later — before Alison put the kibosh on processed foods — Charles taught Cody to make this dish, re-christened as *Cody's* Chicken of the Sea Surprise.)

This Saturday, however, his parents were hosting a tailgate party at the house from ten o'clock until twelve thirty, so Catherine would be arriving later.

A little after eight thirty in the morning, while Charles was still lingering in bed reading comic books, he heard the front door open and close; there were heavy footsteps in the foyer accompanied by the sound of labored breathing, and then his mother's voice erupted from the kitchen:

Damn it! she yelled. Damn it, *Garrett! What the hell did you do?*

. . .

What?

The responses to her tirade were too quiet to understand.

. . . You're lucky you didn't kill yourself!

. . .

Did you have to start before they got here? Look at this! We're going to run out of gin before they even get here.

. . .

Stop that.

. . .

I said, Stop it! *I'm going to have to go to the liquor store.*

. . .

Are you crazy? You can't drive. Goddamn it, they'll be here in an hour.

It turned out that, after downing a few drinks, Garrett Marlow had decided that the front yard needed mowing. He'd stumbled into the deep well of one of the daylight basement windows. Fortunately, the lawn mower hadn't fallen in with him.

Charles's mother left him with strict instructions to take the olive cheese puffs out of the oven the *moment* the timer went off; she then snatched up her handbag and rushed out.

Garrett Marlow limped a meandering path out to the patio, collapsed into one of the lounge chairs, rolled up his pants, and stuck his injured foot into the big Coleman cooler that was already packed with ice and beer. After turning the radio to the pregame broadcast, he sat back and closed his eyes.

The timer went off. Charles pulled the olive cheese puffs out of the oven, burning his hand in the process.

Hey, Charlie! Make me a drink, will you, now that your mother is gone?

After calling out the instructions for rimming a glass with salt, Garrett Marlow talked Charles through the rest of the process, including the celery-stick garnish.

Well, look at that, he said. *You just made your first bloody mary, Chuck. Bravo.*

Having fulfilled his responsibilities, Charles retreated to his room.

A few minutes later, there was a knock on his door; his mother poked her head in, her face pink and sweaty, her lipstick worn off.

Charles, I need you to come out here and do the things your father would be doing if he weren't such a useless SOB.

Garrett Marlow spent the duration of the party with his foot in the cooler, wearing his purple-and-gold hat with the *W* on the front at a jaunty angle, holding court while his wife and son served as caterers. At one point, emerging from the kitchen with another tray of olive cheese puffs, Charles discovered that Mrs. Helmsdorfer was snuggled into his father's lap, nuzzling his neck.

Mr. Helmsdorfer didn't seem to mind. *Shit, Garrett!* he bellowed. *You're gonna get frostbite, leaving your leg in there so long. You'd better pull that thing outta there or we might have to cut it off!*

For no reason Charles could think of, the adults found this wildly funny.

❖

After winning the certificate of merit, Charles was awarded the role of fourth-grade teacher's assistant. He hadn't bargained on this result; it was one he'd soon come to rue.

Mrs. Braxton now expected him to stand at the blackboard not only during penmanship practice but also during lessons in world studies, reading, science, and spelling. This allowed her to patrol the room as she lectured — slowing her speech and emphasizing words or phrases that she wanted transcribed on the board — and exert her fierce, up-close-and-personal vigilance over the class in a nonstop manner.

The Republic of Congo, the Soviet Union, Puerto Rico, Cuba . . .

Other perks followed:

She had a desk and chair set up beside hers. It was not an adult desk, nor was it the cramped, standard-issue all-in-one chair/desk that everyone else inhabited. Charles wondered if it had been stolen from some poor unwitting sixth-grader, possibly a former certificate-of-merit holder whose penmanship had lapsed.

She bestowed upon him with unprecedented liberality the much-coveted hall pass so that he could fetch supplies, refill her coffee cup, and deliver messages. This freedom would have been exhilarating had it not been won at such a cost.

Bradley's and Mitchell's contempt ratcheted up several notches.

Astrida Pukis continued to emit an embittered loathing that abated only during math, when she exerted her dominance during blackboard multiplication races.

Class morale plummeted. The students of room 104 began to look haggard —

Fidel Castro, Nikita Khrushchev, Cape Canaveral, the Iron Curtain . . .

— with the exception of Dana, who seemed to expand under these conditions, maintaining his snaggletoothed insouciance even as his white suits became grimier and his fingernails continued to grow unchecked, accumulating a yellowish, gritty opacity.

Underdeveloped country, gross national product, crop rotation, drought belt . . .

As the de facto class clown, Dana provided the only leavening element during those long, grim days.

Montgomery, Alabama; Anchorage, Alaska; Phoenix, Arizona . . .

Charles now understood that his tenuous social position — which had been compromised from the very beginning, when he'd shown up on the first day of school without Donnie Bothwell at his side and then exchanged words with Dana McGucken — was now cemented: he was a toady, a sycophant, a Jewish policeman in the Warsaw ghetto.

It is of course not always the case that teachers' pets become social outcasts. Had Mrs. Braxton been more popular, less feared, it's possible that being anointed as her favorite would not have carried such a stigma.

As it was, however, because Mrs. Braxton's leadership style recalled that of the Old Testament Jehovah, her preferential treatment brought into high relief the sufferings of the poor and unfortunate: God's un-chosen people.

In the classroom, Charles occupied the pinnacle seat, but once removed from that setting — in the cafeteria at lunchtime, on the playground during recess — he sank to the bottom, into the special hell reserved for certain elementary-school children: the leper colony of the tribeless.

❖

There was always something terribly hollow and disturbing about the end of the broadcast day. Seeing the rippling American flag in black-and-white and hearing "The Star-Spangled Banner" made Charles feel as though the world had ended. Still, he felt compelled to remain and watch until the flickering test pattern appeared and the airwaves went silent.

After turning off the TV, he brushed his teeth and turned the back-porch light on and off three times; that was Catherine's cue, and she emerged from her boyfriend's car within moments, waving to him as he drove away. Charles never did meet him, but Catherine revealed that he was twenty-seven years old, rolled his own cigarettes, and worked for the railroad, bare-bones facts that only enhanced his mystery.

How was the movie? Scary?

Uh-huh.

What was it tonight?

The Mummy.

Oh, I've seen that . . . That is *scary. You didn't mind watching alone?*

No.

After firmly tucking the covers around him, Catherine leaned down to pet Charles's hair. Her small gold crucifix dangled close enough that he could move it with his breath.

Did you say your prayers?

Yes.

Good boy. Good night. Sweet dreams. Sleep tight.

She left the door slightly ajar so that a long thin spindle of gold from the hallway illuminated Charles's room. It must have been Catherine Ryan's experience, having mothered many of her siblings, that young children are solaced by light and connection.

When Garrett and Rita Marlow got home, Charles always woke up.

Did you have any problems?

Was he good?

Pleasantries were exchanged.

How much do we owe you?

Thanks so much.

Charles's door was still open, admitting that yellow ribbon of light.

See you next week.

We'll watch till you get home.

He pictured Catherine walking home to her large, sleeping family.

Good night! Garrett and Rita Marlow called. *Thanks again!*

He pictured his parents, side by side, waving woodenly, their faces fixed in atrocious, mummified smiles.

The front door closed. They were entombed.

His mother would tiptoe down the hall and close the door to his room. It was a thoughtful gesture, uncharacteristically tender, but did she seriously believe that a closed door would shield him from what always happened next?

. . . fucking tramp . . .

. . . selfish bastard . . .

. . . you and your big mouth . . .

. . . arrogant son of a bitch . . .

That's how it was for couples like the Marlows: they attended tailgate parties, dinner dances, hospital-benefit headdress balls. They played pinochle and golf; they went bowling. In summer, they sunned themselves on backyard patios or next to country-club pools; in winter, they hosted fondue parties by the fire.

When they got home — and somehow they did, blood-alcohol levels notwithstanding — they paid the babysitters, looked in on the children. The next morning they woke up with hangovers, told their kids it was the flu.

They steadfastly maintained an active social life even if they hated each other, even if what played out between pre-party preparations and the next morning was a horror show.

Claim Check

Charles was carrying another load up from the crawlspace; in spite of his efforts, the boxes seemed to be *multiplying.* (*Because if there are boy boxes and girl boxes,* he heard Emmy say, following up on her earlier question, *that means that boxes can have babies, right?*) Arriving in the living room, he was startled by a series of loud, insistent knocks on the front door.

He offloaded onto a plat of open floor space near his office and removed his respirator before opening the door.

It was Alison.

"I didn't see you pull up," Charles said. "Have you been here long?"

"A few minutes."

Rain was coming down, torrential, with no sign of abatement, but she remained on the front step, grasping her coat at the center back collar and pulling it up and over her head so that it formed a small, ineffective shelter.

"Sorry," Charles said. "I was doing laundry."

"You ready?"

She stood beyond the protection of the roof overhang, at the farthest edge of the porch landing, her expression fearful, as if this were the entrance to a house infected with some biblically lethal contagion — cholera, leprosy, Ebola — and under quarantine. Asking her to come inside would be pointless; Alison hadn't stepped foot in the house since she'd moved out.

She peered past him.

"What's with all the boxes?"

"What? Oh. I've been doing some . . . you know, *purging.* I'm . . . thinking of having a yard sale."

"Now?"

"No. Of course not. In the spring, maybe. It will take a lot of organizing."

"Well, if you find anything of mine, get rid of it. If I haven't used it in a decade, it's nothing I need." She started backing away and down the steps, as if even *speaking* in such close proximity to the house was hazardous. "We should get going. The first place is up near Snohomish. Not that far, but traffic might be bad in this weather."

❖

So stupid, to have forgotten to wear boots.

They'd barely arrived and already Charles's shoes and the bottoms of his khakis were soaked and muddied. The other parents on the tour were all wearing appropriate footwear. He felt like a fool.

The first of three planned visits of the day was to Foxglove Farm, an ICF.

"I don't think this rain is going to stop any time soon," the executive director said once they were all gathered at the main building entrance, "so we might as well start outside and then make our way in. There will be coffee, tea, and hot chocolate waiting for you at the end of the tour, so I promise you'll all have a chance to warm up and ask questions then. Would anyone like an umbrella?"

The tour participants included one singleton mom plus three other parental units besides Charles and Alison. As they all trudged through the field to the outbuildings, Charles wondered about the couples, if any of them were like him and Ali: divorced, but reunited under these circumstances, collaborating on their children's distant futures when everything else about their marriages had eroded.

They arrived in the stable, the tangy smells of manure, cedar, horse sweat, and hay made denser by the damp. The rain was falling so hard on the tin roof that the executive director had to shout:

"The stable and outlying farm buildings constitute the heart of our program; every resident has tasks related to our agricultural and animal-husbandry programs."

Husbandry, Charles thought. It struck him as a lovely, old-fashioned word, one that wasn't heard nearly enough.

The director — who had the broad, strong physique of a rancher's wife and squarish, unmanicured hands — relaxed visibly in this environment; it was as though they'd started the tour at a country-club gala and had now arrived at the block-party barbecue.

After calling out a greeting to a group of four people at the back of the stable — two residents, each paired with a caregiver — she said, "As you can see, residents groom and feed the horses. Those who are able take riding lessons." She snatched up some hay and offered it to a large brown-and-white horse that was nosing its head insistently over the top of its stall gate toward her.

"Cody would love this," Charles murmured to Alison.

"Hmmm," she replied.

The director started herding them back to the stable entrance. "We give our residents every opportunity to participate in the routines of farm life to whatever extent they are capable."

"Great philosophy," Charles said. "She hasn't said the word *autism* even once."

"Hmmm," Alison repeated.

"Okay, we'll walk over to the organic garden and the chicken house, and then we'll head inside. I'm sure you're all ready to dry off and warm up."

They were still slogging through the open field, maybe two hundred feet from the shelter of their destination, when Alison spoke up.

"It's very isolated."

"Sorry?" the director said, turning around. "Did someone say something?"

Alison raised her hand and shouted, *"It's very isolated."*

Charles was irritated with her. Hadn't the director made it clear that questions would be taken once they got back inside?

"I'm just wondering how often residents get off campus."

Why couldn't she wait? Why was she inconveniencing everyone like this? She knew there was a Q&A scheduled after the tour. It seemed to Charles that Alison wasn't really asking a question but showing off, asserting some kind of alpha-female bullshit.

"I'd be happy to answer that," the director shouted in reply, her voice amicable, her expression pokerfaced, *"once we get inside . . ."*

They trudged on.

"Jesus, Alison," Charles muttered.

"What?"

"Never mind."

They arrived in the chicken house and shook off their parkas and raincoats and umbrellas — a pack of Labrador retrievers who'd just emerged from Lake Washington.

"So," the director began, now competing vocally with both the rainfall and the brood hens. "In answer to that question from . . . ?"

Alison raised her hand and announced her name with a prim reserve; she seemed to be channeling the spirit of Astrida Pukis.

"We occasionally schedule trips into Snohomish," the director said, "even into Seattle, but mostly our residents stay on campus. We have art, music, and woodworking classes. We have ice cream socials and dances, game and movie nights. The craft program supplies residents with not only the satisfaction of making things but the knowledge that the things they produce — the rugs, brooms, hats, and so on — are valued, and visible. We don't, for example, have our residents doing things like wiping down tables in church basements. Does that answer your question?"

"Yes," Alison replied. "Thank you."

They looked in on resident bedrooms, recreational and community spaces; Charles was struck by words like *campus, pods, dorms*. Language you'd hear on a college tour. Language they *would* have heard on a college tour, had things gone differently.

"Okay," the director said as they returned to the entrance. "That wraps up the facilities tour. Please help yourself to refreshments and then meet me in the conference room."

They didn't stay. Charles wasn't surprised. "You've made

up your mind already, haven't you?" he said once they were in the car.

"No," Alison answered defensively. "I have not. It's just so far from everything. Can you imagine yourself coming all the way out here to visit him?"

"Yes."

"On a regular basis?"

"Yes."

"Well, that's not the point. It's as if they want to separate them from the rest of the world. Cody already does a lot of the things they offer here — and he gets to do them while he's out in the world instead of hidden away . . ."

Charles stared at the highway. The rain pounded against the windshield. A semi pulled past, sending up a blinding spray.

"Why are we even doing this, Alison?"

"Don't be like that, Charles, or this is going to be a long day."

"It's already been a long day. If we're just going through the motions, if you've already made a choice, then please take me home. I've got work to do. Let's not waste time pretending that there's some kind of collaboration going on here."

"A waste of time? You consider looking for places for our son to spend the rest of his life a *waste of time?*"

It was hopeless. Charles shut up.

He thought about the young woman he'd noticed in the stable, one of the residents, probably close to Cody's age: pale skin, long dark hair, dazzling smile, nonverbal. She'd been grooming one of the horses, stopping now and then to press her forehead against his whiskered muzzle.

Charles was reminded of Eulalie, the special relationship she had had with Cody, their shared love of horses. Maybe it was that more than anything that seemed to so instantly sour Alison on Foxglove Farm; God forbid she should make a choice that would have pleased her Kentucky-born-and-bred equestrian mother.

Eulalie had died nine years ago, suddenly, of a hemorrhagic stroke. There was no suffering, but neither was there time to say goodbye.

Cody still missed her, Charles knew; whenever Eulalie was spoken of, whenever Cody saw a photograph of her, he signed her name by gently touching his nose, forehead, and eyelashes.

Eskimo. Horse. Butterfly.

◆

The next visit was to a typical adult group home about eight miles north of Seattle, in Bothell. It was a neat-looking structure on a big wooded lot.

At the door, they were greeted by an enormously tall, lantern-jawed man who bore an astonishing resemblance to the actor who'd played Lurch in *The Addams Family.* He smiled at them with expansive, genuine warmth and then urinated on the floor.

The final visit was to one of Seattle's oldest and largest facilities, a place that occupied several acres up in Shoreline. It was a state-run institution that had had a horrible reputation in the past but, according to Alison, had recently undergone major reform.

It certainly wasn't as bad as Charles had expected, but he couldn't believe that she was honestly considering putting Cody in a place like this.

Eventually, he figured out her strategy: she was showing him the worst possible scenario so he'd offer no resistance to the *other possible option* she'd outlined on their date night, which basically involved co-purchasing a house and establishing a privately funded facility.

It wasn't that Charles didn't want the very best for Cody. Of course he did. He should feel grateful that money was no object when it came to their son.

But instead, he felt angry.

Maybe because it was Alison's pretense that the playing field was level. Maybe it was because he'd let himself be suckered into this whole day, this prolonged charade, this emasculation.

They arrived at the house around four. It was already dark. It felt like midnight.

"Let me know what you decide," Charles sniped as he exited the car.

"You are such a baby," Ali shot back.

❖

They used to refer jokingly to that claim check — the one she'd handed him the night they met — as their prenuptial agreement.

As it turned out, the final article of that document, *I'll want to have children right away*, wasn't entirely true, but in contrast to what was expected in the arena of legal counsel (where, as Charles understood it, withholding certain key demands was essential in ensuring a successful outcome for one's clients), Alison believed that when it came to matters of the heart, it was important to state the deal-breaker from the outset.

Their courtship might have been unorthodox, but after they married, their lives conformed to a traditional template: they didn't start trying to have kids until Alison's law practice was established and Charles was hired full-time at City Prana; and then, it was so easy, it took no time at all. Alison always said that it was like Cody was right there, watching, ready to jump into their lives the very moment they made room for him. He chose them, he wanted them; they were the parents he was meant to have.

There were some problems early on: Cody did not nurse well; his growth was somewhat behind the curve; his movements were slow, but purposeful — something Charles attributed to a patient temperament.

At each office visit, they ran through the list of social, emotional, linguistic, cognitive, and physical expectations and were always reassured: *He's hitting all the major developmental milestones. See you in three months.*

But Charles was not reassured. He pretended to be, but he knew something was amiss; he even knew *why* — although for a long time, he couldn't admit it to himself, much less to anyone else:

Dana McGucken had returned. Dana, who had waited and waited and waited and waited. He had come for Cody, whisking him away, bit by bit, replacing him with the inscrutable changeling child who would from that time forward be Charles's son.

Club Membership

"Sorry I'm late," Charles said. "Lost track of time." He sneezed, his habitual reaction to arriving in Pam's class-room, where the atmosphere was filled with pottery dust and paint fumes.

"Bless you," Pam said. "No worries, we just got started."

"Hi, Mr. Marlow."

Charles sneezed again.

"Bless you," Pam repeated. "Romy and I were talking about the incident."

They were gathered for a senior-project update meeting, meant to assure all concerned parties that Bertleson, Romy Andrea, was on track.

"What incident?" Charles asked, reaching into his satchel for his pen and notepad.

"Romy had some trouble with one of the participants at Art Without Boundaries."

"A participant?" *Oh God,* he thought, *please let it not be Cody.*

"One of the dementia patients."

Romy jumped in. "Really, the whole thing got blown way out of proportion. I mean, yes, it was upsetting, but it was just a little slap. She got frustrated, the way little kids do when they can't find their words."

"Someone *slapped* you?" Charles interjected.

Romy continued. "I just don't want to give up on her. I mean, that's the whole point of the program, right? To help people *connect* through art?"

"Some people don't want to connect," Charles said.

Pam and Romy turned in unison to look at him. Charles doodled a row of loops across his notepad.

"Let's look at your photos," Pam said brightly. "You have prints for us, right?"

Romy laid out the twenty or so portraits that she was considering for inclusion in the May exhibit: black-and-white, mostly close-ups of individuals. The subjects were sharply polarized by age.

At first, Charles didn't see any pictures of Cody; he wasn't sure whether he felt relieved or offended. Was Cody so unremarkable that he didn't warrant photographic notice? It was hard for Charles to imagine Cody as anything other than the center of attention, but maybe for once, at least in this setting, his son was *blending in.*

But then Charles spotted him in the background of one photo, one of many featuring the same elderly woman. He recognized her from an earlier batch of photos Romy had taken.

"That's her," Romy said, pointing. "That's Mrs. D'Amati."

The angle of the photograph suggested the viewpoint of

a small child; Romy must have crouched below the tabletop on which Mrs. D'Amati was writing — for that was what the woman's downward-focused gaze and posture suggested she was doing, although she didn't appear to be holding a writing implement. Cody was standing in the background. His face was out of focus, and anyone who didn't know him as Charles did wouldn't have been able to read his expression and stance: whatever Mrs. D'Amati was doing, Cody was riveted.

"How did you get this one?" Pam asked. "I thought the groups take classes separately."

"They eat lunch together."

Pam ran the rest of the meeting. Charles nodded and made occasional nonverbal interjections, but in truth he was barely in the room; his eyes kept wandering to the photo, to the blurred but rapt expression on his son's face.

❖

Charles and Donnie used to conduct experiments that might have been published under the title "Factors Affecting the Speed of Elementary-School Lunch Consumption."

What kind of meat sandwich went down quicker, bologna or olive loaf? (Bologna. Donnie almost choked to death testing this one day.)

Which combination could you eat faster, peanut butter and jelly or peanut butter and marshmallow fluff? (Surprisingly, PB&J; they discovered that fluff expands rapidly in the belly, giving it appetite-suppressant qualities.)

Vegetables: Carrots sticks or celery sticks? (A tossup in the speed category, but they observed that celery makes you have to pee more.)

Charles held the record for overall lunch speed, once

downing his entire meal — tuna sandwich, potato chips, banana, and two Hostess Cupcakes — in two minutes and fifty-seven seconds. (The secret to his success was layering the potato chips inside the sandwich.)

Another lunchroom entertainment was the result of a deal that had likely been brokered in the halls of state government: every public-elementary-school student, whether the child brought his or her own lunch or went through the lunch line, was entitled to a free half-pint carton of milk. This is how the Washington State Dairy Association ended up aiding and abetting the universally beloved lunchtime activity/science experiment Adventures in Milk Aeration.

For this activity, the boys weren't really interested in measurable results, just in the sheer joy of creating a lava flow of translucent bubbles and seeing how far they could make the devastation extend on a single, controlled out-breath.

These lunchroom experiments could be conducted only in the absence of the single other adult whose reputation matched that of Mrs. Braxton's: Nellie Goodhue's principal, Miss Vanderkolk.

Miss V. was probably much younger than she looked, but the severity of her disposition and her anachronistic appearance made her seem ancient — indeed, the oldest adult at the school.

She wore her dun-colored hair chin-length, parted with precision, its brittle waves smashed against her head and immobilized by a transparent net. A bulky, flesh-colored hearing aid was lodged behind one of her ears. Her eyeglasses were wire-rimmed ovals that magnified her blue, marble-like eyes to a disturbing degree. She dressed in short-sleeved belted shirtwaists that were so bland as to be indistinguishable from one another. Her footwear was practical, geriatric, and ugly — beige, rubber-soled, lace-up flats with bulldog toe boxes — and her opaque support hose gave her legs the artificial look of a storefront mannequin's.

These features made Miss Vanderkolk unappealing, but what qualified her as truly terrifying — even more terrifying than Mrs. Braxton — was the fact that she was missing parts of two fingers on her right hand; what remained were two truncated, blunt-ended structures that moved slightly whenever she gestured.

Charles and Donnie had debated the possible causes of this disfigurement endlessly. One slew of scenarios placed Miss Vanderkolk in wilderness settings:

1. She'd lost her fingers in a logging accident — a misaimed ax, a falling Douglas fir. (Miss Vanderkolk bore herself in an unfeminine manner that made her seem well suited to the life of a lumberjack.)

2. Her fingers had been crushed by a falling boulder as she scaled Mount Rainier. Undeterred from her goal of being the first solo woman to accomplish this feat, she amputated the fingers herself with a bowie knife and continued on her way after burying them in a secret location. They were still up there, somewhere.

3. She'd tussled with a cougar — no, a *grizzly* — vanquishing the unfortunate animal by breaking its neck with her bare hands, but in its death throes, the poor beast exacted its final revenge.

The boys went so far as to tape down their middle and ring fingers in order to get a better sense of Miss Vanderkolk's capabilities. Writing was difficult, but they imagined that she could hold her own in a fistfight; she could definitely operate a small firearm.

This gave rise to another set of stories that revolved around Miss Vanderkolk's secret life as a Russian spy, a devious KGB operative — decommissioned after getting her fingers shot off in a gun battle, she was now undercover, an ever-loyal Communist, a double agent infiltrating America via the Seattle school system.

Ingenious!

Charles imagined her going home at the end of the day and communicating her latest discoveries via ham radio to her comrades behind the Iron Curtain sounding exactly like Natasha in *The Rocky and Bullwinkle Show.*

Were both of Miss Vanderkolk's mannequin-looking legs real? Or was one of them hollow, a receptacle for smuggling secret documents?

Was that thing behind her ear really a hearing aid? Or was it a recording device, a hidden camera, a canister of tear gas — or a vial containing a single cyanide pill? A Russian spy would never let herself get taken alive.

School lunches post-Donnie were a dreary affair.

Charles's police-detective notebook remained at home, gathering dust, its final entry made on one of the last days of third grade, when he and Donnie expanded its use to list all the fun things they planned to do over summer vacation, unaware that Donnie would be moving to the Land of Sky-Blue Waters in a matter of weeks.

Charles no longer kept his eyes glued to the minute hand of the cafeteria clock while eating lunch; why bother? There was no one to bedazzle with his two-minute-fifty-seven-second record.

And although it remained a popular illicit activity for everyone else, milk aeration had lost its appeal.

Lacking a partner in anarchy, Charles completely lost his antic nature.

One day — lingering so long over lunch that even the Lonelies and the Fatties had left for midday recess and the cafeteria ladies had started to close up the kitchen — Charles found himself alone with Dana McGucken.

Dana was in his regular place, in the corner nearest the boys' bathroom. From a distance — and because Dana wasn't doing anything out of the ordinary at that particular moment, just sitting quietly before his lunch tray — Charles received a quite new and different impression of him.

Dana's white suit gave him a posh, dignified appearance. He might have been a solo diner at an upscale establishment, a gentleman who, having just finished a fine meal, was patiently waiting for the check. Remembering a place where he'd once dined with his parents, Charles conjured a red-and-white-checkered tablecloth, a red rose in a vase, a lit candle stuck into a wine bottle.

Everybody knew what Dana was — a *ree*-tard.

And yet, Charles wondered, what if they *hadn't* known that?

What if this instant, right now, was the first time Charles saw him?

What if, instead of meeting Dana as everyone had on that first day of school — a kid marked as *bad* by his front-row placement (no wonder Mitchell and Bradley hated him so much; in Mrs. Braxton's seating chart, Bullies and Ree-Tards sat together) — Charles had met him differently?

What if there had been no adult present through whom to interpret Dana's identity, no Mrs. Braxton (a biased judge who should have recused herself from the proceedings)?

Dana looked up and locked eyes with Charles. Instantly, his face turned impish; he hunched down theatrically in his turtle-like way and started blowing bubbles into his carton of milk.

Feeling a twinge of fear, knowing that Comrade Vanderkolk might be lurking in the janitor's closet, Charles shook his head violently and mouthed *No!*

Dana laughed. "Hi, Char-Lee!" he called across the lunchroom. "Look! Look at this!" He went back to blowing bubbles; soon, the lava flow of his lactating volcano filled his entire tray.

Realizing that Dana wouldn't stop as long as he had an audience, Charles looked down and started to finish off his lunch quickly, as in the old days.

Dana called again, "Char-Lee! Char-Lee Mar-Low! Look!"

When Charles didn't respond, Dana left his table and crossed the room.

"Loo!" he announced, arriving at Charles's table. He held out a package of Hostess Cupcakes. "Loo."

"Okay, okay, I'll open it for you." Charles fumbled with the wrapping and then handed the cupcakes back.

"No, Char-Lee," Dana said, shaking his head. "See? It's *loo!*" He pointed.

"Yeah, I know. Hostess Cupcakes. They're good. I had one today too."

"No! *Loo!*" Dana repeated. Slowly, delicately, he extended his index finger (Charles noticed with relief that his nails were clean) and started tracing the row of white icing.

Charles finally understood what Dana was trying to say. It was so obvious, he felt like an idiot for not figuring it out sooner.

"See?" Dana asked. "Loo!"

"Yeah, I see. Loops."

"Here, Char-Lee." Dana forced one of the cupcakes into Charles's hand. "You have this one. You like loo."

"Loops," Charles repeated, giving a special emphasis to the *p* and the *s*. "You say it."

"Looooooooo-*puh*-zzzzz!"

"Yeah, loops. I like peeling them off sometimes. You ever do that?"

"No." Dana sat down. "Show."

"You have to go real slow or they break. See?"

Dana gave it a try; it was the most concentrated, dexterous, purposeful movement Charles had ever seen him execute. He removed his loops in one piece and then carefully set them on the table.

"Hey, you did it!" Charles said. "Attaboy!"

"Yeah! Attaboy! I did!"

They spent the last few minutes of midday recess eating their loops, then the chocolate icing. When Charles got down to the cake — his least favorite part — he offered it to Dana.

"No, thank you, Char-Lee," he said. "Show me those other loops. *Pah*-mer loops."

"Oh, okay, sure." Charles didn't have any paper, so he mimed the action along the length of the table's edge. Dana watched and then mimicked the movements perfectly.

From then on, they sat together every day and began having informal Palmer penmanship tutoring sessions. At home, Charles requested Hostess Cupcakes as a lunchtime staple. He and Dana competed to see who could successfully peel off his loops in one piece; the winner got to eat both sets.

Charles retrieved his flip-top detective's notebook from home and used it to demonstrate. He brought in a drawing pad for Dana, thinking he might have an easier time working on unlined paper; Dana gleefully filled page after page in a way that would not have earned a Brax the Ax seal of approval.

Charles came to love Dana's joyfully chaotic loops, tumbling and stumbling in all directions, intersecting and overlapping randomly so many times that they were impossible to separate. In places, dense confluences of lines created the feeling of shadows and depth. Sometimes, if he stared long and hard enough, squinted a little and tilted his head this way and that, he saw images within this seeming randomness: fat ladies wheeling madly past on roller skates; battalions of soldiers in profile; balding superheroes wearing boxing gloves.

In class, Charles continued to endure the undisguised hatred of Astrida Pukis and the sotto voce taunts of Bradley and Mitchell, but he found himself caring less and less about what anyone thought; at last, he had a friend.

And that was how he became a member of another two-boy club at the Nellie Goodhue School.

The Ree-Tards.

First, Middle, Last

Saturday. Cold and rainy.

Charles was home, grading one of the last batches of student work before winter break. It was already three o'clock, late enough so that it seemed permissible to uncork another highbrow selection from the wine rack — something German and white this time.

After rinsing and refilling his coffee mug, he took a sip; *high minerality, fine notes of apricot, surprisingly dry.* He'd recently tucked a delightful new word into his vocabulary: *oenology;* its variations and argot would come in handy whenever he and Emmy felt bold enough to tackle the Sunday *New York Times* crossword.

Alison would be coming by soon to pick him up; they were going to the group home to have a transition-planning session with Cody's caregivers, caseworkers, et al. — and to visit Cody, of course.

Following that, they'd be looking at a classic midcentury

brick rambler (*Perfect Pinehurst!*) that was up for short sale: four bedrooms; two baths; lower-level mother-in-law apartment; 3,220 square feet; fireplace, yes; forced air; built in 1962.

Gil Bjornson and his son had, as usual, been hard at work all day on their restoration project, hunkered down in the shelter of the garage, welding sparks flying, radio blaring. The Best Hits of the '60s, '70s, and '80s were muted today, overlaid with the scratch and warp of a steady downpour.

When Charles was growing up, Seattle residents could accurately refer to most precipitation events as *mist. Now*, Charles mused, *we get* rain *like everybody else.*

He'd just encountered the word *flense* for the third time that day. If he hadn't known otherwise, he would have assumed that *flense* was a recent arrival on the shores of the English language and was getting a good workout, as new words do.

He set the student papers aside and took up a sheet of stationery.

Dear Emmy,

Listen, honey, I just wanted to follow up. If I sounded disappointed, I apologize. I'm happy you've met a boy you like, really I am, and I think it's terrific he's invited you home to meet his family over Christmas break.

I know you're holding off on accepting the invitation because you're worried about me, but please, sweetheart, don't be. You're doing exactly what you're supposed to be doing: growing away from me, establishing a new circle of friends and your own holiday rituals. I promise: I'll be just fine.

How could you possibly turn down an invitation to go skiing in Vermont? The setting for one of our favorite holiday movies! "The Christianas and the stemming and the plotzing and the shushing," as Danny Kaye and Bing Crosby say right before breaking into time steps and joyous yodels. "Hot buttered rum, light on the butter . . ."

I mean, really, sweetheart: Why shouldn't you absent yourself from your family's odd holiday gatherings, which are dominated by your mother's need to include Cody in everything even though he hasn't the slightest idea why one day is different from any other, and all the seasonal hoopla can be downright upsetting. And as far as that goes, Hanukkah will be even worse — instead of one out-of-the-ordinary day, there will be eight! Has your mother even considered this? Dreidel spinning, hora dancing . . . It will be a disaster.

I hardly need remind you that your brother values routine above all, and any variation from the external norms — visual, auditory, olfactory, tactile, whatever — can send him wildly out of orbit, and we all know I'm not speaking metaphorically.

At best, holidays chez Marlow are characterized by an overarching trepidation.

There certainly isn't any yodeling.

Charles took another swig of wine, swiveled around in his desk chair, and surveyed the rampart of low-stacked cardboard boxes that were arrayed around him in a semicircle; it struck him that he'd essentially marooned himself in his office.

When Alison had asked about the boxes a while back and he'd improvised about having a yard sale, there were only four or five of them up here; now there were probably . . . what? Twenty? Thirty?

He had yet to locate Emmy's artifacts.

But there was still a lot more down there to bring up and examine.

So here he was, stranded on the desert isle of his office. There were worse places to be shipwrecked, he supposed.

Flense was an old word, ancient. The notes on its origin were lengthier than the definition itself, which was "to strip an animal of blubber or skin."

Charles was always loath to suspect his students of wrong-doing; however, this in-triplicate appearance of *flense* was not, he believed, the kind of coincidence that arose when nimble, receptive minds dove into the vast pool of human subconsciousness and emerged waving a common banner emblazoned with the expression of a potent, shared eureka.

Charles's guess was that the authors involved met over Red Bulls and breakfast burritos at the 7-Eleven, realized they hadn't done their homework, and convened in the library for a last-minute collaboration. These weren't stupid boys, just lazy, although Charles had to wonder: Did they think he wouldn't notice? Or that he wouldn't care? Either assumption saddened him.

> *"Eek!" screamed the girl when she saw the cat flensing the mouse.*

> *There is debate about whether Native American tribes have the right to flense whales.*

> *Downtown at the Lusty Lady, the low-lifes applauded as the strippers flensed.*

The assignment was part of a unit called First, Middle, Last. Students were asked to scour the dictionary for three juicy, unfamiliar words, one for each of their initials, and write them into sentences.

It was essentially a vocabulary assignment, but Charles always hoped that the kids would take it seriously, make the effort to find words they were genuinely drawn to, whether because of their look or sound or definition, he really didn't care; he just wanted the students to find words they were head over heels crazy about and eager to put to use, the way kids did when they were little and graduated from the small box of primary-color Crayolas to the big one containing crayons with names like Cerulean Blue.

Charles wondered if there were people whose job it was to seek out and follow the progress of emerging words, to study aspects of usage, monitor frequency, track movements, chart evolution — above all, recognize when a word had reached its linguistic tipping point, completed its mission, and infiltrated the general population to become *one of them.* It was sad in a way, when you thought about it, this acceptance, this legitimacy, because at that moment, a word's life as a covert, rogue element in the language came to an end.

There was a kind of death — at least that's how Charles saw it — when a word permeated the lexicon to a degree that warranted its inclusion in the dictionary; instead of this renegade entity darting around, furtive but unbound, it became just another gray-flannel suit trudging through the book of common usage.

Charles's habit was to read student assignments in ascending-grade order. The fact that it was nearly happy hour and he hadn't yet started on the sophomores said something about the quality of his attention.

A Norwegian variation on *flense, flans,* meant "horse's pizzle," and the Icelandic riff, *flanni,* meant "penis" — leading Charles to wonder if these boys had more of a sense of humor than he'd thought.

He was tempted to let it go this time.

He loved the way each of the authors — Finn Gregory Evans, Thanh Fenton Kerrigan, and Alexander Terrell Epstein (who'd apparently been so carried away that he'd forgotten his own monogram was *F*-less) — revealed an authentic voice, a stylistic confidence.

And *flense* was a remarkable word, one whose sound belied its meaning: the soft sustaining consonants —*f, l, n*, and *s* — standing in sharp contrast to the savagery of the definition.

What the hell? Charles asked himself, wielding Alison's Montegrappa Italia with a flourish as he marked the boys' papers.

"A's for everyone! On to the sophomores!"

It occurred to him that perhaps Cody could be said to be flensed of speech.

But no, that would be inaccurate.

One cannot be stripped of something one never really had.

❖

"You're awfully quiet, Charles. Is everything all right?"

It turned out that Charles had misunderstood the sequence of planned events; they'd looked at perfect-Pinehurst-four-bedroom-rambler-on-quiet-corner first; now they were driving to the group home.

Post–daylight saving time; five o'clock and it was already dark. Charles was reminded that suicide rates in Seattle and Stockholm were roughly the same.

"I know it's a lot for one day," Alison continued, "a lot to take in."

"It's fine," Charles said. The rain had stopped and started several times in the past hour, sudden downpours followed by sudden cessations, as if there were a poorly sutured incision in the sky that kept opening up, being restitched by the same incompetent surgeon, and then tearing open again, a perpetual malpractice suit. "I'm fine."

They'd spent almost an hour rambling through the mid-century rambler. The sound of the rain's dramatic stop-start was amplified by a large blue tarp spread out in the backyard, covering a swimming pool. The pool was a feature Charles had missed when he looked the property up on the Internet. Its presence left him doubting — atypically — Alison's judgment.

Of course, it wasn't just *her* judgment at work, and Charles had to assume that she and her potential partners had discussed the wisdom of buying a house with a swimming pool in the backyard for three soon-to-be-technically-adult autistics.

Another rain-letting began; Alison turned the windshield wipers up to full speed.

"So, what do you think?" she asked. "About the house."

"It seems to meet most of your criteria."

"I know you think my mind is made up, Charles, but your opinion matters . . ."

Charles found himself incapable of responding. *Do I have an opinion?* he wondered. *Surely I do.*

". . . especially as someone who knows about the inner workings of things."

"What are you talking about?"

"You know . . . plumbing, wiring, structural issues, things like that. Like your father."

"My father managed a warehouse, Alison. He sold acoustical ceiling tiles."

"Yes, but you always described him as *handy.* He could *fix* things. You know what I mean."

"I have no idea what you mean. My father and I weren't exactly close, if you remember, and as far as I know, there's no gene for pipe-wrench proficiency."

"You're being purposely obtuse — and disingenuous. You

talked a lot about those kinds of things with Daddy when we remodeled the house."

"I was faking it. I felt a strong need to impress him."

Alison sighed, but trudged on. "Well, in any case, we *are* going to have to make a decision fairly soon . . ."

Why is it possible, Charles wondered, *to recognize certain doomed conversational choreographies — especially the kind that occurs between spouses — and yet remain incapable of changing the steps?* He'd pondered this for years.

"In one sense" — Alison was dancing now in quickening circles; Charles was amazed that the car didn't start listing to the right, given her accelerating buoyancy, his accumulating weight — "we've been really lucky, with the economy the way it is, I mean. It *is* sad to think that, if we do end up buying this property, we'll be capitalizing on the financial misfortunes of others — I told you it's a short sale, right? But we felt as though the timing couldn't be better. It's a lot of house for the money."

"The pool was a surprise."

Alison groaned. "God, that pool! Obviously, we're talking about what to do about that if we end up going through with this. In every other way, though, it's pretty close to perfect, don't you think?"

In using the word *we,* Alison was referring to two sets of still-married couples she'd grown close to over the years, fellow PLAY participants, parents of low-functioning autistic sons who'd been in the group home almost as long as Cody.

"The fact that the Youngs and the Gurnees are willing to do this now, even though Robbie and Myles don't age out for another year, is a huge blessing. I mean, there's the financial piece, of course, but more than that, there would be the whole process of looking for prospective parents, doing interviews, vetting the kids, et cetera. The fact that our boys know each other will make this transition so much easier on them — and on us."

Do they? Charles wondered. *Do our boys actually* know *each other? Autism,* auto, *from the Greek for "self."*

The rain stopped. Alison turned off the wipers and sighed heavily.

"This weather is really something, isn't it?" Charles offered.

Like Alison, the Youngs and the Gurnees were frequent visitors to the group home. Charles had met them only a couple of times, over coffee at the Lake City Starbucks. He tried to remember their first names. He tried to remember their kids' names. Alison had just mentioned them, for Christ's sake.

He realized that Ali had asked him something.

"Sorry, what?"

"You've been drinking, haven't you?"

"What do you mean?"

"I'm not accusing you of anything, Charles, there's no need to bristle."

"I'm not bristling. But yes, in point of fact, I drank a glass or two of Gunderloch Riesling this afternoon while I was grading papers."

They drove on for a while. Cross-town traffic was murder — probably every bit as bad in Seattle as in Manhattan. Charles wondered if Emmy had told Alison about her young man, the Vermonter. *I'm dreaming of a white Christmas, just like the ones I used to know . . .*

"How's school?" Alison said. "What are you working on?"

. . . where the treetops glisten, and children listen . . . "Sorry. What?"

"With your students. What are your students doing?"

Strangely, the effects of the wine were only now starting to kick in; he could feel himself inching toward drunken maudlinity, maudlinness, *wallowing*, whatever, and so he made a concerted effort to enunciate. "First. Middle. Last."

"Oh, I love that one! Any especially good words this year? Any cheaters?"

Charles felt suddenly protective of his *flense* boys and chose not to share their transgression. "No."

"I still remember when you came up with that assignment, how we made lists of everyone's first, middle, and last names: friends, family, celebrities . . ."

"Adjective, adjective, noun, my name, go."

"Okay." Alison squinted. In the flash of passing headlights, Charles noted etched dashes at the corners of her eye: a bulleted list that hadn't been made yet. "Cruciferous Sartorial Manatee."

"Very nice. Now yours . . . Amaranthine Nautical Macaroon."

"Oooh . . . Cogitating Laparoscopic Marzipan!"

"Echopraxic Fulminating Mezuzah!"

Why did I do that? Charles thought. Alison fell silent, bit her lip. She didn't deserve his unintentional cruelty. She missed Emmy just as much as he did.

"You win," she said. They drove the rest of the way in silence.

Why is it, he asked himself, *that family misfortunes tend to arrive in a pileup? Is it really simple cause and effect, or do catastrophes establish a new normal of sorrow to which all subsequent events must conform, a base to which only some things may be added? Once certain ingredients are in the pan, one's choices are limited; you can't make rice pudding once you've started sautéing a head of garlic.*

Charles noticed that the car had stopped.

They were in the group-home parking lot; Alison was

yanking her keys out of the ignition. Looming over them was a giant Douglas fir, boughs saturated with rain, nodding like a giant narcoleptic.

"We're here," Alison said, but it sounded like *Wake up!* "Are you ready?" she asked, priest to prisoner in the moments before an imminent execution.

❖

This person, my son, Charles thought, for the thousandth time. *How do I describe him?*

From where Charles was standing, in the foyer, a short hallway led to the spacious, well-lit combination kitchen/family room at the back of the house where the six residents (four boys, two girls, ranging in age from fourteen to twenty) took their meals and engaged in what passed for social interaction in a group home serving low-functioning autistic children. The house itself was clean but shabby-feeling, with its paucity of homey touches (one of the hallmarks of a state-funded facility); its sharp potpourri of chlorine, laundry softener, urine; its childproofed cupboards and cabinets; the waterproof pads laid out on every upholstered surface.

Even though Charles had been visiting Cody and his various housemates for years, he still felt as though every time he walked through the door, he was entering a new dimension, stepping foot on a planetary surface that was not quite solid but a swirling, liquefying mass through which he was eternally falling.

It was nearly dinnertime.

The senior member of the group — Cody — sat at his TV tray, immobile, eyes downcast. His arms were rigid, right-angled, and held aloft, his forearms framing his face, fists clenched. It looked as if he'd been frozen in the process of wrestling two flailing, disobedient antennae that had sprouted from his temples. Or, a more sedate description: his bent arms defined the parameters of an invisible box into which he'd inserted his head.

This was a signature posture for Cody, and one he took frequently, presumably in the interest of self-containment and/or segregation, although it was impossible to know for sure. What *was* certain was that he could hold this position for hours, whether waiting for food or not. Sometimes he even held a slightly relaxed version of it in his sleep. At least, Charles assumed he still did that; he used to, when he was little.

Alison emerged from the conference room. Their meeting with Cody's team had officially ended ten minutes ago, but she was still talking to the social worker assigned to the task of helping transition Cody out of state-supported care.

Charles tended to lose his civility when speaking with these people. He understood it wasn't their fault but found it beyond absurd that most of the state-funded programs and forms of assistance that were available to Cody as a child would disappear — *poof!* — the moment he turned twenty-one.

He lingered in the shadowed hall, waiting for Alison to finish her conversation. She'd reminded him that his presence in tandem with hers was unusual and thus potentially upsetting; she'd go in first and then gesture him in when she felt that Cody was ready to handle the unusual experience of seeing both Mom *and* Dad in the same room at the same time.

There were five staff members working tonight: Raisa, Benjamin, Malachi, Tami, and someone new: a small, compact, brown-skinned woman who could have been anywhere from thirty to fifty years old and whom Charles guessed to be Filipino. He'd overheard Raisa call her Bettina.

There had been a lot of turnover in the years since Cody had been here. This was understandable — none of these children were easy to care for, most had medical issues compounding their autism, all had very specific limits and conditions in terms of what they could tolerate, and state-employed caregivers in this kind of situation weren't exactly recompensed at a wage commensurate with the work — but it was also unfortunate. Personnel changes were hard on the kids, and every time a new caregiver came onboard there were almost always glitches. High turnover was one of many factors that Alison, the Youngs, and the Gurnees hoped to eradicate.

"Hi, Cody," Alison said, acting and sounding like an ordinary mom entering a regular room greeting a developmentally normal teenager who was hanging out with five close friends. "How are you doing, sweetie? It's me, Cody. It's Mom."

Cody showed no sign of registering either his mother's greeting or her physical presence; he continued to sit absolutely still, his dazed, unlit eyes directed at the empty surface of the TV tray. One of his upheld fists clutched a cloth napkin, the other, a spoon.

Dinner hadn't yet arrived — Raisa would dish it up at the counter and it would be served by the other staff members — but Cody's meal would consist of partially thawed frozen peas, mashed potatoes, room-temperature fried chicken, and a heavily vitamin-supplemented smoothie. Except for that final item — getting him to drink it was a fiercely fought, protracted battle begun when Cody entered adolescence — Cody's evening entree menu hadn't changed since he was thirteen. His food preferences were nonnegotiable.

"Smells great, Raisa," Alison said. She introduced herself to the new caregiver, said hello to Cody's housemates, and then settled into one of the folding chairs that had been set up on either side of Cody. Charles realized with a flicker of anxiety that the second chair was for him.

"Looks like somebody's ready for dinner," Alison said in a joking voice.

No reaction.

They sat side by side; patients in a waiting room, passengers on a train. Cody's posture, in this tableau, suggested an exhausted commuter headed back to the suburbs, escaping the stresses of his day and the proximity of his fellow passengers by hiding behind the pages of the *New York Times*.

Alison looked up briefly and caught Charles's eye. Slightly shifting her body so that it blocked Cody's view of the gesture, she held up her hand: *No, not yet, stay.*

Cody was tall, long-boned, almost plank-like in his slimness; big hands and feet; extremely strong and muscular. Ironically, he'd been gifted with a set of attributes that would have predisposed him to athletic success — tennis player, track star, point guard.

The new woman, Bettina, set Cody's plate on his tray.

A moment, and then, very slowly, he lowered his arms and began the process of feeding himself. The fact that some food did not end up on his bib, his face, the tray, or the floor was a mark of tremendous success.

"Those mashed potatoes look really good, Cody," Alison said. "Be careful. I might have to steal some when you're not looking."

Cody emitted the abrupt, voiceless *Hoo!* that was his version of a laugh; it briefly rocked him back and then forward in his seat. Charles was reminded of those odd, silent, featherless toy birds that balance and bob on the rim of a drinking glass.

Charles watched Alison watching Cody. When another spoonful of potatoes started making its unsteady way toward him, looking like its final destination this time might be

Cody's eye, she rocked sideways, close to him, and opened her mouth. Cody straightened out his spoon's flight path and successfully deposited the potatoes in his own mouth.

"Darn!" Alison said.

Cody found this hysterically funny. Another *Hoo!* propelled him back and forth.

Another *Darn!* tilted Alison from side to side, and then a game began, a cross-species ornithological pantomime with role reversal: baby bird (species A) feeds self, mama bird (species B) feigns disappointment.

This reminded Charles of another favorite book from his children's library, *Are You My Mother?*, in which a baby bird determines who his mother *is* by determining who she is *not*.

Darn! Hoo! Darn! Hoo! Darn! Hoo . . .

Charles loved that story, although he'd always hoped that Mr. P. D. Eastman would publish what would be the obvious companion to that book, *Are You My Father?*

It had been clear for a long time that Charles didn't have the same permissions that Cody granted Alison — Charles's mere *presence* agitated his son in some profound, mysterious way; physical contact was out of the question. Because he and Alison were never here at the same time, Ali couldn't know that reminding Charles to keep his distance was unnecessary; Cody would let him know in no uncertain terms if he was too close. The saddest part of Charles's relationship with his son was this physical banishment. Yes, children need to be held and touched by their parents; it is also true that parents have a reciprocating need to hold and be touched by their children.

Wait. Look. Something is happening.

Cody's spoon was changing course, banking sharply toward Alison. Slowly, slowly, with a redirection of his lowered gaze so that he now seemed to be looking at Alison's shoes, he began tilting toward her — the oozing pace of tree sap on a subzero day — stopping before their bodies could actually touch but allowing his spoon-wielding arm to continue on until it came to the edge of the no-fly zone, the outer reaches of his rigidly maintained personal bubble.

Arm and spoon halted, hovered, and then a tremendous exertion of will allowed Cody to press on, sending his lone, cargo-carrying extremity beyond the limits of his heavily fortressed personal space and into the unknown space of another.

Arm and cargo arrived at their destination, coming to a full stop in front of Alison's gaping, astonished face.

Then Cody did a kind of thing they'd been told over and over again was impossible, beyond the range of his abilities:

He fed his mother a spoonful of mashed potatoes.

Ali chewed, swallowed.

"Yum." The small vessel of that single word contained a sea of gratitude.

No giver-upper, my ex.

Dinner drew to a close. Alison gently wiped Cody's face as Bettina deftly exchanged his dinner plate for a pudding cup.

"Oh boy! Look, Cody. Here's dessert."

As Alison carefully removed a long smear of mashed potatoes from Cody's jawline, she nodded to Charles to let him know he could come in.

"Cody," she went on in a slightly lower, slower voice. "Guess what? I didn't come by myself."

Charles started toward them, careful to strike an energetically neutral balance between stealth and exuberance.

"Cody," Alison continued, "are you listening? I brought someone else along. Someone you'll be happy to see."

His expression relapsed into its default glazed blandness,

his isolation firmly reestablished. Anyone observing the scene now would find it difficult to believe what had happened between mother and son only a few minutes ago.

"Look who's here, Cody." Alison signed the letter *D* at her forehead. "It's Dad."

Charles arrived, on cue, and ventured a small smile. "Hi, Cody."

A globule of pudding slid off Cody's spoon, hit his solar plexus — *splat!* — and started to migrate, sluglike, down the front of his bib. When Alison reached toward him with her napkin, he grunted and shrugged his chest into concavity, away from her hand. She immediately pulled back. Cody scooped up another spoonful and slammed it sideways against his mouth.

"Wow," Charles said, trying to imitate the playful tone Alison had been using, "somebody really likes his dessert."

"Your dad is talking to you, Cody," Alison said. "Cody Larson Marlow."

Cody moaned and bowed low to the surface of his tray, briefly submersing the tip of his nose in his pudding cup. Then, in a wide-ranging motion, he swept his head up and back: a startled horse carving an arc through space, mane tossing, whites of eyes exposed, assessing quickly and efficiently the possible presence of a predator.

At the end of this movement, Cody froze, body torqued, vacant eyes aimed toward the door leading to the backyard, as if he were longing to escape into the black, drenched night.

Bettina was making the rounds, moving among the diners, helping those who needed help.

Noticing that Cody had made a mess, she said cheerily, "Here, Cody, let's get you a new bib," and before Charles or Alison could stop her, she had her hands on the bare skin of his neck, his shoulders, and Charles thought, *No*, no, *she hasn't been told, how can they not have told her, she doesn't know.*

For one moment, there was a subtle undulation in Cody's face, the effect of an idly drifting cottonwood tuft landing on a perfectly unperturbed pool.

And then: thrashing, screaming, the sudden stench of loosed bowels, Cody reaching into the back of his pants, smearing face, hair, body with feces; Bettina backed away in horror and confusion as Charles and Alison tried to restrain him.

Among the other children, a cacophony arose: empathetic moans, giggles, gibbering incomprehensibilities; a wordless, savage wilderness expressing extremes of terror and jubilation.

"Didn't anyone *tell* her?" Alison was shouting, furious. "*Damn it,* I cannot *believe* that no one told her! He cannot, cannot, *cannot* be touched on his scars!"

❧

It is an odd but demonstrable truth that there are times in Earth's history when a shadow falls over the planet. (Charles always thought of the blackness enveloping Earth in *A Wrinkle in Time*, a book that is for many young girls — as it was for Emmy — an early favorite.)

The shadow manifests in large-scale devastation and suffering: environmental, cultural, political; earthquakes, fires, tsunamis; the rape and mutilation of innocents; acts of genocide; acts of terrorism. And although sometimes these catastrophes are glimpsed from a distance and our sympathies extend no further than writing a check, often the shadow falls on us in a personal way. The darkness finds us at home; personal suffering occurs in tandem with the larger tragedy and is forever after associated with it.

It was in the wake of 9/11. Alison especially had been devastated — she had enduring connections with many people in Manhattan and lost two dear friends in the Towers.

Charles didn't know how to reach her. His connection to the event was less direct than Alison's, and at times he felt that perhaps she resented him for that. But it was also that distance that allowed him to keep functioning when she could not.

Alison spent the rest of September on the living-room sofa in a kind of coma, unable to extricate herself from the nonstop television and radio coverage even though the effects were basically those of an inexorable wasting disease.

Charles brought her tea and broth, the only nourishment she would take for days on end. She occasionally accepted some partially ground uncooked ramen noodles from Cody. But during those few weeks, her ongoing obsession with curing Cody's autism became completely supplanted by her grief over the state of the planet.

Charles couldn't convince her to go with him and the children to the Seattle Center memorial. They brought flowers and herbs from the garden: asters and mums, rosemary boughs for remembrance, and sprigs of fennel, which Cody loved picking and carrying about, brushing the feathery fronds across his cheeks. It was eerie: thousands of people gathered in silence around the fountain. Cody's muteness that day was a kind of blessing; for once, his inability to speak was not stigmatizing or isolating — he was just one more citizen of a world that had been stunned into a voiceless, impotent grief.

Eventually, Charles managed to get Alison out of the house, driving her to an aikido class. She was resistant at first, but reconnecting with aikido was what finally filled the hole and brought her back. He thought, briefly, of joining her, that perhaps he should make another effort to learn to fall, but he knew from experience that when going through hell, Alison preferred to go alone.

By mid-October, she'd started an intensive six-week teacher-training program and was gone five nights a week and from ten until five on Saturdays and Sundays. It was hard, being essentially a single parent during that time, but Charles truly felt that it was saving Alison's life.

On weeknights, Alison's classes went until nine, sometimes later. It was especially late when she came home that particular night, almost eleven.

Emmy was asleep. Charles and Cody were in Cody's room. Charles was on Cody's bed, reading; Cody was sitting cross-legged on the floor, grinding, showing no sign of being the least bit tired and resisting any effort to get him under the covers. Charles thought perhaps Cody wanted his mother to put him to bed. He'd seen little enough of her the past few weeks.

Usually Ali came home animated, keyed up, quickened in body and spirit, but tonight, all the typical sounds of her homecoming — the opening of the front door, keys dropping on the table, briefcase and gym bag hitting the floor, coat being hung in the closet, footsteps coming up the stairs — were separated by long pauses, as if she were moving very slowly, laden with some enormously heavy cargo.

"I saw Cody's light on from outside," she said, appearing in the doorway. "I can't believe you're still up."

"You okay?"

"Fine. Just tired."

"Look, Cody," Charles said. "It's Mom."

"Hi, Cody. How are you, sweetheart?"

Cody grunted, signed *Hi, Mom* without looking up, and continued grinding.

Alison leaned against the doorjamb and slipped off her shoes. She went straight from work to the dojo, changed into her *gi*, and then put her business suit and heels back on after class, so she was wearing a business suit and heels. Now that she was finally off the sofa and back in the world, her stamina was astonishing. Charles couldn't fathom how she managed these thirteen-hour days.

"So," she said. "What have you guys been doing?"

"Not much. Just hanging. We made pesto for dinner, didn't we, Cody? Watched a video . . . read . . . you know, the usual."

"Has he had his bath?"

"Yes."

"Did he brush his teeth?"

"Yes, Alison. We've got the routine down."

"Hey, Cody." She squatted and signed her greeting this time. "Have you been having fun with Dad?"

Cody reached for another package of noodles. Alison grabbed it and hid it behind her back before he could get to it.

"Cody, look at me. What have you and Dad been doing?"

"Mom's talking to you, son. Can you take a break?"

Alison handed off the package of noodles to Charles; she then tried to take Cody's mortar and pestle, but he let out a screech and clutched them fast.

The two of them tussled for a while, their respective energies stubborn, straight-lined, rigid, in unassailable collision.

Alison gave up. Cody went back to grinding.

"Goddamn it, Charles." Alison stood, stomped to the hall closet, returned with a whiskbroom and dustpan, and made a show of sweeping up the noodles that had spilled during their struggle.

"What? What's the matter? Here, I'll get that."

"Don't bother. Come on, Cody. Say good night to Dad. Mom will put you to bed."

Alison reached for him. Cody started to protest, a series of short, aggressive, staccato caws, like a Steller's jay protecting a brood of nestlings.

"Good night, Cody." Charles snapped up the noodles and the mortar and pestle while Cody was distracted. "I love you, son. See you in the morning."

As Charles went down to the kitchen, he heard more noises of protest from Cody — for a kid who didn't speak, he had an amazing range of sounds when it came to expressing objection: screeching, barking, keening, yawping, howling (thank God that Emmy had proven herself since birth to be a sound sleeper) — but by the time Charles removed all the necessary childproofing locks, lit the gas stove, put on the kettle for Alison's tea, and spooned the leftover gluten-free pasta and pesto into a saucepan to heat, all was quiet.

The storybook-cottage kitchen had, by this time, been scaled down to something resembling the interior of a typical home in a Plymouth Rock reenactment village: at the center, a big unadorned wood table; countertops bare of appliances, bare of anything, for that matter; what few bits of crockery had survived years of tantrums and accidents were locked up, ditto the flatware and knives; no glassware whatsoever, and not a microwave or BPA-containing plastic item in sight.

In the years since Cody's diagnosis, Alison had spent much of her downtime investigating various theories concerning possible causes of autism, many of which were related to diet, nutrition, and environmental toxins. Charles frequently arrived in the kitchen in the morning to find a stack of highlighted articles she'd printed out from the Internet sometime in the wee hours.

The day after Alison read about how microwaving *distorts* and *deforms* the molecules of whatever substance is subjected to it (as proof of this, a woman had died after receiving a transfusion of microwaved blood in 1991), Charles came home to find the microwave sitting outside on the curb with a FREE sign.

The evening after they'd spent one date night in the City Prana auditorium watching *Bag It!*, a documentary that the Environmental Studies Department had made schoolwide required viewing, she jettisoned every plastic food container in the house.

You never know what's going to make a difference, she always said. *It could be the smallest change, one little thing that seems completely insignificant, but the one little thing that's going to make him better.*

Alison came downstairs. Charles knew she was irritated about Cody being up so late but he didn't feel like getting into it. She wasn't the only one who was tired.

"Cody in bed?" he asked.

"Yes."

"How was class?"

"Fine."

Charles stirred the pasta. "This will be ready in a couple of minutes."

Alison pulled a bottle of wine off the rack, uncorked it, and filled a coffee mug.

"So, are you going to tell me how long?" she said.

"How long what?"

"How long you've been letting him stim?"

"What do you mean? The grinding thing?"

"The grinding thing." She firmed her mouth and took a swig of wine. "Yes, Charles, the *grinding thing*. Jesus."

"All right, Alison, so I didn't set the timer. Christ. Is that why you're so upset? He's happy, or he was until you got home and started programming him."

The pasta was starting to stick. Charles added water from the kettle and stirred.

Alison topped off her mug and began to pace.

"I don't understand why it's so hard for you to comply with the rules. We talk about this, all of this, all the time. We have conversations, over and over again. What is it with you? Is this your way of punishing me?"

"What the hell are you talking about?"

"I'm talking about how I do this one thing, this *one fucking thing* for myself, going to aikido, and —"

"This *one thing?* Alison, it's taking up all your free time, and that's fine, I'm happy to support you if it helps you out of that black place you were in after —"

"Oh, great. Here we go, how happy you are to support me, how much you're giving up so I can do this, how perfectly okay it is that you're doing all the child care, all by yourself, blah-blah-blah. It's not called *child care* when they're your kids, Charles; it's called *parenting,* and you signed up for it. This teacher training will be over in two weeks. Two weeks! It's not as though I haven't carried the load for you now and then. It's not as though I haven't logged just as many hours with him, but at least I stay present, I keep him engaged, I don't just let him stim for hours on end."

"He did not stim for hours on end, Alison! Jesus! He was just having trouble winding down, and it helps him, what the hell is wrong with that? Christ, how many nights do you play computer solitaire until two in the morning? How many nights do you cruise the Web, looking for . . . who the hell knows?"

The teakettle was starting to whistle. Charles turned down the flame.

"Don't. Don't do that. Don't make this about me. We're

talking about Cody." She poured another mugful of wine and muttered, "I just don't know how the hell I'm supposed to trust you."

"What? What did you say?"

"I'm tired. I'm going to bed."

"How you are supposed to *trust me?*"

Alison snatched up the wine bottle and the coffee mug and marched out of the kitchen, but Charles followed her, waylaying her at the base of the stairs.

"No," he said, taking her by the arm and leading her down to the laundry room. He struggled to keep his voice under control so as not to wake Cody. "You do not get to walk away from this conversation. I don't care how late it is or how tired you are."

"I just want a straight answer. How long did you let him sit there and stim?"

"Why can't you just accept him the way he is?"

"How can you even say that? Accept him the way he is? The way he is is *sick* Charles. He's *sick.* Would you accept him *the way he is* if he had cancer? Would you just shrug your shoulders and say, Oh, well, what the fuck, it's just the way things are."

"It's not the same, Alison."

"It *is* the same, Charles. It's always the same with you, the same old bullshit. You might as well still be a pothead bartender working at the country club, coasting along, not a care in the world. Floating. Just *floating.* Don't you ever feel the need to *steer* your life, for God's sake? Don't you ever want to once, just once, take charge of something? Life is just one big fucking surrender for you, and I can't take it. I can't take it anymore. Cody needs us to *fight* for him. Where the hell is your *fight?*"

"I work just as hard as you do with him."

"Really? Really? All I see is you sitting around reading while he tears up his magazines and smashes noodles. You call that *working* with him?"

"Everything doesn't have to be so goddamn *hard* for him all the time, Alison. Why can't he have some downtime like everybody else? Why can't he just spend time doing things that make him happy?"

"And that's really it, isn't it? Because as long as he's happy — in other words, sitting in a corner with his version of a pacifier jammed in his mouth — he's manageable, he causes no problems. Of course, he never grows, he never learns, he never advances. But then, that's the way *you* are. You just want him to be a mirror of you: no cares, no challenges, just hours and hours of solitude and —"

"Fuck you. You are so spoiled."

"What?"

"If you weren't constantly asking Daddy for this or for that, we'd actually have to handle this on our own, together, instead of you always bringing in some new specialist, spending money on some new bogus miracle cure —"

"Wait. Quiet."

"What? I don't get to speak?"

"No, wait. Do you smell something?"

The smoke detector went off.

"Did you —" Alison said, suddenly sober, her face ashen. "The stove."

"Oh God. Oh no . . ."

They rushed up the stairs to find Cody in the kitchen, standing in front of the lit stove, holding the teakettle, his pajama top in flames, his mouth open in a silent scream.

Had he heard them fighting? The savagery in their voices?

Had he been hoping to comfort his mother, as he'd seen Charles do, by bringing her a cup of tea? Or had he been trying to comfort himself, coming to look for his mortar and pestle, his noodles?

They would never know. Never. Only this: their son would wear a hair shirt of burn scars for the rest of his life.

❧

The two male caregivers intervened and started trying to restrain Cody. Raisa and Tami dealt with the others, calming them, keeping them in their seats; Bettina stood in shocked stillness and kept repeating, *I'm sorry, I'm so sorry,* until Raisa barked at her to fetch some towels. Charles cleared the remains of Cody's dinner.

"Can you get home?" Alison asked. "Call a cab or something?"

"I'll be fine."

"I'll call you later." She followed Ben and Malachi as they carried Cody, still thrashing and screaming, toward the bathroom.

Not yet ready to leave, Charles filled a bucket with soap and water, located a scrub brush, and went to work on the carpet. Beneath the sounds of Cody's screams and moans was the steady, low-pitched obbligato of Alison's voice trying to soothe him.

Charles felt a light touch on his shoulder. "Leave that, Mr. Marlow," Raisa said. He wasn't sure how long he'd been scrubbing, but the TV trays were gone and the other children were quieted now and watching a video. Bettina had returned with the towels; Tami was loading the dishwasher. "You go on. It's okay. We take care of it."

Outside, the temperature had dropped and the rain had turned to sleet: a spate of sharpened quills. He could have gone back in for a coat, an umbrella, but he didn't. He walked. It was only a few miles.

When he got home, he was shivering, soaked to the bone.

He began prying the plywood off the fireplace, his hands bloodying with the effort, opening the long-closed flue, stuffing in newspapers, flattened boxes, whatever he could find in the recycling bin that could be set alight, striking the match.

Then he hefted one box up and out from among the others and carried it to the hearth.

Sitting down on the tiles (they were warm now and felt good against the cold clamminess of his soaked khakis), Charles began feeding "Flipper Boy" into the fire, one page at a time, as if he could unwrite the story, the tale he'd told as a prescient child, the fictional masterpiece that had come true.

Paper burns hot, quickly. There was so much smoke.

Charles heard a voice in his head, his own voice reciting the opening line of the fireman narrator of *Fahrenheit 451* — "It was a pleasure to burn" — and then a vision appeared: his ten-year-old son being transfigured by fire.

Once upon a time in a small town in the Land of Sky-Blue Waters a boy was born to a husband and wife . . .

Page after page went in; more splintered plywood; the sound of the fire growing louder, but never loud enough to drown out the trapped-animal shriek of Cody's inchoate screams.

They sounded exactly like Dana's.

Homo Faber

Whereas some sense can be make of my brother's noodle-pulverizing habit (from the first time he watched our father use a mortar and pestle to grind herbs from the garden, he was mesmerized), the reason behind his other primary occupation has remained a mystery.

Beginning around the time I was born, whenever a magazine or catalog came into the house, Cody would snatch it up and rip it to shreds if it wasn't immediately intercepted.

What is further puzzling about this obsession is Cody's fussiness about the kind of magazines he prefers to destroy. My parents endured many violent tantrums when they offered up periodicals that did not meet Cody's criteria — whatever they were. They learned through extensive trial and error that only certain publications were acceptable. For example:

People magazine, yes; *Vogue,* no.

The Sundance catalog, yes; Bas Bleu, no.

The New Yorker, yes; *Newsweek,* no.

Cooking Light, yes; the *Enquirer,* decidedly no.

As with the noodle-grinding, my mother impresses upon all of Cody's caregivers the protocols surrounding magazine-tearing: it is an activity that must be strictly monitored; he is to be given only *one* magazine at a time; he is allowed to engage with the magazine for *no longer* than ten minutes.

These hard-and-fast rules, however, have never been communicated to anyone involved in Art Without Boundaries.

The guest artist volunteering this month arrives early and — assisted by Romy Bertleson — begins hauling the needed supplies out of his car and into the church basement. It's a good bit of material, carefully organized into plastic bins of various sizes and weights; getting all of it inside requires three trips to and from the parking lot with the help of a handcart.

There are stacks of precut posterboard, mat board, and card stock, packaged glue sticks, bottles of rubber cement, watercolor paints and brushes, used hardback and paperback books of all genres and sizes, boxes of greeting cards, calendars, stickers, photographs, catalogs, vintage sheet music, travel brochures, posters, junk mail. There is also an assortment of the collage artist's most valuable tool: magazines.

❖

As soon as Roma offers up a copy of *The Knot,* Giorgia immediately knows the story they are enacting today, a prequel to "The Sunflower Bride": she and Roma-as-Felice are studying hairstyles and makeup and wedding gowns so that Giorgia can learn how to dress like a proper American bride and make her husband-to-be proud. She mustn't look like a peasant.

"Devo carina per lui," Giorgia murmurs. *"O almeno il più*

carina possibile . . ." The models are all blondes. And so skinny! Don't American girls have any curves at all?

Giorgia turns the page. "Ah," she says, relieved.

"You like that picture?" Felice asks. "Should I cut it out for you?

Giorgia pats her hand. *"Sei tanto cara, sorella mia."* She looks at more pages.

"How about this one?" Felice asks.

"Hmmm." Giorgia squints at the image appraisingly, tilting her head this way and that. *"Forse no. Troppo fantasioso. Vediamo se c'è n' è uno più semplice . . ."* She turns to another page. *"Quest'ultimo!"* she announces happily. *"Potrei farne uno come questo!"*

"Oh! That one's beautiful!"

"Bee-*you*-tee-fohla!"

Giorgia finds more pictures she likes. Felice cuts them out.

After they come to the last page of the magazine, Felice sets it aside and places a piece of posterboard on the table. "Where do you think this should go?" she asks, holding one of the cut-out bride faces in the palm of her hand.

"Che vuoi dire?"

"Remember? You're going to take these little pictures — The ones we cut out? All the ones you said you liked? — and glue them to this" — Felice smoothes her hand across the posterboard — "to make a new, bigger picture. A *collage.*"

"Colla?"

"Where should this one go? Here? Here?"

Giorgia pushes the posterboard aside and points to the middle of her white triptych screen.

"You want to glue it there?" Felice looks around the room. *Ah,* Giorgia thinks, *she has always been the most timid of all Papa's girls, so worried about making him mad.*

Giorgia pats her hand again.

"Well . . . okay. Why not? Where? Where should it go?"

Giorgia takes the cut-out picture and pins it to the screen with her finger.

"There? Okay. Perfect. May I have it?"

Giorgia watches with interest as Felice turns the cutout face-down and rubs its surface with something that looks like a lipstick tube. *"Sei così attenta,"* she says with fondness. *"Mi ero dimenticata che fossi così, sorella mia."*

This is not exactly what Giorgia expected — in fact, this might be a new story altogether, one that doesn't yet have a title — but she doesn't mind. She is remembering when they were little girls playing with paper cutouts this way, except they had to make their own *colla* — when Papa wasn't around, they collected the leftover flour from the *panificio* counters and floors, carefully brushed it into a bowl, and then mixed it with water. Their glue didn't work as well as this, but at least it didn't cost any money.

Felice positions the picture on the screen.

"How's that?"

Giorgia nods. *"Perfetto."*

"Show me where another one should go . . ."

By the time class is over, the center of Giorgia's triptych is dappled with cutouts of veiled and unveiled faces, bouquets, shoes, bridal gowns, and bridesmaids' dresses.

"You like it so far?" Felice asks.

"Bene . . . Mi piace finora," Giorgia answers.

After Felice excuses herself from the table, Giorgia studies what they have made.

Yes, this is definitely a new story. It lacks a title. The whole is not yet clear. There are many white spaces. But Giorgia has faith. What is needed at such times of confusion and uncertainty is what is always needed: patience and prayer.

And look: Felice has left something behind! This in itself

is a sign; an answer, at last, to Giorgia's many entreaties to the patron saint of penmanship: *Dear Saint Lorenzo* — how many times she prayed for his assistance — *Please make my labors visible to those who cannot see, please manifest in my humble empty hands the pen, and on this barren table the paper.*

And lo! Here they are, the tools she has longed for.

"Grazie a Dio," she murmurs, taking up the pen, rolling up her sleeves, resettling herself in the correct position.

When Cody arrives, he immediately heads for Giorgia's table; she is making marks on the posterboard.

Romy arrives, pushing a cart with food for the not-Cody group. "Here's your lunch, Mrs. D'Amati," she says, setting a plate on the table. "Hello, Cody. See the collage she made?" As she moves on, she adds, "You'll get to make a collage today too."

Giorgia pats the table top next to her. *"Col-la,"* she says.

Cody sits. "Coh-dee," he replies.

After lunch is over, Mrs. D'Amati and her group leave.

The teacher introduces himself to Cody's group and begins talking about the day's activity. Moving among the tables, volunteers deliver the needed supplies to the students, two dozen PWAs ranging in age from fourteen to sixty. Each student is given posterboard and a magazine.

When a volunteer arrives at Cody's table, he leaps up, grabs the entire stack of magazines, and scurries away.

"Hey! Cody!" Big Mal says. "Take a seat."

Clasping the magazines to his chest, Cody scoots under a table.

"Cody! Where you goin', big guy?"

Cody puts the magazines on the floor and then sits on them.

Big Mal walks over. "Give those to me, Cody. You know the rules." He takes Cody by the arm and tries to get him to come out. Cody grunts, thrashes, and pulls himself into a tight ball: chin to chest, arms bent, elbows touching, forearms pressed against his cheekbones, fists like corks in his ears.

"It's okay," the teacher says. "He can have all of those if he wants. I've got plenty of magazines."

❖

For the next ninety minutes, Cody is oblivious to anything but his work. Here is how it goes:

He takes the top magazine off the stack and sets the others aside.

He tears out the pages one by one, placing them in a stack. Their edges must be lined up.

He puts one page on the table in front of him. He tears this page into strips, sometimes the long way, sometimes the short way, but never on the diagonal. He takes great care with this part of the process — the strips can be different widths, but a single strip cannot be wider in some places and narrower in others; its shape cannot undulate noticeably. If that happens, Cody seems to consider the strip ruined, since he immediately crumples it up and throws it away.

He goes on like this until every page of the magazine has been torn into strips.

Today he does something he's never had enough time to do before: he weaves the strips together into a bowl-shaped tangle that looks like a bird's nest.

He picks it up carefully and, cradling it in his hands, carries it around the room.

"Ga," he says each time he holds it out to one of his classmates. "Ga."

Egg-SHEP-Shun-All!

Charles arrived on the doorstep of Cloud City Café, waved to Sunny the cook to announce his presence, poured himself a cup of coffee, settled into his corner, and opened up the Sunday edition of the *Seattle Times*.

As was his custom, he read the first section while waiting for his food to arrive. There wasn't much of interest today, with the exception of a page-six story that filled him with a potent melancholy: it was about the recently announced bankruptcy of an iconic American bakery.

After greeting Jamie the waitress as she delivered his breakfast, Charles extracted the *Pacific Magazine* section. On the front page was a photo of him, Astrida Pukis, and the other three Nellie Goodhue interviewees, positioned within the Gothic-style niches of the Fisher Pavilion.

These 1963 classmates did a fair job of predicting twenty-first-century life.

Inside was the story, with Mike Bernauer's byline:

A half century ago, just after the Seattle World's Fair, a reporter from the Seattle Times visited the Nellie Goodhue School in North Seattle to ask a group of ten fourth-grade Language Arts students what they thought life would be like in the twenty-first century.

The article included a small partial reprint of the original piece, a photo of the class arranged in their reading circle, and captioned, close-up individual portraits the photographer had taken as they were being interviewed.

Beneath Astrida's picture: *Robots will be used to do everything from cooking to taking people's tonsils out.*

Beneath Charles's: *Everyone will take drugs that will grow new muscles and turn them into superhumans.*

Charles began skimming the article, hoping he wouldn't find much mention of himself or his fictional masterpiece.

These students — part of what was then a radical new reading and writing curriculum called Language Arts — first came to the attention of the Seattle Times when their teacher, Mrs. Eloise Braxton, submitted their creative writing for a citywide contest the newspaper sponsored that year: "Who will be the next century's storytellers?" The winner of that contest was one of Mrs. Braxton's students, Charles Marlow.

Seeing his name in the newspaper was like hearing it broadcast in the room, a summons to the principal's office for some behavioral infraction; Charles sank a bit lower in his chair and read on with trepidation.

Mr. Marlow, 59, still lives in Seattle and for over 20 years has been a Language Arts teacher at City Prana, a grade 6–12 private alternative school. When asked if his experiences in that inaugural program influenced his career choice, Mr. Marlow chuckled and said, "I suppose so. Mrs. Braxton was certainly a dedicated and memorable teacher and her methods probably had a great impact on all of us."

That was the extent of it, thankfully.

Of those ten members of Mrs. Eloise Braxton's Language Arts class, eight were named in the original article; five of them gathered at the Seattle Center for this interview. A striking aspect of Mrs. Braxton's fourth-grade Language Arts class is how accomplished these former students have become, in a wide array of fields.

The article went on to list the credentials of the other interviewees — Astrid was referenced as *a Seattle neurosurgeon who lectures at teaching hospitals throughout the world* — and quote their reflections on their former predictions:

> *We'll be going to the moon and other planets in our solar system!*
> *There will be lots of inventions that will help us learn things faster!*
> *Everyone will have a telephone in their pocket!*
> *We'll have ways of traveling underground like subways only much faster!*
> *Seattle will be famous! Everyone will want to move here!*
> *Cars will have a new kind of fuel!*

And to those ebullient, optimistic predictions, Charles silently cataloged his own, as laid out in "Flipper Boy" — a great many of which had also come true.

❖

At the parent-teacher conference in the fall of 1962, Mrs. Braxton began by praising Charles extravagantly for his academic excellence, exemplary citizenship, and prodigious affinity for the Palmer Method. In all her years of teaching, she'd never seen anything like it, especially from a boy.

"Penmanship mastery seems to present a special challenge for males," Mrs. Braxton remarked as she walked Rita Marlow around the classroom, "which is a great irony considering that both the Palmer system and its antecedent, Spencerian script, were male inventions. I have wondered from time to time if there isn't some physiologic reason for the gender disparity, some organic cause that could account for the way boy students consistently lag behind the girls in this area of study."

Charles sat, waiting, a nonentity. Teacher and parent continued their tour of the room; Mrs. Braxton pointed with obvious pride to the many examples of Charles's handwriting on display throughout the room.

On a strip of orange construction paper thumbtacked to the wall where Mrs. Braxton exhibited art projects, Charles had lettered "The Monsters, Witches, Goblins, and Ghouls of Room 104." Below this were class self-portraits. Charles had done a stiff, uninspired drawing of himself as a wizard; Dana's picture consisted of exuberant scribbles rendered in white crayon — they were essentially bedspring ovals grafted together to form something that looked like an electrified snowman with numerous extraneous appendages. Because this self-portrait had been the result of one of their lunch-time lessons, Charles knew that Dana had meant to draw himself as the White Rabbit from *Alice's Adventures in Wonderland.*

Rita Marlow nodded and emitted an occasional mono-syllabic sound. Her eyes kept darting between the door and the wall clock, and she moved with jittery hyperawareness, like a spooked animal. Although she was by far the lighter of the two women, her stiletto heels struck heavily against the floor; in the morning, Charles would be able to track her movements by following a smudgy trail of black, half-moon-shaped scuff marks.

"Shall we wait a few more minutes for your husband to arrive, Mrs. Marlow?" Mrs. Braxton asked.

"No. That's fine." Rita Marlow's voice was burred, crenu-late, shiny, like the aluminum rim of a Swanson Turkey Pot Pie pan.

"Perhaps he'll be along later? Perhaps he's been delayed."

"Yes, well, in any case, let's do get started. I know you have other families to see this evening."

"All right, then." Mrs. Braxton indicated the chair where Mrs. Marlow should sit, waited for her to extract her ciga-rettes and lighter, supplied her with an ashtray, and then took her place behind her desk. "I must begin, Mrs. Mar-low, by saying what an absolute delight it has been having Charles in my classroom this year . . ."

Out came the cursive-writing tablets and reports and spelling tests and attendance book; Mrs. Braxton droned on about Charles's successes. His mother inhaled deeply on her cigarette; she seemed to relax slightly, but did not smile. The minutes passed. Still no one acknowledged the subject of all this praise. Still Mr. Marlow didn't come.

"In conclusion," Mrs. Braxton said, "Charles is a model

student, a great help to me, someone the rest of the class looks up to and emulates."

That's a joke, Charles thought.

Mrs. Braxton fixed her eyes on him for the first time that evening, and for one heart-arrested moment he thought she'd mind-read his unvoiced smart-aleck observation.

"Charles, I've selected you to be part of a pilot program at our school, an experimental curriculum that will be introduced in January. It's called Language Arts."

She held up a textbook: *Language Arts: A New Approach to Discovering the Joys of Reading and the Elements of Creative Writing.* Its cover illustration showed a small group of wholesome-looking children sitting in a circle that included a very pretty young woman, presumably their teacher. The children held opened books in their laps; one child was reading, and the others were raptly attentive. Everyone looked very happy.

Mrs. Braxton went on to explain that a small number of fourth-graders — "only the very best and brightest children, you understand, from each of the two fourth-grade classes" — would be leaving their classrooms each day for a period of thirty minutes; they would spend this time in the library with her.

Charles understood that this was meant to represent some kind of award, another rung on the ladder toward academic heights, but he was concerned. *Who will be teaching everybody else?* he wondered.

In answer to this unspoken question, Mrs. Braxton added that Mrs. Hurd, the other fourth-grade teacher, would be working with the remaining students on learning to *diagram sentences.* Charles had no idea what that meant, but it did sound less appealing than *Language Arts.*

Rita Marlow, by this point, had all but left the premises.

Her eyes were glazed, her teeth were clenched, and the quieting effects of smoking had abated; she'd begun jiggling and circling her foot, frequently switching the cross of her legs, the way she habitually did when Charles's father was late or, as in this case, a no-show. All that was missing from this portrait was her martini glass.

But upon hearing the phrase *diagram sentences,* she roused herself to quasi-attentiveness. "Sentence diagramming," she said. "We learned that in parochial school. Isn't that important?"

"Well, yes, indeed, it is true that in the past, sentence diagramming has been a feature of elementary-school education" — and now it was Mrs. Braxton's turn to glance at the clock — "but this new curriculum gives children the chance to absorb the mechanics of language in an intuitive manner. The thinking is that by reading excerpts from literature, they will come to understand what constitutes good writing, well-crafted sentence structure; this will enable them to be better thinkers and more expressive and creative writers."

"I liked diagramming sentences," Charles's mother said. "It was . . . direct."

Mrs. Braxton grinned. "Well . . ."

Rita Marlow stood up and extended her hand. "Thank you for your time, Mrs. Braxton. I'm glad to hear that Charles is doing well."

Mrs. Braxton began walking them to the door. "Oh, and there is one last thing you should know."

"Yes?"

"Charles has taken on quite an unusual and heroic role within the classroom."

Both parent and student looked puzzled. Rita Marlow glanced at her son. "Charles. Heroic," she repeated dully.

"Oh, yes. Without any prompting from me, Charles has become quite a help to Dana McGucken."

Rita Marlow shook her head. "I'm sorry, I don't understand."

Mrs. Braxton looked at Charles and cooed affectionately, "You haven't said anything, have you?" She placed one of her puffy, sharp-nailed hands on Charles's shoulder, a gesture that froze him to the spot. "I suspected as much. That's very like you, Charles, to be so humble."

She addressed the rest of her remarks sotto voce, as if shielding Charles from potentially upsetting information. "Dana is one of our *special* children, Mrs. Marlow. Thanks to Charles's attention and friendship, Dana has shown tremendous improvement. You have a lovely boy there, Mrs. Marlow."

"Ah. Well, thank you again for your time, Mrs. Braxton. Good night."

Mrs. Braxton stood in the doorway, smiled her toothiest smile, and waved. "See you tomorrow, Charles!"

Rita Marlow walked briskly down the hallway toward the exit door that led to the school parking lot; Charles had to jog slightly to keep up. As soon as they were out of hearing range, she reached into her purse for another cigarette and hissed, "Where the *hell* is your goddamn father? And who was that boy your teacher was talking about? Some friend of yours?"

Before she could inquire further, the door swung open and there he was, wearing an impeccably clean suit that made him seem to shine against the dark autumn night.

"Hello, Char-Lee!" Dana bellowed, rushing toward them willy-nilly but coming to a full stop at the last possible moment. He began bouncing excitedly on his toes. "Mom!

Look!" he called. "Look at this boy! It's Char-Lee Mar-Low! Come on, Mom! Say hi to Char-Lee!"

Following behind Dana was a diminutive, pale-complexioned woman wearing a dark pink coat with a matching hat, white gloves, and sensible low-heeled shoes. Her facial features were delicate, unremarkable, and almost completely overpowered by large black-rimmed glasses. But she gave off a feeling of great calm and kindness. Charles had expected something more eccentric, more flamboyant from a person who let her child wear white suits to school every day.

"Hello," she said as she drew near. Dana straightened his arm to its full length and pointed, his finger coming within inches of Charles's nose. "It's Char-Lee Mar-Low, Mom!" he announced again. "We make loooo-*puh*-*zzzzz*!"

"It's very good to meet you, Charles," Mrs. McGucken said. "Dana has told me so much about you." She extended her hand. "How do you do, I'm Sylvie McGucken."

Rita Marlow — who'd been caught unaware by these social niceties — struggled clumsily to re-situate her handbag on her forearm and free her hands from her pack of Camels, lighter, car keys. She averted her face to exhale a cloud of smoke over her right shoulder and then took Mrs. McGucken's hand. "I'm Rita Marlow. Nice to meet you."

"Charles has been such a wonderful friend to my son."

"Oh?"

Dana continued to bounce on his toes and began pivoting from side to side, smiling broadly, breathing quickly, his eyes roaming the ceiling in a happy way, as if following the movements of a monarch migration. "*Aaaaahhhh!*" he sang. His mother touched him lightly on the padded shoulder of his white suit coat. "Aaaaahhhh," he said again, at half volume.

Rita Marlow kept smiling aggressively at Mrs. McGucken

in a way that went far beyond mere exclusion. She wasn't just ignoring Dana, Charles realized; she was *repelling* him.

"Char-Lee is my friend," Dana said.

She was *afraid* of him.

"Dana talks about your son all the time," Mrs. McGucken said.

"Me and Char-Lee make *loops!*" Dana added.

"Dana has never been so excited about coming to school."

"We *eat* loops!"

"That's nice," Rita Marlow offered, her smile beginning to fossilize. "Well, we don't want to keep you. Good night."

"All right, Dana," Mrs. McGucken said. "Let's say goodbye to Charlie and his mom and go see Mrs. Braxton."

"Goodbye, Char-Lee, goodbye, Char-Lee mom, hello, Mrs. Brack-ton, we are heeeeere!"

Dana resumed singing his butterfly song as he and his mother made their way down the hall. Charles turned around just before the heavy double doors of the building swung closed to see that Dana's head was craned back toward him and he was waving.

◆

When he got to school Monday morning, Charles found that there was already another voicemail message from Alison reminding him of their appointment at the bank.

. . . and I hope you'll be willing to go out for drinks afterwards. They're really nice people, Charles, you'll like them when you get to know them, and besides, we're going to be spending a lot of time together over the next few years. Maybe — actually, hopefully — the rest of our lives, *if things work out, and please God, let that be the case . . . Oh! Nice article in yesterday's paper. What a surprise. You didn't tell me about that. Okay, have a good day, see you later, here we go!*

Charles wished he could share Alison's exuberance over this whole house-buying, going-into-the-residential-health-care-industry-for-themselves business — truly, he hadn't seen her this happy in years — but there was something about the degree of the commitment: *We're going to be spending a lot of time together . . . the rest of our* lives, *if things work out.* Having failed to sustain a traditional marriage, Charles felt understandably wary about wedding himself to four other people he'd barely met — and to their sons too, for that was part of the equation. Her earnest invocation, *please God,* troubled him. He'd also felt a sting of irritation when she mentioned the newspaper article. Of *course* he hadn't told her about it. Why would he?

Charles headed for the teachers' lounge. As he was putting his lunch into the fridge, he felt a hand on his shoulder.

"Good morning, Charles." It was the school principal, Emmett Willoughby, an educator who'd come to City Prana by way of Cambridge and who normally exuded an aloof, monarchical presence that perfectly matched his pear-shaped tones and garnered great credibility in fundraising situations.

He clapped Charles on the shoulder with fellow-crew-member camaraderie and said, "Terrific article in the newspaper, Charles! Well done. I hope you're planning on sharing with the students . . ."

More teachers came in. Everyone seemed unusually perky and loquacious — energized from Christmas break, perhaps. Many mentioned seeing the story in the newspaper and wanted to engage Charles in conversation about it. It was all very congenial and well-intentioned, but really, he just wanted to get to his classroom and have a few moments of quiet before the students' arrival.

As he poured another cup of coffee and looked for an

escape route, Pam joined him, her hands wrapped around yet another failed pottery project, but at least this one was glazed in cheerful saffron yellow.

"Walk me to my room?" she asked quietly. "You look like you need an out."

"Thanks," Charles answered.

As they traversed the halls, Charles was hailed again and again — by both teachers and early-bird students — with greetings like *Great story in the paper; How fun to read about you in the news; You're a star, Mr. Marlow!* Charles had no idea that there were so many people who'd remained diligent consumers of newsprint.

"Well, off to the races," Pam said when they arrived at her classroom door. "Have a good day."

Charles experienced a surprising impulse to follow Pam inside and hide out among the shelves of unglazed pottery.

After hastening to his room and closing the door — there was still a full half hour before the start of homeroom — he took up his clipboard and legal pad and sank into one of the beanbag chairs.

Dear Emmy,

It is with no little sadness that I am writing today to share an important news development: the demise of the Hostess Baking Company.

You and Cody never experienced the thrill of eagerly opening your lunchboxes on a daily basis to discover which treat had been tucked inside.

Sno Ball? Twinkie? Hostess Cupcake?

These nutrition-free items were a beloved element of my childhood; nevertheless, I understood and supported your mother's rejection of all things processed. The dietary deprivations we enforced so stringently with you and your brother — sugar, dairy, soy, tree nuts, peanuts, wheat, corn, eggs—sweetheart, I hope you know that they were made out of love and concern, with the best of parental intentions. However, let me go on the record and say this: I sincerely hope that by now you've been able to experi-ence the joys of peanut butter. There's really nothing like it.

Knowing that Hostess factories will soon close, I went to the QFC late last night and purchased a substantial and varied supply of snack cakes to supplement our earthquake-preparedness kit. I don't know why I didn't think to do this sooner; even canned goods can go bad, but Twinkies never expire.

❖

"What was *that* all about?" Rita Marlow asked as she started the car.

"What do you mean?"

Charles pretended to look through a big construction-pa-per folder Mrs. Braxton had sent home; it contained a sam-pling of his fourth-grade work to date. He'd achieved good citizenship, commendable penmanship, a promotion to Lan-guage Arts. His report card was filled with words like *ex-emplary, excellent,* and *superlative.* And — although it wasn't written down anywhere — he was, in addition, *a lovely boy.* So why was his mother so angry?

"That child we met on the way out," she prompted. "That Dana. Is he really a friend of yours?"

"Yes. Well, kind of."

She glanced at him. "I'd be careful if I were you. About spending too much time with him. I mean, a boy like that."

Why? he wanted to ask, but didn't.

As anxious as his mother had been all night, Charles assumed she'd be racing to get home, so he was surprised when she asked if he wanted to stop at the Dairy Queen. "I think we deserve a little *treat*," she said.

They sat in the car in the parking lot. Rita Marlow sipped a chocolate milk shake and smoked two more cigarettes while Charles ate his Buster Bar.

"I'm proud of you, Charles," she said after they started home again. "Really, I am. And it's nice about Language Arts, you being picked for that. That's really something. I didn't know I gave birth to a genius."

As they pulled into the driveway, she pushed the button on the new garage-door opener. The door lifted slowly, like a theater curtain rising to reveal the scenery for the last act: Garrett Marlow's car.

"But then," she added, "I don't know why I should be surprised." She turned off the car, yanked the keys out of the ignition, grabbed her purse, and started getting out. "Your father is a big goddamn smarty-pants."

There was a bowling bag sitting in the foyer. Charles's father came out of the TV room, holding a bottle of beer.

"Where the hell have you been?" he said.

"Where the hell have *you* been?" she answered.

Charles walked down the hall, brushed his teeth, and went to bed. He closed the door himself that night.

❖

Up until the past half hour or so, the six of them had been having a pleasant enough evening over half-price drinks and small plates at a Northgate Mall restaurant — although, once again, Charles found himself on the receiving end of compliments about the *Seattle Times* article. After finishing his first glass of wine, he finally just gave in and started speaking more freely about the whole experience, including "Flipper Boy."

He kept a careful eye on Alison, trying to gauge her reaction; he'd never shared the details of his early literary fame and was, frankly, looking for some indication that she found these revelations impressive in an endearing, winning sort of way.

"It sounds like you were quite the wunderkind," Robbie's mom said.

"Remarkable," Robbie's dad concurred.

Alison made no comment. She stared at Charles as if looking through a miasmic fog, uncertain whether the person in view was Dr. Jekyll or Mr. Hyde.

Jumping in to fill the silence, the Gurnees delivered their tandem responses:

"What a story . . ." (Gurnee dad).

"So imaginative . . ." (Gurnee mom).

"Oh, hardly," Charles answered. "You know what it was like in '63. We were all preoccupied with science . . ." But then, realizing that no one else at the table had even been *born* in 1963, he dropped that conversational thread.

They moved on to other topics, mostly related to the boys, of course: their collective hopes for this new living situation, the things that needed to be accomplished in the next few months in order to have the house ready in time.

Probably Charles shouldn't have had that third glass of wine.

But it seemed to him that if there was ever an audience to which the question could be put, a circumstance that supported a lively and informed discussion of that question, it was this one.

"Have you ever thought about *why*?" he asked. "Why *these* children, why *our* children? And I'm not talking about the medical-genetic-environmental-dietary-nature-versus-nurture *why*, because as we all know, those kinds of questions get us absolutely *nowhere*. I'm talking about the deeper, more . . ." Running out of words, Charles gestured in a spontaneous, reflexive way; the gesture felt so right that he did it several more times, upturning his hands and arcing them away from each other, as if describing the opening of a book that got bigger and bigger with each unfolding. By the time he stopped, his hands — and the cover-to-cover expanse of the imaginary tome they described — stretched well into the personal spaces of Robbie's mom to his left and Myles's dad to his right.

"I mean," Charles concluded, "I'm just curious: Where do you all stand on the issue of God?"

The question had the unexpected effect of bringing all conversation to a full stop.

"Sorry," Myles's dad said after a few moments. "God?"

"Are you folks practitioners of any kind of organized . . . organization around all that?"

"You mean church?"

"Charles," Alison said quietly. "Maybe this isn't —"

"Well, yes," Charles went on. "Isn't that what church is supposed to do? Organize our notions of God? Give us some kind of an outline, guideline, rubric?"

Myles's dad shrugged and smiled. "I'm not sure about that . . ."

"Have you found it helpful?"

"Found what helpful?"

"Your belief in God. I mean, I'm sorry, maybe I'm misinformed here, but I've always assumed people who go to church believe in God."

"We're Unitarians," Myles's mom put in.

"Ah! Well, I'll spare you my repertoire of Unitarian jokes."

"We've probably heard most of them," Myles's dad said affably.

"I bet you have, but what I'm wondering is: Have you found it a comfort? Your membership in the God Club? The Higher Power Club. Or . . . what *do* Unitarians say? The Good-That-Some-Call-God Club?"

"Charles," Alison interjected.

"Yes," Myles's dad said.

"Really?"

"Yes."

"I'm sorry," Alison said. "Charles, I think —"

"How about you?" Charles said, appealing to the Youngs.

"We don't go to church," Robbie's mom answered, "but it's not out of any kind of lack of faith or religious belief, we were both raised with that, it has more to do with time, really, how we want to spend our Sundays."

"So it's a matter of convenience?"

"Well, when you put it like that . . ."

Alison cleared her throat loudly. She reached across the table, gripped Charles's wrist — a reprimand disguised as a display of affection; there was no mistaking her subtext now — and started making exaggerated, focus-stealing movements, as if their waiter were wandering the Russian steppes.

"I'm curious because *Alison*, for example" — Charles withdrew his hand — "has gone full tilt in that direction. The religious direction, I mean. Have you told your friends about that, honey?"

This brought Alison's diversionary tactics to a halt. Clenching her jaw, she grinned tightly and said, "I'm in the process of converting to Judaism."

"Really?" the Young/Gurnees responded in sync; poster children for passivity and tact.

"Isn't that wonderful?" Charles said. "I find it wonderful.

I mean, all else aside, being Jewish is going to do so much for her sense of humor."

This comment spurred delayed tepid laughter, followed by comments like *Well, it's getting late, I suppose we should be heading home,* and then generalized business involving wallets and a resumed effort to locate their exiled-to-Siberia waiter.

"I've got this," Alison said, insistently waving her credit card as if bidding on some especially coveted auction item.

After the Young/Gurnees were out the door she turned to Charles and hissed, "I cannot *believe* that you did that, Charles, ambushed me like that, embarrassed me — and on a night that was supposed to be a celebration."

"Did *what* to you? We celebrated. Didn't we? I don't understand why you're so upset."

"You don't understand why I'm so upset? You've got to be kidding."

"What? My bringing up the religion thing? Are you ashamed about it?"

"It's not that and you know it. You promised me, you *promised* when I first told you about converting, that you wouldn't make fun. It was cruel. It was spiteful."

"Don't you think you're overreacting just a little bit?"

"Do not do that. Do not use that word. I am *reacting,* and my reactions are perfectly appropriate."

"Well, touché, darling, and I cannot be responsible for your reactions."

Alison inhaled sharply, as if she were about to deliver some stinging retort. Instead, she bowed her head and stopped her mouth with the back of her hand.

"You promised," she repeated softly, and then she stood, gathered her things, and headed away.

"I prefer written correspondence to dramatic exits!" Charles shouted at her back.

He took out his pen and inscribed a short sentence on his cocktail napkin.

You promised too.

Then he signaled the waiter to bring him another glass of wine.

PART THREE

101 Names of God

I dreamed I had a child, and even in the dream I saw it was my life, and it was an idiot, and I ran away. But it always crept onto my lap again, clutched at my clothes. Until I thought, if I could kiss it, whatever in it was my own, perhaps I could sleep. And I bent to its broken face, and it was horrible . . . but I kissed it. I think one must finally take one's life in one's arms.

— Arthur Miller, *After the Fall*

You have asked for and been given enough words — it is now time to live them.

— Meher Baba

Personal Reflections on the Value of Penmanship as a Biographical Tool

Have you ever tracked the progress of your handwriting over the course of your life? If you have access to personal archival writings, you might consider making a study of the way your penmanship has evolved over the years; it can be an interesting undertaking, very revelatory.

In an opinion I share with my father, not nearly enough credence is given to graphology as a supplementary tool in the study of personal development. I think there's an argument to be made that, for those seeking degrees in psychology or psychiatry, required course work should include a class in graphology; how much those students could enhance their understanding by looking at that most direct and revealing expression of the self.

Among the books in my father's library related to this subject is one he especially likes because of its chapter on presidential penmanship. Richard Nixon's mental decline,

Abraham Lincoln's melancholia — all are clearly demonstrated. Even a novice would be able to sense a sickening, a shift.

On Thursday, February 14, 1884, the day his wife, Alice, died, Teddy Roosevelt's diary entry reads as follows:

The script is quavering, the lines broken, the penman too weak to add a period.

If great men are not immune to the effects of personality on penmanship, then surely neither are the rest of us.

You're Carrying Some Slight Magic

It was nearly time for Charles's senior-project assessment meeting (SPAM) with Pam Hamilton and Romy Bertleson, their last before the school holiday known as midwinter break; an unfortunate title, conjuring (as it did for Charles, anyway) that nineteenth-century hymn "In the Bleak Midwinter," with its mellifluous but woeful lyrics: *Snow had fallen, snow on snow, snow on snow* . . . In Seattle, rain was falling, rain on rain . . .

Charles filled the electric kettle with water in case Pam wanted some tea. Outside, another weather system — one that had been drenching the city for days — seemed expressly designed to authenticate Al Gore's dire hypotheses about the effects of global warming.

At this vitamin D–deprived point in the life cycle of Seattle's citizenry, almost everyone who didn't have the good sense to invest in a full-spectrum light-therapy system was stumbling around in a stupor of depression, lethargy, mental cloudiness, and unfulfilled expectations. Charles found that, more than at any other time of year, late January through March was when it was most difficult to avoid feeling as though he had let everyone down. The relentlessly gray, damp outer world revealed the projected truth of one's innermost character flaws, an irremediable structural rot that was the deserved result of being foolish enough to seat one's support beams in soggy ground instead of dry concrete.

Many folks took heart at this time of year in the emergence of daffodils and crocuses, grape hyacinths and snowdrops; to Charles, they were accusatory, shaming reminders of neglect. Years ago, he and Alison had planted all kinds of early-flowering bulbs. Charles knew that there was a point at which he was supposed to dig them up and separate them, but he could never remember when that was, and by the time he did remember, they'd already pushed out of the ground and were huddled together in overcrowded clumps, like tenement families, smacking their yellow- and purple- and white-bonneted heads against one another in the wind with such ferocity that their blooms survived only a couple of days.

Even City Prana's most stalwart, reliable, and rain-proof students seemed to languish. Creative-writing assignments were filled with phrases like *weeping trees* and *lachrymose moss.*

Many students and their families — younger versions of that special class of retirees known as *snowbirds* — fled the Pacific Northwest for an infusion of sun. Some of Charles's colleagues migrated as well.

Pam Hamilton, for example; some years she visited one of her far-flung brood of children and grandchildren; other times she attended the Cowboy Poetry Festival in Elko, Nevada, doing a lot of plein-air sketching and returning with emerging freckles and sketchbooks filled with vividly colored drawings of horses, mountains, and desert plants.

She'd given Cody one of these drawings years ago — a herd of amethyst-colored wild mustangs, grazing and becalmed before the backdrop of a fantastically colored western sky. Cody couldn't stop staring at it when Charles brought him into Pam's art room once for a visit, so she'd had it framed and given it to him when they moved him into his first group home. The picture hung in his bedroom there, and in the three subsequent bedrooms he'd occupied since then, four homes in ten years, a visual touchstone through all the upheavals that Alison felt compelled to put Cody through — always with the best of intentions, always with the hope that the next situation would be better.

None of Cody's homes were *bad* in the sense of being unfit, abusive, or criminal, thank God; never did they have to move him because they were faced with one of the worst-case scenarios featured in those newspaper exposés Charles was always finding.

What drove Ali, what she really hoped, of course, was that *Cody* would be better, that these perennial change-ups in environment and personnel would spark some transformation. They never did. Cody, like those wild purple ponies, remained fixed, static, as if he too were held within a mitered wooden frame.

Charles wondered what Pam was doing over midwinter break this year.

His plans mostly involved helping Alison and the Young/Gurnees ready the house for the boys' moving-in day, which was set for mid-April.

Beyond that, he'd be grading papers and watching DVDs of films that took place in sun-drenched settings. It was the perfect time of year to revisit those Merchant Ivory adaptations, stories in which repressed, tightly wound Englishmen traveled to the Italian countryside, shed their inhibitions and their waistcoats, and magically transformed into skinny-dipping, freewheeling hedonists.

❖

"There's this new movement called photolanthropy," Romy was saying, "photography that draws attention to a cause or an issue . . ."

You mean photojournalism, Charles almost said, but he stopped himself; *photolanthropy* was a catchy word, one that would certainly be a dashing addition to the common-usage dictionary.

"You have to make yourself invisible, let the camera do the work," Romy continued.

"What happened to that woman you were having trouble with?" Pam asked.

"Mrs. D'Amati? Oh, I thought I already told you. She and . . ." — Romy darted her eyes to Charles — "another artist have started to collaborate. I'm hoping to get a portrait of the two of them working together. It just hasn't happened yet."

"Well, you've already got a lot of terrific images to choose from," Pam said. "As far as I can tell, you're right on track." She glanced at Charles. "How is the written component of the project coming together?"

"I'm still planning on writing American Sentence captions for the photos . . ."

Charles knew he was being distant, preoccupied, not at his senior-project-adviser best, essentially forcing Pam to

conduct the meeting without his help. But in his own defense, he was acting as adviser on *seven* other senior projects this year, a record number. Surely it wasn't a sin to coast
a bit on this particular occasion. Pam was the one who'd
suggested they do this as a team, after all. She was the one
who'd said co-advising would allow them to *share the load.*

He needed someone to share the load right now. It had
finally dawned on him just what he had signed up for in the
next ten days: a remodeling assault on Perfect Pinehurst.

The magnitude of what lay ahead — Merchant Ivory films
notwithstanding — suddenly fell on him like a circus tent
collapsing under the weight of a monsoon.

"Yes. Right on track," he blurted, sweeping Romy's paperwork into a pile and thrusting it in her direction.

Pam and Romy stared at him. Charles realized that he'd
not been following their conversation and had perhaps spoken inappropriately. A compliment was in order.

"You're very gifted, Romy," he said.

"Oh, I don't think it's me," she replied. "There's something Diane Arbus said, about how having this thing" — she
indicated her camera, which was positioned, as usual, at the
center of her chest — "gives you an advantage. She said, 'It's
like you're carrying some slight magic.'"

Romy smiled, radiantly.

Charles's breath grew suddenly shallow; he found himself staring. Romy's use of the word *magic* — unusual in this
setting — along with the measured, mature emphasis she'd
used when speaking the quote, her satsuma aura, and the
fact that she *so* resembled Emmy had the unexpected and
embarrassing effect of bringing tears to his eyes.

"Will you excuse me?" he said, abruptly taking up his
school satchel and flimsy umbrella and heading for the door.

"I completely forgot that I have an appointment. Please, if you don't mind, finish up without me, and then, Ms. Hamilton, could you lock up when you're done?" He left without waiting for a reply.

Language Arts class did not prove to be the earthshattering experience Charles expected, although it was fundamentally different from the rest of the school day in at least one way:

Before lunch that first day, ten *exceptional* children trooped to the library — no hall passes required — and joined Mrs. Braxton, who was already seated, not behind a desk but in one of eleven chairs that were arranged in a *circle,* each chair seat containing a pristine copy of *Language Arts: A New Approach to Discovering the Joys of Reading and the Elements of Creative Writing.*

Mrs. Braxton did not direct the arriving students to any particular place; they could sit, she said, wherever they wanted.

Initially, Charles found this egalitarian setup and radical freedom distressing. There was nowhere to hide from either Mrs. Braxton or his fellow classmates; he'd had quite enough of center stage at this point and had begun to feel nostalgic for his era of academic invisibility. He had other concerns as well: Were they supposed to sit somewhere different every day? Was the place each chose to sit some kind of a test?

For the first week, these questions filled him with anxiety. If being chosen for Language Arts was supposed to be some kind of *honor,* he'd rather do without.

As time passed, however, and it became clear that most children preferred to occupy the same seat day after day (especially Astrida, who consistently rushed to station herself at Mrs. Braxton's side) and weren't penalized for it, he relaxed, grateful for the fact that, given this configuration, *everyone* was in the front row, *everyone* was noticed. In a sense, *everyone* was a teacher's pet.

The class format was simple and unvarying: Mrs. Braxton greeted the children as they got settled and then directed them to open their textbooks to the day's lesson, which had titles like "Story Basics: Protagonist and Problem," "Conflict: The Heart of Story," and "Character Attributes: Dreamers and Doers." They began by reading a story aloud, one paragraph at a time, going around the circle so that everyone got a turn; this was followed by a discussion of the accompanying study questions, vocabulary words, and concepts.

The stories themselves weren't that great — Charles still preferred the fantastic narratives and characters of comic books and sci-fi/horror movies — but they weren't bad either, *Reader's Digest*–type excerpts from English-language classics like *Huckleberry Finn, Uncle Tom's Cabin,* even *Moby-Dick.* More and more, he found himself looking forward to Language Arts.

There were never any tests, and there was a definite sense that Language Arts class questions didn't have right or wrong answers.

In your opinion, what makes a character heroic?

Who are the heroes in your life? Do you consider yourself to be a hero? Why or why not?

What does it mean to be a dreamer? What does it mean to be a doer? Which are you?

What is an example of an internal conflict? What is an example of an external conflict? In your opinion, which kind of conflict makes for the best kind of story?

What is a climax? Give an example of a climax in a story you've read or a movie you've seen.

Have you ever wanted something really badly? Was there

*something in the way of getting what you wanted? How far would
you go to get something you really want?*

The other great surprise of Language Arts was Mrs. Braxton herself. A completely different side of her personality
emerged during those thirty minutes; she was calm, relaxed,
congenial — more like a tea-party hostess than a despot.

A protagonist is someone you root for. Pro = *"for, in favor of."*

An antagonist is the protagonist's enemy. Anti = *"against, opposed to."*

Astrida raised her hand. "Why isn't it *anti-agonist?*"

"What a good question, Astrida!" Mrs. Braxton replied. "I
can't say that I know the answer to that . . ." She shrugged,
sighed, and added with obvious fondness, "Ah, well. You will
find, children, that this English language of ours is full of idiosyncrasies."

The best and brightest had no idea what *idiosyncrasies*
meant, nor did they care; they were too busy being bowled
over by the fact that Mrs. Braxton had just admitted to a
roomful of fourth-graders that she didn't know everything.

Describe yourself using the prefixes pro- *and* anti-.

*I am pro-American! I am anti-Communist! I am pro-math! I
am anti–fish sticks!*

Sometimes the discussions got a little rowdy, but Mrs.
Braxton did nothing to squelch the enthusiasm so long as
the children took turns, raised their hands, and listened with
open minds to everyone's opinion. She actually appeared
happy — even happier than when Charles produced a perfect row of Palmer loops. What a *relief* it was to know that he
and Mr. Austin Norman Palmer weren't the only sources of
pleasure in Mrs. Braxton's life.

Language Arts remained enjoyable right up to the Friday
when class began not with a story but with Mrs. Braxton in-
structing the children to turn to page 60 and read aloud the

guidelines listed under "Unit One Assignment: Writing Your First Short Story."

"But . . . what is our story supposed to be *about?*" Astrida asked.

Mrs. Braxton smiled, tolerantly. "Well, one of the things we all seem to agree on is that good stories feature an extraordinary protagonist, so why don't you begin there?" Astrida opened her mouth to protest, but Mrs. Braxton held up her hand and addressed the group at large. "Don't worry, you'll have plenty of time."

It was at that moment Charles realized there was a downside to questions that had no right or wrong answers.

He and Dana continued to meet in the lunchroom, peeling icing and practicing unusual approaches to the Palmer Method, but as the days passed and Charles remained unable to come up with an *extraordinary protagonist,* he left Language Arts class feeling worried and often arrived at Dana's table subdued and preoccupied.

Dana seemed to sense this, and he began bringing a new fervency to their noontime lessons. "Let's make *loopuhzzz!*" he suggested. And by *loopuhzzz* he meant any kind of writing.

"Okay. Try this." Charles demonstrated. "Start to make a regular loop, so go up, but then stop at the top, and when you come back down, don't let the loop be fat. Make it skinny."

"Ha! Not fat," Dana stage-whispered, "like Mrs. Braxton."

"Then put a dot up here, like . . . a cherry on a sundae."

"Or a sun."

"Son?"

"Sun!" Dana repeated happily. He added a series of jagged lines. "See?"

"Oh, right," Charles replied, but he wasn't seeing the sun. The addition of Dana's zigzags emanating from the dot instead reminded him of the RKO radio tower at the start of one of his favorite horror movies, *The Thing*. Donnie Bothwell was the person who'd informed him that the weird clicking noise accompanying the image of the radio tower wasn't part of the movie soundtrack but Morse code spelling out *An RKO Radio Picture*. Donnie had a merit badge in Signaling.

"I'll try now!" Dana proclaimed.

He inscribed his version of a lowercase *i*, going slowly and smoothly through the up-down part, and then executing the dot by stabbing at the paper as if wielding an épée. His aim wasn't perfect, but he had the right idea. He practiced making more *i*'s, soon filling another page in his Big Chief drawing tablet. Charles made a mental note to bring another one to school soon; Dana went through them so quickly.

Dana had come a long way with his penmanship — but he only demonstrated this when the two of them were alone together in the cafeteria. Charles always wondered why Dana never revealed to Mrs. Braxton, or the rest of the children in room 104, how good he could be.

To keep himself busy while Dana practiced, Charles started making a list: *it, is, in, if, ill* . . .

"What you do?" Dana asked. Simple dots had become too boring; he'd taken to topping his *i*'s with energetically scribbled orbs that were the size of dimes.

Inch, itch . . . "Huh?"

Dana continued. "In that class. What you do in that class when you go away with *Ass*-trid?"

IQ, idea, Iron Man . . .

"You mean Language Arts?"

"Yes, that place you go with the other smart kids."

"I'm not smart," Charles replied. *Invisible, instant, insane* . . .

"Yes you *are* smart, Char-Lee. You best at *loopuhz*. Better than Brax the Ax!"

Invincible, interior, interrupt . . . Charles thought about telling Dana that just because he could make loops didn't mean he was smart, but he had a feeling it would hurt Dana's feelings.

Intelligence.

"We're supposed to write a story."

"Supposed to write a story. Supposed to write a story about what?"

"I don't know. That's the problem. A hero. Somebody special. Somebody you root for . . . I can't think of anything good to write about."

"You'll think of something, Char-Lee," Dana said, giving a final spiraling flourish to a dot that was the size of a half-dollar. "You'll think of something good to write about for your story. I root for *you*."

The collaborators do not speak to each other; they do not look each other in the eye; their time together is limited to thirty minutes twice a week. They sit side by side behind a white trifold screen that will gradually be transformed through their efforts. Sometimes they finish a particular section in only two sessions; sometimes it takes longer.

Mrs. D'Amati arrives. She might gesture to Romy, in which case Romy delivers magazines, scissors, and adhesives; she might prefer solitude, and on those occasions Giorgia busies herself inscribing long rows of loops, up-down, and bedspring ovals on any of the many textures and colors of plain paper made available to her. She might do a little of both activities during the hour she works alone. By her choice of pictures, Mrs. D'Amati determines the theme of these constructions.

When Cody arrives, he walks quickly to Mrs. D'Amati's table, sits next to her at a distance of about four feet, and starts tearing whatever is available: magazines, Mrs. D'Amati's practice pages. Romy is there to help; she glues the scissored bits and torn strips to the screen as directed.

At some point in every class, Mrs. D'Amati makes at least one attempt to get Cody to take up a pen or pencil and write; he refuses these overtures.

Mrs. D'Amati leaves. Cody keeps going.

The end result: large triptych collages jam-packed with alternating stripes of color and text — irregularly shaped images and bits of handwriting.

Babies and mothers, fathers and daughters, baked goods, flowers, churches, fields, teachers and students, soldiers, sisters, and all things bridal: dresses, gloves, veils, ribbons, shoes, bouquets, and kissing couples.

Anyone who looks closely begins to suspect that buried within this visual cacophony are heroes and villains; comedies; tragedies; commingled mysteries waiting to be solved.

Things Like Fingers

The Youngs, the Gurnees, and Charles and Alison gathered at the Pinehurst house at eight o'clock in the morning; the plan for the weekend was to put in two ten-hour days.

As soon as everyone arrived, Alison presented them all with copies of her SUGGESTED DIVISION OF LABOR list. There were three major tasks that needed doing in advance of the upcoming deliveries: repainting all the rooms with zero–volatile-organic-compound paint, pulling up the old stained and mildewed carpeting throughout the house, and deep cleaning with an assortment of nontoxic products.

It turned out that Ted Gurnee was a handy sort of fellow with a varied skill set. He seemed to know a little about everything related to construction: electricity, plumbing, carpentry. He was also meticulous and detail-minded, someone who obviously thrived on *sweating the small stuff* and so was forever finding small, noncritical, but still (in his mind at least) important tasks — none of which were on Alison's list.

Within a few hours, it was obvious that Ted's preoccupations with things like polishing door hardware to a high gloss and acquiring matching switch-plate covers were driving Alison crazy. *Ted,* she kept saying, *I think it's more important right now that we focus on accomplishing the large, overarching jobs; there will be plenty of time later for small projects,* to which Ted always replied, *Oh, absolutely, I agree, this won't take long at all, I'll be done in ten minutes,* a sure indication that whatever it was would take at least an hour and a half and involve several unscheduled trips to Home Depot.

Ted's affable cluelessness when it came to Alison's management style caused Charles to develop a certain fondness for him; he began acting as Ted's ad hoc apprentice, accompanying him on his hardware-store jaunts, pairing up with him once they returned, taking lessons in Wiring and Plumbing 101, often in direct violation of Alison's work assignments. In addition to enjoying Ted's company, Charles found it perversely rewarding, thwarting Alison in this way, seeing the look on her face every time he made his own decision about what to do and when to do it.

Although Charles had written a brief note of apology —

Dear Alison, I'm sorry if my comments about your conversion activities upset you and/or seemed insensitive. I hope becoming a Jew brings you every happiness. Mazel tov. Sincerely, C.

— she hadn't responded, and he could tell that she was still angry. Her phony cordiality in front of the others riled him, inciting what he knew to be a completely immature desire to aggravate, but in Charles's opinion he had as much of a right to immaturity in this situation as she did.

Of course, they'd have plenty of time to argue over the coming week, if they chose: the Youngs and the Gurnees had traditional jobs, but Charles (on vacation) and Alison (self-employed) could work at the house from eight to five

Monday through Friday, adding to their labors the roles of contractor managers and shipment-receiving clerks.

On Monday, Charles made a point of arriving half an hour early. Alison wasn't the only one who had a key. He was already pulling up staples in the living-room floor when she arrived. They did not greet each other.

The house was large; it was easy enough to stay separated as the week wore on. The delivery people and contractors came and went; Charles let Alison handle them.

Midweek, Charles started to wonder where Alison's beau was during all this. If he was such an important character in her life, why the hell wasn't he *here,* helping?

He decided to ask.

"Where's your friend?"

"My friend?"

"That guy you've been seeing."

"You mean my *fiancé?*"

"Yes. Him."

"You're asking now? After all this time?"

About an hour later, she sought him out in the basement, where he was scrubbing down the concrete floor, and added, "He's in California, teaching a weeklong aikido intensive."

Charles wondered why Steven/Jackie/Jean-Claude had to go all the way to California; it was plenty intense right here.

They worked every day, holding space and silence between them, until around four o'clock, when some combination of the Young/Gurnees arrived, there was a discussion of what had been done, what still needed doing, and then Charles went home, exhausted, too tired even for Merchant Ivory.

"What are you doing in here?" Alison asked toward the end of the week, finding Charles in Cody's room opening up a recently purchased can of paint that was not part of the supply Alison had selected (although it *was* zero–VOC).

After spending years in various room whose walls were inevitably some shade of dingy white, Cody could tolerate a little color, Charles felt, something soothing; he'd selected a deep powdery blue that he thought would go nicely with Pam's mustang picture.

"What does it look like I'm doing?" He didn't mean to sound snippy, but this unending assault, this tension between them — it was exhausting.

He expected some witty and/or cutting rejoinder; instead, she slunk off to another corner of the house. Charles was still painting Cody's room when he heard her leave.

Alison had brought a radio and kept it constantly tuned to a local NPR affiliate, one that was light on music and heavy on conversation. After she left, he switched to the Best Hits of the '60s, '70s, and '80s and, experiencing a surge of energy, worked through the night and well into the wee hours of Sunday morning.

❖

Biographers make informed, factual, well-researched connections between their subjects' lives and work: *The writing of So-and-So during this period took a dark turn, likely because of the cataclysmic occurrences within the family circle . . .* and so on.

My father cannot provide a subjective biography of his own life; he has *designed* his memories, built them into a structure that supports the whole.

Memory — uncorrected, uncorroborated, and (by its very nature) unreliable — is what allows us to retroactively create the blueprints of our lives, because it is often impossible to make sense of our lives when we're inside them, when the narratives are still unfolding: *This can't be happening. Why is this happening? Why is this happening* now?

Only by looking backward are we able answer those questions, only through the assist of memory. And who knows how memory will answer? Who will it blame? Who will it forgive?

Perhaps the most important character in everyone's life — and the one with whom we have the most ambiguous relationship — is memory itself.

In my father's mind, all the most significant elements of his fourth-grade year were irreversibly grafted together in a single night and the next morning.

A weeknight? A weekend?

Let's make it a Saturday.

❖

The Marlows were fighting. Charles took up his flashlight and tried to distract himself with images of more benevolent-looking monsters: the sweet-faced children in *Life* magazine with Janet Leigh and the eleven red fezzes.

THE FULL STORY OF THE DRUG THALIDOMIDE

Outside his door, muttered, guttural incomprehensibilities alternated with articulate savageries:

. . . *fucking selfish* . . .

. . . *turning him against me* . . .

A thump, a slam, a gasp, a grunt . . .

THE 5,000 DEFORMED BABIES

He pulled his blanket closer, resettled his crucifix over his heart.

Although he'd survived countless other monstrosities — vampires, werewolves, giant mutant ants, radioactive blobs, pod people, creatures risen from black lagoons and Japanese seas — they'd been viewed from a safe distance.

A TRAIL OF HEARTBREAK

Charles didn't dare come out of his room; if the *sounds* were terrifying, what he might *see* was too horrifying to contemplate.

In Arizona, Mrs. Sherri Finkbine discovered suddenly that her unborn child would be cheated of its arms and legs.

If he needed to go to the bathroom, he was prepared: he'd appropriated a Tupperware container and placed it under his bed.

Thalidomide, deformity, phocomelia, seal limbs, stumps . . .

When his mother removed her shoes before she tiptoed down the hall and closed his door, she wasn't just quieting her footsteps; it was the beginning of a skin-shedding . . .

Some think the babies should be mercifully killed.

The sounds were a symphony played over and over; its structure never varied.

YOU CAN'T KEEP YOUR GODDAMN MOUTH SHUT
YOU CAN'T KEEP YOUR FUCKING HANDS OFF

Charles turned the pages, studied the photos illuminated by the bilious, quavering glow of his plastic flashlight.

Things like fingers extrude from odd places . . .

It was easy to tell when the war was over — it ended not with atomic explosions or bloodcurdling screams but with the sounds of his father storming into the night and his mother weeping as she went to bed.

The final pages of the August 10, 1962, issue of *Life* featured an especially odd pairing.

On the left: a two-year-old German girl fitted with a vest-like contraption with two steel arms capped with mittenlike appendages. (Looking closely, Charles saw them: the *things like fingers,* just beneath her armpit.)

On the right: a smiling, aproned mother, arms and hands intact, bracing the sides of a box of Albers New Deluxe Flapjack Mix: *Like No Other!* And in small print beneath: *Visit the Carnation Exhibit at Century 21 Exposition, Seattle World's Fair/ April 21 to October 21, 1962.*

❖

Sunday morning, Charles awoke to the smells of coffee and buttered toast. He padded down the hall and found his father standing at the kitchen stove, squinting through the smoke from his cigarette, cooking an army breakfast special: canned corned-beef hash topped with two fried eggs.

"Morning, Chuck. Hope you're hungry."

Aside from being unshaven and looking tired, Garrett Marlow appeared the same as always. His feet were bare; he wore pajama bottoms and a sleeveless T-shirt that showed off his arm muscles and the tattoo he'd gotten in Korea. There was no trace of whatever he had transformed into the night before.

"There you go."

"Thanks, Dad."

His father poured a cup of coffee, lit another cigarette, sat down at the table, and opened up the Sunday paper.

"You want the funnies?" he asked.

"Sure."

Charles listened for any indication that his mother was up and about. But aside from the dead-leaf sounds of his father turning newspaper pages, the house was eerily still.

"Your mother's not feeling well," Garrett Marlow finally said. "Touch of the flu, so it'll be just you and me at Mass."

"Okay."

Charles was used to this deception; he understood that, behind the door of his parents' room, his mother had not yet changed back into human form.

Around five in the morning, Charles finished painting Cody's room. Too tired to drive, he lay down on the living-room sofa and slept for a few hours. Then he headed home — but not before making a quick stop at the grocery store to pick up Cody's housewarming gift of noodles and magazines.

He stopped at the curb to collect yesterday's mail. There was the usual array of bills and non-Cody-approved catalogs, but among these items was a card, addressed by hand, originally sent to him at City Prana and presumably forwarded to him here at home by the school secretary. The return address bore the name S. McGucken.

Charles's knees began to tremble; he sat down on the curb. His hands were shaking as well. Eventually, using one of his keys as a letter opener, he carefully razored around the edge of the envelope flap.

> Dear Charles,
>
> I hope this letter finds you, and finds you well.
>
> I was delighted to see your name and photograph in the recent *Seattle Times* article about the students of Nellie Goodhue School.
>
> I'm not sure if you will remember my son, Dana, but he was a classmate of yours, and at the time, the two of you struck up a friendship.

I've thought of you often over the years and wanted to say how pleased I was to learn of your success as a teacher. I remember well how very patient you were with Dana; it is no surprise that you ended up finding your calling in the teaching profession.

I'm sure your life is very full, but if you would ever care to meet, I live at the Foss Home in North Seattle and would be delighted to offer you coffee or tea some afternoon at your convenience.

Again, Charles, I send my congratulations to you and wish you and yours all the very best.

Sincerely yours,
Sylvie McGucken

How could anyone *not* remember Dana? It seemed inconceivable.

Did Bradley and Mitch remember him? Provided they were still alive, which somehow seemed doubtful. Charles imagined that they'd graduated to criminal careers and then met with violent ends, but perhaps that wasn't their fate. Perhaps they'd become insurance salesmen, upstanding members of the Rotary Club, toiling away to end malaria; maybe they even belonged to the country club where Charles had bartended.

Charles's attention was redirected by the sound of a truck coming up the street: it was his next-door neighbor Gil Bjornson. He got up, stiffly, and waved.

Gil rolled down his window. "Hey, Charles! You mind being my set of eyes? I need to back this thing in."

"Sure, no problem." Charles stationed himself in front of the garage door and used hand signals to help Gil maneuver his newest restoration project into the driveway.

It was probably the most hopeless-looking vehicle yet, barely a shell. The only clue to its former glory was a small silver icon on the right front wheel well: a sleek, stylized horse in profile, running with such speed that all four of its legs were off the ground, as if it were flying.

Gil got out of the truck. "Thanks, neighbor," he said, shaking Charles's hand. "Good to see you."

"You too, Gil. So, what do we have here?"

"Mustang, 1970 Mach One." Gil held up a preemptive hand, as if Charles were about to ask something. "You don't wanna know, but trust me, after we get this baby restored, it'll be worth every penny."

"I believe you." Charles strolled around the heap of metal that would be his regular view from the kitchen window for possibly the next decade. There were few traces of the poppy-red paint that must have once graced the car's exterior; it had no driver's side door; its transmission was sitting in the back seat, on upholstery that at one time had probably been a pristine white but was now riddled with grime and grease.

"Four-twenty-eight Cobra Jet . . . ," Gil said as he unhitched the trailer.

This made no sense to Charles, but he could tell that Gil was elated. "Sounds like you found yourself a treasure," he said.

"Had to drive all the way to Ellensburg to get it, but yeah, it's a treasure, all right. I haven't told Erik about it yet. It's a surprise." Gil stood up and stretched. "Thanks again for your help."

"You bet. No problem. Have fun." Charles started heading to his front porch.

"Say," Gil called out, "you planning on being around this summer?"

Charles found this question amusing, as he and Gil had been neighbors for twenty years.

"I'll be here."

"Well, we'd love to have an extra set of hands on this thing."

"Oh, that's nice of you, Gil, but I don't really know much about . . . what you do."

"Hell, Charlie, most of what we do, in the beginning, anyway, is apply tons of elbow grease. You'd do fine at that. You could even bring Cody. I've been meaning to ask how he's doing."

"We're moving him into a new house, actually. Not too far. Over in Pinehurst."

"That's good. Must be hard, what you and Alison have had to go through . . ."

"We've had some challenges, it's true."

"Well, you do your best. It's not like these kids come with an owner's manual."

Charles laughed.

"You want some coffee? I texted Erik and he's on his way. I'm sure he'd love to see you."

Charles considered. What exactly was waiting inside that he needed to rush to? Piles of boxes, a nearly empty crawlspace, another DVD from Netflix, student papers . . .

"Sure," he said. "Why not?"

"You take it regular?"

"Sounds good."

Charles had forgotten that Gil was originally from New York City, so when he came back outside and delivered the mug of coffee *regular,* Charles discovered that it was generously laced with cream and heavily sugared. He drank it anyway.

Notice of Proposed
Land-Use Action

It was late afternoon. They were putting the final touches on Cody's room.

"Can you find his comforter, Charles?" Alison asked as the bed sheet billowed and snapped. "I think it's in that box over there."

It had been a frantic day, one that began early: Cody and Robbie and Myles were roused, readied, and loaded into the van for a daylong outing with their caregivers; once they were gone, their parents, along with Robbie's and Myles's siblings and friends, moved the boys' furniture and personal items out of the old group home and into Pinehurst Palace — an efficient team of benevolent burglars.

Everyone agreed that it was important to execute this transition with sensitivity and care. It was decided they would tell the boys that, after their trip to the riding center and the park and the pea patch, they'd be coming home to a new place. *You're going to like it so much!* But of course, there was no way to know whether this made any sense or how the boys would react when faced with the reality. In each mother/father unit, one parent had a consistently better track record in terms of meltdown management, so these three parents would form the welcoming committee. Charles would be departing along with Robbie's mom and Myles's dad. It was really for the best.

Alison received Cody's freshly laundered, threadbare Toy Story comforter from Charles and cast it onto his bed. A few days ago, standing in Bed, Bath, and Beyond, they had seriously debated buying a new comforter to commemorate Cody's legal advancement into adulthood but had decided against it. One small step at a time.

With the exception of the wall color, Cody's new room was a near exact duplicate of his old one. They'd arranged his furniture in the same configuration as before: twin bed against the wall; cowboy light on the nightstand; small shelf stocked with board books, some still bearing the bite marks of Cody's pre-changeling, teething self; and, hanging on the wall opposite his headboard, where he could see it first thing every morning, Pam's pastel drawing of purple ponies.

"How's that girl's project coming along?" Alison said.

"Which girl?"

"The one who's taking pictures? Pam told me that one of your students is photographing Cody's art classes."

"She did?"

"You needn't look so shocked. Pam and I are still friends."

"I know that."

"Have you seen the photos?"

"Some. She's showing them at the fundraiser in May."

"That's always a nice event."

"You could come, if you want."

Alison rubbed her eyes. "Maybe. I'm not sure."

After Ali spread out the comforter, they started tucking in the edges; tight, military-style, the way Cody required.

Charles made a last quick sweep of the floor with the broom; Ali plumped the pillows, stood back from the bed, surveyed the room, and tossed a couple of small moving boxes into the big one. The gesture seemed to drain her of energy. She sighed heavily.

"You ready for a break?" Charles asked.

"Yes." She sat down on Cody's bed, smoothed her hands across its surface.

"I brought wine; you want a glass?"

She sighed again. "Sure."

Charles went into the kitchen and pulled a couple of plastic juice glasses out of the cupboard. In the other two bedrooms, he could hear the Youngs and the Gurnees murmuring to each other in quiet, exhausted voices.

He returned to Cody's room, sat on the bed with Ali, and opened the wine (another bottle recovered from the wine rack, which had emptied significantly since the start of the school year): *Santa Margherita*, a pinot grigio. Margaret was the patron saint of women in childbirth.

"This color," Alison said, her eyes ranging around the room in invisible curving lines, "it's nice. Very peaceful."

Charles knew that she meant this belated compliment as an apology. "Thank you," he replied.

There were twenty-year-old photos somewhere, in a drawer probably, of the two of them getting Cody's room ready in the storybook cottage before he was born: painting the floor, stenciling the walls, hanging the mobile, laying the cross-stitched comforter over the arm of the antique wicker rocking chair. They'd built the bassinet and the swing. They childproofed the electrical outlets, locked up the poisons. They planted bulbs, an herb garden, cherry tomatoes, an Italian plum tree. All those gestures of tenderness for the guest they had yet to meet.

They did many of those same things again in preparation for Emmy's arrival — a different room, a different set of colors, but with regenerated, hopeful hearts.

"Do you think we'll ever be able to die?" Alison asked. Her voice was without affect, as tired as Charles had ever heard it. "Do you think we'll ever be able to let go as long as he's like this?"

"Of course not," he answered.

"Immortality it is, then," she said, letting herself lean against him.

Charles moved an arm around her and settled his palm on the bed beside her hip.

If things went as planned, their son would turn twenty-one years old while living in this house; he would wake up looking at Pam's drawing of wild horses on the day he turned thirty; he would be smashing ramen noodles and tearing magazine pages here when he turned forty. He would perhaps spend all the birthdays of the rest of his life here. *And what,* Charles wondered, *will those years add up to? A life has to mean something, doesn't it?*

They continued to sit, still and speechless. Their clothes were damp with sweat from the exertions of the day, and Alison gave off a scent Charles hadn't smelled for years: an exotic, thin-skinned fruit that was slightly overripe.

He became aware that Alison had shifted her gaze so that she was looking at his chest; he'd undone the first few buttons of his shirt at some point during the day.

"You still wear that," Alison said flatly. "After all this time."

"Of course."

Gently, she lifted the necklace away from his skin, lightly fingering the paper clips and translucent colored beads.

"I forget sometimes," she said, "how sentimental you are."

◆

It was 1995. Charles and Alison had been married for seven years.

Cody was three.

No longer talking, socializing, or imitating; no longer making eye contact; not smiling, not laughing, not toilet-trained, not interested in other children; eating only certain foods; sometimes eating his own feces.

The diagnosis of autism had already been offered up several times, but Alison would not accept it.

Or, rather, she'd accepted the diagnosis but not what it meant.

She was pregnant and having an ultrasound and she wanted to bring Cody.

He won't understand, Alison, Charles said. *The setting is unfamiliar; there will be too many new people, too much stimulation.*

But she fought him. She fought him all the time now, whenever he dared to question decisions involving Cody. A pattern had been established: he proposed, she rejected; he suggested, she modified, and Charles kept asking himself how he had lost all voting rights when it came to their son.

Cody now shrank from his father's touch. No one knew why. Perhaps Charles exuded some energy — like a radio signal — that Cody found upsetting. Perhaps Charles's fears were palpable, his love for Cody too desperate.

And now Cody was going to have a little brother or sister, and Alison felt it was important to include him as much as possible, even if that meant the occasional disruption of his routine.

Can't you see that, Charles? she'd argued. *Yes, he might have a tantrum; in fact, he probably will, but what is it you're really worried about? Disrupting Cody's schedule or being looked at? Being judged? If people are going to be educated about children like Cody, they have to encounter them in everyday situations.*

But this isn't *an everyday situation,* Charles longed to shout, *this is us, getting a chance to see our new baby for the first time. Can we not have that experience for ourselves, just the two of us? Can we not for this one moment — I'm not talking about pretending or denying — can we not just, you and I, without complication, enjoy some peace? Can we not give all our attention to this child? This he or she who is already doomed to be banished to the suburbs of our attention?*

Alison had recently purchased noise-reduction headphones for Cody; these sometimes helped when he was in situations with unfamiliar sounds. They weren't helping today; Cody had planted himself in the hospital foyer and was screaming.

Charles and Alison flanked him, but they couldn't take his hands, so what was Charles to do but pick him up — a big, manhandling bully — and carry him up the stairs while Alison glared at every person who looked at them askance.

No, we are not child beaters, her expression said. *No, we are not refrigerator parents. And no, we will not hide, we will not cower; we will fight to be seen as a family because that is our right.*

All Charles could see was that their son was clearly very unhappy.

Finally, they checked in at the ultrasound suite, raising their voices so their names could be heard above Cody's anguished screams. They made their way to the small room, where the technician tried to be kind, tried to engage Cody in conversation. She offered him a sucker; he threw it in her face.

And then Alison was on the table, belly bared, saying, *Cody, Cody, Cody,* and Charles had to keep him from biting her, hitting her. *Look, Cody,* Ali went on. *Look here, you're going to get to see a picture of your baby brother or sister on this TV. Look!*

The technician slathered the mound of Ali's belly with an orange gel that Cody instantly found irresistible, so again Charles had to manhandle him, and then, *finally,* it was beginning.

The screen lit up. Cody fell silent.

The auditory assault had gone on for so long that Charles didn't trust Cody's sudden compliance, although he recognized this state of being; when he shut off quickly like this, it was because he was truly engaged in something, making his parents' next worry *Will we ever be able to get him out of here?*

Alison smiled at Charles as if to say, *See? Didn't I tell you it would all be fine?*

Cody was staring at the screen. *Do you want to know the sex?* the technician asked. In unison, Alison said no and Charles said yes and then they laughed — but quietly, so as not to disturb Cody's concentration.

See, Cody? Charles said. *The baby is floating, like you when you go swimming. The baby loves to swim too, and when the baby comes out, you'll be able to swim together.*

Cody's body had relaxed. Charles wondered if he dared release his hold. Cody seemed so calm, and Charles's arms were tiring, so he set Cody down, and then they were standing together, in close, light physical contact.

Let's get a nice picture for you, the technician said, moving the wand around Alison's belly. *Everything looks perfectly normal, by the way, no cause for worry.*

I'm not worried, Alison said.

The tech pointed at the screen: *See? There's the baby's*

*head, there's the heart, there's the femur . . . I'm just going to take
a little measurement . . .*

Is it all right, Alison asked, *if our son touches the screen?*

No! Charles wanted to say. Cody might push something
over, flip a crucial switch, press the wrong button, but Cody
was already reaching up, touching the place where the technician had pointed to the baby's head.

His hand lingered there, completely still, chubby fingers spread wide against the screen — *Gaaaaaah,* he murmured — and when he withdrew his hand, his fingerprints
remained, and his face reflected a rare lightness, almost
transcendence. Charles thought of J. D. Salinger's *Seymour:
An Introduction,* about how, after placing a hand on his baby
sister's downy pate, Seymour Glass became happily scarred
for life.

With a leap of spirit that Charles hadn't felt for years, not
even at his wedding, he thought: *Maybe this baby will be our
salvation, drawing out of our mystery child something that neither
Alison nor I have succeeded in accessing; maybe this baby —*

(*It's a girl!* read the Post-it note the ultrasound tech
pressed into his palm as they left.)

— maybe this baby girl will save us all.

◆

"Do you regret it?" Charles asked as he poured the wine.

"Regret what?"

"Our life together, our marriage."

"How can you ask that?"

"It hasn't exactly been an easy life."

She accepted her glass, swirled its contents, took an expansive inhale, and then sighed. "I don't think you can regret anything once you have children."

"How do you mean?"

She shrugged. "Well, everything you've done up to that moment, every detour, every . . ." Charles could read her mind; he knew she'd pulled up short before saying the word *mistake.* "Every *choice* . . . it's all led to getting them. To regret anything, to wish any of it changed, would mean a different outcome, wouldn't it?"

How Charles yearned to get drunk with his ex-wife and explore this issue, but suddenly she was standing, shaking her head, saying, *No, what am I thinking, I can't stay, I'm sorry.* She needed to rush home, take a shower, get a second wind, and then hurry back so she could have Cody's favorite meal ready.

Thanks again, said the mother of Charles's children as she hastened away. *I'll take a rain check on the wine.*

Charles left shortly afterward, walking stiffly to his car (the muscles of his thighs, arms, and lower back were already sore) and meeting up with the other de-selected parents: Robbie's mom and Myles's dad.

The young people who'd lent their help — Robbie's and Myles's older siblings and their friends — had already gone out for pizza and beer, suctioning away any residual feelings of festivity.

Charles could tell that Dr. Young and Ted Gurnee were just as exhausted and eager to leave as he was — they still had to return the U-Haul — but Charles was experiencing a kind of postperformance letdown; he felt as if he were in the company of fellow reality-show competitors who'd almost made the final cut. Couldn't they spend a few minutes commiserating over their shared fatigue and failures?

But they were non-*wallowing* types, and so they said their farewells.

As Charles watched them drive away, his back spasmed. He wished he'd asked for some pharmaceutical assistance from Dr. Young — a bit of Percocet, a smidgen of Ambien, a little something to get him through the night. Ah, well, at least there was the wine.

Suddenly, he knew what his plans were.

It was only a couple of miles away.

❦

The houses were still here. But the Nellie Goodhue School was gone.

All but one of the huge old poplars that had bordered the east side of the property had been cut down. What remained was an empty lot surrounded by a rental chainlink fence with wild, straggly up-shoots of poplar suckers forming a young forest within this fortified landscape. The big birch was still there, as was the rockery and the stone steps leading up from Meridian Avenue.

At the six-way stop — the star formed by the intersection of 137th and Roosevelt and Meridian — there stood a large, heavily tagged NOTICE OF PROPOSED LAND-USE ACTION sign informing the citizenry that there was a project under review, #3005091. The surrounding grass was mostly lush and overlong here, but someone — some self-designated caretaker from the neighborhood — had thoughtfully cut a swath up from Meridian and across the property to a spot in front of the sign.

A fat bumblebee stumbled by, a house finch sang from the branches of the old birch, and Charles read that there was a proposed construction of a CHPD (clustered housing planned development), a subdivision of twenty-six single-family units. There was a map of the Goodhue Plat, and at the bottom, contact information for the Seattle Department of Planning and Development. *Comment period ends _____ but may be extended to _____ by written request.* Charles wondered why the blanks had not been filled in.

He walked the perimeter of the grounds, finding a pair of
size eleven men's black shoes, an abandoned car, food wrap-
pers, discarded condoms, a child's mitten, a torn envelope
addressed to someone in St. Paul, Minnesota, broken bottles, and a dead mallard. Coming around to the back side
of the property, he noticed that the snowberry bushes still
stood, an untended tangle, and had leafed out, as they did
each April.

There were no hornets' nests that Charles could see, but
still, from the bushes' snarled innards, a faint buzzing ema-
nated and then crescendoed, like a tinnitus.

Charles stood by the bushes, hypnotized by the eerie
sounds they emitted, compelled to draw closer and seek
out tiny openings within their dense mass of leaves and
branches, trying to discern movement, a flash of white, half
yearning, half terrified to discover that there was something
inside, trapped, and peering out.

There wasn't.

And so he drove home, finished off the Santa Margherita,
and wrote a reply to Mrs. McGucken, accepting her invitation.

Fictional Masterpiece

Charles finally came up with an *extraordinary protagonist.*

He didn't set out to write a fictional masterpiece. He didn't aspire to the celebrity that would soon come his way, elevating him to an even greater degree of visibility and scorn.

He simply started to write and, like all enthusiastic first-time novelists, crammed perhaps a few too many themes and concerns into his debut opus. But his fervor was sincere, and all those weeks of Palmer practice allowed him to write easily and without tiring for long stretches.

He worked on his story at home after school, in the library during Language Arts class, and in the cafeteria during lunch.

"I win!" Dana yelled, holding up another perfectly peeled row of loops from his Hostess Cupcake. "Look, Char-Lee! I did it *again!* Attaboy me!"

"Yeah, Dana, I see." He found himself getting cross with Dana lately.

"*You* try, Char-Lee."

"No, that's okay, you win. I'm gonna work on this right now."

"What's this? What are you working on, Char-Lee?"

"Just something we're doing in Language Arts."

"What you do? Show."

"Maybe later. Here. Take my cupcake. I'll show you when I'm done."

"Okay. You show me when you done."

As Bradley and Mitchell passed by, they muttered their usual insults — *faggot, queer, ree-tards* — and made loud farting noises on their hands and forearms. Dana guffawed delightedly.

"Hey!" he called after them. "Wait for me!" And he lurched outside, leaving the mess of his lunch behind.

Charles couldn't care less. Something about writing his story was important, more important than entertaining Dana.

With every stroke of his pencil, he felt that he was stacking gold in heaven, shoring up a place of safety, bounty, and salvation.

He was becoming both a dreamer *and* a doer.

❖

He finished his story and turned it in, on time and without ceremony, depositing it on the seat of his chair before leaving class as per Mrs. Braxton's instructions.

The following afternoon, Rita Marlow received a phone call; she answered it in the kitchen, where Charles was eating his one-person snack. (His mother had finally inquired about Donnie Bothwell's whereabouts.)

"This is Mrs. Marlow speaking . . . Yes, I'm Charles's mother . . ."

She listened intently, nodding and frowning. Her expression was not one that Charles had seen before.

"I understand . . . No, I don't see any problem with that . . . I'll let him know . . . Thank you for calling, Mrs. Braxton. Goodbye."

Charles took an extra-large bite of his peanut butter sandwich.

His mother lit a cigarette, shaking her match several times while regarding him through narrowed eyes.

"So what's this *story* about," she began, "the one you wrote for your Language Arts class? It seems to have made quite an impression on your teacher." She flicked the match away, sideways and behind her, a blind but perfect aim; it landed in the kitchen sink and made a muffled *psst,* as if it were trying to get her attention.

Charles indicated that his speech mechanism was gummed up with Wonder Bread, Welch's, and Skippy, and he'd respond when it would be polite to do so.

"She was calling to say that your story is so amazing, so *extraordinary,* that she wants to enter it in some kind of contest. She needed to ask my permission."

"What kind of contest?" Charles asked, hoping to buy some time, since his mother's expression still revealed nothing of her thoughts or feelings about what Mrs. Braxton had said. After quickly assessing his mother's face, he realized that her inscrutability arose from that slightly furrowed space between her brows. He'd noticed this in his father too, and Mrs. Braxton. That was what most distinguished an adult from a child — not age or size or fashion or responsibility, but that tiny physiognomic plat between the brows. It seemed to hold so much mystery, so much import: the Bermuda Triangle of the adult face.

She shrugged noncommittally, expelling a puff of smoke.

"Who knows? Something the *Seattle Times* is sponsoring, apparently. You didn't know about it?"

Charles shook his head and reapplied his attention to his sandwich.

"So, what's it about?" she asked. "Your story."

"Just a kid," he mumbled, "who goes on a trip."

She waited.

"That's it, really," he added.

His mother gave a short, deep-pitched *hm*, like she'd just done a sit-up. "Can you tell me the *title*, at least?"

He answered between mouthfuls with exaggerated difficulty: "'Flipper [*swallow*] Boy' [*swallow*]." He made gulping motions several more times and worked his tongue around the inside of his mouth in a way he hoped would indicate that further communication might be hazardous.

Rita Marlow asked no more questions but continued to stare at him while he finished his snack.

"May I go watch some cartoons, please?" he asked.

She pointed to his mouth and then her own and mimed wiping at it; Charles mirrored the gesture, leaving a smear of peanut butter and jelly on his napkin.

She started shaking her head, as if the answer to his question were no, but then she said, "Yes, Charles, you may watch cartoons."

"Thank you."

As he got up to clear his place, she leaned across the table, took his hand lightly, and gave it a little squeeze.

"Funny boy," she said, looking up at him. "You are such an *enigma*."

◆

The next phone call came on a school night after dinner, a rare evening in that Garrett Marlow had come home right after work. They'd eaten together and were now all gathered in the TV room watching *Ben Casey, M.D.*

Rita Marlow took the call in the kitchen.

"Yes, this is she . . . Hello, Mrs. Braxton . . . Really? Well, that is exciting news . . . How nice . . . Friday afternoon at two thirty? I'll check with my husband. Yes, of course, I understand. We'll try our best to both be there . . . Thank you."

"Who was that?" Charles's father yelled once the commercial came on.

There was a muffled *pop* from the kitchen.

"Rita!" Garrett yelled again. "Who the hell was on the phone?"

Charles's mother appeared in the doorway. She'd reapplied her lipstick and was holding a silver tray, the one from the hutch in the dining room that came out only at Thanksgiving and Christmas. On the tray were three long-stemmed, slender glasses filled with something clear, like water. The bubbles in the glasses rose magically, perpetually: shining, uprising galaxies suspended in liquid.

She didn't ask permission to turn off the TV. She just did it.

Then she said, "We have something to celebrate."

❖

The next day, Mrs. Braxton informed the class that at the end of the week, they'd be entertaining a group of special visitors that would include Charles Marlow's parents and, possibly, their principal, Miss Vanderkolk.

If the initial part of this announcement didn't earn any special note, the mention of the dreaded Miss V. caused a collective shudder to pass through the room. Charles worried that his story had set in motion something rather larger than he'd intended.

"For this reason," Mrs. Braxton went on, "I'm expecting all of you" — she looked beadily at Mitchell and Bradley — "to be on especially good behavior."

"*I will! I will!*" Dana shouted.

Astrida raised her hand.

"Why are they all coming? What did Charles *do?*"

Mrs. Braxton grinned. "I'm going to keep that as a surprise."

Two guests arrived first thing on Friday: a tall man with the straightforward name of Jim Rupp (he looked like the lead actor in *The War of the Worlds*) and a never-identified young woman carrying a camera who was almost as pretty as Catherine Ryan. They remained quietly on the sidelines through math and social studies. When it came time for Language Arts, they followed Charles and his classmates to the library.

Once everyone was seated, Mrs. Braxton began.

"Children, as you know, our Language Arts program is the first of its kind in Seattle. When I learned that the *Seattle Times* was sponsoring a citywide creative-writing contest, I decided to submit your short stories."

Apparently not everyone's parents had shared this information with their children; there were mutterings of surprise and excitement. (Say what you will about Brax the Ax, but she had an unerring sense of theatricality. That woman could work a room.)

Mrs. Braxton continued. "You ten children have represented our school admirably. In fact, our own Charles Marlow has been chosen as the *winner* of that contest. Because of this, the *Seattle Times* has sent a reporter to interview you and a photographer to take pictures. I'm going to turn the class over to them now. Please give them your full attention."

Mr. Rupp asked a lot of questions about what students thought the world would be like in fifty years. (Charles wondered if he'd even still be *alive* in the year 2013. It seemed doubtful.) At lunchtime, Charles was allowed to eat at his desk while Mr. Rupp interviewed him privately, asking more specific questions about "Flipper Boy"; for example, where did he get all those wild ideas?

Charles told him that he didn't think his ideas were that wild; he got most of them from reading magazines. When Mr. Rupp asked *which* magazines, Charles answered truthfully before remembering the contraband nature of his periodical library and realizing that this might not be a wise revelation.

"Could you please leave out that part about *Playboy*?" he asked.

"Sure." Mr. Rupp made a show of crossing something out in his notebook and then winked.

At two thirty sharp, Rita and Garrett Marlow arrived; Mrs. Braxton led them to the back of the room, where four folding chairs had been set up, and introduced them to Mr. Rupp. The pretty photographer roamed around the class taking pictures. As people began to settle, Charles noted with relief that the last folding chair remained empty; perhaps Miss Vanderkolk was out of the country, engaged in a top-secret KGB mission.

"All right, children," Mrs. Braxton started, clapping her hands briskly. "Please put your things away. Our program is about to begin."

What program? Charles wondered.

"We are celebrating the fact that Charles Marlow has won a citywide creative-writing contest sponsored by the *Seattle Times*. His story was selected out of hundreds of stories submitted, and at the end of our presentation today —"

What presentation?

"— Charles will be receiving a certificate and a special prize. But first"— and at this point, Mrs. Braxton balanced her bulbous figure on a stool at the center of the front of the room — "I will be reading Charles's story, beginning to end. Is everyone ready?"

Appalled, Charles dove for his writing tablet and began making loops.

"'Flipper Boy,'" she began. "'By Charles Marlow.'"

❖

CHAPTER ONE: Once upon a time in a small town in the Land of Sky-Blue Waters a boy was born to a husband and wife whose names were Vincent and Barbara Hefner and they named the baby Kennedy. At first, Kennedy was like every other boy in the town. He went to school and liked eating Hostess Cupcakes and watching TV and swimming and reading comic books. He was not special except that he had no brothers or sisters or even any pets. One fine summer day Kennedy came inside and found his mother sitting at the kitchen table crying but she stopped as soon as she saw him. Kennedy asked her why she was sad and she said I'm not sad let me fix you something to eat. While Kennedy's mother made him a tuna sandwich with potato chips and a dill pickle which was Kennedy's favorite, Kennedy asked his mother if he was spoiled because sometimes he was teased about not having brothers and sisters. (Kennedy was the only boy in all of the Land of Sky-Blue Waters who didn't have brothers or sisters but you already know that from before.) Barbara said no because if I had ten children I would love them all the same way I love you and make them all tuna sandwiches or whatever their favorite was. And then Kennedy asked why she and his father didn't have more children and she told him it was because God knew that she could only be a Really Good Mother to One Child, like Mary. (And Vincent and Barbara never did have another baby.) After that Kennedy's mother said I'm a little tired do you mind if I take a nap you can watch some cartoons. While Kennedy was eating a sliver of dill pickle in front of the television, it seemed to him that his two little fingers looked a little bit littler than usual but maybe it was just his imagination. But then that night, when Kennedy kneeled by the side of his bed and folded his hands to say his prayers, he was sure that his little fingers had shrunk and that was when it started and Kennedy Hefner was no longer ordinary but becoming truly special.

CHAPTER TWO: Kennedy grew older and wanted someone to play with but he knew that if God thought his mother could only be a good mother to one boy then probably God also knew that he couldn't be a good brother, but still he was lonely and so he asked for a pet. His mother said, ask your father. So Kennedy did, but his father said no, it's cruel to keep animals as pets unless you live on a farm, so Kennedy was not allowed to have pets except sometimes his mother took him to the pet store and he got a turtle which soon died. Kennedy enjoyed creating habitats for the turtles and did his best to take care of them but they all died and then parents everywhere learned that turtles carry a deadly germ called salmonella and that was the end of all turtles for the boy Kennedy and he had to content himself with television and magazines for company. One night Kennedy heard his parents outside the door of his bedroom arguing about pets. Barbara said it would mean so much to him and Vincent said I don't want a filthy animal in our house who do you think is going to end up taking care of it. And that was when Kennedy felt something funny about his toes, like all of a sudden he was wearing socks that were too tight. He fell asleep and forgot about it but in the morning when he went to put on his flip-flops so he could go outside he saw that his little toes had shrunk just like his little fingers so he put on Keds instead and told his mother he didn't feel like swimming today.

CHAPTER THREE: One time when it was late at night and Kennedy was in bed he woke up and it wasn't because he was having a bad dream but because his parents were having a fight. It scared him when his parents had fights because he knew that if they had a really bad fight they might get a divorce and then the three of them couldn't be together at the end of the world in the bomb shelter that Kennedy's father had ordered from the catalog to protect them from the atomic blast that was coming one day. Kennedy put his pillow around his ears so that he couldn't hear anything, but it was no use and when he got up the next morning his ears had shrunk. And what was even worse, the tops were curled down, like they were plants closing up.

CHAPTER FOUR: By now you can probably guess what was happening to Kennedy. Every night his parents fought or told a lie, some part of his body got smaller or deformed. For a while he was able to hide this because it was his little fingers and little toes first as I already told you and then his ears which he covered with a hat and by combing his hair differently, but one day when his mother who had been crying put his tuna sandwich down in front of him she looked into his face and screamed.

Mom, what is it, Kennedy asked. But she didn't answer because she had fainted. Kennedy held a pickle under her nose because it was the strongest-smelling thing he could think of and when his mother woke up she didn't look at him but said I'm sorry Kennedy I must be seeing things but for one second you looked exactly like your father.

❖

It went on like that: sixty-eight single-spaced pages written in Charles's best Palmer penmanship. As promised, Mrs. Braxton read the whole thing.

In summary, "Flipper Boy" was the story of a boy whose parents' fights worked like a magic potion. Each time they spoke a harsh word to each other, there was a corresponding change to young Kennedy's anatomy, specifically his extremities. Soon, he started noticing changes in his limbs: subtle distortions, subluxations, shrinkages. By the time his parents stopped fighting long enough to notice, it was too late; Kennedy Hefner had fully transformed into Flipper Boy.

His parents shrieked with disgust and horror.

Realizing that his mother and father were incapable of loving him in his flawed condition, Kennedy ran away from home and had a series of adventures set in exotic locales like Transylvania, Antarctica, and Havana.

Finally, in Japan, Kennedy met a large family of rice farmers who were suffering from the disfiguring effects of mercury poisoning. They took young Kennedy in. They cherished him in spite of his horrific deformities.

The force of their communal love, combined with the intervention of a beautiful fairy — modeled, in countenance only, on the September 1962 Playgirl of the Month — resulted in the miraculous straightening and regeneration of young Kennedy's limbs.

Kennedy grew up to be a fabulously wealthy, benevolent doctor who married all his nurses and invented cures for cancer, leprosy, thalidomide babies, and the flu.

And then, one day, Kennedy's parents showed up at his clinic as patients. They were blind, infected with leprosy, monstrous to behold.

Kennedy cured them, not revealing his identity.

But when their sight was restored and they saw the gold crucifix Kennedy wore at all times around his neck, they recognized him as the long-lost son they had wronged so terribly all those many years ago.

All wrongs were forgiven. They fell weeping into one another's arms and lived happily ever after.

❧

"'The End,'" Mrs. Braxton said. She reached into the sleeve of her shirtwaist dress, produced a balled-up handkerchief, and began dabbing at her eyes.

Except for the sound of her intermittent sniffles, the room was completely still. The self-designated emcee seemed utterly drained of her leadership abilities, and no one was quite sure how to proceed.

It was Dana McGucken (who had listened intently the entire time, not fidgeting, not punctuating Mrs. Braxton's reading with a single vocal or flatulent outburst) who finally took charge and initiated the applause.

"Yay, Char-*Lee!*" he yelled. "Yay! Yay! Yay! I like that story!" The rest of the class joined in, the pretty photographer snapped pictures, and Mrs. Braxton, still rendered mute by emotion, indicated to Charles that he should stand.

It was then, with a hopeful heart, that he turned around to see his parents' reaction.

Because they were both seated and clapping politely in near perfect synchronization, Charles's first thought was that at least they were *unified* in their response. If his unconscious intent had been to shore up and strengthen the bonds of his parents' marriage, to lead them to whatever common ground they'd occupied before becoming combatants, antagonists, in a brutal civil war, then he had succeeded, brilliantly.

Their expressions — soon to be captured by the camera and published in the *Seattle Times* as part of the article titled "Fourth-Graders Predict the Future" and subtitled "Nellie Goodhue Students Earn Attention Thanks to Controversial Prize-Winning Story" — did not reflect jubilation, pride, or even moderate approval.

Garrett and Rita Marlow's faces looked exactly as Charles imagined Kennedy Hefner's parents' did when they first beheld their grotesquely transfigured son:

Perfect expressions of unadulterated horror.

That Arrow Grinding

Over the years, a few people have dared to puzzle over some of Mr. Palmer's recommendations. For a man who was allegedly concerned with speed and efficiency, some of his letter forms require time-consuming care. A few are nearly indecipherable because of their resemblance to other letters. Others are frankly difficult, even awkward, to execute, in some cases downright counterintuitive.

For example: a capital *X*.

It's a powerful letter, one that often has unpleasant and/or illicit connotations: X-rated movies; X marks the spot; exile; excommunication.

Because the pharmaceutical industry relies heavily on the letter in its brand names (Sominex, Ex-Lax, Xanax, Lexapro), it is associated with ill health.

Teddy Roosevelt marked his diary with a slashing, irrevocable **X** to articulate darkness, unspeakable grief.

Mr. Palmer's uppercase *X* consists of two C-shaped curves that touch, just barely, but do not cross.

And yet, what could be simpler or quicker than two intersecting diagonal slashes?

It's as if Mr. Palmer's variants are inside jokes, put there for his personal amusement. He couldn't really have believed, could he, that these variations were timesaving? They are flouncing, fancy choices.

Perhaps Mr. Palmer wanted to demonstrate that he too, like his predecessor Mr. Spencer, had an appreciation for the finer things in life; beauty for beauty's sake, flourishes that serve no purpose beyond loveliness.

The most baffling example of these odd lapses occurs in three letters when they appear in a terminal position.

A Palmer *t* is uncrossed;

the up-swinging curve of a *w* is severed (this being the variant present in my father's signature);

and the tail of a *g* is reduced to a single stroke, a pessimistic downward slash, an animal's tail stripped of feathers or fur.

Sister Giorgia Maria Fiducia D'Amati knows better than to
try teaching her boys these complex refinements. At the island convent school, they celebrate small successes; for the
majority, the execution of a single loop constitutes reason
for rejoicing.

That it often takes months or even years for one of Giorgia's boys to take up a writing implement is fine. Sometimes
they never do, and that is all right too.

But there was one boy.

He'd come to the island long ago, in the 1960s, but when
Giorgia remembers him —

(and she remembers him frequently now, whenever she's
in the presence of the silent boy who tears magazines during
his lessons)

— it is as if it were yesterday: his odd way of dressing;
his shining, pale face; his gregarious, joyful spirit; his pure
heart.

Before he was put into their care — after whatever
trauma or tragedy sent his parents in search of an alternative school — someone had taught him to write, and taught
him well. The joy he took in that simple skill! He inspired all
the sisters. He inspired the other boys too.

His presence was proof of what Giorgia had known since
childhood:

Even a backward girl

(*dummy* was what Papa called her: *manichino*),

an unloved girl

(who'd killed her mother in childbirth, forever depriving
Papa of a son),

but strong, like a man, almost

(raped by soldiers, sent away to bear her baby in shame),

such a girl can survive, learn, pray, forgive, serve, receive
love, give thanks.

Such a girl can grow to be a bride of Christ, a friend, a teacher.

Such a girl knows that God cherishes the backward no less than the genius.

❖

The playground of the Nellie Goodhue School was a large, flat rectangle of land that tilted sharply at its far end, where it sloped up to abut an odd convergence of dead-end streets. What vegetation there was had a weedy, wild, untended look; the northern border was dotted by several large, dense, shapeless shrubs that stood a few feet from a chainlink fence.

In the winter, the bare branches of these shrubs and their white, BB-size berries provided a tangled cage and a ready food supply for small, overwintering birds. In the spring, they leafed out, forming a dense, inscrutable barrier, giving rise to terrifying rumors of bees, wasps, and hornets lying in wait within and inciting stern warnings from Miss Vanderkolk.

The school year was almost over. The fuss over "Flipper Boy" had died down. Charles wrote another story, "The Sad Donkey," but — as is often the case with second novels — it was not received with the same acclaim; furthermore, his sophomore effort shared the spotlight with a debut story by Astrida Pukis entitled "The Wonderful Dove."

Penmanship lessons had shortened in length; however, Mrs. Braxton still set aside five minutes every day for some form of Palmer practice. "Next year, when you are fifth-graders," she cautioned, "you will not have the time that we have enjoyed this year to further your penmanship skills."

Charles remained her unofficial teacher's assistant, and whenever she required a demonstration, she merely nodded, signaling him to rise and take his place.

"Today we will review the three special letters that are

executed in a different manner when occurring in the terminal, meaning *final,* position of a word. Who remembers what those letters are?"

Astrida Pukis shot her hand up.

"*T! W! G!*" Dana shouted.

"That's correct," Mrs. Braxton replied, "but please raise your hand if you wish to respond to a question."

Dana thrust his hand skyward and repeated, "*T! W! G!*"

Mrs. Braxton sighed.

"Astrida, can you list the words that we use when practicing these variations?"

Astrida rattled off the three words, snippily.

Mrs. Braxton said, "Exactly right. Let us all inscribe this phrase ten times."

On the blackboard, Charles wrote *that arrow grinding, that arrow grinding, that arrow grinding,* demonstrating the atypical endings that were the focus of the lesson.

What arrow? What did it grind?

It's a savage image, really, one Charles has pondered through the years. Why couldn't Mr. Austin Norman Palmer have come up with some gentler phrase to demonstrate those three letter variants?

Why not
that swallow singing or
what callow rejoicing or
that sorrow abating?

By the end of the year, Charles's friendship with Dana had undergone a change.

They still ate together, but Dana now joined Bradley and Mitchell for lunch recess.

"Come play with us!" Dana yelled on his way out the

door. "Come *on*, Char-Lee! Come play with me and Brad and Mitch! We make loops too!"

Charles had no idea what that meant — and he might never have learned had he not been hustled out to the playground one day by Miss Vanderkolk.

"Charles," she said, appearing with terrifying suddenness after the lunchroom had emptied, "I appreciate your diligence, but it is a beautiful day. Leave your reading for now and join the other children."

Charles looked for Dana among the thronging, giddy hordes of kids. He looked for Bradley and Mitchell too, but didn't see any of them.

Miss Vanderkolk had already issued her seasonal warning about the bushes on the far end of the property, but when Charles spotted a flicker of white behind them, he headed out that way. He soon heard Mitchell speaking in an exaggerated, falsetto parody of Mrs. Braxton:

"Up and down and around again, up and down and around again!"

Peering behind bushes, Charles saw Brad, Mitch, and Dana, flies open, penises out, inscribing loops of pee against the concrete retaining wall.

"Hey, spaz!" Mitchell called out. "Come make Palmer loops with us."

"Hi, Char-Lee!"

Charles looked down the corridor that was formed between the bushes and the retaining wall; at the opposite end was Astrida Pukis, staring.

"Dana. Come on," Charles said. "Come out of there now."

"No, Char-Lee. It's *fun!*"

The next day, Charles tried to keep Dana from going outside. "Stay in here with me today," he said. "We could practice, we could have a cupcake race . . ."

"Awwww, the faggot is *jealous*," Mitchell said.

"The faggot misses his *girlfriend*," Bradley added.

"Come on, Char-Lee!" Dana said, and so Charles went outside, but when he tried to get Dana to play a game of foursquare or tetherball, Dana said, "*No!* Too many kids there. I like the other place," and there was no changing his mind.

The next time Charles ventured to look behind the bushes, Dana was the only one with his penis on display. Mitchell and Bradley were flanking him, looking on. Bradley was sniggering as usual, but Mitchell's face was deadpan.

"That's it, faggot," Mitchell's voice was no longer a parody of Mrs. Braxton's; it was flat and joyless. "Up and down and around, that's it. Up and down and around. Now do some push-pulls. Good. Now do some bedspring ovals . . ."

"Dana!" Charles called. "Come out of there."

"Hi, Char-Lee! No! You come *in!* Come make loops with me!"

Mitchell perked up. "Yeah, come *on*, Char-Lee Mar-Low," he echoed. "Don't you want to do some *Pah*-mer *looooooopuzzz?*"

Dana laughed.

Charles realized then that he had lost Dana McGucken; their two-boy club was no longer enough. Dana had achieved and embraced membership in a new club — except he was too much of a *spaz* to realize that he wasn't really a member, he was a pawn, a fool, a sacrificial lamb.

He hated Dana McGucken for going with those boys, those bullies.

Let him get what he deserves, Charles thought, walking away, *that ree-tard.*

A week went by.

Charles kept an eye on the three of them. They didn't always disappear behind the bushes, and when they did, it was for short periods only. They reemerged after what Charles calculated to be the length of an average piss, with Dana trailing in Brad and Mitchell's wake, bounding and uncoordinated and always happy, an oversize white puppy.

It was clear that Bradley and Mitchell had come to regard Dana as an embarrassment, a pest, and they began trying to ditch him, flat-out ignoring him, rolling their eyes and exchanging frustrated looks as he stood too close and babbled loudly into their averted faces, his energetic, penetrating cries —

Miss-Shel! *Bra*-Deee! *Less* play! *Less make* loops!

— cutting through the chorus of playground voices, making Mitchell and Bradley even more mortified by the awkward social situation they'd brought upon themselves.

Now you know what it's like to have a ree-tard for a friend, Charles thought. *Ha-ha, creeps; the joke's on you.*

Dana was undaunted, though; the only time he didn't cling to them was when they ventured into the middle of the playground. At those times, he remained on the perimeter, massaging that web of skin between his thumb and forefinger, his expression anxious and forlorn.

❖

During the final two weeks of that school year, the ranks of room 104 began to diminish.

This kind of attrition was common as summer neared. The assumption was that the absent children were lucky ducks whose parents had already whisked them away on fun-filled family vacations.

The next-to-last Friday of every school year was Field Day, a free-for-all of outdoor activities for the entire school, with every child on the playground from nine o'clock until two, drinking pop for once instead of milk, eating hot dogs and hamburgers and potato chips and cookies supplied by the PTA. The thinking was probably that if the students were given this last hurrah, they'd tolerate one more week filled with sedate, end-of-year chores — emptying out cubbies, lockers, and desks; taking down bulletin-board displays; all the joyless but necessary labors involved when the circus leaves town.

On that morning, Mrs. Braxton noted several absences in her attendance book, including that of Mitchell Rudd. Charles didn't care where Mitchell was; he was just hopeful that he didn't plan to return before the end of the year.

Out on the playground, Dana was easy to spot — especially so that day, since it was warm outside; the girls were bare-legged and sleeveless, and many of the boys wore shorts. He was following Bradley around. Brad looked smaller and less threatening without Mitchell by his side, and he didn't seem to have the energy to deflect Dana's attentions in the usual forceful way; he kept looking around as if he didn't quite know what to do.

Charles participated, a little, in the festivities. There were ringtosses and races, fun challenges that were organized, run, and supervised by the dozens of parents who were volunteering their time.

There is some horrifying statistic about children drowning during parties, how — incredibly — the odds of such a thing happening increase in direct proportion to the number of adults present.

When Charles couldn't locate Dana, he knew where to look, so he started to make his way through the throngs of happy children and oblivious adults to the far, quiet end of the playground where the bushes were, where the hornets nested.

Miss Vanderkolk had ordered the bushes cordoned off; a makeshift fence of caution cones and rope had been erected, and a sign reading DANGER OF BEES HORNETS YELLOW JACKETS AND WASPS! STAY AWAY! had successfully kept everyone at a distance.

There was no one close enough to see or hear anything of interest; there was nothing to give a single clue as to what Charles would find when he finally came around the corner.

Mitchell Rudd *had* come to school that day after all; there he was, with Bradley and Dana — whose hands and feet were bound with the fabric strips Mrs. Braxton had used earlier in the year in service of the immobilizing technique.

"Hi, Char-Lee!" Dana cried with exuberance. "We're playing a *new* game!"

Before Charles could register what was happening, Mitch trapped him within the vise grip of his arms. Bradley went to work binding his hands and feet while Mitchell slapped a hand over his mouth. But then, realizing that Charles's screams wouldn't attract any special attention, he let go.

"We're playing cowboys and Indians," he said.

"I thought we were playing dam-*sell* in this-*dress!*"

"Yeah," Mitch said, considering. "I suppose we could keep playing that . . ."

Charles realized that Mitchell didn't really have a plan beyond luring him here. If he kept his mouth shut, things might be all right.

Then Mitchell noticed Charles's police-detective notebook.

"What's this?" he asked, withdrawing the notebook from Charles's shirt pocket. Charles's favorite pencil, sharpened to a fine point, was wedged into the spiral coils; Mitchell pushed it out and flipped the notebook open.

There it was, the damning evidence: all the notes Charles

had taken, the clubs and their members (BULLIES: MITCH-
ELL RUDD AND BRADLEY WILCOX), the list of summer plans
he and Donnie had made last year, the loops he'd demonstrated for Dana.

Charles expected Mitchell to react, to get angry, to say
something, but he just kept reading, looking up every now
and then.

Finally he said, "You really like making those Palmer
loops, don't you?" His eyes slid from Charles to Dana and
back again. "Know what? Now that Charlie's here, I think we
should do some Palmer practice."

"*Yay!*" Dana shouted.

"So," Mitchell said, smiling, "which one of you wants to
make Palmer loops?" Charles understood that now Mitchell *did* have a plan; he'd solved whatever problem he'd been
wrestling with.

"I do! I do!" Dana raised his bound hands.

"But wait," Mitchell said. "It's a special challenge, because
it's Field Day."

Dana bellowed, "I *like* Feed Day!"

"You have to make Palmer loops without holding the
pencil in your hands."

"*Ha!*" Dana said. "How we do *that?* How we make *loops*
without *hands*, Miss-*Shel?*"

"How do you think, Dana?"

"Don't *know! Show!*"

"Well . . . ," Mitchell said — and it wasn't just the absence
of malice in his voice that was chilling, it was the perfectly
modulated evenness with which he spoke, as if he were a be-
nevolent nursery-school teacher: a perfect mimicry of compassion. "You could put your pencil in your ear, like this." He
demonstrated; Dana giggled.

Mitchell put the pencil between his teeth, like a cigar,

and tried to articulate around it. "Or you could put it in your mouth, like this . . ."

Dana howled even louder. "You *fun*-eee, Miss-*Shel!*"

"Or in your nose, *or,*" Mitchell said enticingly, "you could do it another way."

"What?" Dana asked, entranced. "What way?"

"Stop," Charles said.

"But he wants to know," Mitchell said. "Don't you, Dana?"

"I *do. Show!*"

"Do *you* know, Char-Lee? Do *you* know where a pencil can go besides your ear or your nose or your mouth?"

"Stop," Charles said again, weakly. It was hot; he'd eaten too much.

"I bet you do. Maybe *you* want to show him."

Charles threw up.

"Char-Lee sick," Dana stated, his face serious.

It kept coming, everything Charles had eaten that day, hot dogs and relish and potato chips and brownies; the enclosed space and the heat intensified the smell, and even after there was nothing left, he kept heaving.

"Jesus," Bradley said, plugging his nose with his fingers.

"*Jeeeee*-zuhs!" Dana added, and then, "Char-Lee sick."

"So which one of you is going to do the special challenge?"

"Me," Dana volunteered. "I make loops. Char-Lee sick."

"Okay, Dana. Attaboy."

Mitchell started pulling down Dana's pants. Bradley looked surprised but didn't say anything.

Stop, Charles tried to say, but the sight and smell of the vomit was awful, and the convulsions kept coming.

"Char-Lee," Dana asked, "Char-Lee Mar-Low, you okay?"

Mitchell said, "Okay now, Dana, get on your knees."

Dana complied, still looking at Charles.

"Now bend over . . . that's right. Just like a dog."

Bradley spoke. "Shit, Mitch. Are you sure —"

Mitchell pinched the pencil between his fingers, as if it were a dart he was trying to align with the bull's-eye, and studied Dana's bottom.

Bradley spoke again. "Geez, Mitch, are you sure you should do that?"

"Christ, Brad. Don't be such a faggot. Didn't your mommy ever take your temperature when you were a little-bitty baby? Shut up, it's fine. Get over here and help me. Spread his butt cheeks."

Bradley cast a dubious look in Charles's direction but obeyed.

Mitchell shoved the ground-down eraser end of the pencil into Dana's bottom. Then he sat back with a bemused look on his face, as if he had no connection to what he was seeing.

"There you go, faggot," he said, his voice expressionless.

Dana frowned; he looked puzzled.

"Okay, you're ready," Mitchell said, his voice growing impatient. "What are you waiting for? Get to work, *ree-tard!* Make those Palmer loops!"

Dana's voice was small. "How?" he said.

"Oh, come on. You know what to do. Charlie here, he taught you how to make Palmer loops, didn't he?"

"Yes. We make loops. Char-Lee teach me all the time."

Mitchell gazed quizzically at Charles, as if seeking guidance, as if *he* were the one running the show. Then, slowly, a look of realization and delight spread across his face. "*You* tell him, Charlie," he said. "You're the teacher. He's not listening to me."

"What?"

"Tell the *ree-tard* to make loops."

"Char-Lee?" Dana asked.

"What —"

"Or maybe *you* want to do the challenge too. Brad, get another pencil."

"No!"

"Okay, then. Tell him. If you tell him, I'll untie you."

"Char-Lee?" Dana repeated, his voice now tinged with fear.

"Tell him, *faggot,* or you're next."

"Dana," Charles said. "Make loops."

"Noooooo!" Mitchell's voice had resumed its expressive malice. "His name isn't *Dana.* It's Ree-tard. Say it: *Ree-tard.*"

"Ree-tard."

"Now say, 'Ree-tard, Charlie says make loops.'"

"Ree-tard. Charlie says. Make loops."

Mitchell grabbed Dana from behind and started moving his bottom in circles.

"That's it! Now say, 'Faggot, make loops.'"

"Faggot."

"What? I didn't hear that."

"You said you were going to untie me."

"Not yet. The *ree-tard* needs more practice. Come on!"

"Faggot. Make loops."

"Now say, 'Queer.'"

"Queer. Make loops . . ."

Mitchell kept moving Dana's bottom around in ever larger, quickening circles so that Dana lost his balance; he pitched forward beyond his bound forearms and ended up lying on his face, his cheek grinding into the dirt.

"Hey!" someone called. It was Astrida, standing at the end of the tunnel, slack-jawed, beady-eyed. "Someone's coming. You better quit that. You better get out of there right now!" Then she ran out of view.

"Shit," Bradley said.

"Goddamn it," Mitchell said. He yanked Dana up off the ground, but Dana fell back and sat down hard. Mitchell hauled him to standing, pulled up his trousers, and unbound his arms and feet. "Untie the other one, stupid!" he barked.

Bradley rushed over to Charles and started freeing him.

"You feel better, Char-Lee? I did Feed Day loops for you. Did you see?"

Charles stumbled out of the bushes in time to see Miss Vanderkolk striding across the playground with Astrida jogging beside her.

Mitchell and Bradley emerged from the other end of the hedge, flanking Dana, arms around him, propping him up as if they were designated drivers seeing a soused pal home at the end of an evening.

"What's going on out here," Miss Vanderkolk called as she approached.

"Sorry, Miss Vanderkolk," Mitchell said, his voice nauseating in its unctuousness. "We found Dana playing out here and we were trying to bring him back."

Miss Vanderkolk looked skeptical but said, "All right, then. Go back and join the others. Charles? What's wrong with you?"

"I'm sick."

She accompanied Charles to the nurse's office, where he was given a bromide and some apple juice — *No Vanilla Wafers for you, young man,* the nurse said, *not until your stomach settles down* — and from there into the Quiet Room, where he recuperated on one of the army cots until his mother arrived to take him home.

❖

When Mrs. Braxton took attendance the following Monday, neither Mitchell nor Bradley was present. Dana was there, less ebullient than usual, but otherwise the same as always.

After their final Language Arts class of the year, Mrs. Braxton and the other children trooped back into room 104, where Mrs. Hurd was finishing up her lesson on sentence diagramming, whatever that was, and where Dana had his head on his desk. He seemed to be taking a nap.

As Charles passed by, Dana roused himself and said weakly, "Char-Lee. Char-Lee Mar-Low." He reached out, stood up, and then fell, slumping into Charles's arms.

Immediately, there were gasps from the children behind him, then screams, then they started pointing: on the backside of Dana's white linen trousers, a blooming splotch of blood.

"Oh my God," Mrs. Braxton said, rushing over to help keep Dana upright, putting a hand on his forehead. His eyes were glazed. His face was blotchy and slick with sweat. "Oh my God," she repeated. "He's burning up."

She kicked off her too-small high-heeled shoes, hoisted him into her arms, and took off running. "Char-Lee, Char-Lee Mar-Low," Dana continued to cry, his strange voice, normally so joyous, now a keening, hollow moan that reverberated through the halls of Nellie Goodhue.

❖

Not long after Charles got home and sat down in front of his snack, there was a phone call.

"Hello? Yes, this is Charles's mother, Mrs. Marlow . . . No, he didn't mention anything . . . I'm sorry, what did you say? What happened? When? Are you telling me that Charles was involved? . . . I see . . . Yes, yes, of course, I'll speak to him about it . . . I understand, thank you very much for calling."

Generously buttered saltines alternating in a semicircle with precisely cut squares of processed cheese, a julienned dill pickle, a cup of tomato soup, two Fig Newtons, Rita Marlow's signature apple rosette.

It had been three days since the playground, but the lingering taste of vomit (or its memory) made Charles barely able to look at this display, much less eat any of it.

His mother lit a cigarette and leaned against the counter. "That was your school principal," she began, her voice quiet, impartial. "She said you were in some kind of a fight during Field Day, a disturbance . . . Why didn't you say anything?"

Charles wished he could get up — he wanted to brush his teeth — but his body felt like cement.

"Charles? Charles. Look at me. What happened?"

He opened his mouth, but then, fearing he might gag on the air itself, closed it.

"One of your classmates, that *Dana*, has been very seriously injured. No one knew he'd been hurt until today. He's in the hospital, in intensive care. They're saying he might . . ." She paused and took a deep drag on her cigarette. "Were you involved with any of this?"

"Not exactly."

"What do you mean, not exactly?"

"Some other boys, they . . . did something to Dana."

She paused again to draw on her cigarette. "Did you see what they did?"

Charles nodded his head. He felt dizzy.

"Did they do it to you too?"

He shook his head no.

"Did you try to stop it? Charles?"

He shook his head again.

"Well, that's good," she said. "That's very good. You might have been seriously injured yourself if you'd tried to intervene."

I didn't intervene, Charles thought. *I didn't do anything except call Dana McGucken a ree-tard and a faggot and a queer and now he's going to die.*

The next day, midmorning, Mrs. Braxton sent Charles to the office on some errand, and there, standing at the main counter, was Mrs. McGucken.

She looked destitute: a wrinkled, untucked sleeveless blouse over a pair of too-long slacks, soot-smeared Keds, oily, uncombed hair.

The moment she saw him she pulled him into her arms.

"Oh," she sobbed. "Charles."

To this day, Charles remembers the way she prolonged and filled the sounds of those two words, and in the years since, having spent so much time trying to impart to his students the brilliance of Shakespeare's language — not as fancy, pretentious poetry for poetry's sake, but as simple, potent physical expression — he has often heard echoes of Mrs. McGucken's voice in Ophelia's *Oh, woe is me;* Juliet's *Oh, be some other name!;* Romeo's *Oh, teach me how I should forget to think!*

"I am so glad I ran into you," she went on. "I came by to pick up Dana's things."

She released Charles to arm's length, then squatted and regarded him at close range. Charles noticed things about her face that he hadn't seen before: she was slightly wall-eyed, a flaw that somehow only enhanced the qualities of compassion and serenity that her countenance expressed; her pale skin, unlike Dana's, bore a light dusting of cinnamon-colored freckles; precisely centered in the space between her brows was a small mole.

"Dana is at Children's Hospital," she continued, "and I'm sure he'd love to see you, before . . ." She started to cry again.

Before he dies, Charles thought.

She stood, removed her glasses, pressed her palms against her eyes — Charles saw then that, though tiny, she had the long-boned, elegant fingers of a much taller person. Dana had inherited his hands from her.

"You have been such a wonderful friend, Charles," she said. "All this year."

"Here you are, Mrs. McGucken," one of the office ladies said, sliding a small sack across the counter.

"Thank you," she said, with the slightest hint of coldness. Then she looked down and stroked the side of Charles's face; her hands had the feel of warm silk. "Goodbye, Charles." She briefly cupped his chin, smiled, and was gone.

Even after she passed through the office door and out of view, Charles could somehow still see her, a shimmering remnant of embodied sorrow.

"Can I help you, Charles?" the school secretary asked.

"Charles?" the nurse said, emerging from the Quiet Room. "Are you all right?"

He took off running: out the door, across the playground, up Meridian to 145th, across the freeway bridge, right on 15th, down the hill, and into the sanctuary, where the pews of St. Matthew's were empty.

He stood in the foyer, catching his breath. Now that he was there, he wasn't sure what to do.

Light a candle? People sometimes did that when they came to church.

Pray? He'd only ever said prayers in his room at bedtime or in church on Sunday. It had never occurred to him that the need for prayer could strike at any time. Would God show up at this unaccustomed hour, and for a solitary ten-year-old child? It seemed unlikely. Still, assuming it couldn't hurt, he whispered the Lord's Prayer and then, *Please God, please don't let Dana McGucken di*e.

He waited.

Perhaps the key — as with handwriting practice — was repetition.

Please God, please don't let Dana McGucken die, please God, please don't let Dana McGucken die, please God, please don't let Dana McGucken die, please God . . .

After a while, the words seemed to gain density but lose potency, overfilling the space, crowding God out. Was there no other way?

In the back of the sanctuary was a notebook, an ordinary three-ring binder filled with lined paper. Charles had seen his mother write something inside it once, one Sunday morning when she didn't have the flu. He opened it.

There were all kinds of prayers in there, all kinds of handwriting . . .

Please God, look after my family, especially my father, who is suffering so much . . .

Please God, teach me to be a better mother to my children . . .

Please God, help my husband stop drinking . . .

Please God, watch over and protect my son . . .

Please God, heal my daughter . . .

Please God . . .

Please . . .

Maybe *writing* his prayer would make it more likely to be heard and answered, so he picked up the pen.

But something was wrong. He could not make his hand obey.

Again and again he tried to write his prayer for Dana; again and again, he failed.

❖

Hours later, when the St. Matthew's priest began to prepare for evening Mass, he discovered a boy with a tearstained face fast asleep on the floor in the back of the sanctuary. He was clutching the book of prayer intentions.

Gently, carefully, the priest extracted the binder from the boy's grasp.

Inside, he found page after page of writing, a collapsed mess, a chaos of scrawled, angular, graceless lines, the same words over and over again, just barely legible:

Please God forgive me

It's a Girl!

When Mrs. McGucken answered the door, Charles couldn't bring himself to linger on her face; instead, his eyes immediately went to a large window on the wall opposite. It had been fitted with a system of floor-to-ceiling glass shelves that were entirely given over to dozens of small pots of variously colored flowers.

"Charles," she said, "Charles Marlow. Thank you so much for coming."

The flowers did not obscure what little light came into the room — Charles determined it to be north-facing — but rather filtered it in a lovely way, the backlit petals and velvety leaves glowing, small snatches of color that gave the effect of intricate stained glass.

"I've made coffee, but I also have hot water for tea if you'd prefer," she said.

"Coffee would be perfect," Charles said.

"Please, sit down."

There were three rooms from what Charles could tell:
this one — serving as a combination living/kitchen/eating
area — a bathroom, and (presumably) a bedroom behind a
partial wall. Charles couldn't help it; he found himself looking for evidence of Dana, but there was none. The bookcase
held only books. With the exception of two large colorful
framed art prints, the walls were bare.

"Do you take cream and sugar?" she asked.

"Black would be fine."

Foss Home was on Greenwood Avenue in North Seattle;
it was Lutheran-run, as were many assisted-living facilities,
something Charles had learned when he moved his mother
back to Seattle from Coeur d'Alene, Idaho, after the death
of her second husband, a sweet, uncomplicated, retired Jewish grocer named Leo with whom she'd been very happy.
Garrett Marlow experienced neither a second marriage nor
a happy ending; he died at forty-eight, two years after the divorce, in a car accident.

"Here you are, Charles."

"Thank you," he said. "I cannot stop staring at those flowers."

"Oh, yes," Mrs. McGucken said. "My violets . . . they do
keep me busy . . ."

Charles followed her over to the window and was treated
to an impromptu lecture on the joys of *Saintpaulia ionantha.*
Mrs. McGucken identified each distinct plant variety and
spoke about their soil and light requirements, emphasizing that although African violets had a reputation for being
horticultural prima donnas, it was completely undeserved;
they were, in fact, *easy* to grow — certainly less high-mainte-
nance than *orchids.* They were also long-lived (some of her
specimens were decades old), and, perhaps best of all, their

diminutive size made them perfect for small, dimly lit dwell-
ings such as this.

She was obviously an expert, but Charles had the sense
that the subject of flowers wasn't a source of pride for Mrs.
McGucken so much as a way of initiating a conversation
with someone she hadn't seen for fifty years. It had taken all
his courage to come. Possibly, inviting him had taken all of
hers.

"You've converted me," Charles said as she concluded
her lecture, eliciting from Mrs. McGucken the most delightful and surprising response: a low-pitched, throaty chuckle.

"I so enjoyed that article in the newspaper," she said,
leading Charles to the sofa and settling herself in a nearby
chair.

They went on to chat about all the expected, safe topics. At Mrs. McGucken's urging, Charles talked about his
long history as a City Prana teacher, his students, this year's
impressive slate of senior-project advisees. Mrs. McGucken
filled in the details of what sounded like a very busy life, especially for someone who had to be in her eighties: her volunteering obligations at the nearby elementary school and
the public library, her active membership in a society of fellow African violet enthusiasts.

About forty-five minutes into their visit, she got up to
pour them each another cup of coffee and then said, "Come."

Charles followed her around the partial wall; on the
other side, as he'd expected, was Mrs. McGucken's bedroom.
What he hadn't expected were the photographs; in this private area of her tiny apartment, the walls were covered with
them.

"I don't like to talk about him with everyone," she said
by way of explanation, "so I keep these out of sight. Please,
look."

Charles immediately recognized Dana in baby pictures, as a toddler, and of course at elementary-school age, but then — *it couldn't be* — there were pictures of Dana as an adolescent, a teenager, a young man.

"What is it, Charles? Are you all right?"

"These pictures," he said, pointing. "Is this . . . ?"

"Yes, that's Dana. He must be, oh, maybe twelve or thirteen in that one."

"But I thought . . . I thought . . ."

"Charles. Sit down, please. You've gone quite pale. Let me get you something."

Charles sank onto the bed, staring. It *was* Dana, without question: older, grown far past the age Charles had continued to imagine him for almost fifty years, but still, the same face, the same radiance, the same white suit in gradually larger sizes.

"Here," Mrs. McGucken said, returning with a glass of water.

"I thought . . . ," Charles began again, but his mouth was parched; he had to take a drink before he was able to go on. "After what happened on the playground . . . when I saw you in the office that day and you told me he was in the hospital . . . I just thought . . ."

"You thought he'd died? Oh, no, Charles, I'm so sorry." She placed one of her hands over his. "No. No, dear, Dana recovered from those injuries. He had a severe infection, and it was touch-and-go for a while, but . . . I thought you knew. I called your mother to tell her, in case you were worried."

"You told my mother?"

"Yes, I —"

"You told my mother that Dana was all right."

"Yes. I'm sorry, Charles. I'm really so very sorry that you

didn't know. I kept Dana at home for a while after what happened, but then a school opened up on Shaw Island, a school for special children run by an order of Benedictine nuns. Dana lived there until he was eighteen — those were very good years for him; here's a picture of him there — and then he moved back in with me."

In the photo, Dana looked to be about sixteen. He was sitting at a picnic table next to a nun. She was writing; he was watching. In the far distance was an expansive view of undulating pastures dotted with grazing sheep; in the midground, a plain wooden structure, the schoolhouse, perhaps; on the porch, another nun was helping a young child hold a watering can over a window box filled with flowers.

Charles looked up and began surveying the photos again. It was then that he noticed: there was a certain point after which Dana did not advance in age.

"What happened to him?" he asked.

"He died in 1980, at home. He was twenty-seven years old. The diagnosis was sudden unexplained death in epilepsy. It's not uncommon for children like Dana, who have a history of seizures, to go that way. He died in his sleep, very peacefully, from what I could tell. I didn't hear him cry out that night, and I always did, I always heard him. When I went to rouse him in the morning, as usual, he was gone."

"I'm so sorry."

"Oh, don't be. Really. Brief as Dana's life was, it was very rich. He was loved; he had friends." She gave Charles's hand a gentle pressure. "And as far as what happened at Nellie Goodhue, he seemed to completely recover. It didn't change him in the least. But then, as you might remember, Dana had a great gift for . . . Oh, how can I say this? For *happiness*, you know? He was so utterly himself, so completely at home in his own body and spirit. He was a kind of angel, I think. An angel on earth. At least, he was in my life."

She reached up and rubbed the tears from her eyes, temporarily displacing those large, black-rimmed eyeglasses Charles remembered so clearly.

"Here," she said. "I have something for you." She opened a bureau drawer and brought out a framed photograph: their fourth-grade class picture. "That's yours to keep. I had a copy made. I thought you might like it."

An objective observer would give the photograph no special weight except as documentary evidence of 1960s fashion and haircuts. But to Charles, the photo was revelatory:

It wasn't him who occupied the choice position in that photograph, the place that, in the 1960s, was always given to the teacher's pet. Nor was it the brilliant and myopic Astrida Pukis. The person standing next to Brax the Ax and holding her hand was Dana McGucken.

Here too was a window into a possibility that Charles had never considered: in her way, Mrs. Braxton loved Dana.

"I've gone on and on about my family," Mrs. McGucken said after they returned to the living room. "So rude of me not to ask about yours. Did you marry?"

"Yes, I did."

"Children?"

There was a story he could tell, about his son and daughter, but instead he nodded and said, "Two. One boy, one girl."

They talked a while longer, until it became clear that Mrs. McGucken was tiring.

But Charles was tiring too, he realized; there was a strange, weighted feeling in his body, not exactly unpleasant, as if he were a boat that had been filled with water but was now emptying.

"I'd best be going," he said, getting up, and the water emptied, downward, a liquid weight pooling briefly in his feet and then releasing into someplace far below.

Mrs. McGucken made as if to stand; when she seemed to be having difficulty, Charles reached out and took her lightly by the elbow.

"I have one last thing to give you."

She reached down and laid hold of a decoupaged wood box that had been sitting on the coffee table between them.

"Inside are Dana's letters to me, from the time he lived on Shaw Island." She held the box out to him. "I'd like you to take some."

"Oh, Mrs. McGucken, I can't —"

"Please, don't worry," she said, smiling. "Dana wrote lots of letters."

Charles opened the box; it was filled with half sheets of lined manila paper, the very kind they'd used in Mrs. Braxton's class.

"I wish I could translate what all of it means," Mrs. McGucken said, "and it surely all meant something to him. I just wanted you to know that you taught him well; he made those loops right up until the day he died."

As they stood at the door, she clasped his hand. "Your mother," she said. "Is she still alive?"

"Oh, no. She's been gone a long time."

Mrs. McGucken nodded, and then looked intently into his eyes. "Don't be too hard on the dead, Charles. It's not easy for them to say they're sorry or ask for forgiveness, although I do believe they try."

She gave him a quick kiss on the cheek before saying goodbye.

Charles sat in the car for a long time looking at Dana's

letters to his mother. At the end of every indecipherable piece of correspondence, he had written his signature:

Dana McDucken

❖

Dear Emmy,

I'm sitting on the front-porch steps watching the first blush of morning light, a rose-colored flatline on the near horizon.

It's been another insomniac night. I've just come home from watching a movie at Pinehurst Palace; there's a VCR player over there, and the movie is an old one, available only in that format.

My sleeplessness commenced around midnight, when I awoke from a dream, a version of which I've had frequently over the years. This time, however, there were several significant changes.

The dream began with me standing at the base of a huge, towering fortress of mildewing cardboard boxes. I was aware, as always, that my mother was inside, but I had no idea if her seclusion was forced or voluntary. Was I meant to rescue her or let her be? (These are questions that plagued me when she was alive; they remain unanswered, so it's no wonder that they've continued to haunt me long after her death.)

I noticed a space, a small point of entry, a gap in the fortress's façade that I'd not seen before, just big enough to crawl through.

I heard my mother's voice—"Charles? Charles, is that you?"—and the tinkling of ice cubes. I saw spiraling wisps of smoke rising from inside the enclosure and knew them to be a signal of some sort—but this time, they were not a sign of distress but a kind of visual prayer, an offering.

"Charles," my mother repeated. "Why are you standing out there? Come inside."

And so I crawled in, becoming younger as I did, and once inside I found myself in the living room of a house I'd lived in until I was ten. My mother was dressed up—wearing an outfit I remembered watching her iron one night before she went out on a date with my father—and there, laid out on the glass-top coffee table, was a silver tray of face snacks, the kind I used to make for your brother.

"Hi, Dad," another voice said. I turned, and it was you! Seventeen years old, dressed entirely in white, in the corseted, long-skirted style of a nineteenth-century lady. A cartoon bubble hovered over your head; your words appeared inside the bubble as you spoke them. "Here," you said, "wear these." And you handed me a tall stack of tasseled caps in an assortment of colors.

As you and your grandmother and I sat down to Hamm's beer served in tiny porcelain cups, I could hear, not too far away, the sound of young boys laughing, of paper being torn, of noodles being smashed, of clinking glasses . . .

After awakening, I knew it would be difficult to go back to sleep, and I decided not to try, no homeopathics, no herbal teas; there was nothing for it but to get up and go down there, downstairs, down to the crawlspace. It was time to open the last boxes.

I knew where to find your things, as well as a few other items of significance, archival documentation of our little family's history.

In fact, I'd known all along.

And there they were. Not a towering fortress of boxes, just three.

I brought them upstairs and out here to the front porch, one at a time. They're sitting next to me.

In the first box (the one on which I found your tea set resting way back in September when I first began this archaeological project): the bluebird mobile, the yellow-and-green layette, the silver rattle, the Beatrix Potter books sized for a child's hands—a gift from my mother.

The contents of the second: the Post-it note (*It's a girl!*); the ultrasound image (*Hi, Daddy!*); the photograph album your mother assembled after your baby shower; the congratulatory cards; the videotape I watched earlier this evening. These items went into the box in the crawlspace a few months after you were born.

I'd come home from school one day to discover your mother's car in the driveway; when I walked in, there she was, lying on the living-room sofa, dozing, a cup of tea on the table next to her.

"Hey. You're home."

"Yes," she said drowsily, "I'm home." Her eyes were puffy, her face flushed.

"You sick?" I dropped my school satchel next to my office desk and went to her to feel her forehead. It was clammy but cool.

She shook her head, rubbed the back of her neck, and readjusted herself on the sofa. She was holding a heating pad to her abdomen.

"Where's Cody?" I asked.

"Next door. I called Erik Bjornson and asked if he could watch him until you got home."

"Did you work today?"

"No. I mean, yes, I went in, but I left early."

"What's wrong?"

"I'm just a little tired is all."

"I'll start dinner."

"Don't fix anything for me. I'm not hungry."

I was headed to the kitchen when I noticed a box by the front door.

"What's this?"

"Some things for the thrift. I meant to drive it over this afternoon, but . . ." She started to cry, quietly.

I opened the box flaps.

I remember feeling a sudden, sickening loss of equilibrium

when I saw what was inside, as if I'd stepped into an elevator that immediately began plummeting from the top floor of a very tall building.

"Why are you giving this away?"

Your mother didn't answer.

"These are Emmy's things. Why are you giving them away?"

"We're not having any more babies."

"You don't know that. We haven't talked about that."

"We're not going to talk about it. That's where I was today. That's what I was doing. Making sure. No more babies."

And that was when she told me she'd had surgery, a tubal ligation. She and I weren't supposed to have any more children, she said; Cody, your brother, was going to take all of our strength, and if I didn't see that, if I didn't accept that, well, I had to, there was no choice.

I remember thinking that I should feel very angry about the fact that your mother had made such a momentous, irrevocable decision without asking me, her husband, her supposed partner; that she'd drastically altered the blueprint of a life that we'd agreed upon, that we'd quite literally put our hands to on that first night we met — "I'll want to have children right away," and I'd said yes, yes; to her, to the miracle of that possibility.

What I felt instead was a kind of stunned panic, an animal protectiveness, an urgent compulsion to shield you, hide you, get you as far away as possible from this person, this weak-seeming, weeping person on the sofa who had once been your mother but had somehow transformed into a predator.

"Where's the rest of it?" I asked.

"Charles . . ."

"You didn't," I said. "Alison. Tell me you didn't."

When she didn't answer, I rushed outside, pulled off the garbage-can lid, and made another horrifying discovery. I began extracting the remaining evidence of your existence.

When I passed through the living room carrying your things, she was still on the sofa, crying more fiercely now, but also saying something, words, I suppose, but whatever it was made no sense and I interrupted her. "We're not getting rid of Emmy's things," I said. "We are not getting rid of her."

I brought everything downstairs and hid it in the farthest, darkest corner of our meticulously remodeled, mycotoxin-free crawlspace. I didn't want your mother finding your things again; I suspected that she'd once more try to dispose of them, that someday in the future I'd come home to find that she'd erased you forever. This was a terrible thought to have about a person I loved.

So. The last box. It too has a story. It too represents a signifi-cant vertical slash on our family's timeline.

A few years later — you would have been about seven years old — I once again came home from school to find your moth-er's car in the driveway in the middle of a workday; again, she was waiting for me on the living-room sofa, upright this time and looking far from vulnerable.

Next to the door were two suitcases. Cody had already been moved into his first group home at this point, so the suitcases did not belong to him.

Next to the suitcases was this third box.

"I hadn't decided to leave, really, I hadn't," your mother began. Her voice, I remember, was very matter-of-fact and practiced, a voice I realized she probably used often when deposing a witness for the defense, perhaps, or cross-examining an alleged rapist. "I was only thinking about it. I went downstairs, I'm not sure why, I told myself it was to see if there was anything down there I might want to take with me if I decided to go. And then I found them."

She nodded her head toward the damning evidence.

There was no need for me to open the flaps of that box; I knew exactly what it contained. Not the treasure chest of sentimental savings that I started looking for months ago—those lost relics documenting your journey from toddlerhood through high school, the handmade birthday/Valentine's Day/Father's Day/get-well cards, the letters from camp, the school projects—but seven years' worth of unsent one-way correspondence, tucked into envelopes addressed to Emerson Faith Marlow.

Your mother went on to say that anyone who was this obsessed with a fictional child could not possibly be a good parent to a real one. "No wonder you can't be a father to Cody," she said. "No wonder this marriage has failed. You wanted Cody out of the house—you've wanted that since the diagnosis—and now he's gone. You've wanted to be alone with a fictional, perfect daughter—fine, have at it . . ."

She said a lot of things that afternoon. I prefer not to remember most of them.

"It's *sick,* Charles," she went on. "It's *pathological,* carrying her around like this, *thinking* about her, *writing* to her, *imagining* her like she's some kind of . . . I don't know . . . *character* in a story . . ."

I heard her words. I understood that she was upset. And even then I knew that the person your mother was, and is, would never, ever understand.

But it cannot be that, Emmy. Emerson Faith, can it?

You and I; it cannot be a pathology.

I used to think that it just happened; there wasn't a specific moment when it started.

But I know now: it began the day your mother boxed up your things with the intention of giving them away.

From then on, you began inserting yourself into my consciousness. At odd and unexpected moments, you'd materialize in my imagination. Scenes would present themselves; conversations would arrive fully formed, as if they were memories, not fabrications. It seemed to be out of my control.

And when I first brought your box down here and laid eyes

on that never-to-be-used tea set (a gift from your other grand-mother), suddenly, you were there:

"Would you care for a cucumber sandwich, Mr. Charles?"

"Yes, indeed, Miss Emerson. Thank you ever so much."

As for that movie I watched at Cody's tonight, the videotape that was part of your mother's Discard pile:

It has no title, no musical soundtrack, no opening credits, no RKO tower emitting Morse code signals.

This movie begins and ends with a master shot: the interior of a small room in the neonatal intensive care unit of Seattle Children's Hospital.

The view is of a bed on which a newborn baby is lying. The baby is intubated. Her eyes are closed; if there is a question to be answered in this film, a narrative engine powering the plot, it is this: Will she ever open them?

Beyond that, the movie has no dramatic arc; its unedited footage shows the parents and sibling of this babe — floating in and out of frame — along with a succession of friends and family who are coming to both meet the baby and say goodbye.

Propped-up and brave-faced at the start, the visitors offer the gifts they have come to deliver — hugs, flowers, words of well-intentioned comfort — but soon, whatever inner scaffolding they've erected for the occasion gives way, and they make their exits housed in broken bodies, features buckled by grief.

Many of the visitors comment on the baby's expression — "She looks like she's smiling," they say, or "She looks like she's about to laugh" — and the baby's mother takes a photograph of her at one such moment.

It is not until the film's final act that the parents and sibling insert themselves into the center of the action.

Mother, played by Alison Marlow.

Father, played by Charles Marlow.

Mute Child, played by Cody Marlow.

The father settles by the bedside and begins reading the baby a story, "On the Day You Were Born." He succumbs to a wordless assault of tears long before the story ends.

And then, in the final minutes, a cameo appearance by the pediatrician; she enters the frame and speaks to the gathered threesome, including Mute Child, who is being held between his parents, in both sets of arms. He has been seen previously in the film, initially a scene-stealer (thrashing and screaming whenever someone tries to remove him to an offstage location), but eventually a quiet, pacified, mostly ignored presence at a corner table, where he has occupied himself with an assortment of non-toy items that the rotating cast of kindly nurses bring for him: waiting-room magazines, plastic containers and lids, craft and office supplies.

"Say goodbye, Cody," Mother whispers, "say goodbye to your baby sister, can you? Goodbye, Emmy. Goodbye, Emerson Faith Marlow . . ."

The baby is extubated.

Her eyelids quiver briefly—two small, shimmering aspen leaves—the color drains from her face, and then she is still.

Father sobs.

Mother weeps.

Over Father's bowed head, Mute Child gently drapes a paper-clip necklace.

THE END.

Dear Emmy. Emerson Faith Marlow.

I've given the six-word-short-story assignment to my students often enough over the years, modeled on Hemingway's "For sale: baby shoes, never worn."

I could not allow the story of your life to be so brief.

After the video ended tonight, I went into your brother's room and watched him sleep for a while.

I do so wish that he could have known you.

But maybe he did. Maybe he does.

Maybe he dreams of you.

Maybe the two of you communicate in some way, and during those frequent times when Cody lifts his eyes to the sky, he sees something I don't.

On his bedside table, in the album he keeps to help him communicate, there is that single photograph of you, the one your mother took before you were extubated: your face pink, your small mouth bowed into what looks for all the world like a smile. Sometimes your brother points to this photo, as if asking to see you, expecting to see you; I believe as much as I believe anything that you are still alive for him as well.

Is that a pathology?

Is writing and reciting your name a pathology? Do not the observant recite Kaddish? Do not the faithful attend the Funeral Mass?

Dear Emmy. Emerson Faith Marlow.

You, in truth, are my greatest fictional masterpiece.

My one comfort is in thinking that perhaps you chose to leave us. Maybe you wanted to be born into a different family, one in which you wouldn't have so much to bear. Maybe you knew, as your mother seemed to, that your brother would require all of our strength. Maybe your choice was for yourself.

Still, I am left with these questions:

If I stop talking to you, will you cease to exist?

Or:

If I stop talking to you, will you finally be free?

Unbind the Body

Charles was not, by nature, a partygoing type.

Which was a shame, in a way, since the city of his birth and lifelong residence is enthralled by celebrations of the large-scale variety.

Seattle's two oldest, biggest, and most established blow-outs — Folklife and Bumbershoot — bookend the summer, the former a high-octane, bare-midriff marathon of dance and world music that takes place over Memorial Day week-end, the latter an only slightly more sedate lollapalooza of literary and cultural offerings that stretches over Labor Day weekend, the last huzzah before the rainy season sets in.

Charles was a regular no-show.

However, on those weekends, inevitably hunkered down at home in his Maple Leaf neighborhood, he could almost hear the drums, smell the kebabs, visualize the profusion of swirling colors, absorb a diffuse but palpable energetic wave generated by hundreds of thousands of people congregating near and around the base of the Space Needle, that Seattle icon, standing alone on the horizon, the vestige of an imagined architectural future that never came to pass.

Odd but true: Charles did not attend the 1962 World's Fair, possibly because his parents weren't festival-going types either. Just as the maximum occupancy of their social life was the size of a cocktail party, the largest population Charles could comfortably tolerate was fifteen, the average class size at City Prana, a school that prided itself on its low student/ teacher ratio — that being, of course, one of the reasons he'd applied there in the first place, and why he'd remained so long.

As far as Charles could remember, all the other students he'd mentored over the past twenty years had fulfilled their final senior-project requirements by giving classroom presentations.

Today, however, thanks to the unusual nature of Romy Bertleson's project, he was obliged to vacate the metaphorical comforts of his beanbag chair for a very different kind of finale: the annual Art Without Boundaries exhibition fundraiser, which was scheduled to take advantage of a monthly neighborhood event known as the Capitol Hill Arts Walk.

◆

He left much later than he should have. Even though it was Thursday, not even a holiday weekend, southbound I-5 was a grinding mess; he'd had to exit the interstate and make his way via a series of surface streets, clogged with freeway escapees like himself, so by the time he got to the church, the exhibition had been in progress for almost an hour and the parking lot was full.

What if Romy thought he wasn't coming? What if she'd already left?

Charles drove around for another ten minutes before finally finding a spot a few blocks away, and then he had to weave in and out of the dense, leisurely parade of urban art seekers strolling the sidewalks and the barricaded cross-town streets.

The mood was celebratory but not frenetic, and in addition to the edgy, single, fashion-in-extremis types Charles expected to see in this part of the city, there were lots of parents with young children. True, many of the mothers and fathers were heavily inked and/or liberally pierced, but besides that, they and their offspring looked like typical migratory family units charged with safekeeping their most vulnerable members; they transported their young in strollers, wagons, backpacks, nestled in body-hugging slings (either kangarooed in the front or caboosed in the back), hoisted on shoulders, cradled in arms.

Watching them, Charles experienced a rare sense of commonality: *I've done that*, he thought, smiling. *I've had that gift, that privilege.*

The weather was cloudy and cool; the temperature hovered around sixty; shops and restaurants, with their doors and windows flung open, seemed to be smiling.

On the sidewalk outside the church, a large sandwich board advertised the ANNUAL ART WITHOUT BOUNDARIES EXHIBITION FUNDRAISER. Charles slowed his pace and allowed himself to be carried along by the crowd toward the entrance.

Once they were inside, another sign directed them around a corner and into a huge open space with gleaming wood-plank floors and a bank of enormous west-facing windows.

Charles's recent feelings of ease and community quickly began to evaporate; the sensation of intruding into a situation where he didn't belong was an all-too-familiar one.

He stepped aside, adhered himself to the wall immediately

to the left of the large double doors, and allowed other, more confident partygoers past.

A long table was situated nearby. Charles began perusing the spread of written materials on display: informational literature about church programs, e-mail sign-up sheets, colorful brochures that advertised the Art Without Boundaries mission and offered ways to get involved.

"Would you like an exhibition guide?" he heard a voice say.

He looked up to see a young woman holding out a large, glossy catalog.

It was Romy, seated, smiling impishly. "Hi, Mr. Marlow," she said.

As unrecognizable as she'd been at the start of the school year, her transformation today from the gawky young person who'd come through the doors of City Prana six years ago was even more remarkable.

"Romy," Charles said. "Congratulations."

She stood, walked around the table, and drew him into a hug.

"Thanks for coming," she said graciously — as if his presence weren't mandated by article 18, paragraph 25 of *The City Prana Senior-Project Guide for Teachers.* "Let me find someone to man the table," she said, stepping away. "There are some people I want you to meet."

She'd assembled a look that combined vintage and modern elements in a sophisticated, balanced way: a 1940s jacket and wool beret, loose pleated trousers, a soft rayon shirt, a colorful scarf. The ensemble suited her, reflecting the inside-out expression of a young woman who was starting to know herself and beginning to put her personal style in the service of an authentic, inner substance.

Charles wished he could comment on her appearance

but feared that would violate the contract of teacher-student relations, especially when the teacher was male. Pam Hamilton could say it, but not Charles; the words *You look beautiful* belonged to Romy's father, wherever he was. Still, Charles could *think* them, and he did: *You look absolutely beautiful, sweetheart. I'm so proud of you.*

When she rejoined him, taking his arm, Charles realized that the biggest change in her appearance was the absence of her camera; in place of the wide, bandolier-slung strap that usually crossed her torso, she wore a lanyard with an ID badge that read ROMY BERTLESON, AWB VOLUNTEER AND EXHIBITING ARTIST.

❖

The room was set up as a large exhibition hall: the walls were densely hung with two-dimensional pieces that were expertly illuminated by track lighting; standalone stacked white cubes displayed pieces of sculpture. It was all very polished-looking, which made sense; in his brief perusal of the AWB materials, Charles had learned that much of the work and the program support came from professional artists with ties to the gallery world.

The event itself had clearly been designed with elegance in mind, but although there were a few people who were dressed up and obviously here specifically for this event, most of the crowd was part of the drop-in Art Walk group, and — typically for Seattle — dressed down.

And then he saw the nuns: two stark, substantial, black-and-white islets in a sea of muted REI outerwear. Romy was leading him directly toward them.

"There are a couple of people who have been hoping to meet you," she said, "and they have to leave soon . . ."

The sisters stood near the food and drink tables by the windows, holding glasses of plum-colored wine and looking up at a large mobile suspended from the ceiling: a piece of upcycled artwork, its elements were hundreds of bird shapes that looked as if they'd been scissored out of colorful tin cans. The nuns' upturned faces and obvious delight with the mobile made them look very young.

"Sister Martha, Sister Frances, this is my teacher Mr. Marlow," Romy began. "He and Ms. Hamilton were co-advisers on the project."

"How do you do," Charles said, extending his hand to each of them in turn.

The sisters greeted him with warm smiles. Sister Martha had a piece of kale stuck to one of her bicuspids; Sister Frances sported a faint mustache and soul patch.

Romy continued. "Mr. Marlow's son, Cody, is the person who collaborated with Mrs. D'Amati — sorry, I mean Sister Giorgia — on the collages."

Oh yes!

Of course!

Lovely boy.

Beautiful work.

We'd love to meet him.

Perhaps we could arrange a visit?

I'm afraid we must be leaving.

We have to catch a ferry.

So good to meet you.

Such a pleasure.

Take care.

God bless.

Charles managed to utter brief polite responses to these comments and questions —

"I'm going to walk the sisters to their car," Romy was saying. "Be right back."

— but inwardly he was trying to come to terms with the fact that Romy had somehow learned that Cody was his son.

Feeling suddenly woozy, Charles moved to lean against one of the catering tables. The next few minutes were an ongoing blur of pithy, pleasant social interactions: several City Prana students and friends of Romy's came along to say hello; a woman who introduced herself as Romy's mother thanked him for his support; the AWB program director — Charles had no idea how she knew who he was — congratulated him on fostering such a remarkable young person. Of all these compliments, Charles felt completely undeserving; it had always been his feeling as a teacher that, whatever his students did right, wherever they succeeded, that was all *their* accomplishment, nothing to do with him; he took responsibility only for his students' failings.

"Ms. Hamilton told me," Romy announced without preamble upon her return. "About Cody, I mean. I hope you don't mind. I was already taking lots of photos of him so it wasn't like I chose him because he's your son."

"What do you mean, *chose* him?"

"I only got to exhibit five pictures, and the ones I liked the best were ones of Cody and Mrs. D'Amati."

Charles wasn't sure what to do with this information, especially since he hadn't seen the pictures yet. He noticed Romy looking past him and turned to find Alison arriving to join their twosome.

"Hi again," she said to Romy. "Hello, Charles."

"Romy," Charles began, "this is —"

"Cody's mom," Romy finished, nodding. "Ms. Hamilton introduced us before she left. Listen, I need to get back up front, but first I wanted to give you something." She handed Charles a small wrapped gift. "See you Monday, Mr. Marlow. Nice to meet you, Mrs. Marlow," she added.

"You as well, Romy," Alison replied. "Good luck."

Charles opened Romy's gift; it was a volume of Mary Oliver poems. Inside was an inscription: *To Mr. Marlow, my teacher. Thank you so much for the inspiration and support — and for having faith in me. Love, Romy B.*

"I've been trying to say hello for a few minutes," Alison said, "but I couldn't get to you, you're so popular. Have you looked at the art yet?"

"I'm about to. Have you?"

She took his arm and started leading him across the room.

"You want to go for coffee or something after this is over?" Charles asked.

"Oh, thanks, Charles, but I'm here with James. We have dinner plans."

"James. Right."

"Here we are."

They'd arrived in front of Cody and Mrs. D'Amati's collages, *Untitled 1* and *Untitled 2.*

"He did these?" Charles asked, aghast.

"Yeah. Can you believe it?" Alison shook her head and chuckled. "Apparently the ten-minute magazine rule has been revoked."

Charles wasn't sure which was more astonishing: that Cody had had a hand in creating a piece of art that was this sophisticated or that his ex-wife was amused about the repeal of a fifteen-year injunction against an activity she used to condemn as *stimming.*

After studying the triptychs a while longer, they walked on until they came to three of Romy's pieces: black-and-white photographs captioned with handwritten American Sentences.

In the first image, Mrs. D'Amati stood in a pose reminiscent of the Statue of Liberty: one small but strong-looking hand held a cloth napkin pinned loosely to her heart center; her other hand was directed heavenward, fingers arranged in a specific but mysterious shape, a kind of mudra. Her expression was confident, triumphant.

You babblers well may rule the earth, but heaven's the kingdom of the mute!

Another portrait of Mrs. D'Amati was taken from behind with the camera looking down on her from over her left shoulder. She was sitting, her hand resting on an empty table in the exact shape it would take if she were holding a pen.

When memory fails, cast the truth aside and then unbind the body.

Finally, there was Cody, with his mortar and pestle, grinding.

Charles turned to Alison. "How — "

Alison shrugged. "Don't ask me." She chuckled. "I have no idea how ramen noodles made their way into art class, but apparently the grinding rule is kaput too."

Their son's face was lit with a soft glow. He was completely focused on his work and on whatever inner conversation that work evoked.

This meditation, over olive wood and wheat, is a voiceless hymn.

None of the photos were traditionally composed; they were conspicuously empty in places, or at least unpopulated. Charles was reminded that there were always vacancies in the construct of a life: blank spaces occupied by the unseen guest, the absent friend.

"I've been meaning to ask you," he said as they looked at their son's portrait. "How is it going?"

"How's what going?"

"You know. The conversion thing."

"The conversion thing." Alison smiled. "It's going fine."

"Good."

"You know, I think about you sometimes, in class. There are certain ideas, certain aspects that you might like."

"Really."

"I don't know. Maybe."

"Like what?"

"Like . . . oh, the whole idea of confining It, Him, Whatever, to a single name: *God.*"

"What do you call It, then?"

"Oh, so many things. It's fairly overwhelming. Understand, I'm talking Judaism 101 when it comes to all this, but . . . there's *El, Elohim, Elohaynu . . . Yahweh, Ehyeh, Hajak, 'ilah, Jehovah, Adonai, El Shaddai, Ha Shem . . .* It's intriguing; giving It lots of different names almost has the effect of giving It no name at all — which, really, when you think about it, is as it should be. Does that make sense?"

"It does."

She sighed. "Or maybe it's about finding the *right* name for It? A name you can live with? Maybe that's another way of getting to belief. I don't know. What do I know?"

Charles heard Cody calling out to them from the distant past: *Gaaaa . . .* He saw him touching Emmy's head on the ultrasound screen.

"So you're a believer now?" he said.

"I don't know that I can say that, Charles. But I decided it might be all right to seek comfort. It might be all right to say *Help,* because just saying it implies that something is listening — and also because saying it is a kind of comfort in itself. That might be selfish, but it also might be enough. A place to start, anyway."

"And are you comforted?"

"Yes. I am."

"Well. There you go, then."

"Thank you for asking."

Charles noticed the SOLD sticker on the photograph. "You bought his, didn't you?"

"You can borrow it anytime."

"Thanks."

"Listen, Charles," she said, putting a hand on his arm, "I've got to go, but I'm really glad I saw you here." She gave him a light kiss on the cheek and then gestured to another spot in the room. "The other photos are over there. Talk soon?"

"Yes."

He followed her figure through the crowd, toward the double doors, where a tall man with a lined face and excellent posture stood smiling at her. She stumbled briefly on the entrance threshold; he clasped her arm and steadied her; they laughed, his face falling into the shape those lines described. Then he guided her into the hall, not in an overly authoritative manner, but with assuredness. They joined the exiting procession and moved out of sight.

Charles looked at a few more pieces of art and then came to Romy's last two pictures in the exhibit: matted and framed together, the photos were dual portraits of Cody and Mrs. D'Amati, sitting side by side, not touching, each obviously absorbed in his or her own work —

Speak in tempests of torn paper; I will answer with flurries of loops.

— but also clearly experiencing a sense of intimacy and connection.

Tell me your story in stillness; I'll answer with a grinding of wheat.

Charles was reminded of an early developmental milestone, one of many items on a list that, in Cody's case, was never checked off.

Does your child engage in parallel play?

Yes, Charles thought. *Yes, he does.*

Are You My Father?

Dear Alison,

Since the Art Without Boundaries fundraiser, I've found my-self frequently replaying our conversation. Your comment about "finding the right name" struck a resonant chord, for that is in-deed a huge part of my problem. The word itself is irreparably despoiled, a Trojan horse packed with a garrison of desolate con-notations. Regenerating any kind of belief in It/Him/Whatever is really impossible until that central problem is addressed.

So, earlier this evening, I initiated a Web search: The Names of God.

Among the articles I perused in the ensuing cyberspace jour-ney was one on Meher Baba, a twentieth-century Indian spiritual master who claimed to be an avatar of God. His name means "be-nevolent father."

The good works of Meher Baba, a world traveler and con-temporary of Gandhi, were legion. In 1927, he announced that he would adopt a practice of silence; he maintained that silence for the remaining forty-four years of his life, using an alphabet board and a unique sign language to communicate. Mary Pickford and Tallulah Bankhead hosted parties for him. Pete Townshend was a devotee. He is the originator of the phrase "Don't worry. Be happy." There is newsreel film of him twirling his alphabet board with the dexterity of an NBA point guard, washing and kissing the feet of lepers, playfully tossing cashews and raisins to throngs of children, embracing horses.

What drew my interest as much as anything was the man's abiding facial expression: an irresistibly impish glint in his eyes, a perpetually pleased grin. He looks like the doppelgänger of Zero Mostel.

Given these factors, I've decided that the name Baba is acceptable—or, as you so wisely said, "a place to start, anyway."

My feeling: it's never too late to try a new approach to learning anything, and just because one has no expectations doesn't mean one has no hope.

Ali. Alison Nadine Forché. I hope you're having a wonderful time. If anyone deserves a honeymoon, it's you.

Give my very best to James. I'll see you in a few weeks.

Love, Charles

He could not believe the turnout.

True, it was an exceptionally beautiful day for this early in the summer, only the third weekend in June: a light breeze, temps in the upper seventies, a slow, stately march of story-inspiring cloud shapes moving up from the southwest. But such weather usually sent Seattleites out of the city to the mountains or to the water or to one of the many weekend summer festivals — not to a Maple Leaf yard sale.

He hadn't done that much advertising either, only some hand-lettered posters at his usual neighborhood haunts (Cloud City, the video store, the hardware store); a few more a couple of miles away at the other places he frequented, the QFC on Roosevelt, the library and community center across the street from the mall, the Northgate Village Starbucks; and one more on the bulletin board of the City Prana teachers' lounge.

No newspaper ads. No street signage.

Where had all these people come from? There had been no fewer than ten customers at a time all morning, sometimes as many as twenty.

One of the first arrivals was a bearded, leather-clad, bandanna-wearing fellow who'd driven up on a Harley. He browsed for a while and then, encountering the children's section, picked up Cody's old board-book copies of *Brown Bear, Brown Bear, What Do You See?* and *Runaway Bunny.*

"How much?" he asked.

"Take them," Charles replied.

"What?"

"They're free."

Harley scowled, replaced the books, and moved on to inspect a box of electrical supplies left over from one of the storybook cottage's many remodels.

Charles had given a lot of consideration as to how to best publicize this event, finally coming down on the side of Yard Sale — even though that was a blatant violation of the truth-in-advertising concept. What he planned, in fact, was a Yard Giveaway.

"How about a quarter each?" Charles asked the biker when he looked like he was about to leave. "For the books?"

"Oh. Sure. Okay."

It became a fascinating lesson in psychology: most of the people who dropped by during those first hours refused to take things they obviously wanted, needed, or were interested in after asking the price and hearing the word *free.* Among the few items Charles was able to successfully give away were a couple of coffee mugs, a faux-leather desk set whose origins were completely unknown to him, and a stack of partially completed *New York Times* crossword puzzle books.

Nobody took the furniture, the sports equipment, the never-used wedding presents . . .

"Come back tomorrow!" Charles yelled amiably as people drifted away, empty-handed. "Everything will be half off!"

As the day progressed, there still remained a sizable inventory. Charles decided he'd better change tactics or risk finding himself at four o'clock tomorrow afternoon with a yard that was still full of merchandise — and a repeat of the wrenching dilemma of what to do with it all.

A young couple started making their way to Charles's table; they were probably nineteen or twenty years old, and they exuded the unmistakably comfortable but magnetized energy of two people in like *and* in love. He'd been watching them for some time; they used their voices, but they also spoke in sign language.

The boy was holding a pair of cross-country skis and boots Alison had bought Charles for Christmas one year.

"Hey," the boy said, setting the boots down and propping the skis against Charles's table, signing as he spoke. "I was wondering, what size are these?"

"Ten and a half," Charles answered.

The boy's hands translated, the girl's face brightened, and she gave him a playful hip check.

The boy grinned at her. "How much?"

Charles considered. They were probably students, probably poor. The boy especially had that undernourished, tired-and-overcaffeinated look, so Charles quoted him the price of a triple venti latte.

The boy looked puzzled. "For just the boots, right?" he said.

"No, the skis too," Charles said. "And here . . ." He walked them over to the clothing department and pulled out the ski jacket Alison had given him that same year. "I'll throw this in too. It looks like it'll fit you."

"Seriously?"

"Seriously."

A look of delight broke across the girl's face. Her expression was so purely radiant, for a moment she reminded him of Dana. *Thank you!* she said to Charles, using a simple sign that he recognized and remembered.

You're welcome, he signed back.

As they walked away, the girl took the boy's arm. Her hands moved with a wonderful grace and rapidity as she spoke, her voice denasal but clear and expressive: "I promise you, babe, you're gonna *love* cross-country. I know it's not snowboarding, but nobody gets a compound fracture doing Nordic . . ."

Charles checked his watch. Three thirty. Only a half hour to go.

Tomorrow would be a shorter day, not only because it was Sunday and he expected a smaller crowd, but because Cody would be with him. And although Charles planned to set Cody up at a table in a semiprivate area of the yard and provide him with plenty of timed noodle-smashing and magazine-tearing opportunities (alternating with snacks and lunch), he didn't want to test the limits of Cody's patience.

Charles wondered if Pam Hamilton would be dropping by again. She'd been here early this morning and stayed until the sale opened.

Isn't that yard sale of yours coming up? she'd asked during those last, student-less days of school when teachers cleaned out their classrooms for the summer and attended a few mandated end-of-year meetings.

Yes, it is, Charles answered. *Next weekend,* he added. *Saturday from nine o'clock until four; Sunday from ten until three.*

Sunday.

Yes.

This coming Sunday.

That's right.

Isn't that Father's Day?

Is it? I hadn't realized. Charles wondered if business would be adversely affected by the holiday.

Do you have someone to help you?

Help me?

Your poster said the sale included a lot of furniture. Do you have someone to help you get everything outside?

Charles hadn't considered this. An extra set of hands would probably be useful. He supposed he could ask Gil from next door . . .

What time does the sale start again? Pam asked.

Nine, Charles replied.

Okay, Pam said, considering. *I'll be there at six thirty.*

Six thirty?

Actually, six.

And she was, toting a cardboard traveler of Starbucks coffee and, surprisingly, a baker's dozen of Krispy Kreme doughnuts; Charles had figured her as more the yogurt-and-granola type.

It would indeed have been difficult for Charles to manage the furniture on his own; it would also have taken twice as long to get things set up. Without Pam's help, he never would have been ready by nine o'clock. It always amazed him: time passed so quickly before a deadline was met; so slowly afterward.

At seven thirty, they were hauling the combination changing table/bureau out onto the lawn when Cody arrived promptly and as planned with one of his caregivers, the only customer to be granted early-bird status.

Charles had arranged this stopover, a brief and hopefully not-too-upsetting blip in the schedule before Cody headed to Kirkland for his weekly riding lesson.

There were still lots of items to get outside, but in preparation for Cody's visit, Charles had made sure that the box of children's books had come out early.

"Hey, Cody!" Pam said. "How are you?"

Cody dropped his chin to his chest and signed, *Hello, Pam!* Since he was three, he'd been greeting her with an exuberant signing of the word *pony.*

"Come on over here, son," Charles said, leading him to the front porch. "Take a look at these. You get to take the ones you want to keep."

Cody plopped down in his habitual odd manner — long limbs folding and collapsing quickly, a marionette with cut strings — and immediately went to work. The caregiver stood guard while Pam and Charles continued to haul things outside.

Fifteen minutes later, Cody stood up, suddenly, decisively, clasping a stack of books to his chest.

"All done? Find some good ones?" Charles asked. He was pleased to see that in Cody's save pile were *Caps for Sale, On the Day You Were Born,* and *Are You My Mother?*

Some of these books, Charles knew, had torn pages and teeth marks. He and Alison had both reprimanded Cody again and again, gently, firmly, but to no avail. *No biting, Cody! No tearing! Books are treasures!* Now, in retrospect, seeing the possessive and reverent manner in which Cody cradled the books, Charles wondered if they'd misunderstood; perhaps Cody's literary vandalism wasn't an expression of disrespect but rather his way of demonstrating an intense affection — and then, later, after he'd lost his words, an even more intense anguish.

Cody turned and started back toward the van.

"Thanks for bringing him by," Charles said to the care-giver. "Bye, Cody!" he called to Cody's unresponsive figure. "See you tomorrow!"

"Bye, Cody!" Pam added. "Adios, cowboy!"

They finished setting up by eight thirty, a whole half hour early.

Grateful for her help and company, Charles found himself hoping that Pam might stay longer — he could fix her a cup of tea, give her chance to relax; she'd worked so hard — so he was disappointed when she said she'd be taking off, meeting a friend for a walk around Green Lake and then heading to a yoga class.

She certainly was an *active* person.

"Oh. Well. Thanks for your help, Pam."

"You're welcome, Charles. Good luck with the sale."

Next door, right on schedule, the Bjornsons' garage door rumbled open and the current Best Hit — "Desperado," by the Eagles — crescendoed dramatically.

"Morning, Charles!" Gil called, emerging from the garage. "You're up bright and early for a Saturday. Yard sale?"

"That's right."

"Well, Erik'll be here soon. We might have to take a break and stop over."

"Please do. I'll be here."

"Was that Cody I just saw leaving?"

"It was."

"Shoot. Sorry I missed him."

"He'll be back tomorrow, most of the day."

"Oh, good! Erik would love to see him."

All that Saturday, the Bjornsons provided a soundtrack for Charles's customers. Charles kept expecting them to come over (there were some old tools of his father's that he thought Gil might like), but they stayed put, looking up every now and then to wave but mostly elbow-deep in the Mustang's innards, apparently at a critical juncture, a surgical team performing a multiple-organ transplant.

When Charles closed up shop at four o'clock — leaving everything out in the yard (there was no rain in the forecast, and he certainly wasn't worried about thieves) — the two of them were still out there, working away.

❖

The next morning, another Pinehurst Palace caregiver delivered Cody at nine thirty. After reviewing the list of what medications Cody took and when, Charles thanked him and then turned his attention to Cody; he seemed less than thrilled about being there.

Charles had rented two long, sturdy tables for the sale, but one of them had emptied yesterday, so he was able to provide Cody with an extra-large work surface. He wanted to get him set up and occupied before customers started arriving.

"Okay, buddy," Charles said, bringing out his porcelain mortar and pestle — one wedding gift that wouldn't be part of the yard giveaway. "I'm setting the timer now; when it goes off, you have to stop and have a snack. Deal?"

Charles produced the block of noodles he'd stashed under the table, and Cody set to work.

It was another beautiful day. There was, as Charles had expected, a slightly smaller turnout, but his rock-bottom pricing strategy continued to move merchandise at a successful and steady clip.

A few folks from Cloud City came over. Jamie, the waitress, was thrilled to acquire the baby things: crib, Beatrix Potter bedding, and changing table; Charles hadn't known she was expecting. (*Five dollars? Mr. Marlow, are you sure?*)

Sonny gratefully took the salad spinner, industrial-strength juicer, and one of the three deluxe Cuisinarts Charles and Alison had received as wedding presents, and two women Charles recognized as early-morning café regulars picked up the bulk of the camping equipment.

Gil and Erik weren't in the driveway when the sale began, but they pulled up in Erik's four-by-four around noon. Erik got out and immediately walked over, extending his hand.

"Hi, Mr. Marlow. Mind if I say hello to Cody?"

"No, of course not."

Erik ambled through the half dozen customers to Cody's table. He stood there for a few moments before speaking.

"Hey there, Cody. Remember me? I'm Erik, from next door, your old babysitter. You're such a big guy now, I barely recognized you."

Cody didn't look up.

"Sorry," Charles said.

"No worries," Erik replied.

Several customers later, Cody sat up straight, looked across the yard toward the Bjornsons', raised his arm in a salute, and yelled, *"Gaaah!"*

❖

When the timer went off, Cody, thankfully, was compliant as Charles removed the mortar, pestle, and noodles and set down a stainless-steel bento box filled with Cody's lunch-time favorites. Charles affixed a sticker to the sheet of poster-board that served as Cody's portable reward record when he was out and about.

"Good job, buddy. Well done."

Business picked up. Cody dove into his lunch. Charles mingled.

At one point, while Charles was conversing with a woman

who was interested in the Hardy Boys collection, he noticed that Cody had left his sequestered spot and was wandering through the yard, looking like any other customer. "You should know," Charles said, keeping an eye on him as he spoke, "several of these books are slightly damaged . . ."

"Oh, that's okay," the woman answered. "They'd be going to a shelter for kids awaiting foster care. We've got some voracious readers. How much?"

When Cody came upon Charles's *Life* magazine collection, he immediately took hold of the box flaps and dragged it back to his table. Then, surprisingly (Charles would have been sure that the smell alone would have put Cody off, never mind the flimsy paper quality), Cody began reducing Janet Leigh and the thalidomide babies to a pile of ragged-edged strips.

❖

"You look surprised," Pam said when she arrived around one o'clock, bearing two bags from Chipotle. "I thought I told you I was coming by after church and bringing lunch . . . Here you go. I hope you like *carnitas*. And there's Cody again! Hi, buddy!"

Cody greeted her but less enthusiastically than he had yesterday, involved as he was in his new *Life* magazine–tearing project. Pam sat down next to him and started eating her lunch.

Charles continued to stroll through the yard, chatting with customers and quoting absurdly low prices to interested parties while stealing glances at Cody and Pam. She occasionally offered him bits of her lunch — a chip dipped in guacamole, a forkful of salad, a spoonful of beans and rice — and he (incredibly) occasionally accepted.

After about half an hour, Pam announced that she was leaving again, not wanting to miss her daughter's regular Sunday-afternoon telephone call.

"Listen, Charles," she said, "I've been meaning to ask: Would you be interested in coming to a meditation class sometime?"

"Meditation. That's when you sit for hours and try to think about nothing?"

She laughed. "Basically, yes, that's the idea."

"Sounds impossible."

"Oh, it is, completely. And as it happens, there are lots of varieties of impossible: Zen, mindfulness, zazen, koan . . ."

"When and where?"

"Wednesday night, six to seven, University Unitarian Church. I can pick you up if you like."

"No," Charles said, surprising himself as much as anyone when he reached out and took her hand. "I'll come to you."

◈

By two thirty, the yard was empty of customers. Charles was a bit disappointed at how much was left, but still, as yard giveaways go, this one had gone all right.

In addition to clearing out much of the crawlspace and streamlining the house's contents, he'd netted sixty-three dollars and fifty-five cents, enough money to keep Cody in double-dip waffle cones for weeks. (They'd recently started having father-son dates at the Baskin-Robbins, which was within walking distance of Pinehurst Palace. Cody eating ice cream was an intensely messy affair, but the employees earned Charles's loyalty when they came up with the idea of wedging a marshmallow into the bottom tip of the cone to minimize leakage.)

Just as Charles started to think that it might be time to bring things to a close, a van pulled up at the curb: un-marked, dark blue, liberally dented, with an engine that had a twitchy, labored sound. It coughed asthmatically for a few seconds after being turned off.

A pair of nuns stepped out. The sight was so surreal that Charles wondered for a moment if he was hallucinating, but then he recognized them: Sister Martha and Sister Frances, the two women he'd met at the art exhibit.

"Hello," Charles said.

"Hello," the sisters answered.

"I hope you don't mind us stopping by," Sister Frances said, extending her hand. She was the tall, stoic, strapping one, and on this occasion Charles noticed her slight resemblance to Principal Vanderkolk.

"Not at all," he said. He couldn't help himself; he quickly glanced down and was relieved to see that Sister Frances was in possession of all of her fingers.

Sister Martha — dewy-complexioned and cupcake-round — added, "We came to the mainland to take Sister Giorgia to Mass. We thought we'd take a chance that you were home. We did so want to see you again, and to meet your son, Cody."

"I'm glad you came."

Sister Frances slid open the rear door of the van and assisted a third woman down onto the sidewalk. Charles immediately recognized her from Romy's photos: this was Cody's artistic collaborator, the notoriously spirited Mrs. D'Amati.

"Giorgia," Sister Martha began, "this is —"

But as soon as Giorgia alighted on the sidewalk and looked at the house, she gave a gasp of surprise and delight and then — sprite-like, with a nimble speed that left Charles and the sisters slack-jawed — scampered across the yard, past Cody, up the porch steps, and through the unlocked front door.

The Dream-Ladder Kitchen

There can be a kind of tipping point when it comes to the souls' yearnings, a moment when it is no longer possible to keep waiting for fate or coincidence or design or It/Him/ Whatever to reward our patience. To go on becomes untenable, unbearable. We must seize by an act of will the experience that has been so long denied, so wished for, whatever it is.

It might be reunion, with others, with self.

It might be some small cherished ritual, forgotten, denied.

At such times, when the soul wearies of waiting, she throws an image of that longed-for experience out ahead of her: an avatar, a hologram, a dream. She engineers, if you will, an answer to her prayer. She projects her yearning onto a stage and then — with a heart full of faith, expectation, and courage — rushes into it.

This house! Sister Giorgia Maria Fiducia D'Amati rejoices the moment she sees Charles's storybook cottage. *It is like something from a fairy tale!*

But no fairy tale she has ever heard before or found herself within; this is something else, something new (or something old), and as she runs, she prays: *Dear Father in heaven, thank You for that which I am about to receive, I know it is Your goodness that has brought me to this place and that whatever I find inside will be Your doing, Your gift, Your blessing, and for this, dear God, I am truly thankful, amen!*

Charles gives chase. The sisters hike up their black serge tunics and follow.

"I am so sorry!" Sister Martha says breathlessly.

"Giorgia!" Sister Frances calls. "Come back here!"

Cody has remained occupied with reconfiguring Charles's *Life* collection, but even he glances up when he hears the hullabaloo of panicked voices, and is confronted with the unprecedented sight of four adults (led by the tiny woman who sits with him at art class) running pell-mell into the house. He gets up and joins the procession.

Charles arrives inside first and immediately hears Mrs. D'Amati in the kitchen; she is opening and closing cupboards and drawers with terrific energy and purpose.

(*At last! No locks!*)

"I cannot apologize enough," Sister Frances says. "She's never done anything like this before."

"Oh dear," Sister Martha says, breathless, despairing, beginning to sob.

(*Finally, she can get to the tools she needs!*)

"No harm done," Charles says. Nevertheless, given what little he knows of Mrs. D'Amati's history, he considers it prudent to ease his way into the kitchen and take up a position blocking the knife drawer.

Giorgia is muttering as she continues to open and close the cupboards: *"Farina, sale, uova, lardo — o olio d'oliva — latte, lievito in polvere . . ."*

"Giorgia!" Sister Frances admonishes. "Come along now. This is no way to act."

"It's all right, really," Charles says.

"What should we do?" Sister Martha asks, looking anxiously from person to person. "I've never seen her this way."

"She seems happy enough," Charles observes.

"True," says Sister Frances.

"Mrs. D'Amati? Mrs. D'Amati, can I help you with something?" Charles asks.

Giorgia comes to a dead stop, turns, and begins to peruse his face.

Her eyes are the first indication of her infirmity, or rather that she resides in more than one world; they seem to be directed inward as much as outward, as if they are sightless decoys and she is actually watching an old print of a favorite movie playing inside her own head. Who knows what she sees in there? Memories? Fantasies? Personal history, revised? The truth, redacted? Whatever it is, Charles understands that she has chosen to cast him in the film. And this close to her, he is certain she poses no danger, no threat; there is nothing to worry about.

"Avete del lievito?" she asks. *"E del lardo?"*

When Charles doesn't immediately answer, she gestures in a dismissive way, pats him on the shoulder, and says, *"Va bene. Posso fare un altro tipo di pane . . ."*

"Bread," Sister Frances says. "I think she wants to make bread."

"Pane, si!" Giorgia extends her arms and smiles broadly. *"Benvenuti alla Panetteria D'Amati!"* She then resumes her search of the cupboards.

(Flour . . . Here it is! . . . Baking soda, salt . . .)

"Conosci la storia di 'Un Amore Come il Sale'?" Giorgia asks no one in particular. *"Racconta di un papà che bandisce la sua figlia più giovane . . ."* She prattles on quietly as she locates the things she needs and starts placing them on the kitchen table.

"What can you tell me about her?" Charles asks.

"It's a sad story," Sister Martha says, her eyes glistening.

"Indeed," Sister Frances adds. "But not unusual . . ."

(From the refrigerator: milk and eggs. Such a well-stocked kitchen. Simple and plain too, like Papa's . . .)

They go on to tell what little they know: Giorgia's rape by soldiers, her pregnancy, a baby boy given up for adoption . . .

(No need for cups or measuring spoons, only her hands and their old wisdom — so long neglected.)

. . . being forced to enter the convent and banished to America — a banishment that ironically saved her life, for within a short time, her family, her family's *panificio,* the small village in Tuscany where she grew up, the surrounding countryside . . . all were bombed, all became casualties of World War II, documented in magazine photos and clippings they found among her personal possessions, after her disease required them to move her out of the convent and into the city . . .

(But now the war is over! The bakery is open! Business is good!)

So sad, so very sad.

"Niente strutto, niente lardo ma . . . ," Giorgia murmurs. But then: *"Ah! Con l'olio d'oliva sarà altrettanto buono!"* She pulls out a bottle of olive oil, adds it to the other items on the table, plants herself in a strong, authoritative stance, and then claps her hands for attention. *"Guardate da vicino e imparate!"*

With a theatrical flourish, she grabs a handful of flour from the canister and scatters it across the table.

And so she begins. For the next few minutes, Sister Martha, Sister Frances, Charles, and Cody receive expert, perfectly clear instructions (in a language none of them understand) on assembling the unleavened bread known as *piadina Romagnola*.

Once Giorgia has fashioned the dough into several uniformly sized and shaped balls, she says, *"Ora, il pane si lascia a riposare e noi andiamo a lavorare!"*

Clapping her hands again brusquely, she begins ordering them around: gesticulating, nudging, shoving, miming directives with the clarity of a commanding officer, leaving no doubt as to what is expected.

Charles is to light and preheat the oven and find other things to go with the bread: *"Formaggio, erbe, basilico, del buon parmigiano, e rucola andrebbero bene, e del prosciutto, se lo avete."*

Her sisters are to set the table.

And to Cody, who has been lingering just outside the kitchen door, she says playfully, *"Anche tu, figlio! Vai a lavorare, pigrone!"* Charles doesn't notice when she grasps Cody's sleeve and draws him to the table. And by the time Charles turns around, he is too far away to stop her when she pushes Cody down by his shoulders into a chair and leans down to nuzzle his cheek and hug him round the neck.

Cody does not scream. He does not flinch.

He ducks his head and smiles.

Then Giorgia brings over Cody's granite mortar and pestle and places it in front of him. *"Fai del pesto da servire con il pane. Mettiti a lavoro, Cody. Tempo da sprecare . . ."*

After thirty minutes, Giorgia moves on to the next part of the lesson. She is rolling out flat, uniform disks of dough when the doorbell rings.

Charles opens the door to a worried-looking Gil and Erik.

"Hey, Charlie," Gil says. "We noticed that nobody's been outside minding the store for a while. Just wanted to make sure everything's okay . . ."

"Ci sono altri ospiti?" Giorgia calls from the kitchen. *"Li invito a entrare! C'è n'è per tutti!"*

❧

The kitchen is warm, filled with what Giorgia's sister Felice called *l'odore che è il cielo sulla terra,* "the smell that is heaven on earth." Charles opens the windows, bringing in the sound of Nat King Cole singing "That Sunday, That Summer."

Giorgia gestures for everyone to sit. She stands at the head of the table, bows her head, and then begins. *"Benedici, o Signore, noi e questi doni che la tua bontà ci elargisce —"*

Suddenly she stops, surveys the table, and scowls.

"No, no, no, no, no! Ci stiamo perdendo la cosa più importante!" She points at Charles and then gestures toward the wine rack. *"Signore, per favore potrebbe portare due bottiglie."*

It is only after Charles has selected two bottles and presented them for Giorgia's approval —

"Sangiovese? Bene, bene! Bisogna esser un paesano in fondo al cuore."

— that they are finally able to begin, and Charles's decades-long moratorium on hosting dinner parties finally comes to an end.

"Evviva!" Giorgia says, raising her glass.

"Evviva!" the others echo.

The unseen photographer snaps the picture, and the feast begins.

Giorgia has lost so much: her baby son, her father, her uncles, her sisters; the *panificio,* the sunflower fields, the village, the island schoolhouse; she has lost the company of schoolchildren, the community of her sisters in Christ.

She has lost mobility, autonomy, independence; access to the kitchen, permission to use the bread knife, to go to the bathroom without assistance; she has lost solitude, common sense, the right to push a grocery cart, to check things off her list, to acquire the ingredients.

So she focuses on what she has, right here, in this moment: the unexpected blessing of sitting at a big, sturdy, plain wood table eating good bread, drinking good wine, in the company of friends and family, in this kitchen, in this storybook cottage where, for all this time — who would have believed it? — everything, *everything* has been waiting for her.

❖

"It's almost time to say goodbye, Sister Giorgia," Sister Martha says.

"Okay," Giorgia replies.

After finishing dinner, Charles, Cody, Sister Martha, and Giorgia cleaned the kitchen; Gil, Erik, and Sister Frances went outside, gave the van's engine a quick tune-up, and loaded up the remaining yard-giveaway items. The sisters were delighted to accept Charles's donation to the island convent's thrift store.

No longer employed, empty-handed, Giorgia appears restless. She has started roaming the periphery of the living room.

Cody stands in the dining room, watching her. In Giorgia's presence, Charles has noticed, Cody is like an astronomer, constantly recalibrating the telescope to keep her in sight, as if she's an unidentified celestial body whose existence he's determined to prove.

"May I please use the facilities?" Sister Martha asks.

"Right through there," Charles says.

"Sister Giorgia? Sister Giorgia. Do you need to go?"

"No," Giorgia answers. *"Io sto bene."*

"You'll keep an eye on her?" Sister Martha whispers. "I'll be right back."

Charles nods.

Giorgia has alighted in Charles's office and is staring at the framed photo on his desk: his fourth-grade class picture, Sylvie McGucken's gift. Charles picks it up.

"That's me," he says, pointing. "And this was my best friend."

Giorgia stares and smiles, nodding.

And then, once again, she looks into Charles's eyes, but this time, she does not seem to be seeing someone else. Charles has the sense that she is absolutely conscious of her surroundings. She reaches out, lightly taps his Montegrappa Italia — always at the ready, clipped to his left shirt pocket, over his heart — and smiles. *"Paesano,"* she says.

What she says next is, of course, in Italian, but even though Charles has no idea what her words mean (and the name Dana will go by so quickly that he won't notice), their effect will be perpetual.

I knew there was something special about you, signore. I knew it when I saw you, and this house, and now there is proof. She points at the photo. *This picture of you and Dana, my best student. He was a blessing while he was with us. We remember him always. And you, signore, you were his friend, his teacher, his hero. He told me all about you. He loves you still. Never doubt it. He roots for* you, *Charlie Marlow . . .*

She pats his chest again.

Then she turns to Cody and wraps him in an embrace. *"Addio, bello,"* she says. *"Ci vedremo presto."* She takes his face in her hands, gently pulls him down so that they are eye to eye, and plants a kiss on the center of his forehead.

Sister Martha returns to collect her, they say their good-byes, and then Giorgia is gone, leaving a light dusting of flour on Cody's cheeks.

What is it? Charles thinks. *That word for the fine, soft, downy hair that sometimes covers a newborn baby's body? Emmy had it . . .*

And then it comes to him:

From the Latin, *lana,* for wool:

Lanugo.

◈

After everyone left, Charles was suddenly aware of his bone-weariness.

Should he take Cody back to Pinehurst Palace first, or finish up outside? He should probably fold up the rental tables and bring them in.

Cody still stood in the spot where Mrs. D'Amati had delivered her farewell kiss; now he too was staring at the school photo.

"Hey, Cody, I know you're probably tired, but can you hang here with me for a few more minutes? I've got a couple of things to do and then I can take you home. You wanna watch some TV? No? Okay, well, I need you to come outside with me, then. This won't take long."

Charles went out to the curb and retrieved the sign. When he turned around, he discovered that Cody had planted himself at one of the tables and was looking down at a legal pad; he must have picked it up off Charles's desk.

"No, buddy, you can't sit there. I have to fold up this table and bring it inside."

The sky was completely cloudless. The days were lengthening, but it had started to get dark, and the stars were arriving. The moon — nearly full — was a softened spoonful of vanilla ice cream.

"Buddy. Come on now. Please get up."

Cody didn't budge. He had a look on his face that Charles had come to recognize as the prelude to one of his refusal tactics: on little notice, he could transform into a one-hundred-and-seventy-five-pound conscientious objector. As strategies go, it was very effective. The caregivers had started calling it the Cody Sit-In.

"Cody. Cody, I need you to move. Maybe you could help me."

"Ga," he grunted with unusual emphasis, still staring down at the table.

"Yes, buddy, I'm right here, and I need you to get up now."

"Ga!" he grunted again, and Charles thought, *Oh no, here we go . . .*

But instead, Cody thrust his arm in Charles's direction. Then he slapped the palm of his hand against the table surface.

"What is it, Cody? You want me to sit down?"

"Ga."

"Okay, but just for a minute. Dad's tired, and I'd really like to get this done."

Next door, Gil and Erik were gathering up their tools, closing the car hood, chatting quietly.

Cody grabbed Charles's hand, yanked it closer, and held it firm against the tabletop for a few moments. Then he made a motion: *Stay.*

Charles sighed. There was nothing to do but try to figure out what his son wanted.

Tilting closer, giving Charles's chest a sideways glance, Cody reached out again, slowly this time.

His hand brushed against Charles's chest, paused there for a moment when he encountered the paper-clip necklace, and then moved on to the Montegrappa. He took hold of it and dropped it on the table.

Charles sat, stunned. "Cody? What —"

Cody tilted closer and nudged his nose toward the pen.

Charles picked it up.

Cody laid his hand atop his father's.

Charles waited.

Cody began moving Charles's hand for him, slowly: *up, down, around . . . up, down, around . . .*

"Gaaaaaaah," he said, the sound both an inhale and an exhale, and as their hands continued to move together, Charles discovered that his own breath felt light, ragged, irregular; eddying handfuls of shredded paper.

Cody squinted at the sky. "Gaaaaaah," he said again; a different inflection, a different meaning. His eyes widened with recognition and delight, as if he'd achieved whatever celestial contact he'd been seeking.

And then, just when Charles thought the miracle was complete, Cody took hold of the pen, lightly, and his hand started to disengage, as if propelled by a very gentle rocket-booster system.

Tentatively, it floated and circled upward; ever upward.

Charles looked on, entranced, bearing witness as Cody gained confidence until eventually he was making grand, joyous, looping gestures in space, his pen a lariat, lassoing the lopsided moon.

THE END

Acknowledgments

If you're reading this, perhaps you are, like me, a person who stays seated at the end of a movie and watches the credits roll, taking painstaking note of every name, all the way to the appearance of the IATSE logo and the assurance that no animals were harmed in the making of this production. Perhaps you even continue to linger — marveling at just how many people it takes to make a film — until the lights come up and the theater is empty of everyone but you and a couple of theater employees carrying brooms and dustpans, smiling benignly but obviously wishing you'd remove your odd loitering self from the premises so they can finish sweeping up the popcorn and setting up for the next show.

Filmmakers often speak about the many fingerprints on a movie; the same holds true for books — although in a slightly different way, since the people who support a book's creation aren't necessarily in evidence. I get the byline, but an enormous debt is owed to the many uncredited friends and colleagues whose unflagging encouragement sustained me throughout the four years it took to write this book. They listened while I kvetched, hugged me when I cried, and kept my wineglass full of *piquepoul* while I babbled.

Here then, with gratitude, is a list of people who have left their fingerprints on *Language Arts.* I hope you'll stay in your seat and read all the way to the end.

To my pals in Seattle7Writers: Carol Cassella, Dave Boling, Erica Bauermeister, Jamie Ford, Jim Lynch, Kevin O'Brien, Thea Cooper, and Laurie Frankel.

To my band mates in The Rejections: Garth Stein, Jennie Shortridge, Matt Gani, Paul Mariz, and Ben Bauermeister.

Playwright Steven Dietz defines *friend* as "someone who reads your first drafts." With that truth in mind, I extend deepest thanks to those who read various drafts and offered invaluable insights: Cindy Heidemann, Cheryl McKeon, Kate Carroll de Gutes, Kevin McIlvoy, Kit Bakke, Sheri Holman, and Maria Semple. Special hugs and love to my "sister from another mother," Randy Sue Coburn, whose friendship has been an anchor throughout this tumultuous process; she cheered with me, mourned with me, drank with me, and is one of the chief reasons that this book is finally seeing the light of day. Thank you, Petunia.

To "the Computer Doctor," Boegart Bibby, for saving my work when Microsoft Word "hung" — a term I learned while writing this book and one I hope never to have to use again.

To my colleagues and friends in the 2013 Jack Straw Writers Program for their support during an especially difficult time; to the friendly, accommodating staff at Starbucks Store no. 358, who allowed me to nurse my lattes and journal for hours on end; and to Christina Janssen's third-grade class at Sand Point Elementary for providing the handwriting samples that inspired Charles's and Dana's youthful signatures.

To the following authors, whose writings on spiritual matters were nourishing sources of wisdom, solace, and laughter: Anne Lamott, David Whyte, Doris Grumbach, and Sue Monk Kidd.

To my knitting buddies: Alexandra Immel, Carol Cooper, Julie Hiers, Sarah Ketchley, and Wendy Dell.

To Tom Bothwell, for being the brother I never had and always wanted.

To Kelly Harland, Kate Buzard, and Barbara Burnett for speaking openheartedly with me about the challenges of parenting a child with autism.

The works of the following documentary makers provided special inspiration: Todd Drezner (*Loving Lampposts*); David E. Simpson (*Refrigerator Mothers*); Fridrik Thor Fridriksson (*A Mother's Courage*); and Susan Hamovitch (*Without Apology*), who was especially generous in allowing me access to her film.

To Timothy Archibald and Elijah Archibald for their inspiring photographic collaboration, *Echolilia*.

To Beniamino Ambrosi, who kept Giorgia's Italian from reading like English run through Google Translate.

Thanks to Amara Najera for Dana McGucken's signature, to Noah Johns for Charles's prayer, and to Samuel L. Jianokopolous for re-creating Teddy Roosevelt's diary entry.

To the following arts colonies and staff, each of which provided much-needed time, space, and solitude: Hedgebrook (Amy Wheeler), Ragdale (Susan Page Tillett), and the Aspen Writers' Foundation (Mo LaMee, Adrienne Brodeur, and Jamie Kravitz).

A very special thanks to Isa Cato Shaw and Daniel Shaw for opening their beautiful home and glorious gardens to me in August of 2013. Much of the most difficult work on this book was possible because of the sanctity, magic, and sanctuary I experienced while living in Parliament House.

Gratitude to Bruce Nichols at Houghton Mifflin Harcourt for having faith in me and in this project, and, as always, I offer deep and abiding thanks to my beloved editor and friend Lauren Wein. Huzzahs as well to the amazing Tracy "Dr. Eagle Eyes" Roe for her copyediting expertise and artistry.

To the boychiks, Rabbi Simon and Fab Dan: thank you for your good counsel, noodging, and integrity. I love you both dearly.

To my wonderful family: my husband, Bill; my boys, Noah, Sam, and (occasionally) Jack; my girls, Brynn and Amara. This work that I do would be meaningless without your love and support. Thank you, thank you, thank you.

To you, the reader, because novels are collaborations; it is only through your imagination that Charles, Dana, and the rest can come to life.

And finally, reaching into my past, I give thanks to the many dedicated elementary, junior high, and high school teachers who modeled the very best and highest aims of their profession: Mrs. Prohaska, Mrs. Axthelm, Mrs. Hurd, Mrs. Carol Gross, Mr. Paul Guidry, Mr. Steve Lahr, Mr. Jon Peterson, Mrs. June Williams, and many others whose names I've sadly forgotten but whose indelible fingerprints shaped me for the better. This book is my small attempt to pay that debt forward.